JAMES PHELAN

DARK HEART

CONSTABLE • LONDON

CONSTABLE

First published in Australia and New Zealand in 2016 by Hachette Australia,
an imprint of Hachette Australia Pty Limited.

First published in Great Britain in 2018 by Constable

13 5 7 9 10 8 6 4 2

A CIP catalogue record for this book
is available from the British Library.

ISBN: 978-1-47212-720-4

Typeset in Simoncini Garamond by Bookhouse, Sydney
Printed and bound in Great Britain by CPI Group (UK), Croydon CR0 4YY

Papers used by Constable are from well-managed forests
and other responsible sources.

MIX
Paper from
responsible sources
FSC® C104740

Constable
An imprint of
Little, Brown Book Group
Carmelite House
50 Victoria Embankment
London EC4Y 0DZ

An Hachette UK Company
www.hachette.co.uk

www.littlebrown.co.uk

James .... g author of twenty-nine novels and one work of non-fiction. From his teens he wanted to be a novelist but first tried his hand at a real job, studying and working in architecture before

ALSO BY JAMES PHELAN

PROLOGUE

Freeing herself from under the bodies would not be easy. It would take all the strength she had. The blood made it harder. She closed her eyes and pictured a different time and place. The tangle of lifeless arms and legs, the weight of leaking torsos and heads, became friends playing a childhood game of stacks-on. *Move*, she thought. *Get out of here.* She slipped, and shifted, and slid. Got nowhere.

It's useless. I'm trapped.

She could smell the death around her. Could taste the coppery blood, like an old penny in her mouth. Hear the silence. She couldn't move her arms enough to be useful – they were pinned beneath hundreds of pounds of dead weight. She squirmed and wriggled. The blood was tacky and thick. Gallons of it. Multiple gunshot wounds. High-powered assault rifles. New weapons, nothing like the ones the militia used. The cacophony still rang in her ears; the screams echoed. Otherwise, it was silent. She moved fast and shuffled on her back, but she was getting nowhere on the slick ground, and a body above her shifted, blood pooling onto her face, forcing her to cough and gag and start to hyperventilate.

You'll die like this.

Rachel Muertos kept her head tilted to the side and closed her eyes and slowed her breathing. *Something else. Anything else. Somewhere happy. Another time.* She pictured her mother, a career librarian in

San Francisco elementary schools, and it worked better than the image of the playground. Her mother had been through hell to get into America, and she'd survived. She'd thrived. Thinking of her mother's smiling face took her away from the reality around her as she lay still. Her breathing relaxed. Her senses settled. The screaming, black silence gave way to actuality. First came noises. She heard dripping, and the wind that blew through the long-ago bombed-out warehouse. The dripping sound was blood. Rachel fought to stay composed. She pictured her mother's face, that familiar smile, and thought back to being in bed as a child in Los Angeles when they'd first arrived in the United States. It was a few months before they'd moved north and settled and she'd started preschool and she could remember her mother reading her books in English. It was like they were both still there, in that moment long ago. The memory calmed her. She felt hope.

Move, bit by bit.

She started to roll her shoulders; her arms were pinned to her sides. She tried her feet; her heels moved up and down like paddles. She shifted and slipped and tried to move, just a little, away from the blood that now drizzled onto her neck. In her mind's eye it was like trying to get out from beneath an avalanche of bookshelves, all that mass, all those words not spoken, her mother cheering her on. The reality seemed made-up, unreal, but she knew what happened. She'd seen it. Heard it. Real-time. Hyper real, really, because when the killing had started, everything had amplified.

Stop. Rest. Relax. Try again.

She managed to move just enough to keep her face clear, and then stopped moving to regain her strength. The heat kept the blood slick and viscous, even now, almost two hours after the event. Drip-drip-drip. The heady funk of body fluids created a humid environment. Rachel breathed through her mouth to avoid the smell. She heard a noise. A bird, perhaps, or a person. Far off. Like shuffling. Rachel made a noise. Not a call for help, but a faint hello. She felt it was safe now. To make noise. To create movement. To try to emerge from the tangle of death that had kept her alive. To find safety. But her fright and initial reaction, which was to play dead as the bodies piled around and then upon her, was proving her downfall. The strength had gone out of her. All that mass. Her arms and legs tingled. The weight pressing on her body meant her chest could only rise and fall in small, rapid motions. She knew that if she breathed out fully, her lungs would not have the power to inflate again. She was hot and tired and getting more and more light-headed.

You have to keep trying. You have to save yourself.

It took her ten minutes of wriggling and paddling and shifting to realise that she couldn't get out. Not on her own. She didn't have the strength. She'd spent too long in the one spot, with five, or six, or more, bodies piled on her. Then her breath started to quicken as she thought that maybe she'd been shot and couldn't feel the pain of the wound for the numbness of the weight upon her and the time elapsed. Maybe her spine was compromised. She started to scream but knew it was useless because she could barely let any sound out. No-one had heard the gunshots and carnage and thought to investigate it. No-one would hear her scream and investigate it. But it was all she could do, and she had to do something. She screamed. The sound was pitiful. Her lungs could inflate maybe halfway, and she could only expel half that. The sound was of a small child, and she again pictured herself sitting up reading with her mother not long after they'd arrived in the United States to make a new life.

Your mother went through hell. Get out of this, for her.

She yelled. A little louder this time. Stopped. Kept still.

Movement. A noise. Hope. Or a threat.

Then, one of the bodies shifted. Slid right off. Thumped as it landed. And then another. The release of pressure was like being born again. She could breathe, and see, and hear, and move. Another body fell to the concrete floor. And another.

And then a face, above her. One of the other Americans. He'd come back, to help her. He shifted the bodies and helped her up to a seated position, and looked her in the eyes as he spoke.

'Find Jed Walker.'

1

Seven thousand miles away, Jed Walker took his first unaided steps in four days. The nurse was close by, as was the physiotherapist, and he waved them away and gave a thumbs up. This was nothing. A nick. A ricochet of a pistol round. Through the quad. Along it, actually, a groove half an inch wide and three inches long. Surface muscle damage, some skin grafted from his hip to make the cosmetic repair. Plenty of physiotherapy to regain full functionality. Walker was prepared for that. He'd been shot before, twice in fact, and he'd got through both those rehabs just fine. This was nothing on those instances. Besides, being shot wasn't the worst that had happened to him. He stopped and turned and headed back down the corridor of UCSF Medical Center in San Francisco and he knew that even with the full weight on his leg he'd be fine to go home soon. He'd be slowed down for a while, sure, but as long as the stitches held and the wound heeled, he'd be up to speed in no time. He wouldn't be anywhere near full capacity for a few weeks, then he might have a slight limp for a couple of months after that while his muscles adjusted to their new arrangement, but he'd be fine.

Which is fine, Walker figured. *So long as nothing urgent comes up.*

•

Rachel Muertos woke to the beep of intensive-care equipment.

'Good morning,' a voice said. 'Do you remember your name? Where you are?'

She saw that the speaker was a man in military uniform. ACUs, to be precise – the US Army Combat Uniform, all patterned and baggy and ready to see action. He was a veteran from the campaign in Afghanistan, because he was wearing a legacy camouflage pattern that had since been replaced. Officer's rank sewn on his bib, but she didn't know what it meant. Army Surgeon's patch attached above his name plate and on his left sleeve pocket flap. She knew that symbol. He stood next to her bed. Close. Her eyes lingered over the medical patch, which depicted a modified caduceus, with snakes entwining a winged sword rather than the conventional staff. The sum of it all was a relief to see, and she smiled inwardly at the recognition. Being here meant she was no longer in Syria. *But where?*

'What do you remember?' he asked.

'Your medical patch,' Muertos said. 'It's wrong.'

'What do you mean, wrong?'

'It's not your fault; it's the Army's mistake, from way back. In the US Army context, the staff is replaced by a sword. But the caduceus symbol is the wrong symbol: it has nothing to do with medicine. The Rod of Asclepius, that's what should have been used. That has a single snake, rather than the two-snake caduceus design; it has ancient associations with trade, trickery and eloquence.'

The army doctor was quiet, watching Muertos. Beyond the surgeon and his pen light that was following her eyes, she could see a building. Not a field hospital. There was airconditioning. The bleep of medical equipment. Overhead lighting. A sterile smell.

'Your name?'

'Rachel,' she replied. 'My name is Rachel Maria Muertos.'

'Do you know where you are, Rachel?' As he spoke he pocketed his pen light and then made notes on her medical chart.

'A hospital.'

'Specifically?'

'Specifically?'

'You've been told.'

'Told? When?'

'We had this same chat yesterday,' he replied, taking a step closer, again shining the light in her eyes, then moved back. 'I told you where you were. Do you remember that? Do you recall what I told you?'

Rachel paused, then shook her head. Then went still. She became aware of another presence in the room. Another man. A big man. In the far corner. In shadows. Dressed in a suit. Official.

Rachel said to the surgeon, 'Where am I?'

The doctor moved away and turned towards the other man. 'She's not ready for questioning. She needs more time. Her memory, it's coming and going, but she's not ready yet.'

The suited man stepped from the shadows. Rachel could just make him out. Unfamiliar. Beyond big. He was huge. Broad shoulders. When he got closer, she looked away. There was something about him. He was aged about forty, his head shiny under the lights. Strong jaw. A nose that had been broken more than once. Wide-set dark eyes. A brute.

'Two minutes,' he said to the doctor, who shrugged and moved back to give him room. The suited man's voice was deep, gruff. American, but unspecific. Maybe west coast. But he had no tan, and there was nothing relaxed about him, which were things Muertos associated with her adopted home state of California. This guy looked like he had a high degree of Neanderthal in his DNA make-up. He was easily as wide and tall as a door. No fat. All muscle. His suit bulged at the biceps. He didn't wear a tie, because there was no tailor in the world who could make a dress shirt to button up around a neck that size, let alone a tie long enough to wrap around it. A chill ran through Muertos as she felt the man staring at her.

'Rachel, I'm with Homeland Security,' he said. 'We spoke yesterday, you and I.'

'We . . . did?' She looked up at him, and forced herself not to look away. She searched his face, and though she saw nothing familiar she now knew why there was something odd about him. He was bald, completely bald – no eyebrows, no eyelashes, no shadow of a beard. Just dark eyes set in a big face. The eyes were calculating. Fixed on her, like a predator.

'Yes,' he said. 'What do you remember?'

'Where am I?'

'You're at Ramstein, Germany. Military hospital. You were told that yesterday. What do you remember about how you got here?'

'How'd I get here?'

He paused, his eyes searching her face, then said, 'You remembered all that crap about the US Army medical patch, and you don't remember what brought you here?'

'What? No. No, I don't. How'd I get here? Please, tell me.'

He looked around the room like he was frustrated. She could see a pulse ticking away at a thick vein in his temple.

'You showed up in hospital in Damascus, Syria, two days ago,' he said. He looked at her. His eyes, set back below a big boney brow, searched her own for any sort of telling sign. 'When you were brought in, you were covered in blood.'

'Blood?'

'Yes. A doctor from Médecins Sans Frontiéres thought to run checks on it. It was the blood of at least six separate people.'

'I . . .'

'Whose blood was it?'

'I don't know.'

'What do you remember about Syria?'

'I don't remember.'

'Don't play with me.'

'I don't remember. What did I say yesterday?'

He watched her in silence. Five seconds. Ten. Then he said, 'That doctor from MSF said that you were talking, in some kind of a delirious state, from the time you were brought in to when he had to sedate you. You were saying the same thing, over and over.'

'What was I saying?'

'You can't remember?'

'Could I remember it yesterday?'

The man watched her, as though her question were a test. The vein ticked away, the pulse escalated, as if Muertos's lack of memory was making him angry.

He eventually said, 'You were in severe shock, but you're otherwise unharmed. Delirious, they said. But I need you to think, Rachel. Do you remember anything of what happened in Damascus? Anything at all?'

'Why was I in Damascus? How did I get there?' She looked across to the doctor. 'How – how did I get here?'

'Look at *me*,' the Homeland agent said. 'Rachel, look at me. That's it. Now, think. Do you remember anything that can help us?'

Rachel Muertos was silent.

'Find Jed Walker,' he said. 'Over and over. That's what you were saying. *Find Jed Walker*.'

Rachel's eyes were blank. 'Find . . . Jed Walker?'

The Homeland agent nodded and leaned closer. Then, in a tone that suggested she should summon an answer, said, 'Who is Jed Walker?'

'I . . . I don't . . .' Muertos started to breathe fast, and the heart-rate monitor spiked. 'I don't . . . where . . . How am I . . . Who . . .'

'Agent Krycek, she's not ready,' the doctor said, moving back into the light and taking Muertos's wrist in his hand. Her heart rate started to calm. 'She needs more time.'

Agent Krycek stared at the army doctor.

The doctor looked down to Muertos. 'Rachel, we'll give you more time. You need rest. And time.'

Rachel was silent. She watched the Homeland agent, Krycek, as he stared at the doctor. The doctor was unflinching amid the weird, close to volatile, tension.

Krycek's face turned to Muertos and he gave her a look that could have been read as wary. Certainly serious. Curious. Suspicious.

'I'll be back, same time tomorrow morning,' he said to her. 'We'll talk more then. You will remember.'

2

Jed Walker left hospital a day after Rachel Muertos, but he didn't know it and he wouldn't know her name for another five minutes.

The woman standing in front of him he did know. As well as you could know a person. And then some.

'Hello there,' Eve said to Walker, and wrapped her arms around him. He was 230 pounds and six-three, and Eve's hands barely touched around his back as he leaned his chin on her head. He was in his hospital gown, standing next to his bed. She wore a yellow dress that showed off her tanned arms and legs. Her chestnut hair was back in a ponytail and smelled of the ocean. Her eyes were lined with black ink and framed by long eyelashes. Walker was lost in the moment. 'Husband.'

Walker said, 'You haven't called me that in . . .'

'Probably since we separated.' Eva let go and looked up at him. 'How'd we ever let that happen?'

'I'm pretty sure I let it happen, and you forced it to happen.'

The smile was still on her face. 'I can't even remember why now. Can you?'

'Something to do with you not being able to share me with all my work out there, you know, saving the world and all.' Walker stripped off his gown and pulled on his black cotton shirt, buttoned it up.

'Oh, *that's* what you used to do . . .' Eve stood on tiptoe and kissed his lips.

11

'Used to do. I like that. Past tense.' Walker sat on the edge of the bed and started with his jeans. 'So, why is it that you're so enamoured with me again?'

'Enamoured? No. Relieved.'

'Same-same.' He leaned back on the bed as Eve helped him with his jeans and socks and boots.

'You didn't have your meds?' Eve asked, motioning to the plastic cup of pills by the bed.

'Don't you read the news? Opiates like that are a gateway drug to addiction. Next thing you know I'm vicodined up to my eyeballs. Uh-uh. Too many of my old buddies in the Air Force got hooked on the stuff.'

'Too many of them died, too. Before they got the chance to see the inside of a hospital.'

'So, what's that mean? I should take my meds because I'm the lucky one?'

'I'm saying the medical staff know what they're doing, Jed.'

'I'd rather feel what my leg can do. It's fine.'

Eve was quiet as she pulled his boots on, then said, '*You* nearly died on me.'

'*On* you?'

'You know what I mean.'

'If I'm going to go,' Walker said, standing up and pulling on the jacket Eve had brought him; like the rest of his new outfit, it fit like it was tailored for him. It suited the airconditioned environment of the hospital, not needed outside if the bright shiny morning out his window and Eve's dress were anything to go by. 'That's how I want to go. On you. Or you on me. That's probably better for you, right? Don't want to be squashed.'

'Can you stop joking around?' Eve pushed him playfully in the chest. 'You're a thirty-nine-year-old man, and I'm being serious. And by serious I mean this is the last time I'm picking you up from hospital. Ever.'

'Okay, sure, play the age card.' Walker puller her in close. 'But aren't you older than me?'

'I think I'll go get the doctor,' Eve said, smiling. 'I think you're having memory problems.'

'Six months older?'

'Respect your elders, that's all I'll say.' She kissed him again.

'I've had worse injuries,' he said, his arms around her. 'And been in far worse situations.'

'Ten tours in Iraq and Afghanistan; yes, the whole ward has heard your stories.' Eve shifted her arms up around his neck. 'But those wars were not like this. This was different.'

'I've been shot before.'

'Twice, yes; all the pretty nurses here have heard your boasting.'

'It'd take more than a bullet or three to stop me.'

'You nearly bled to death, you big oaf, you know that?'

'You underestimate my liver. And blood stores. And passion.'

'Passion?'

'Not to die.'

'Jed . . .'

'Baby steps.' He squeezed her tighter. 'Besides, not wanting to die? That right there is a state of mind that's kept me alive all this time.'

'You sure picked a funny occupation with that kind of outlook and drive.'

'Most of the people I served with didn't want to die young.'

'Most?'

'There's some bat-shit crazy people in the military, just like anywhere else.'

'Right.'

He let her go and they headed out of the room, Eve leading the way and reaching back to hold Walker's hand. As they stood in the large open reception area of the fourth floor, Walker paused and looked back. The unmade bed. The EKG machine on its stand. The small table covered in newspapers and the pen he'd used for the crossword and Sudoku. The window with the impossibly blue sky beckoning beyond.

'You look like you're going to miss this place,' Eve said.

Walker looked to her and smiled. 'One last look, since I won't see the inside of an emergency or recovery room until I'm about ninety, right?'

Eve looked at him sideways. 'Your father's still out there, so I know you're just saying what I want to hear right now.' She took a step in to him and placed a finger over his mouth when he was about to speak. 'No, let me finish. Maybe you have in your mind some kind of plan to *not* run out there and find your father. Okay. That's great. Or maybe it's just the painkillers, or lack of, doing the thinking for you. But Jed, look, I get it, and you know that. I was an Army brat; I know duty and honour and service better than any of the girls you ever met way back when, and I still get it. And I understand that you can never turn your back on that. But you need time off from it all, okay? Time away. It'll be good for you. Your father and whatever he was a part of be damned, right? Right?'

'Right.' He kissed the top of her head. 'You're right. But now is beyond being just good for me. It's good for us.'

'Long time coming, some might say.' Eve smiled up at him and squeezed him tight. 'Some might even say it's a lifetime too long.'

Walker knew that Eve was referring to his military service, and beyond. About something he'd said to her, way back when, on their engagement shorty after he'd graduated from the Air Force Academy: *My work won't pull me away forever.* But it had. The war on terror led to his transition from the Air Force to near-on a decade in the CIA's pointy end of things. Then there was that last year of federal employment, of not quite being able to let things go, in the form of a short stint at the State Department, trying to unravel what his father had started. But try as he might, pretend as he did, he could never fully turn his back and shirk all responsibility. He didn't have a choice in the matter – he'd been dragged along, by his father, and he couldn't let it go until he had answers that were well overdue. But in that moment, right then, where he was holding onto Eve, all else seemed superfluous to life. He no longer felt the need to put his own life on the line to save people he didn't know. Not now. Not when he had this. He'd be mad otherwise. But . . .

'That's all behind me,' Walker said, looking around the ward from where they stood in the negative space between the nurses' station and the lift lobby. It was a constant hum of activity, the medical staff talking and trading information and passing tablet computers and old-school files and clipboards to various hospital staff, assigning activities and chores with professional aplomb. Near the lifts was a seating area with vending machines and old magazines in a rack, next to the three sets of stainless-steel lift doors, and the fire stairs. 'So, where to from here?'

'I got us a hotel downtown with views over the Bay. Figured we can live off room service and binge watch some TV for a week or so. You wait here, invalid. I'll bring the car to the pick-up area, call you when I'm there.'

'I can walk fine.'

'Do as I say,' Eve said, passing him his cell phone. 'You're going to do as I say, all week, Mister Walker, you got that? It's time someone looked after you for a change.'

Walker smiled. 'Sounds too good to be true.'

Eve headed for the lift and pressed the call button, then looked over her shoulder and gave him a look. *That* look. He'd seen it a thousand times, and it never failed. It was a sense of *I get you, and don't you ever believe otherwise.*

Walker was silent. He'd known Eve since high school, and they'd been the best of friends before anything or anyone else important had entered his life. And that seemed to hold true now, in this truce of sorts. Reconciliation. But he felt, in his gut, that it was illusory. He watched her wave a brief goodbye and then walk into the lift. He worried that he was still unable to commit to anything like the normal life and mutual love and respect that she deserved. Not while his father was out there, with Zodiac. It nagged and clawed at him.

The lift pinged. Out of the opening doors came a woman, and she brushed past Eve and scanned the room. Eve went into the lift and waved at him and the doors closed again.

The woman looked around the recovery ward and then started towards the nurses' station, but then stopped – she did a double-take, looking to her left, eyeing up Walker. Her eyes locked on his face and she headed straight for him. She was about the same height and size as Eve, about the same age, her hair jet black and cut at her shoulders. Her skin was a dark tan and her features and her body shape broadcast that she had Central or South American roots in her family.

'Jed Walker,' she said, stopping close into his personal space. There was a panic in her eyes, urgency in her demeanour. 'My name's Rachel Muertos. You need to listen to me, and follow what I say. I'm here to get you out of here. Your life's in danger and time's ticking, so listen hard.'

'Excuse me?' Walker said. He looked from the woman who introduced herself as Rachel Muertos and glanced around the ward. The scene, which he'd taken in over the past couple of weeks, was purely normal. The lift pinged again. An orderly wheeled in a guy Walker knew from rehab.

'We don't have much time,' Muertos said, glancing over her shoulder. 'There are people coming here to kill you.'

3

It wasn't the first time someone had told Walker that he was going to be killed, and he suspected – for all he'd just said to Eve – that it would not be the last. Military service never really let you go. Neither did working for the CIA. And he had a third thing, a trifecta of sorts, something about which no matter how hard he may have wanted to leave this life behind, Eve was right: as long as his father was out there, a man who'd been an expert on global terror and the unwitting brainchild of the Zodiac terror cells, Walker was bound to live by the gun. But right then, right there, he didn't see it; there was something about the setting of the San Francisco hospital that made him more sceptical than usual. And maybe the trace of the previous few days of pain medication was dulling his senses. Something about this Muertos woman, what she said, and the way she said it, seemed like a prank from a friend still in the service.

'People are coming here to kill me?' Walker said.

Rachel Muertos nodded. She looked spooked.

'Look, if you're referring to the hospital catering department,' Walker said, 'you needn't worry. They've done their best to kill me all week, and nearly succeeded with what they call meatloaf, but I'm still here. I might just be invincible.'

Muertos looked at Walker like he was speaking another language.

'I've seen your photo,' she said. 'You *are* Jed Walker. Please, believe what I say – you're in danger here.'

Statement. Definitive. Official. *Legitimate?* Plenty of people had seen Walker's face in the news recently, following the event that had hospitalised him earlier in the week. He'd received flowers and cards from people he didn't know nor ever would, thanking him for putting a bad guy down. There was more to it than that, of course, and Walker knew better – those people were thanking him for keeping the Internet chugging along so that they could respond to friend requests and look up pictures of cats. Among all those notes had been some threats from anarchist groups, which Eve had tried to keep from him as she helped him open the mail. But threats on paper were not the same thing as physical reality. The former were from gutless wannabes; the latter often from unstable or deranged loners. It wasn't a stretch to make Muertos as some kind of sycophant.

'Yes, you've got the right guy,' he said. 'Okay. Where are you from, Muertos?'

'I'm with the State Department.' She showed her ID. 'This is all very complicated, but right now I need you to—'

Walker inspected the ID, saw it was legit. 'Look, Muertos, I don't work for the government anymore. And if someone's coming for me in a hospital in San Francisco, well, bring them on, let's see what they've got.'

Muertos paused a beat, then said, 'I'm here to get you someplace safe. I'll explain everything as we're on the move. This place is compromised.'

Walker gestured around. 'This is hardly Benghazi.'

'I'm not joking around.'

'Okay. So, who's coming to kill me?'

'Men.'

'Men?'

Muertos nodded. 'At least three. Maybe more.'

'And who are these men?'

'I – I don't really know. One of them claims to be from Homeland Security.'

'Are you here alone?'

'I have two cars in the eastern plaza and the drivers waiting for us. Can we go now?'

'Why would someone want to kill me?'

'Walker, please—'

'I really need more,' Walker said, but he could see that Muertos was genuinely scared. 'Where's this threat come from?'

'I was hoping you could shed some light on that,' Muertos said, checking over her shoulder again, and doing little hops, almost imperceptible, from foot to foot. 'Please, we really need to get out of here.'

Walker was silent.

'Follow me out, and we drive around and we talk. Five minutes. If you think it's no good, then, fine, walk away. But at least I told you, warned you.' Muertos looked to the lift lobby for a moment and then focused on him again. 'But you won't think that. Not you. I've read your file. You need to hear this. I've travelled from Syria just to speak to you.'

'Rachel, look. I've been out of government work for a couple of years. You've got more up-to-date people than me who can help you out right now. Besides, I've not been to Syria since the start of all that mess. Find an expert who knows the present lay of the land.'

'This work is stateside,' Rachel said.

'I need more, here and now,' Walker said, picking up his small backpack. 'Tell me more, before I walk over there and press that button and get in the lift. Give me a decent reason to hear you out.'

'Okay,' she said. She bit her lip as though fighting to find the right words in the moment. 'So, I need your help, and I think you need mine.'

Walker shook his head. 'Like I said, I'm out.'

'You did a year for State after you left the Agency, kicking around the Mid East for us.'

Which meant that Rachel Muertos had high-level clearance, because the area of his posting for the State Department was classified above Top Secret.

'Look, Muertos, I'm not the guy you need to help out with something. If you can see, I'm just now getting out of hospital.'

'So did I, just this week. In Syria. And I travelled here via a military hospital in Germany. Now I'm here.'

'Well, you don't look that bad for it.'

Rachel paused, then said, 'Some wounds aren't obvious on the outside.'

'What is it you want from me?' Walker looked at the lift lobby, then his cell phone, waiting for Eve's call to say the car was ready and to head down. He looked up and Rachel Muertos was quiet. It still niggled at him, maybe it was a set-up. Some of the guys back at State or the Agency having a laugh, thinking they'd get him to rush down to the main lobby, where there'd be some kind of 'Surprise!' yelled out and a belated retirement cake and streamers. 'Are there really men, at least three, one claiming to be from Homeland, headed here to kill me?'

'Yes,' Muertos replied, her tone flat and her shoulders hunched a little, as though resigned to the fact that she'd missed her chance to get him out. 'I . . . I might have led them here. In a way. I'm not sure. But indirectly I guess I did – but I can't remember it and—'

Walker held up a hand to signal he'd heard enough and started for the lifts.

'So, I got here as soon as I could, you've got to believe me,' Muertos said, moving to keep in step with him. 'And then I saw them, in the lobby, downstairs. Definitely two guys, with a – a leader, I guess you'd call him. A guy named Krycek, from Homeland. But there may be others. If they're waiting for you to leave the hospital, or if they're coming up here to get you, I don't know.'

Walker stopped and turned to her. 'Then how about I go to the lobby and see what's what?'

Muertos was silent.

'Really,' Walker said. 'If someone's after me, they'd have had their best chance up here, when I was alone in my room, out of sight of the rest of the staff and wards here.'

The lift pinged. Two nurses came out. No-one else. Muertos looked relieved. Walker smiled.

'Walker, I really need your help.'

'Something to do with Syria?'

'Ye— Yes.'

'Why the hesitation just then?'

'I forgot that I mentioned Syria before. That I was there, I mean. The hospital. Then Germany.'

'You okay? Maybe you should still be in hospital?'

'My memory, I – it's complicated. But it was in Germany that I met Krycek. And he spooked the hell out of me. But I'd told him, or some other doctors, your name, so he was a threat to you too, right? So, I broke out, to come and find you – I had to warn you that he might be coming. See? And he's here – I've seen him, he's downstairs with at least two others!'

Walker looked around as a doctor passed. 'So, you're here because you feel guilty about giving my name to a guy from Homeland?'

Rachel fell silent.

'Sorry, Muertos. It's still a no.'

'Walker, you can't say no.' Muertos's voice was full of despair now. '*Please*.'

Walker shook his head and went to the lift and pressed the call button.

Muertos called out, 'It's because of your father.'

Walker turned to Rachel Muertos of the State Department.

She said, 'He told me to find you.'

4

The lift pinged. Two men got out: dark suits, white shirts with dark ties, rubber-soled dress shoes. Both military-age Caucasian. Crew cuts and clean shaven. They looked like they should be wearing fatigues and carrying assault rifles. Each guy looked around, saw Walker and headed straight for him, in step, looking around the ward as they moved. They were both shorter than Walker but not by much. They were maybe ten years younger. Each seemed jacked, ready for action, adrenaline overriding reason. Their eyes took in all the scenery.

'Jed Walker,' the closer one said.

Walker was silent.

'We need to talk, sir,' the other one said, stopping to stand in line with his colleague. They seemed to relax a little. Then he gestured with his ID. 'We're with Homeland Security.'

'Good for you,' Walker said. 'I'll make this simple: I'm leaving.'

'This won't take a minute,' the other guy said. 'In private, if you don't mind. Back in your room, if you will. Promise it won't take a minute. Sir.'

Walker looked at the two men, then back to his empty room, then around the ward still busy with nurses and doctors, then to Muertos. A curious little gang of four people standing in the middle of a working hospital ward. Most of the other patients, from what

Walker had picked up during his few days there, were recovering from elective surgery. A couple had new knees, someone got a new hip, others needed tendon and ligament grafts and repair work. All in all, a place to get things fixed – it could end up being handy, for these two, if they insisted on annoying him.

Walker looked again at Muertos.

Damn.

He could see sweat beaded on her forehead. And in that moment he knew. It's like he could smell her fear, and with that, the legitimacy of what she'd said.

At least three. Maybe more . . . One of them claims to be from Homeland Security.

They'd have had their best chance up here, when I was alone in my room, out of sight.

'You guys wouldn't know an Agent Krycek, would you?' Walker asked.

The two suited men shared a look, which was all the answer he needed. Then, Walker's cell phone rang. He pulled it from his pocket and answered it as the two guys started to object.

'Hey, look,' Walker said to Eve. 'Something's come up. Yep. I'm gonna meet you there. I'll take a cab.'

Walker ended the call. *Something's come up.* Every couple had their codes. Usually it was the kind of line that would get them out of an annoying situation. For the Walkers, it was short-hand to follow instructions due to an imminent threat. *Something's come up* meant that Eve would do as he instructed, no questions asked. They'd used it maybe four times over almost two decades. She'd be in shock right now, given her previous giddy mood, and Walker planned to call her back soon to allay any fears and to set things right.

'Okay,' Walker said to the two Homeland guys, stepping back and glancing towards his empty room. 'After you.'

The two agents hesitated, then one said to Muertos, 'With us, please ma'am.'

Walker nodded to Muertos. He could tell that she sensed he'd changed gears, that he was going to act. The four of them moved as a group, the two Homeland agents up ahead followed by Walker then Muertos. The guy closest to Walker kept glancing back, and when they reached the room and the lead agent held the door open to let everyone pass, the briefest of nods passed between the two Homeland men. Like couples have their coded communications, so did partners in the field, to ensure efficiency. Military and law enforcement used all kinds of looks and gestures as shortcuts to action. And Walker knew that the look and gesture between them was a bad tell. And it told him that he had to act first.

When it came to unarmed combat, Walker had few rules other than to be the one to walk away afterwards. Things could and would change in the blink of an eye, and just when you thought you had an opponent sized up and their moves predicted, they would enter a phase of unpredictability as they attempted to regain control. Wanting to preserve your life would do that. It made even the best training go out the window. That's why any fighter in the world, no matter the martial art or boxing style, trained long and hard, repeating the same moves with monotony so that when the time came, they could rely on muscle memory to move their body the way it had been trained: efficiently, purposefully. Action and reaction, drilled until it became second nature. When you started to mess with those instructions, you inevitably failed. And this was no fight in a ring with rules and procedures to follow.

Take these two guys. In three seconds Walker would know that they had each been Marines at some recent point in their lives for the fighting stance that each went to employ – and three seconds, in a fight, was too long a reaction time. No sooner had Muertos entered the room than the guy at the doorway shut the door and reached out and grabbed her. He had one hand around her neck in a choke hold and the other reaching for the holstered pistol at his hip. That was the first second of action. Walker saw that and kept his concentration on the agent closer to him. By the second second, this one had a weapon already at hand – he'd had it concealed up his left sleeve the entire time, and brought it out and was turning in a wide pivot on his right foot and right arm reaching for Walker to pull him into a headlock.

The weapon was a hypodermic needle in the form of an auto-injector pen, designed by the US military to be able to stab through clothing hard and fast in the event of an emergency, such as administering anti-nerve agents. It was also used by various government agencies to inject barbiturates to render a person unconscious, to later be detained and, perhaps, tortured. Eventually the technology became available to the public, where it was broadly known as an EpiPen or Adrenaclick. Walker caught the guy's wrist, just below the flying needle, and squeezed as hard as he could until he felt the bones compress together and the guy slowed, his face reddened with pain. As he started to react and engage in a fight with his free hand, inside the third second, where he displayed his moves as a former US Marine by the grapple hold he attempted, Walker grasped the guy's other arm and pulled the two wrists together while twisting and turning him around. With his back to Walker and his arms crossed, Walker yanked the arms so that the guy injected himself in the chest.

Three seconds. One threat down, one to go.

As the guy was collapsing to the floor, his colleague had drawn his sidearm and was bringing it up – Walker was moving for him, and Muertos stomped on her captor's foot, a hard sharp blow with the heel of her boot onto the toes of the cheap dress shoes. The guy grunted at the sound of tiny bones snapping, and he let Muertos go.

Walker closed the gap and with his left hand on the inside of the guy's rising gun hand he squeezed and twisted. A shot rang out. Walker kept twisting, and the weapon clattered to the ground. The guy punched at Walker, so Walker grabbed that wrist too.

'You can get out of this okay,' Walker said to him, twisting his hands out and down, putting more pain on the guy's wrist and elbow and shoulder joints while bringing him closer in. 'What do you want here?'

'You're trapped here, Walker . . .' The guy was deep red in the face with the exertion of trying to fight the twisting motion on his arms, and Walker didn't stop. This was no compliance hold. This was an action to put this guy down, and out of the fight, for a long, long time. Major reconstructive work was in this guy's near future. Walker's hands were tight around the guy's wrists and he twisted all the way, well beyond any arresting cop would, twisting and turning and increasing the pressure until the guy's shoulders dislocated, forearm bones shattering on the way, tendons snapped, and as he came rushing downwards desperately trying to relieve the pressure, Walker kneed him in the face. The guy fell to the floor, unconscious.

Five seconds, beginning to end. Two ex-Marines posing as Homeland Security agents down and out.

'What was . . .' Muertos stood there, trying to find the words. 'Disgusting.'

'He's in a good place for the medical attention he's gonna need,' Walker said. He checked pulses on both the agents: both were alive. He put each into the recovery position, and then he picked up the fired pistol, a Glock 19, and field stripped it, pocketing the recoil spring. He checked their pockets. Each wallet contained what looked like legitimate Homeland Security Agency ID. Both cell phones seemed the kind of bland government-issue Blackberry that Homeland agents would receive. The hypodermic was labelled *Etorphine*, which Walker knew well was used by the CIA to render suspects unconscious. He'd seen enough. 'Let's get out of here.'

'How?' Muertos asked.

Outside the room, the nurses' station was still. Four staff stood and stared, the phones and pagers ringing and bleeping around them.

The gunshot. Walker headed past the lifts to the first set of stairs, and as he held the door open for Muertos he pulled the little red lever on the wall, then followed her through as the hospital fire alarm started to shriek.

5

The klaxon blazed and Walker and Muertos emerged with a mass of staff, patients and visitors onto the eastern concourse.

'This way!' Muertos said over the hubbub, and pushed and ducked her way through various human obstacles.

Walker had a clear path. Crowds have a certain type of hive mind, something innate that makes smaller people move for bigger people –some deeply ingrained survival instinct, rather than good manners. Walker was a big guy making his way ahead like a shark moving through a school of fish – the smaller people, a crowd numbering in the hundreds, shifted and moved out the way. The evacuees ended near the curb. He looked up and down the road: no-one about but pedestrians on a Sunday morning in San Francisco, rubbernecking at the growing mass of people evacuating the hospital. There was a distant siren, but apart from that, there was something reverential about the time. Sunday. As if everything were quieter, calmer. From the cars on the road to the birds in the sky. Life was taking stock. Walker, too.

Two big blacked-out SUVs rolled up and Muertos got in the second vehicle and Walker shuffled in after her. The door closed, and the cars moved off. Smooth, efficient. Melted into the streets. Walker didn't see any other obvious threats.

A suited guy was at the wheel. The vehicle in front kept at the speed limit as they merged onto the 101. Walker figured they were headed for the airport – which, if those guys back there really were from Homeland Security, would be a bad idea. You get on a plane, you have to show ID. If Walker showed ID, and he was for some reason on a Homeland watchlist, then the TSA officers, belonging as they did to a subordinate agency of the Department of Homeland Security, would detain him.

'Okay.' Walker looked across to Muertos. 'What do you know of my father?'

The mention of his father had sealed it. Not the attack. His father. Walker had no choice but to tag along and see where this rabbit hole went. Muertos seemed to compose herself before answering. She let out a deep breath, looked at the scene out the window, then turned to Walker. In Walker's experience, people who needed time to get their thoughts together were forming a lie, or a version of the truth that suited the situation.

'Nothing.'

'But you saw him.'

'Yes.'

'Where?'

'In Syria.'

'Syria? What was happening in Syria?'

'That's a long story.'

'I'm a good listener.' Which was true. Walker preferred to listen than to talk, given the choice; talking just enough to get some good listening in. Listening to someone talk was to sit in judgement. He had been in the business of judging and recruiting agents to oversee and run for the CIA for the best part of a decade – a job he'd proved good at. The Socratic method, as he'd learned at the CIA's trade-craft school at The Point: questioning, seeking answers by making the subject think aloud, drawing out the answer from them. So far, Muertos was someone to mine for information. He'd yet to form a solid opinion of her other than she had given him the heads-up at the hospital – but to what extent that was her doing in the first place he was keen to figure out. 'Just keep it relevant. And tell me how you fit in.'

'Okay. I was in Syria as an undercover, working on an anti-human-trafficking taskforce,' Muertos said to Walker, looking down at her hands as she spoke. 'With the refugee crisis there, it's a big, big business. There are tiers depending on what the person who wants out of the country can offer as payment. For the well heeled, those with hard currency or easily tradable assets, some of them can pay up to a million dollars per person to get to a Western nation like Germany or the US or Canada or Australia, with full ID papers and a new life waiting for them. Then there are those who pay about fifty grand per person to just get into a Western country. Those who can pay about half that can get transit to any Western nation's border. Then there's all the others – that's the ninety-plus per cent, those who can't pay because they've got nothing to give – nothing but their lives. They're making all kinds of deals to get out. You name it: selling kids as slaves; selling wives and mothers and daughters into sex rings. And when they do get into new nations, they're expected to pay off the debt. For years.'

'I'm aware of most of that,' Walker said. 'Saw it happening in Iraq and Afghanistan, though the money involved seemed far less.'

'There are some wealthy people who found themselves on the wrong side of the ledger in the aftermath of the Arab Spring.'

Walker shifted in his seat. 'How does my father fit in?'

'I was at a meet in Damascus,' Muertos said. When she spoke she continued to look down at her hands, her fingers linked together and moving in a stress-related action. 'We'd closed in on a high-level smuggling outfit, were due to meet the local kingpin, who would lead us to his contact back here in the US. That's where I saw your father, at that meet. He came into the building. He met with the guy I was to meet with, which meant he was offering up more money than my local fixer and I were. At least five million US. Then . . .'

Walker let her silent pause hang in the air a moment, then asked, 'What'd he want?'

'I couldn't hear, he was across the warehouse, and it was a noisy place – military jets overhead and small-arms fire nearby. But I made out that he was American because my fixer had met him before.'

'Who was your fixer?'

'Just a local guy wanting to help out,' Muertos said. 'He'd lost his family to this smuggling outfit, so he wanted to see them taken down. Your father had gone to him a few days before me.'

'Saying what?'

'We didn't get to that.'

'What's that mean?'

'The meet went south, right as my fixer was recounting the story. My guy was among the first to die. A lot of people died that day. Five people from State. All our local fixers and support staff. Dozens of refugees.'

'What happened with my father?'

'He got away.'

'Where?'

Muertos shrugged. 'Do you know of him doing any business in Syria?'

'He was meant to be arrested, in Malta, four days ago.'

'Why?'

'Why?' Walker's eyes searched Muertos's and found nothing. 'I find it hard to believe that you know about me, and yet you don't know about my father and that side of things.'

Rachel shook her head. Walker looked from her to the scene outside his window. *Could she really not know? Maybe her security clearance with State was compartmentalised – after all, David Walker's case was outside the wheelhouse.* His father, who'd been a rogue element to the US government for years, was wanted all over the place, with suspected ties to the Zodiac terror group. *Surely she'd know that much . . .*

'Years ago,' Walker said, watching concrete and cars as they sped along the road, 'my father had a hand in creating a program of worse-case terror attacks. It was at a Washington think tank, a post-nine-eleven thing, our brightest Intelligence minds gathered together to try to make sure we weren't taken by surprise again. He developed something that, a long time later, has started playing out for real – it's like he stuffed a genie in a bottle, and then it got out.'

'With or without his help?' Muertos asked. There was genuine interest and concern written on her face.

'I'm trying to figure that out,' Walker said. 'Short version, what he cooked up was code-named Zodiac. Twelve cut-out cells, where each attack would trigger the next, and that was the extent of their connection. A far scarier terror outfit than anything we'd seen, because there was no overriding motive of the attackers, no shared ideology driving them – therefore you couldn't find a pattern to predict and counter future events. Three have already played out. Many believe that my father is an active part of it, and because of that he's a fugitive from the US government.'

'For arranging the terror attacks?'

Walker nodded.

Muertos paused, bit at her lip. 'Do you believe he could be doing that?'

'I'm not sure. I doubted it, but now I'm not sure. He may have a hand in driving it.'

'You want to find out.'

'Of course. And to do that, I need to find him.'

'He told me to find you. *Find Jed Walker.* After things went south, that's what said to me, verbatim. *Find Jed Walker.*'

'I still don't get why he'd say that. When was this?'

'Three days ago.'

'The day after he fled Malta.'

'It's a short boat ride to Syria.'

'What was he doing there, at the meet?'

'Buying.'

'Buying?'

Rachel nodded.

Walker said, 'Buying what?'

'People.'

6

Two thousand miles away on the east coast of the United States, a man called Harvey used a cell phone to call a man named Lewis. Not that they would ever use their names over the airwaves. The phones were new cheap throw-away things, mission specific, untraceable.

'We've got a problem,' Harvey said.

'I knew that when this phone rang,' Lewis said. 'Emergency protocols only, you said.' There wasn't concern or malice in his voice, just a slight tinge of disappointment, and it made Harvey cringe. They were equal partners, but Harvey was handling the logistics and hands-on element of their little enterprise, and it was that which was suffering the problems.

Harvey said, 'It's Rachel Muertos.'

'You found her?'

'She's here, in the US.'

'Well, that's good news, isn't it? Two birds, one stone.'

'I'm not sure yet. We know she entered the country, but we can't find her. But it's her being here that has me worried.'

'Why?'

'How'd she get into the country? It wasn't through a civilian airport, we had her flagged on a watchlist.'

'She's resourceful, you said that when she went missing from Germany,' Lewis said. 'It's a big military base over there, right? And she's a pretty little thing from the State Department. Maybe she traded a favour to get stateside on a military transport rotating back? Bypass customs altogether.'

'You think she stowed away?' Harvey asked.

'You said she was canny.'

'She's surprised me, I suppose. Her husband never said much about her. There was never any talk of her being an investigator or field agent.'

'Well, now you know not to underestimate her. Where is she?'

'San Francisco.'

'Why? What's there?'

'The guy she mentioned in hospital . . .'

There was silence, then Lewis said, 'Jed Walker.'

'Yes.'

'You said he was being taken care of.'

'He got away. With Muertos. They're now together.'

'Well, that's just perfect.'

Harvey was silent.

Lewis said, 'How much does she know?'

'I'm not sure. Can't be much.'

'You need to fix it.'

'I know that.'

'This is your problem.'

'I know that too.'

'Then stop wasting time.'

'They're on a watchlist,' Harvey said. 'If they try to fly anywhere or use their credit cards or ID, I'll have them. That's the best I can do at the moment. Wait for them to turn up.'

'So, what's the problem?'

'Walker. He's got me worried. He's the last person we want coming after us.'

'You're saying that like it's news to me. Look at his father. He's been on a watchlist for two years and he's evaded you. The younger

Walker was pedigree to start with, and it seems he's done all he can in life to hone his skills. You have to fix this, fast.'

'How far do you want me to take this?' Harvey asked.

'What are you saying?'

'If I make him public enemy number one, put his name out to all the local police across the country, we find him quickly. But it might show our hand. Prove whatever he thinks is going on. Make him less predictable.'

There was a pause, then Lewis said, 'What do you imagine I think about that course of action?'

Harvey was silent.

Lewis said, 'Do this quietly. We've come so far in just a couple of years. Too far to risk discovery now. And if Jed Walker manages to work things out with his father, and Muertos points them to us, well, everything we've worked at will come apart at the seams.'

•

Two thousand miles away, on the west coast, the two black SUVs drove on, undetected, no-one in pursuit.

'People?' Walker said. 'Refugees?'

Rachel nodded.

'Why would my father want to buy refugees?'

'I don't know.'

'At what point did he speak to you?'

'I'll get to that. I was there as a broker. The smugglers – the people traffickers – were going to be brought in later. We needed that next-level guy, up the chain. We were giving him marked notes, a new type of nano-tracking tech that the Treasury Department has developed to counter organised crime – they mark the bills with a nano-tech trace designed to rub off on hands and clothing and hair and stay there a hell of a long time – you practically have to burn it out, so I'm told. So, the plan was that we'd track him, watch him, follow him up the chain all the way to his contact back here in the US.'

'And my father?'

'He was a late addition – I had no idea who he was or where he came from. There was another buyer due – a big one, supposed to take out over two thousand people via Russian-flagged cargo ships leaving Syria. Before he and his crew showed, your father appeared. And he had a friend.'

'Who?'

'Big guy. About the same age.'

'Describe him.'

'Your height, maybe six-four, big in the shoulders, looked like an ex-footballer – big all over, maybe four hundred pounds. Mop of red-brown hair. Friendly face. Other side of sixty. Kind of like Orson Welles in the later years. He stuck close to your father the whole time, like he was his best friend and bodyguard rolled into one.'

'Marty Bloom,' Walker said. He pictured the guy who'd been like a second father to him. Former CIA, long ago retired to Croatia. 'That name familiar?'

'I didn't get a name.'

'But you got my father's name.'

'Right. But only after I looked into you, and then in your bio notes I saw a picture of your father. Until then I didn't know the connection.'

'Okay. So, this deal somehow went south and then they told you to find me.'

Muertos shook her head. 'Not they. Just your father. He came back. After it all went to hell. I guess to check on his friend.'

Walker knew the news before she said it.

'They killed your father's friend.'

7

'There was a lot of shooting,' Muertos said. She spoke quickly, seeing Walker's reaction. 'He was killed in the crossfire. Instantly.'

Walker had last seen Bloom in Dubrovnik. The old guy had saved Walker's bacon. He'd helped him track his father, organised papers and transit when there were forces hunting him. It wasn't the first time he'd had a hand in saving his life. But Bloom was a giant. A titan of the Agency. Indestructible. He'd survived wars and incursions and insurrections, outsmarted Ba'ath Party death squads, hunted down and executed Pinochet's evil doers, survived the worst parts of the Serbian war. *And he was killed in crossfire?*

'What was my father after?' Walker said. He let his hands relax in his lap, his knuckles still white with tension.

'A family.'

'Specifically?'

'One with young children. Biggest family available. Five million cash – which he brought with him. He wanted them to be provided with full US papers, legit social security and birth certificates, the works. Apparently the sellers and your father had all this prearranged, because the transaction went by without fuss and was over quickly.'

'But something went wrong.'

Muertos nodded.

'Wrong enough for you to end up in hospital.'

'Pro-government forces arrived,' Muertos said. 'It was a bloodbath.'

'Pro Syrian government?'

Muertos nodded.

'I would assume they'd be in on the take at some level,' Walker said. 'That's been my experience with this kind nothing. If those human traffickers were so good, and making the kind of money you say, they'd need to have guys paid off up the food chain to ensure they were left alone, or at least so they could be tipped off in the event of a raid. Surely the Syrian government and its staffers are desperate for cash.'

'This was the President's personal guard,' Rachel said. 'His secret police. Like Saddam's inner Republican Guard and the Gestapo wrapped into one ugly and tooled-up outfit. They're tight. Well looked after and loyal – as incorruptible as you can get. Their methods make ISIS look tame. They showed up and it went to hell straightaway, with everyone ... it was horrific. The firefight lasted maybe two or three minutes but felt like an hour. A few of the smugglers got out, including the top guy. My State Department team – everyone was killed but me. Somewhere in the mayhem your father got out.'

'And that was it?' Walker said. 'They turned up simply to kill everyone? No arrests? Or it could have been a heist – maybe they wanted the cash?'

'They left the money behind. And no, there were no arrests. Hard to tell at first if your father was wounded or not. There was blood everywhere. When it went down I was taking cover next to him. His friend, Bloom, was already down, and your father was trying to get to him. I still had a State security contractor next to me, laying down suppressing fire. I didn't know who your father was, but he was American, right? I called out to him, told him to come with us – then my guy was dropped. I thought that was it. I told your father that I was with the State Department – that if we got out, I'd work out a deal for him, amnesty, if he told me his involvement. Your father took a pistol, provided cover for me, and told me go. I ran. I didn't make it out of the building. It was an old warehouse and factory, a real rabbit warren. The room I ran into was carnage. The smugglers' guys were down to their last, holding off the government troops.'

Rachel fell silent. Walker stretched out in the seat and watched her, waiting. He could see the trauma, in her eyes. Eyes that never stayed still, always searching. Or wary. The only make-up she wore was lip gloss. Her skin was dark tan and clear, her hair and eyes close to black. She could pass for Syrian or from any of the Mid East countries, a likely candidate for the State Department to send over there to blend in and make contacts. She had the air of someone who'd seen too much and was having trouble processing it. Walker had seen that on too many soldiers. He'd been through it too. There was little you could do for it but allow for the passage of time and maturity. For some it took years to sleep through the night again. For a few it was simply too much to bear. But Muertos had resolve. Drive. Something pushing her on.

'The thing is, when the government guys swept through I survived only because I was hiding under dead bodies. They presumed I was dead. They dumped more on me, then doused it with fuel. I thought that was it – I was going to be burned alive. I was about to scream – better to take a bullet, right? But then gunshots rang out from the main warehouse and they ran to that. I was left there for hours. At first too afraid to move, then unable to, for the mass of bodies. And that's when your father came back, and he helped me out, and he told me to find you.'

'That's all he said?'

'That's all. Three words. *Find Jed Walker.* Like if I did, you'd know what it meant. I ran from the scene and I passed out in a street two miles later – just collapsed and blacked out. Apparently I was taken to hospital in Damascus, where some MSF doctors realised I was American and transferred me to a US military hospital in Germany. That first twenty-four hours are a blur, but I'd been muttering your name. Then I met the Homeland guy, Krycek. He's scary. There was something seriously not right about him, so I busted out. It was there that I used a computer to reach out to a friend back here. Then I got on the next flight I could, a military transport rotating back. I got back and made some calls to friends, and found out where you were. And that's it.'

Walker looked from Muertos to his hands, now relaxed, then out the window at the streets of San Francisco. 'Weird.'

'What?'

'That my father would say that. Only that.' He looked at her and searched her eyes. 'Not even a clue. He wants you to find me. But why?'

Muertos looked away. 'You'll figure it out.'

'All I've got to go by are three words.'

Muertos looked up to him. 'I studied your service record from the Air Force.'

'And?'

'It's impressive. Valuable skills.'

'For warfare.'

'They translate.'

'For what?'

'You found more Taliban and al Qaeda high-value targets in Afghanistan than anyone else.'

'I was part of a team hunting them down. I had the resources of the Defence Department behind me. And all kinds of Intelligence agencies. And NATO. And all you've got is a contact here you want to talk with. I think in forty-eight hours you're going to be right where you started, none the wiser.'

'I'm already doing better than when I started.'

'How?'

'I've found you.'

'So, what's your next step?'

'I want to find the American contact, find out what happened in Syria and why. I think I can get to next up the chain, because there's an undercover agent here, a fixer we'd used back in Syria. He'll have intel to move us forward.'

'Us?'

Muertos nodded.

Walker let it slide. 'How are you so sure?'

'Yeah, about that . . .'

8

Muertos's undercover agent was of Syrian descent with a family in Annapolis, Maryland. He'd been in the US Navy thirteen years and a special advisor to the State Department since. *Special Advisor to State*, which Walker read as CIA.

'His name's Hassan. He wasn't at our meet, but he was meant to be,' Muertos said. 'He was the intermediary. Our local fixer's boss. He'd set it all up for us. And he'd messaged through that he was running late.'

'How late?'

'Twenty minutes, by which time the regime's guys showed and started shooting. And he'd never been late.'

'You couldn't contact him?'

Muertos shook her head. 'Cell network isn't great in Damascus.'

'Speaking of, I need to pick up a new phone. They might track this one.' Walker tapped the phone in his hand; he'd call Eve with it just before he ditched it. He needed something cheap and prepaid, so he could use it with anonymity and trash it soon after.

'You can get one at the airport.'

'Right. We can't take San Francisco; Homeland will be all over it.'

'I know. I've got something quicker. Quieter.'

•

The driver of their SUV pulled up to short-term drop off at Gnoss Field airport in Marin County. The driver of the lead vehicle was already out and moving, and opened Walker's door. As Walker stepped out he saw Muertos pass a fat envelope to their driver.

'What was that?' Walker asked as they stood outside the small private departures terminal and watched the big black SUVs drive off.

'They're contractors,' Muertos replied.

'That you have to pay with cash?'

Muertos looked around. 'I'm trying to be careful here. I think someone on my team at State might be compromised. That could be the reason the meet was blown. With or without Hassan's input.'

'Are you suspicious of anyone?'

Muertos shook her head and led Walker through the small terminal. There was no check-in line or security, because all of the aircraft were owned and operated by the people assigned to fly on them. Inside the big open terminal space was a desk with a couple of staffers to handle questions and bookings and logistical issues, a small convenience store, a cafe, and lounges and armchairs spread about to accommodate around fifty people. Walker bought a pre-paid phone. Muertos didn't bother with the desk and headed straight through to the tarmac, where she spoke to a guy in a high-visibility vest who pointed towards a waiting Gulfstream V two hundred metres away.

Walker's first call was to Eve, and he transcribed some numbers into his new phone while making calls on the old. He told her things were fine, but to keep off the grid for twenty-four hours, when he'd contact her on a new number.

'Can you tell me what's going on?'

'Marty Bloom has been killed,' Walker said.

'Oh Jed, I'm so sorry.'

'I need to find out what's going on,' Walker said. 'Call Paul if you have any hassles.'

'Okay. And Jed? Stay safe.'

'Always.' He ended the call and tried three more numbers. The first two went straight to voicemail. The third number was answered.

'Hey,' the voice said. It belonged to FBI Special Agent Fiona Somerville, a friend and sometime colleague of Walker. While still an active FBI agent, she was assigned to *Room 360*, a small multi-national UN investigative outfit tasked with counter-terror investigations.

'You the only one working today?' Walker asked. 'I just tried McCorkell and Hutchinson.'

'They're somewhere over the Atlantic, headed for Belgium,' Somerville said.

'What's in Belgium?'

'Chocolates.'

'And you know why they invented the chocolates, right?'

'If the punchline is something about child abuse, don't say it.'

'Fine. Why are they headed over there?'

'Work. You know, that thing where someone pays you money in exchange for you doing or making something? You should try it sometime.'

'Thanks, I'll file that one away. Much funnier than my joke.'

'Anyway, I'm out of McCorkell's UN outfit. I'm now back at FBI in New York, working a mind-numbing fraud case. Wanna swap with whatever you've got going on?'

'Depends, is your case a *Wolf of Wall Street* type of thing?'

'Nope. Some guy's been skimming a penny or two per transaction at a company he's worked at for thirty years.'

'A penny?' Walker asked, ditching all the phone packaging and heading outside towards the aircraft.

'Sometimes two, if he felt he could get away with it. There were almost two hundred million transactions over that time. You know what two hundred million transactions of one or two missing pennies looks like?'

'About two million transactions of missing dollars?'

'Right. Like I said, you want a job, we're hiring.'

'Have to take a rain check. I'm onto something . . .' Walker gave her Muertos's name and asked her to look into her background. 'I just had a couple of Homeland agents visit me, and it wasn't a friendly house call. I'll message you their IDs, if you can check them out, see who they report to. Email me what you find. We're headed to Virginia to check a lead. I'm switching phones after this call, I'll call you when we land.'

'Okay.'

Walker ended the call, then pulled his phone apart and pocketed it. As he and Muertos crossed the tarmac, he said, 'Who knows you're back in the US?'

'Someone I trust,' Muertos said.

'Just one person?'

'That's it.'

Walker kept pace with her but didn't say anything. This didn't smell right, but he would make a call of his own within the next twenty-four hours to settle that. The Gulfstream's co-pilot greeted them at the bottom of the stairs, and they were aboard and the stairs folded up into the cabin and the door closed and the business jet taxiing to the runway and taking off all in the time it took them to settle in to oversized seats and buckle their belts. The aircraft took off north-west, into the headwind, and as it quickly climbed it went into a slow and gradual east-bound curve that would have them headed to Virginia.

Walker said, 'So, we get to Norfolk to talk to Hassan?'

'It's the only lead I have.'

'Do you think he's bent?'

'Maybe. It certainly crossed my mind. Like, straightaway, when he was a no-show and the bullets started flying.'

'So, if you had to call it one way or the other?'

'Then yes, he is. Got to be.'

'Had you ever been suspicious of him?'

'No. Other than that day, and then afterwards, when I had time to think back on it. It's just too big a coincidence that he wasn't there when the government forces showed, right?'

'Why do you think he would have sold you out to the regime forces? What's in it for him?'

'I don't know. But that's what I was thinking, when I was under those bodies. How I wanted to face him and question him. Preferably at gunpoint. I lost friends that day.' Muertos paused, then said, 'And you lost a friend too. Sorry.'

'Or maybe they made Hassan?' Walker said, acknowledging her reference to Bloom with a a slight nod. Now was not the time to let his sadness and anger cloud his judgement, and he tried to push Bloom to the back of his mind. He hoped revenge would come soon enough. 'Maybe someone there, on the trafficking side, discovered he wasn't who he said he was. Bled him for information. Syrian regime forces are good at getting people to talk. Especially those with family, like Hassan. So, don't get hell-bent on the idea that he sold you out for profit, or the fun of it.'

'I've since thought about that too. But he's still the best lead, right?'

'Right. He may have sold you out,' Walker said, watching out his window. 'Whether he wanted to or not will prove interesting. I mean, what's his motive? Was he a sleeper for the regime, designed to turn over as many Americans as he could over a long duration? It's happened before. He could have been bent all through his Navy years, selling secrets to the Syrians and their Russian proxies. Or was his hand forced? He might have been taken in by the Syrian government and tortured for intel, or he might have had a flat tyre or got stuck in traffic and had nothing at all to do with what went down – there are any number of other things that might have prevented him from being at that meet. Coincidences do happen, like them or not. Life isn't fiction – there's little to no neatness to it, and it's often stranger than anything some writer could make up.'

'Yes, I get all that. But Hassan's still my first port of call. Well, after I found you.'

'Okay, so we get to Hassan, we question him – we need to know what he was up to that day, and where he stands in the scheme of things,' Walker said. 'But you've got another angle.'

'What's that?'

'The US contact for your smuggling outfit. You said they had a contact back here, the one you were trying to make, and track, via the money handling.'

'But I still don't know who they are,' Muertos replied. 'The meet didn't go through, remember?'

'But you said the guy at the scene got out, the head of the trafficking ring?'

'Right.'

'And he handled the money, laced with your nano-track?'

Muertos was silent.

'My bet is that he's well out of the country now,' Walker said. 'Not out of the game, but out of Syria – no way a cashed-up guy is going to hang around in a place where he knows he's marked by the regime in power. He's cooked, retired from frontline work. So, he flees, to take up a position elsewhere in the network. Somewhere that the current Syrian government, and their Russian allies, can't get to him.'

'Where?'

'Here, I'd say. Could be another Western nation, but here makes more sense, if it's his main money earner as a destination, and he has a contact in place. And for him, the benefit of being in the US is that we have the best security apparatus in the world, so he'll feel safer here, more protected from reprisals or assassination, than he would in the UK or Canada.'

Muertos nodded, like it made sense to her.

'He handled the money,' Walker said. 'So, you can track him, right?'

'I guess.'

'You guess?'

'That's . . .'

'Complicated?'

Muertos nodded, but didn't answer.

'You have to be honest with me,' Walker said. 'If I'm getting into this, you gotta tell me everything.'

9

Harvey called Lewis, who picked up after a few rings.

'This had better be urgent,' Lewis said.

'It's been four hours since we lost them at the hospital,' Harvey said. 'And there's been no sign of them. Nothing. Not at airports, nor at any mass transit terminal.'

'That's why you're calling me?'

'It's important.'

'This hands-on stuff is your role.'

'I know. It's just . . . I need to think out loud. Bounce ideas.'

'Okay. So, you're saying they've disappeared? Gone to ground? Or they're in a private car?'

'I think they're either hiding somewhere, or in transit.'

'What's your gut telling you?'

'They're headed east. Muertos is home. She's found Walker, and teamed up with him. What's next? She reaches out to friends.'

'How?'

'They'll be travelling by car. Or maybe a private flight.'

'So, track the private flights.'

'You know how many there are?'

'I have a rough idea. You've got a big tool at your disposal, now's the time to use it, wouldn't you say?'

'Going down that road, making more noise, will make this public. We can't afford the scrutiny. Not now.' Harvey hesitated, then said, 'Right?'

Silence. Then, 'Where's Krycek?'

'Still in San Francisco. He was there, with two other agents, both of whom are now getting medical attention following their run-in with Walker.'

Lewis sighed. 'So, send Krycek east. Have him wait until they pop up on the grid. They will. And then have him put an end to this little side issue. Use Krycek. Let him do what he does best.'

'But you wanted them alive today.'

'Because you said your guys could do that – *pick them up and see what's what*, isn't that what you said? And how'd that work out?'

This time Harvey was silent.

'We tried your softly-softly approach,' Lewis said. 'Time to adapt. But you're right to be prudent. Keep this in-house, quiet. Let Krycek loose on them. It's only two targets, how hard can it be?'

•

Walker had heard her story in greater detail. How Muertos and a joint-agency and departmental task force was combatting human trafficking in and around Syria and Libya. The difficulties they had on the ground, where there was effectively no government, or a hostile one, and near to everyone was corrupt, and those few who weren't were scared to get involved with American forces. Her story wasn't a new one, and it would be repeated by other agents just like her for many, many years ahead. So long as there was war and conflict, there would be displaced people doing anything they could to flee, and that would create a market for the entrepreneurial predators who emerged in such situations.

'How'd you find me?' Walker asked after about an hour's silence. They were somewhere over one of the Virginias, and the banking meant they were coming around from south-west to north-east on a wide landing approach.

Muertos sat up a little straighter in her chair. 'What do you mean?'

'How'd you know what hospital I was in?'

'I—' Muertos caught herself. But there was something there, Walker saw.

'You could Google me, my name, read some stuff I've done,' Walker said. 'But finding me? That'd take outside help. All those letters and cards of congratulations I got this week went to city hall in SF, or via the FBI. No-one outside my few immediate friends knew where I was.'

Rachel nodded. 'I had a friend help out. She's in the Department of Justice, the same one who was handling the nano-track on the money. I reached out to her from Germany, and by the time I landed in Georgia, she had your location, and some deeper bio info.'

'Sounds like she's a good friend to have.'

'Yes. She owed me one. But now I owe her about ten.'

'You trust her?'

'With my life.'

'Then reach out to her again? About the nano-track? She might have found the US contact by now.'

'She'll be onto that. I can set up a meet with her, but anything further, I've got to do it in person. She made that clear, when I called her from Germany – she's paranoid about security over phone and email, because this was a favour, not a sanctioned thing. It's her career on the line.'

'Where's she at?'

'DC.'

'We'll go there after meeting with Hassan. Hook up a meet.'

Muertos nodded. 'What do you want from her?'

'Let's talk and see where she's at with that nano-track. Find the money, we find the man – either the guy from that meet, or the next up the line, or both.'

10

As they came in for landing, Walker's eyes were closed but he didn't sleep. He compartmentalised all the information Muertos had given him, and ordered it about, then re-ordered it. Looking for a pattern that wasn't obviously apparent. The op in Syria, the missing agent, the mess-up at the meet, his father's appearance and then disappearance, Bloom's death, the off-books favour from the friend in the Justice Department.

What bugged him most about it all, aside from the news of his friend, was his father going back, two hours later, to help Muertos out – and specifically, telling her to find him. Why? Was this in any way related to Zodiac? Could it be? If there was a connection, Walker couldn't see it. Maybe his father wanted that family to get into the US and make contact with him. Maybe they were going to send a message, from father to son, face to face, to avoid detection or interception. But he would never know.

By the time the Gulfstream taxied and came to a stop and the door opened, Walker knew he had to reach out to a friend.

'Had you spent much time with Hassan?'

'No,' Muertos said. 'He was being handled by others on the team. I'd met him maybe four times, each in passing. But the team had nothing but trust in him.'

'So, you'd recognise him.'

'Of course,' Muertos said.

'Good. When we land, do you have access to a vehicle?'

'No, I'll need to get us a rental.'

Walker shook his head. 'Homeland Security will be all over our credit cards and IDs. We'll need to borrow one from somewhere.'

'Borrow?'

'Temporarily.'

'Steal?'

'Only for little bit.'

'I can do better,' Muertos said. She pulled her purse from her small bag. 'I've got State Department emergency ID.'

'Has it ever been used?' Walker knew the type of ID, issued to all operational agents outside the US, usually Canadian passports, should US diplomatic IDs be compromised in an emergency or war-like situation.

'No.'

Walker looked at the passport that Muertos handed over: Rochelle Jones of Canada. It was as legitimate as a real passport because it was made by the Canadian government and issued to their allies, who reciprocated the favour.

Walker said, 'Any chance Homeland has access to this?'

'No. They're completely compartmentalised, for security purposes, and I generated the name myself. It's clean, as is the matching credit card, so we can hire a car.'

'Okay, we'll do it your way,' Walker said, passing the passport back. 'We hustle out to Hassan, then make contact with your Justice Department friend. But keep your eyes and ears open at all times. Those Homeland guys weren't there to quietly ask us questions. Whatever this is leading to, it's bound to get rougher before we're done.'

●

Fiona Somerville used the Department of Homeland Security database of Federal Employees to find out about Rachel Muertos.

Rachel Maria Muertos. Analyst for the State Department. Married, no children. Husband, also in the State Department as a special investigator, listed as KIA in the field three months ago. Rachel had been on stress leave since. Her latest assignment had her working on an inter-agency operation to combat people-smuggling out of the Middle East. There were several pages of information from the Office of Personnel Management's Human Resource team; results from psych evaluations and her security clearance. There were a few reports from her superiors, from notation of jobs well done and comments on her aptitude for certain tasks and ability to work under pressure, to the notations around her husband's death and the recommendation that she be put on indefinite leave pending favourable psych evals.

Somerville copied all the information into an email and sent it to Walker.

•

Rachel Muertos's State Department file was flagged with an electronic trigger. When it was accessed by the FBI on behalf of Special Agent Fiona Somerville, an alert popped up in the internal review service of the Diplomatic Security Service, the policing, protective and investigative arm of the State Department.

The Agent in Charge of the unit made two calls. First, to the FBI field office in New York, where he left a message for the Assistant Director asking for a *please explain* on the unauthorised access.

Then he placed his second call, to the number listed in the flag, to notify that person that the personnel files had been looked into. He ended the call and thought nothing of it; it was all well above his pay grade.

11

As Muertos organised a rental car, Walker checked the email on his new phone.

Two messages, both from Somerville.

The first email from Somerville contained Muertos's bio notes. He scrolled through the bullet points, forming a clearer picture of his new apparent partner. Born in Mexico. Immigrated when she was five years old. Grew up in California, then college in Florida. Poli-science and then graduate school in three languages: Spanish, Arabic, Farsi. Fourteen years in the State Department: South America desk for the first half, then seconded to the Iran desk in DC. Did most of her work stateside but for a couple of postings to the Embassy in Tehran. Her last performance review listed her as 'above competent'. Her security clearance was lower than Walker had assumed. That was it.

The second email from Somerville was also about Muertos, and was not a bio.

Walker, Muertos was on an op that went wrong. She wasn't supposed to be in Syria at all – she left her posting in Iran to take up a role as a back-room agent, working phones and coordinating, on a multi-agency anti-trafficking op. There's little detail, but she ended up in a local Médicins Sans Frontiéres tent hospital in Damascus, in a delirious state. She was sedated and remained unconscious for around twenty-four hours. She was ID'd and shipped to

56

Ramstein for observation. Medical reports there had her as showing signs of amnesia. Muertos skipped out of the military hospital during her second day there and had not been seen since. That was forty-eight hours ago. And she's here? How'd she get back into the country? What was she doing in Syria? State and the FBI want to talk to her. I got chewed out for accessing her file – it was tagged back to Homeland. Be careful.

•

Harvey called Krycek on their mission-specific burner phones.

'They're in Baltimore,' Harvey said.

Krycek was in a chartered Homeland aircraft. 'I'm an hour out from landing.'

'They just rented a car,' Harvey replied. 'She used her State-issued cover ID and credit card. I've just seen footage from the rental agency. Walker's with her.'

'Sloppy,' Krycek said. 'You said he was good.'

'Which makes me think Walker wants us to be on his six,' Harvey said.

'Why?'

'Because they've got no leads of their own, so they're waiting to see who comes for them.'

'They won't see me coming.'

'Good. I've got their vehicle in the Homeland system for you to track it. Call me when you've completed your mission.'

'Yes, boss.'

'And Krycek? You make sure this goes away. For good this time.'

•

'All good?' Muertos said, dangling the car keys in front of Walker. She had her small handbag, and in her other hand was a plug-in satnav system from the rental company.

'Yeah, sure,' Walker said, pocketing his phone. 'You've got the address for Hassan?'

'Putting it in now,' Muertos replied, entering the address and setting the sat-nav system on the centre console.

Walker watched her. *Question her? Challenge her – reveal what he'd learned from the emails?* Or better, see where it goes first. Watch. Listen. Probe. Was she telling the truth about anything? About David Walker? About Bloom being killed? Yes. She was genuine about Syria. There was real trauma there, under the surface, and her story of being in the hospital checked out. She wasn't discharged, as Walker had been, but she told him she'd sneaked out. Walker had skipped out of many hospitals over his career, usually far-away military instillations when he had a desire to stretch his legs and head for the closest Base Exchange to buy a quart of whisky to self-medicate whatever pain or trauma he'd most recently endured. He kind of respected her for that. And there was urgency to her – in that action, and in her manner of recruiting him and pressing forward. So, observe, see where it goes.

Walker asked, 'Did you reach out to your contact about the nano-track of the money?'

'I messaged her to arrange a meet,' Muertos said, pressing the fob of the key as they moved along a line of Ford Explorers until they saw a silver one with the indicators flash in response. 'It was an inter-agency op, so the money was being handled by the Secret Service.'

'Secret Service?'

'They're the ones who developed the technology, to combat money-laundering and financial crime,' Muertos replied. 'My contact was there for years, recently moved over to the DOJ. She'll make time for us, and we'll talk to her in person later today.'

'Secret Service is part of Homeland,' Walker said, looking over the top of the Explorer, but he couldn't even see the top of Muertos's head.

'So?'

'So,' Walker said, getting into the passenger seat, 'I don't really want to be hanging out with Homeland people right now.'

'I trust her, Walker,' Muertos said, sitting next to him.

They shared a look, then Walker said, 'Okay.'

'You need to make calls as I drive?' Muertos asked as she hit the ignition button. The big V6 thrummed to life and the dash flashed up all kinds of lights in the gloom of the overcast DC afternoon. Muertos entered their destination in the sat-nav.

'Nope,' Walker said. 'Let's get this thing moving. See what's what at Hassan's house. Then your Secret Service friend.'

'You don't sound like you're expecting to find out much,' Muertos said as she drove through the rental lot and motored out onto the highway on-ramp. She drove fast. Confident. Eyes always checking the rear-view mirror for tails.

'It's how I always sound,' Walker said, looking out the windscreen as Muertos navigated from lane to lane to try to find a quicker path through the early afternoon rush hour. 'I'll sound satisfied when we get the answers we're after.'

12

'Tell me about this agent that State was using,' Walker said. 'Hassan.'

Muertos took a while to answer. She was driving with the DC traffic towards **Annapolis**. It was a Sunday, and people were heading back into town after a weekend out, or picking up their kids from sport, or maybe it was just regular Sunday DC traffic.

Finally she said, 'There's not much to tell.'

Walker let her have some silence, to see what information she might bring up. He watched out his side window. He had never spent much time in the town as an adult, and his memories of the place were specific to Georgetown and his father's apartment there, which he'd spent many school holidays visiting. As his mother's dementia set in, and she moved to Philadelphia to be with extended family and then went into palliative care, his father spent more and more time working and travelling. It coincided with Walker going to the Air Force Academy, and then being posted in the Mid East. Walker still couldn't reconcile his father's decision, and the more distance from those days, the more he wondered if he wasn't so different from his father himself: distancing himself from the grief of his mother losing herself, and then repeating a similar pattern in his own marriage where work trumped all priorities.

'Like I said before,' Muertos said, 'no-one on the team suspected him.'

Walker said, 'Who brought him into your team?'

'He was already in country. He was a shared asset, and we were down the food chain.'

'CIA.'

'Yep. I heard he got tapped when he was leaving the Navy – they were desperate to find and retain people with his ethnic background.'

'Did you ever meet his superiors?'

'Yes. The Station Chief in Syria, when addressing our team, personally vouched for him. They'd previously had him on the periphery of Syrian guys cycling through some of the training camps in Iran. Insurgents and the like. Then when Syria became a thing he was working for the Agency there. Then our joint taskforce was put together, and he became a shared asset.'

'A periphery player sounds like a small fish for the Station Chief to be spending time on,' Walker said. 'That role's usually just pressing flesh at Embassy events and reaching out to business titans and politicians with big golden handshakes, not low-level intelligence officers being loaned out to State.'

'The directive for Hassan to help us out came from up high,' Muertos said. 'All available hands on deck to get spooks in country to recruit and run agents in Syria. I heard it was the Secretary of State who asked for Agency help.'

'Do you know when he started in Syria?'

'I heard it was around three years ago,' Muertos replied. 'So, he'd been in country a long time, and his reputation was solid.'

'And how'd Hassan get attached to your inter-agency op?'

'Apparently he'd proved his worth. Several times. And we knew he wanted out. He's got a young family, and too many of our people were being caught up in the shit storm of the Arab Spring.'

'He asked to do higher-risk work to get out earlier?'

'Yep. His wife and two kids might be at the house we're going to now. The inter-agency op I was attached to was to be his last task in Syria, then he was due to drive a desk at Langley.'

'Interesting.'

'Interesting?'

'Wife. Two kids. Working for three years without fail. A final op and then he's due to get out – set up back here with a house and a stateside job and a cushy life, I'm sure. Why would he double-cross at that stage? Why would he throw it all away, when he was just about to be given his leave?'

'So, you think he was made, before he was attached to us,' Muertos said. 'Taken by the Syrians and bled for intel? Made a deal to hand us over in exchange for his own life? Maybe even the lives of his family back here?'

'It's leaning that way. Doesn't make sense for him to chuck it all away so close to the finish line. I wonder how the Agency have responded to what went down.'

'Can you ask someone there?'

'Not really. We have a kind of love–hate relationship, the Agency and me. Marty Bloom was my best contact.'

'He was still CIA?'

'He's a lifer. Was.'

'Well, I'm the only surviving witness to what happened there,' Muertos said. 'So, the Agency won't know that Hassan wasn't there, right? Because no-one's debriefed me, and I bugged out when the Homeland agent was quizzing me in Germany.'

And you weren't meant to be there at all, Walker thought. *You were on stress leave.*

'But you know for sure that Hassan's back?' he said.

'My contact at the DOJ had his passport flagged: he came back the day after my op went south.'

Walker was silent.

'You think we're wasting our time with him?' Muertos said, glancing across to Walker. 'And if there's a threat against his family, he might have good reason to keep silent, right?'

'Maybe. But it's still our best place to start. Then your nano-track of the cash handler.'

Muertos sighed. 'I have to say, Walker, that I really doubt that the head of the trafficking ring from Syria, is here in the United States. I mean, to come to the lion's den? It's too risky. Crazy, even. Why not Portugal or Brussels or Greece – somewhere he can hide and that has little to no surveillance and lax security apparatus?'

'In my experience,' Walker said, looking out his side window as a metro police cruiser blasted its way down the emergency lane, lights and siren blaring, 'guys like that, when they feel the heat, they go to the end of the line – and that's here. His money was here, so you say. His biggest market was here. His contacts are here. This is where he was going to bug out to, eventually, and set up a new life of his own, living large on the money he'd fleeced from so many of his own people. What happened at that meeting has meant that his plan was brought forward, is all. And if he's been as successful at what he does for as long as you say, he's got more than enough money stashed away to buy a mouse in Malibu and start producing movies.'

'You think he'd really do that?'

'I'm just painting a picture,' Walker said. 'We'll find out soon enough. What do you know about him?'

'Nothing but a name. Tareq Almasi.'

'Tareq Almasi – we'll ask Hassan. If he's been in country working as long as you say, he's bound to know more.'

'I like your confidence.'

'I'm not here to idly watch. I want answers, about Bloom, and my father.'

Muertos stared ahead as she drove. 'We all want answers.'

13

The house of the Hassan family was a facsimile of the houses either side of it and across the road. Timber double-storey lean-tos with tiny porches atop a small flight of timber stairs. Dark slate grey roofs and battleship-grey walls painted with a white trim. The whole neighbourhood was the same. The streets were named after poets. Walker imagined that if you lived there and were headed home from a big night and you got your poet wrong, you'd end up trying your key in every front door until you found your home. On closer inspection, there were minor details differentiating each house. Decorations and paintwork and junk and trinkets on porches. Things the owners did to remember which house was theirs. Flags were popular. American, mostly. A couple of Navy ensigns. Retirees, Walker figured. Lived near Annapolis while they served and stayed there long after they'd left, near what they knew, with the people they trusted.

Muertos parked the rental at the end of the block beside a fireplug, the car spaces all full, the illegal park the only option. They walked the footpath. It was wet underfoot from an afternoon drizzle that would not let up. There was a chill Atlantic wind blowing up Chesapeake Bay. Walker popped the collar of his jacket around his neck. A quiet Sunday fading away to night, all the kids and grandkids were indoors killing time while waiting for dinner. As they passed the houses Walker heard some kids laughing, a couple of loud arguments, someone yelling for more beer from a backyard, a dish breaking, a football replay blaring. The wind and low-pressure system kept the smell of wood-fires at ground level, making the air heavy. The whole time they headed towards their target house, Walker was checking the street. Observing. Looking for guys sitting in cars who might be watching Hassan's house. The thing was, static surveillance was so tech-driven these days, and manpower so expensive, that if the CIA were watching the house of one of their former intelligence officers, they'd do it remotely. There'd be cameras and mikes hidden everywhere – in the house, and pointed at the house. That's the CIA.

It was Homeland Security that he was worried about.

'You know what you want to ask him?' Walker asked as they neared the house number.

'Where he was that day would be a good start.' Muertos glanced across and up at Walker. 'I want to ask if he sold us out, and got all my colleagues killed.'

'You want me to take the lead?'

'Sure. Though I can't guarantee you I'm not going to punch him in the face if it seems he's responsible for my colleagues' deaths.'

'You know,' Walker said, heading through the hedgerow of evergreen box that formed the fences to the houses, clipped to waist height and each grown square to form a gap where a gate might be at the bottom of the stairs, 'in my previous life, as an Intel officer, some people would say that I was a lot better at destroying things than talking to agents and their families.'

'And what would you say to that?'

Walker winced as he ascended the stairs, the wound in his thigh giving a niggling pain that heralded what would likely become a reminder through life: one of those dull aches that came with the cold weather and hung around through to spring.

'I'd say they were about right,' Walker said. He rang the doorbell. The door was solid timber, no window panes set in it, no windows either side, no peep hole. The kind of door in the kind of neighbourhood that said to all and sundry that things don't happen around here that aren't meant to: the residents were predominantly Navy, or ex-Navy, or civilians connected to the Annapolis Naval Academy, and they stuck together; it would be a fool of a burglar or home invader who tried anything against the Navy family. Walker heard a child's fast footfall on the timber floor beyond. Growing louder. 'Don't mention my name in there.'

'Why?'

'House could be bugged, and you can bet that as soon as we're gone he's going to call his local handler at the CIA and give them every detail.'

'Okay. So, you are?'

'Matthew Dellavedova.'

'And he is?'

'He was a point guard for the Cavaliers. Scrappy and determined fellow.'

'The Cavs? Ew.'

'A hater? Don't tell me – you're Dub Nation?'

'Yep. How'd you guess?'

'I heard the smugness in your voice,' Walker said, as he heard heavier feet coming down the hall, then a bolt sliding on the other wide of the door. *And I read your bio notes, Rachel Muertos, recently of San Francisco.*

The door opened.

A man stood there. He was small and wiry, with wide-open eyes that took in everything.

Hassan. And it was clear from the first look that he wasn't going to play ball.

14

Hassan looked at Walker, and in that look Walker knew that a fight was coming within the next couple of seconds. Here Walker was, taking up the man's whole doorway. From Hassan's point of view – a guy fresh from a couple of years spent as an undercover operative in the Middle East – the men who came knocking on your door and looked tough like Walker were either military or worse, and they never made pleasant house calls unannounced. From Walker's point of view, Hassan didn't look like a guy who'd been through the ringer by the Syrian regime. Quite the contrary. He looked healthy and alert and wary. Then his eyes shifted, to the right, to where Muertos stood, and his eyes went even wider – there was recognition there, and it was clear in that look that he wasn't going to welcome them inside.

•

Harvey called Krycek.

'I'm twenty minutes from landing,' Krycek said.

'They've made contact with a CIA officer in Annapolis, and the Agency is responding.'

'What's that mean?'

'They have their protocols to follow.'

'Which are?'

'A tactical team from the Maryland PD is activated to be first responders. A CIA security detail will be not long behind them.'

'Response time of the police?'

'Soon. They're already moving. Maybe ten minutes.'

'What do you want me to do?'

'We can't stop them, so just keep yourself handy and get to Annapolis. If there's an arrest, I want you to be the first to question Muertos.'

•

Hassan's eyes darted back to Walker, and then, because either he saw them as an immediate threat, or because he really did sell out the joint-agency task force in Syria, he decided to react – Hassan had opened the door, seen them and gone through the motions of responding – all inside two long seconds.

Hassan used his left hand to grip the edge of the door and started to push it closed. The way he moved, the way his body was pivoting across as though his right shoulder was moving backward, told Walker that his right hand was reaching for something on his right hip or behind his back to the right.

Which told Walker: pistol.

A 9-millimetre of some kind, probably a Beretta or Glock, since they were common and affordable. Walker hoped for the Beretta; it had a manual safety, and whether it was on Hassan's hip – though it seemed unlikely he would carry a pistol in a visible holster in the family home – or behind his back, to draw and thumb down the safety and point and shoot would take around two seconds, if Hassan was good. Three seconds if he wasn't. Then again, he may not have the pistol safetied, which would be crazy, not just because stuffing a loaded and cocked pistol down the back of your pants was stupid, but the guy had kids around the house. If it was a Glock, with its two-stage trigger safety system, then the time could be closer to one second from drawing to pulling three-point-five pounds of pressure to bear on the trigger and blasting through the door.

So, Walker gave himself a second. Better to err on the side of caution when going up unarmed against a person drawing a firearm.

There are two kinds of people in the world. Those who think that a second is a long time, and those who don't. Walker was the former. He'd done a lot of things inside a second, and this situation called for that kind of reaction time. It was innate: you either had it or you didn't. Pro baseball batters had it – they were able, in a split second, to see the ball out of the hand, make a calculated judgement on its trajectory and spin and curve, make a choice as to how to dispatch it, and react – with the goal of hitting it over the fence. Honing that kind of ability came down to training, something militaries handed out in spades so that their fighters could retain their lives while taking the lives of others.

Ordinarily Walker's instinct would have called for him to make two movements in this situation – one forward, hands and arms up towards the threat, and another backward, with a swift kick to push Muertos away – but that wasn't going to happen today.

He knew he wasn't a hundred per cent. He put himself at around ninety per cent, overall. Less, if the action in question required the speed and power of his wounded leg. He now put that appendage at seventy-five per cent capacity. So, in theory, he had only three-quarters of a second to raise and kick out with his wounded right leg, which would in turn catapult Muertos off the porch and down the stairs four feet below Hassan's shooting angle. The impact of that was unknown – how would the pain involved alter his other actions, directed towards the threat? So, he was not going to make two movements, front and back.

Just a frontal assault. A reaction at the threat, to neutralise it, all inside a second.

He started with the hand on the door. Walker's right hand gripped over Hassan's fingers and squeezed. At the same time, his right leg took a step forward and up, onto the step that formed the threshold of the doorway. That was a half-second, and the remainder of the time was taken up with brute force and hand speed.

Walker pushed the door, extending his right arm out as hard and fast as he could, basically a right-hand jab while squeezing Hassan's hand around the edge of the door, Walker craning forward on his right leg. The door hit Hassan and pressed him hard against the hallway wall. There was a satisfactory cracking noise as the solid timber connected with Hassan's face; the crunch of cartilage and bone and the eruption of blood from the nose. Hassan let out a noise that Walker would describe as a whelp.

At the same time as the whelp came a clatter to the ground of a pistol. No round went off, so Walker figured it was probably a polymer-framed Glock with a round in the chamber but a multi-stage safety trigger.

'Coming?' Walker asked Muertos as he bundled up Hassan and pinned him face-first against the hallway wall. Muertos stepped inside the house, hesitant. Walker picked up the pistol – a Glock 17 – and tucked it into the waistband at the back of his jeans. 'Lock the door after you.'

15

Walker had Hassan seated on a sofa in the front room of the house. Hassan's Glock was all the persuasion he needed to use. He'd checked the bullets in the clip and saw that it was loaded with Hydra-Shok rounds. Illegal in the military but used by police and civilian shooters all over the country. Decent stopping power for a small round, making the 9-millimetre punch above its weight. There was another option for persuasion, if it came to it, but it was one that Walker had never used, no matter how dire circumstances had been a few times in Afghanistan: the child.

Hassan had a small girl in the house, his daughter, around five years old. She had cried, *'Daddy!'* when she saw her father's smashed nose running with blood and Hassan had pulled her into a tight embrace; they now sat together on the couch. There was no-one else in the house – Muertos checked upstairs and out the back. Hassan said his wife was out at swimming practice with their other daughter.

Walker took a dining chair and straddled it opposite the seated Hassan. 'You need to talk.'

Hassan was silent. He held a kitchen towel to his face. His daughter went back to her tablet computer, occasionally looking up to her father.

'You recognise her?' Walker gestured to Muertos.

Hassan didn't respond.

'What happened in Syria last week?' Walker asked. 'And don't lie to me.'

Hassan was silent.

'Why weren't you where you said you'd be?' Walker asked. 'At the meet? Why?'

Walker watched Hassan as he waited for an answer. The guy's eyes were hard. Like he was never going to answer. Like all he had to do was wait Walker out. And Walker knew why he had that kind of confidence. The clock was ticking.

'Keep an eye on the front,' Walker said to Muertos. He saw her out of his peripheral vision as she headed for the lace-covered windows of the lounge room, which faced the street. 'Okay, Hassan. Your time to set things right is now. Tell me what happened.'

Hassan was silent.

Walker said, 'Tell me about Tareq Almasi.'

There was something then in Hassan's eyes. A tell. It was all Walker needed.

'Right,' Walker said. 'Your time's seriously up. You need to tell me who you sold Muertos and her team out to. Five of her team died there. One of my oldest and closest friends died there. You tell me what I need, and then we leave. No more pain, no-one gets hurt, I'll leave it be with that nose bleed there. You tell me who, and we're gone the next minute. That's the best deal you're gonna get.'

'You think this causes me pain?' Hassan said, his voice nasal through a blood-soaked kitchen towel. 'This is nothing. You are nothing. There's nothing you can do. Either of you. This is too big. Bigger than some State Department crap. Even if I wanted to talk, I can't.'

'I'm not going to hurt your kid,' Walker said after a moment's silence, standing, taking a small cushion off a lounge chair. 'But she doesn't have to see what's going to happen to you. This is your choice, okay?'

Walker put the cushion on Hassan's knee, then pressed the Glock's barrel down against it, hard.

'This will stop some of the mess getting on me,' Walker said. 'But it's going to be loud, and it's gonna hurt, and you're going to scream, and you'll probably fill your pants. And your daughter's going to have nightmares for years about a big bad man kicking in the front door and shooting her daddy's knee out. I'll count to three, to give you a chance to consider it all.'

'Who are you?' Hassan said.

'One.'

'You're State Department, like her?' Hassan said. 'You know the kinds of hell that will come your way for doing this? I was with the CIA!'

'Two.'

'You're nothing.' Hassan smiled through bloody teeth.

Walker pulled the trigger.

16

The 9-millimetre Hydra-Shok round went off with a bang. The cushion absorbed the muzzle flash and some of the noise. Bits of stuffing filled the air with a cloud of fine particulate in front of Walker. The little girl was screaming, the sound like a high-pitched jet engine. Tears were flowing down her cheeks. Hassan pulled her into his embrace and buried her face into his chest and rocked her back and forth, making a slow, murmuring sound that might have been a song.

Walker had shot a little wide. The bullet cleared Hassan's leg and burrowed through the floor between his feet.

Hassan looked to Walker with fire in his eyes. 'Okay.'

It was the girl that did it. If it wasn't for her, Walker would have grazed Hassan's leg with the bullet to get him to talk. He knew they didn't have long here, and things had to move quickly.

'I was ordered out of the meet,' Hassan said, looking over Walker's shoulder to Muertos. 'That's all there is to it, okay? I was ordered not to be there.'

'Who ordered that?' Muertos asked.

'Who do you think?'

'The CIA?'

Hassan gave an exasperated smile and shake of the head.

'They have no sway there,' he said. 'These people, up the chain – they're not doing the smuggling for *money*. It's all about *power*.

They're nationalists, see? They want Syria to remain in the status quo. They want to be there ready to rebuild, ready to rule. That is the power they want. They are playing the long game, something I've learned that the Agency, as it stands, is not interested in.' He looked across to Muertos. 'The other day, when your people died? That was nothing. Just another couple of dozen lives lost – just a drop in the ocean.' Muertos shook her head. Hassan looked to Walker. 'An ocean where hundreds die every day. But it's what's coming that will shock you. Mark my words. There are plans, and they will pay off, a long time from now, in a significant way.'

'What do you know about that?' Walker said.

'Only that it's coming,' Hassan replied.

'What is?'

'Something catastrophic. What, I don't know. I swear. But it's coming. Because the State team got too close, and it was clean-up time.'

'Who ordered you out?' Walker asked. 'Who told you to keep away?'

Hassan searched Walker's face and found no comfort there. The man was conflicted, despite the threat in his home. He kept his daughter close. She was silent but had turned her head and peered out at Walker. Striking blue eyes against tan-coloured skin and sand-coloured hair.

'The CIA had to be in on this,' Muertos said to Hassan, taking a few steps towards the seated man. Her jaw was clenched tightly when she wasn't speaking. Her fists were balls of tension and fury. She wanted to lash out, beat the information out of Hassan, and let go of some grief in the process. 'Because here you are, Hassan, still all nicely tucked up in middle-class America, even after things went to hell.'

'These people . . . they have more power than the CIA.' Hassan shook his head. 'Here in the US, the CIA do as they say.'

'That's crap,' Muertos said.

'No.'

'You're lying!'

'No. I am not.' Hassan leaned back and cradled his daughter in his lap. He used the back of his free hand to wipe blood from his top lip. 'Sure, the CIA can hit targets around the world with its drones, they can kill who they like anywhere in the world, and they can throw millions of dollars around like it is nothing. They can do that day in and day out and until the end of time. But you know what? There are always new targets, just like there is always more money, so nothing will be achieved. But these people in Syria? They have *true* power. Influence. You see? It is life itself that they are trading in, and it's ever perpetuating – it is the history, the present and the future – and unless you kill them all, they will never stop, they will never pack up and go away.'

'Hassan, we need a name,' Walker said. He waited until Hassan was looking him square in the eyes. 'The contact here in the US who called you out. Who was it?'

Hassan looked from Muertos to Walker, then down at his daughter. He bit at his bottom lip, as though weighing the consequences of what he might give up.

'Who ordered you to stay away from the meeting?' Muertos asked. 'Who has more power than the CIA?'

'The name I know, it is . . .' Hassan said finally, looking from his child and back to the intruders in his house. 'The man there, at the meeting, who you thought was just a cog in the machine – well, he is not anything to anyone anymore. It was him.'

'You're talking about Almasi?' Muertos asked, looking from Hassan to Walker and back.

Hassan nodded.

Muertos said, 'But you're speaking like Almasi is dead.'

'He . . . is alive?' Hassan said. There was genuine shock in his eyes.

'He got out,' Muertos said.

Hassan's face turned a shade paler. He used his free hand to pinch the bridge of his nose above the break.

'You didn't know?' Muertos said.

'I heard they were going to clean up everything,' Hassan said, his voice nasal.

'Who's they?' Walker asked.

'The ones back here. I – I don't have a name.'

'But you received an order . . .' Walker said.

'A spoken order, by a local courier, a messenger on a motorbike,' Hassan said. 'The day before that meet – this guy, he passed me a picture of my family – from here, up there.' He gestured with blood-covered fingers to a glass cabinet on which sat dozens of framed photos. 'They were here, in my home, while I was in Syria, working for the CIA. See? Their reach?'

'What was it?' Walker said.

'It was a message – not just to stay away, but a message to me that they had reach, if I disobeyed. That they could get to my family at any time. They asked me where the meet would be, and told me not to turn up. So, I told the guy. I – I had to!'

'They could have killed you after that,' Muertos said. 'Once you gave them the information.'

Hassan shook his head and looked at her, then shifted, tightening the embrace with his daughter. 'Insurance. In case the meeting wasn't where I said it would be. Or if I warned everyone about the threat. Keep me alive, just in case.'

'They'll contact you again,' Muertos said.

'No,' Hassan replied. 'That was it. That was the only group I'd infiltrated – you must know that.' He paused, composed himself and said, 'Look, I'm out of all this now. No more field work for the US government. The CIA has offered me a different job, based here, stateside. My family will be raised with a father, and they're safe. That is all I can say.'

Walker heard a noise. Out the front. He turned and looked to Muertos. She glanced out the window, through the lace curtain. Saw an armoured van pull up. It carried a DC Metro SWAT team, which started to pile out and set up positions.

'Company,' Muertos said. 'Sixty seconds.'

'Name,' Walker said to Hassan as he stood. 'Make this right. Let us get justice against those who took American lives – against those who threatened your family.'

'Almasi,' Hassan said. 'That's all I can think of. If he got out, there's a reason. They're keeping him on. Only he knows the American contact.'

'Who's they?' Walker said again, backing towards the hallway but keeping his eyes on Hassan. 'The people who tipped the Syrian government forces off?'

'It's all one and the same,' Hassan said. He glanced from Walker to Muertos and back again. 'They're cleaning house. The way I see it, no-one was meant to get out of there alive. If Almasi did, well . . .'

Walker heard boots on the footpath outside and led the way, fast down the hall towards the back door, Muertos in tow. They hustled outside, where he shouldered the back fence open and took to the laneway, Muertos close behind. The fine rain continued to mist down, and the air was still full of wood smoke from Sunday evening fires throughout the neighbourhood. To the right would lead them to their car – but the end of the block was a long way off, at least couple of hundred metres, and the SWAT team would clear the house and get through the back and get eyes on them before they rounded the corner at the end of the lane.

So, Walker turned left. Towards the other end of the lane. He didn't make it.

17

Walker was just five paces down the laneway when he realised that there was too much distance to cover – and then a third option presented itself. He took a hard right and dragged Muertos with him. They moved fast through a small, narrow easement between the row of houses that backed onto the other side of the lane. Tall timber fences either side, then house walls, the grass underfoot overgrown through patches of gravel and puddles of mud. He emerged at the street running parallel to where they had parked.

There was no easement directly opposite – but there was a house for sale, the mailbox overstuffed with local letter drops and junk mail. He let go of Muertos and crossed the road and ran up the stairs and shouldered the door open. Muertos was two seconds behind him. He shut the door and continued down the hall.

'The car's the other way!' Muertos called out from behind him.

'Forget the car.'

'We don't have to run from the cops,' Muertos said.

Walker stopped at the back door and turned to her. 'They'll arrest us. We pushed our way into a home, where I fired what's probably an illegal firearm, while holding two people hostage – including a little kid. That's a whole bunch of laws broken right there. And you're an accomplice to all of it. Sure, we'll probably get bail, but all that might take a couple of days at best. Have you got a couple of days to throw down the can? Neither of us does – not if there's someone high up in Homeland Security in on this.'

'Okay. Okay. You're right.' Muertos looked around the kitchen of the deserted house. 'What now? We can't wait here until they all go away. Those cops will start door-knocking, looking for two fugitives. They'll find the door you just kicked in.'

'Give me your phone,' Walker said.

Muertos passed it over and stared as Walker put it down the insinkerator.

'Hey!' she said as he turned it on, the machine's steel blade chewing up the plastic and silicone and glass of the phone.

'They might trace it. We'll get you a new one, pre-paid with cash.'

Muertos looked from the sink to Walker. 'What about your phone?'

'Mine's brand new, and they won't have it yet.'

Muertos nodded, then started to pace, running her hands through her hair. 'That SWAT team showed up too way fast to be in response to the gunshot.'

'It wasn't the gunshot that brought them.'

Muertos stopped and stared at him. 'Hassan's house is under surveillance by his minders.'

Walker nodded.

'The CIA?'

Walker nodded again.

'Shit. Right. Okay.' Muertos said. 'They'll be searching the surrounding area. We have to get moving.'

Walker looked out the back window, from the kitchen, and saw a classic old VW Beetle, in gleaming condition, with no plates. Some kind of showpiece, a labour of love or collector's item. Parked there either to show prospective owners that the paved courtyard could be used to park off the street, or because the present owners of the house didn't have any better place to park it. Right now, it was a way out.

'We get out of here,' Walker said, unlocking the back door.

•

Harvey took the call from Krycek.

'The Metro cops missed them,' Krycek said. 'At Hassan's house.'

'Are you getting the track on their car?'

'I'm looking at their car.'

'What?'

'I'm parked across the street from it. They got away, on foot. I just spoke to the SWAT commander. They're door-knocking the area. Walker and Muertos are close. They'll be hiding, waiting, to come back to the car to bug out.'

Harvey paced around his office, said, 'Walker is no amateur.'

'So?'

'He'll leave the car there. Probably head for a bus or cab.'

'Metro PD are covering public transport,' Krycek said. 'Can you put out a BOLO, to cover the cab and transit companies?'

'Not ideal, not yet,' Harvey said. A BOLO – Broadcast, Out Loud – would mean every cop in the area would be on the lookout. Far too public for what he had in mind. 'That'd let these two know they're onto something. I want you to handle this – you need to be there, when they're found – we can't afford to have Maryland State PD being lead on their arrest interview, got it?'

'Got it. And I just spoke with a contact there. They've got eyes on all the local buses routes, but there's a few of them crisscrossing the neighbourhoods through there. But he confirmed what we know –Maryland State PD won't bust a gut on this, certainly not for the federal government. They've got enough of their own problems to deal with in the city, and my guy suggested, or asked, if we can't take over this one.'

'Good. Works for us. What's your next step?'

'Until I have something else to go on, I'll keep eyes on their vehicle and wait for word. They might circle back here to the car. Or have someone else pick it up and transfer it to them.'

'Okay. Stay put. I've got Walker and Muertos in the Trapwire system. Maryland and DC are wired up the wazoo. They'll turn up soon enough.'

'Call me when you know,' Krycek said, 'and I'll end this.'

18

'We need gas,' Walker said. The needle on the Beetle's gauge had hovered not far over empty since he'd push-started it out of the backyard, and thirty miles of back streets and B-roads later it was below the empty mark. The sun had set, and the yellow headlights of the Beetle gave a warm glow to the crisp spring evening.

'So, pull into a gas station,' Muertos said. 'We've passed about ten of them.'

'Too risky,' Walker said. 'They'll get a make on us, then they'll know what vehicle we're in, and soon after they'll catch us – and as sweet as this little tin can is, it's not what we want to be in during a high-speed pursuit.'

'So, pay for the gas with cash, then they can't trace you.'

'No. Every gas station has cameras. And we have to assume our friends at Homeland have uploaded our faces into the Trapwire network.'

'Trapwire?'

'Not our friend. Think of every Internet-connected camera in the city being fed through Homeland Security, with facial-recognition programs looking for us. The first time they find us, they'll have the ID and location. The next, they'll have an idea of the direction we're headed. And if they get our license plate, well, then they'll get a fix on us in real-time through all the Automatic License Plate Readers you see dotted along every highway and random streets.'

'Well, that's all just great,' Muertos said, and she looked out her side window up at the lamp poles and building corners, as though trying to spot cameras that may be perched up there. 'So, what do we do about the gas situation?'

Walker slowed, then took a left down a street in the outer boroughs of DC. It was a mix of industrial and converted warehousing, all being gentrified as quickly as small-time developers could muster. This street was dark and quiet and backed onto a creek that formed a tributary to the Potomac.

'There's more than one kind of gas station,' Walker said, slowing as he passed a few multi-storey townhouses houses sandwiched between big brick buildings. The area was mainly commercial, and once would have been a bustling centre of business, goods received and packed and dispatched from the warehouses, back when they were built in the nineteenth century, when the waterways served a purpose and barges connected the railroads and docks. Now most of the properties seemed to be converted to short- and long-term storage lots, presumably filled with stuff from people's lives that didn't fit into ever-shrinking silo-like apartments that were sprouting up all around DC like a viral outbreak. He took a right into a cul-de-sac and slowed as he passed a few parked cars, and then came to a stop. 'Wait here.'

Walker moved quickly and quietly, over a short fence and into a front lot of a tiny row of workers' cottages with overgrown front gardens, and came back to the car with a garden hose. He put the Beetle into first and took off, working up the gears and getting up to fifteen miles an hour before coasting in neutral to save gas.

Muertos looked at the roll of rubber hose that Walker had put in her lap and said, 'You're not . . .'

'There's our gas station right there,' Walker said, dropping down to second and turning onto a dark side street, pulling up close behind a big pick-up. He took the hose, went to the pick-up and forced the gas cap open, then took the plastic ends off the hose and started to syphon. He spat out the unleaded gas that touched his mouth and pinched the end of the hose tightly, then put it into the little Beetle's gas tank. In twenty seconds the tank started to overflow and he pulled the hose out the truck's tank, replaced the cap, and put twenty dollars under the petrol flap before closing it.

'An honest thief,' Muertos said as Walker got back into the VW.

'A fair transaction,' Walker said, reversing away from the truck and then heading down the road. 'He probably made a profit.'

'He?'

'The owner of the pick-up.'

'Could have been a woman.'

'Doubt it.'

'Women don't drive pick-ups?'

'Did you see the same truck I did?'

'The one with shiny chrome wheels, and a stencil of a Playboy bunny on the mud-flaps, and a bull horn tied to the front bumper?'

'That was it.'

'And a woman can't have all that?'

Walker paused, then said, 'Fair point.'

'And what about stealing this car?' Muertos said. 'You didn't leave a stack of cash back at that house.'

'We'll park it in a tow-away zone when we're done with it,' Walker replied. 'The owners will be notified to come and pick it up.'

'With a fine and tow-fee to pay.'

'They'll survive.' Walker glanced over at Muertos. She was watching the road ahead, nothing showing in her eyes. He wanted to ask her about skipping out of the hospital in Germany. About claiming she worked for the State Department even though she was ousted six months ago. About her motivation to attach herself to the taskforce in Syria. The continued motivation, because this wasn't a job she was doing, it was personal. But he opted to observe. At least until after this next meeting. 'You still navigating?'

'Yep. Keep going straight. The turn's about a mile ahead.'

'Tell me about this contact of yours we're about to meet.'

'Sally Overton. Old friend. At the Department of Justice, as a liaison officer with the Secret Service. We've got an hour to the meet, and judging by your driving it's about forty minutes away.'

'How do you know her?' Walker said.

'Left up here, then head north onto the Beltway.'

Walker took the instructions, easing the little car onto the main north-east-bound arterial that fed onto the I495 that ringed Washington DC.

'She's like a sister to me,' Muertos said. 'Her father helped my mother, a long time ago, back in Mexico. They became family friends, and we've known each other since we were kids. She's one of those rare friends, the kind you call in the middle of the night when you've done something terrible or embarrassing and she's there to help, no questions asked, no judgement made. She'd do anything for me, and I'd do the same for her.'

Walker thought about Bloom. A life-long friend. A guy who'd literally sewed him up, not to mention all the times he'd given him false papers, money, weapons, a place to stay, a shoulder to lean on, a companion to laugh with, a man to learn from. His knuckles went white on the steering wheel, and in that moment he doubted anyone wanted to find the culprits more than he did.

19

Walker eyed Muertos as he drove. Muertos in turn watched ahead, the blank look quiet in her dark eyes. He could feel that she was tense, stressed to the point of giving up. As though finding Walker, and going to this next meeting, was the last roll of the dice for her. Desperation.

'What Hassan was saying,' Walker said, to focus her attention. 'Did that make sense to you?'

'Which part?'

'The motivation of the smugglers.'

She sighed, her eyes snapping back to the here and now. 'It's a global problem. All those refugees moving out, the money moving hands, the lives lost. It's a dirty economy all of its own, feeding on war, and more often than not a lot of that money goes back into the war. What Almasi was running into America was a tiny part of it, but we'd never seen any actual people arrive, which was frustrating Customs and State, who had evidence from Syria that it was happening. It was estimated he was putting a couple of dozen people into the States at a time, give or take. Compared to thousands into Europe, and thousands elsewhere. And he was just one of hundreds of people traffickers.'

'Hassan was genuinely shocked to hear that Almasi was alive.'

'Right. That was genuine, his reaction. At seeing me, too. And he's spooked.'

'He was spooked to see you alive.'

'Right. And Almasi. Maybe it's even Almasi's reach back here that he's scared of. His US contacts. But there's little to nothing we know about him, other than he was the top of the local food chain.'

'But you knew he was working for others outside the country?'

'Right. The money men, living in luxury somewhere in the West. He was like their local manager on the ground. Buying and selling. The profits went offshore.'

'To the contact here in the US.'

'That was the consensus with all those in country.'

'Someone with contacts inside Homeland.'

'It explains the prices they can charge for setting up what seem to be completely legitimate IDs back here.' Muertos paused, then said, 'I mean, up until today, I'd thought maybe there was no physical connection back here, that there might be a money trail to banks or law firms in the Caymans. But the nano-track was going to answer some of those questions.'

'Does State have any idea who the US contact is?'

'No. That's what we were going to use the nano-track on the money for. We knew Almasi headed here once a month on false passports, but he'd always shake whatever tail they'd put on him. And I'm starting to think he had help in that, from Homeland.'

'Who's we?'

Muertos looked at him. 'The joint taskforce.'

'What's the last contact you had with anyone on that team?' Walker looked across at her. 'They lost some of their own in Syria. They must be pissed.'

Muertos paused a second, then said, 'Why the interrogation?'

'Curiosity. You've been out of contact with them – first the hospital in Damascus, then Germany, then finding me. You said earlier you're unsure if you could trust them.'

'That was my thinking until those Homeland guys jumped us. Now I think the compromise is at Homeland.'

'But you're not in current contact with anyone at State?'

'No. I mean, you're right. I'm out of the loop right now,' Muertos said. She fidgeted with her hands in her lap. 'Medical leave, following what happened in Syria. And, like I said, I thought someone within State might have tipped off the pro-government forces.'

Walker didn't push the point. He navigated the traffic and said, 'Okay. Let's get back to Almasi. What if he wasn't meant to get out of there alive?'

'I'm sure he wasn't,' Muertos said. 'The Syrian regime soldiers came in with every weapon blazing, believe me. It was indiscriminate. No prejudice. No-one was meant to get out of there alive.'

'But you did,' Walker said.

Muertos paused again. She looked across to Walker. 'So did your father. And a few of the mercenary types around Almasi. And the Syrians gave chase – that's the only reason I got out. Same for your father.' Muertos looked to Walker. 'Why didn't you ask Hassan if he'd ever heard of your father?'

'I didn't want to put his name out there.'

'Why?'

'Because, like I said, Hassan's house would be wired for sound,' Walker said. 'Cameras too, at least outside. That's how the CIA had Maryland State SWAT there so fast.'

'Why would the CIA watch one of their own like that?'

'He must have put a request in, after Syria,' Walker said.

'Or,' Muertos said, 'he didn't. And the Agency is *not* in the business of trusting people, right? Maybe they were keeping an eye on him.'

'Possible.'

'Take the next left, it's just up here,' Muertos said.

Walker checked his rear-view mirror as he changed lanes and made the turn, watching, wary of any tail. He didn't see one. But it was what he couldn't see that worried him most.

•

Harvey clicked on the sound file and listened to the CIA recording from Hassan's house. Then he called Lewis.

'Good news, I hope,' Lewis said.

'An update,' Harvey said. 'A development.'

He played him the conversation.

Lewis said, 'Can Hassan lead back to us?'

'No. He only knows Almasi on a surface level.'

'Almasi is here in the US?'

'Yes. He's waiting for us. He wants direction – obviously his place in the program has changed.'

'I think he's at the end of his usefulness. Once you deal with Walker Junior and Rachel Muertos, take care of Almasi and his friend.'

'He's the best contact we've got if we want to get back into Syria.'

'Too bad. It's become too hot – we should have shut it down days ago, when Walker's father showed up. It's been a good op, run far longer than I expected. We've got from this little operation more than we need. So, it's time to pack away all our things, and prepare for the next stage. Which means you need to make sure you clean up after yourself.'

20

Walker pulled the Beetle up to the curb and parked next to a walnut tree erupting with the green buds and sprouts of spring. They were in Logan Circle, a leafy district of junior staffers for people in the capital. Lots of up-and-comers; fashionable meets prime-patch-of-real-estate between Shaw and Dupont Circle. They strolled down 14th Street NW, past wine bars, beer bars, tapas bars, oyster bars; the dining options – reasonably priced bistros and cafes and brew houses that straddled a mix between classics and organic hipster fare – occasionally punctuated by a chic boutique. The side streets held stately old manors that give the neighbourhood a feel of old-school class. The smell of wood smoke was in the heavy night air. Not a star in the sky for the cloud cover.

'Maybe you should wait in the car,' Muertos said as she undid her belt.

'No,' Walker replied. 'I want to hear what your contact has to say, and I might have questions for her.'

Muertos hesitated, not looking at Walker as she opened her door and climbed out.

'What is it?' Walker asked and he got out into the car and looked over the roof.

'I told you, Overton's very cautious.'

'Just tell her I'm a friend, helping you out.'

Muertos looked around the street.

'If you really think she won't talk with me there, I'll stay behind,' Walker said. 'But I think we should stick together when possible, because we don't know what we're going to get thrown at us from Homeland.'

She looked back to Walker. 'Okay. Come with me.'

The night air of Washington was cold, and over his black shirt Walker had the light-weave black cotton jacket from LA that Eve had brought for him to be discharged in. The wind bit at him, and he popped the collar and stuffed his hands in his jeans pockets as he fell into stride with Muertos. Nowhere near as cold as his time at the Air Force Academy in Colorado, nor the mountains of Afghanistan while on tours of duty, but after the warmth of the little Beetle's heated interior it woke him up and sent an ache through the wound in his leg.

The line of restaurants and bistros, lit by fairy lights in the bare-branched trees, was a hubbub of diners tucked in from the cold. Plenty sat outside in al-fresco dining areas wrapped in giant plastic tents to keep the cold night out. Their restaurant was called Le Nook, and it was dark inside, black-stained timber panelling and dim light fixtures with exposed orange-glowing globes. The side walls were lined with booths that sat six apiece, and the centre area of the restaurant was taken up by a long U-shaped bar crammed with suits and pencil skirts. Waiters were dressed in black, liveried like old-school barbers complete with elastic armbands that kept their rolled-up shirt-sleeves in place. Walker and Muertos made their way amid the low background din of people talking in close, conspiratorially, like they were plotting Machiavellian manoeuvres at work or life, or both. The food was deconstructed French fare – not Michelin-star, not a bistro, it was somewhere in between, with portion sizes that would leave Walker wanting a burger on the way home.

Walker followed Muertos around the left of the bar and towards a booth down the back. Each booth was full of animated patrons but for the one Muertos stopped at. There, a small woman sat in solace.

She was about forty years old with short dark hair and porcelain-pale skin, and she bubbled with even more nervous energy than Walker had seen in Muertos. By the shadows thrown by the small candles on the table and dull light globe dangling above, the woman's eyes were big and searching.

'Who's this?' she asked before anything had been said or anyone sat down.

'This is Jed Walker. A friend, who's helping me,' Muertos said. 'Walker, this is Sally Overton.'

'Hi,' Walker said, hand outstretched. Overton hesitated, then took his hand in hers and shook it. Her hand was small, soft, cold.

Muertos slid in first, sitting opposite Overton, and Walker took off his jacket and sat beside Muertos on the worn, tactile leather bench. The table was fixed in place, and the gap between Walker and the table was just big enough to be considered comfortable.

A waiter came and poured sparking water and asked if they were ready for menus.

'Sure,' Walker said, taking them before the women could object. He could feel their eyes on him as he put two menus on the table and opened his. *Eat when you can, rest when you can* was about the only motto he continued to live by from his days in the military.

'I'm sorry,' Overton said, looking to Walker. 'Who are you with?'

'Muertos,' Walker said. 'I'm helping her out.'

'I mean—'

'I don't work for anyone,' Walker said, closing his menu. 'I was with the Air Force and the CIA for near-on twenty years all up, then State for a little bit. Muertos came to me because our interests overlap.'

Overton let silence hang in the air for a moment, as though weighing and computing that information, then said, 'You don't look old enough for all that.'

'Good genes.'

'You went to the Air Force Academy?'

Walker nodded.

'My father went there,' Overton said. 'Missed it so much his whole life he's retired to Colorado.'

'Smart guy, it's a beautiful state,' Walker said.

Overton said, 'And now?'

'Now I freelance.'

'You're a private contractor?'

'No,' Walker said, scanning over the menu. 'I'm not that organised. Or driven. I just help out where I can.'

'And what is it that's driving you now?'

'My father might be connected with this,' Walker said, then looked to Muertos.

'Walker's father was in Syria,' Muertos said to her friend. 'He was there when everything went wrong – when Almasi fled.'

'We need to talk about that,' Overton said looking towards the bar. 'You need to tell me what happened there.'

'Sure,' Muertos said. 'But so you know, Walker is helping me unravel this in the hope he can figure out the connection to his father. We need to find Almasi. Walker wants to find his father.'

'Who's your father?' Overton asked.

'He was an academic,' Walker said. 'In foreign policy and international relations.'

'He was a spook?' Overton said.

'Never confirmed,' Walker said. 'But he did a lot of moonlighting for various administrations over the years, so I'm sure he was on the Agency payroll on and off throughout his career. We've had what you'd call a difficult relationship of late. I just want to find him, get some answers about all this mess.'

Overton looked uneasy when she said, 'Everyone's looking for somebody.'

'What's that mean?' Walker asked.

Overton hesitated, then looked to Muertos and said, 'There was no news from the field about your team being hit, until a couple of hours ago. It's just made the wires now – and it's been spun as something else entirely.'

'Spun as what?' Muertos said. She stared at Overton, who avoided her eye contact by looking to Walker. 'Five of our people were killed there, Sally. What are they saying?'

'State reported it as all five staff lost in an aircraft crash,' Overton said.

There was silence around the table for a full ten seconds.

'Why would they do that?' Muertos asked. 'It's a blatant lie, and it'll get out as a lie, and then it'll look even worse.'

'Officially, if you could get an answer?' Overton said. 'They'd say it was because of operational security.'

'And unofficially?' Muertos asked.

'The State Department's covering someone's arse,' Overton said. 'I think they were ordered to.' She looked from Muertos to Walker, and back, then leaned forward across the table. 'And I think it's because of Almasi.'

21

'When I heard from you,' Overton said to Muertos, 'I asked for a team of my own to track Almasi should he turn up stateside. And hand-picked agents – not just a couple of bumbling Homeland agents – I mean full twenty-four-seven surveillance, by *my* guys. My Director okayed it, but he then rescinded it about an hour later, saying it was out of our hands and I was to cease and desist all enquiries into what he described as *the Syrian problem.*'

'Problem?' Muertos said. She paused to retain a sense of calm. 'We lost American lives, and they're stonewalling?'

Overton looked to her hands, fidgeting on the table in front of her.

'Muertos said you can track the money from that meet?' Walker said. 'Some kind of newfangled nano-tech.'

'That . . .' Overton leaned forward again, and looked from Walker to Muertos, her expression hard. 'That was highly classified, Rach.'

'Almasi handled the money,' Muertos said. She looked at her friend across the table, unflinching. 'Can you track him or not?'

Overton sat back in her booth seat and looked uneasy.

'I assure you,' Walker said to Overton, 'whatever classified stuff is going on, you have nothing to worry about from me.' He tapped the side of his head. 'I've got a whole bunch of big secret stuff up here, and that's where it's staying.'

'And what would you do,' Overton said, glancing back to Walker with a resigned look, 'if you found Almasi? What then?'

'My understanding is that he can lead us to the American connection to the smuggling outfit,' Walker said. 'We need that information to work up the chain. Find where the buck stops. Find what's happening in Homeland – because he's got at least one highly placed contact there. Getting to Almasi will bring answers for all of us.'

'Look, after Syria . . .' Overton said, again looking down at her hands, her fingers tightly interlinked. 'My hands are tied. The multi-agency investigation has been shifted away.'

'Away?' Muertos said.

'Broken up, and put back together into smaller teams, looking at different groups,' Overton said. 'And no longer in Syria; it's deemed far too hot. They've been sent to Egypt and Libya, with smaller outposts in Turkey and Iraq.'

'Jesus . . .' Muertos said, leaning back and shaking her head. 'They really don't give a damn do they?'

'They closed down all Syria operations?' Walker asked.

Overton nodded. 'Like I said – we've got nothing to do with Syria anymore.'

'They can't do that!' Muertos said, then looked around for fear of being overheard. She needn't have worried – the sound of the full restaurant and bar was enough to drown out any eavesdropping. '*Why* would they do that?'

'Officially, it's too dangerous,' Overton said.

'Yeah, Sally, I kinda know that,' Muertos said. 'But that's not what we do. If America ran away from everywhere dangerous, where would we be?'

'I don't make the rules, Rach,' Overton said, and there was sadness or desperation in her eyes. 'I'm sorry. But it was never meant to cost lives.'

'Never meant to – do they know the stakes here?' Muertos shook her head. 'This isn't what we do – we don't turn our backs because we're scared. We double down. They kill our people? We should send in a bigger team, with bigger security. We hurt them, we send in the Marines.'

'They won't allow it,' Overton said. 'I argued where I could.'

'Who's they?' Walker asked.

The waiter came and asked for orders, and to get rid of him Walker orders pomme frites and a bottle of Côtes du Rhône Syrah.

'Who's they?' Walker repeated, once the waiter had departed. 'Who's calling the shots on this?'

Overton said, 'The lead agency is Department of Homeland Security.'

Walker looked to Muertos.

'It's a border-security issue,' Overton said, and it was clear by her demeanour that she was trying to get a read on that look between them. 'State Department handled the inter-country liaison and the joint taskforces in the field. We, via Treasury, handled the money. FBI had investigators on it, there were a few CIA liaisons, as well as Naval Intelligence, DIA and NSA all putting resources to the table. But ultimately the buck stops with Homeland.'

Walker said, 'Do you know who it is at Homeland?'

'I don't, but it falls within Deputy Secretary Daniel Harvey's wheelhouse, though he's probably too holier-than-thou to have any direct hand in it.'

Walker and Muertos shared another look.

'What?' Overton said.

'Nothing,' Walker replied. 'It's just we had a run-in with a couple guys earlier today. They paid me a not-so-pleasant hospital visit.'

'A couple guys . . .' Overton said.

'A couple of Homeland agents,' Muertos said. 'They attacked us.'

'Why would they do that?" Overton said.

Muertos shrugged.

Walker watched her, and Muertos shot him a sideways glance and he kept quiet. He wondered about the dynamic between them. He knew that there were things Muertos was keeping from him, now he knew that she was keeping information from a long-time friend. And not just any friend – a friend on whom she was relying to provide answers and intel that would propel them onwards.

'Right, well, the joke is that Homeland are populated by agents the other departments and agencies reject,' Overton said, shaking her head. 'It'd be funny if it wasn't half-true. But the thing is, Homeland modelling puts the illegal immigration at about half a million per year. Which is down from five years ago, and that success means they're being given all that they ask for.'

Walker said, 'How much of that success is because they're policing the borders more?'

'A big part,' Overton said. 'But we suspect there's a big increase in those with false papers, even getting through our biometric scans with legitimate-looking ID.'

'How are they beating the biometrics?' Walker asked.

'It didn't make news,' Overton said, 'but our border fingerprints and retinal scans have gone through some glitches the past two years. At one point they reckoned one in ten passing through customs was not properly identified or tagged. Homeland says they've got it patched now, and that it's somewhere outside their one-in-a-thousand mandated ratio of acceptable error.'

'Where are the refugees facilitated by Almasi getting through?' Walker asked.

'Refugees in name only,' Overton replied. 'I'm sure Rach knows more about it than me.'

'I told Walker about those paying the big bucks for the new lives here,' Muertos said. 'With all the trimmings when they arrive.'

Overton shook her head. 'There are taskforces on that, and a lot of it's driven by DEA as much as Homeland. But Homeland has their own Counter-Narc Department, which steps on the DEA's toes and cuts their lunch all the time – believe me, I'm well aware at every turn that I'm in the Department of Justice umbrella, and that we won't be that surprised if the DEA and FBI and the rest of us are all absorbed into Homeland one day soon. Whatever, all our agencies have got arrangements in place with smuggling networks on the other side of the Mexican border. If there was ever a big influx of Mid East illegals via those channels all hell would break loose, and they know that. So, there's kind of an unofficial alliance in place.'

'Right,' Walker said. 'So, unlike the others, who are using the coasts and the Mexican and Canadian borders, Almasi's illegals are getting through at airports, right through TSA?'

'Yes,' Overton said. 'Right under Homeland's nose. That was always the joint taskforce's driving force, to find out how.'

'He's getting them in through the front door,' Muertos said, for the benefit of Walker. 'Social security, IDs, housing, jobs, the works.'

'Yep,' Overton said. 'He's more connected to legit IDs on a scale we've not seen, hence the green light to put our nano-tracked cash out in the field.'

'And the big multi-agency taskforce,' Muertos added. She shook her head. 'I can't believe they've shut it down. After all the work . . .'

'Did you track Almasi, via the money?' Walker asked Overton.

'That's . . .' Overton looked from Walker to Muertos, and her voice wavered when she said, 'not that simple.'

22

The waiter came and poured the wine. Overton wrung her hands, took a few breaths. Muertos reached over the table and put a hand on Overton's and squeezed. The waiter departed.

'It's okay,' Muertos said. 'Tell us what you can, and we'll do everything we can to fix it.'

Overton nodded, sipped her wine, and then said, 'Okay, we tracked the cash. The nano-tracers attach to anyone who comes in contact with those people – shaking hands, brushing against them. A day after your meet, the cash was put through a casino in Monaco to be laundered. The trick was tracking the right contact up until that point – Almasi and three others handled the money that day in Syria, so we kept on all four of those. We tracked them until yesterday, until when it was shut down. Now I don't have access. No-one does.'

Muertos asked, 'Who ordered that?'

'Harvey, at Homeland?' Walker said.

Overton nodded and was silent for a beat. Then she said, 'Two of the contacts – both known to us – stayed in Syria, then crossed into Israel, where they remained. Mossad had eyeballs on them, and we crossed them off. The other two we tracked went to Monaco, via boat. They stayed a night there, and we had them ID'd at the same hotel, two different levels of accommodation – standard room, and presidential suite. We took the presidential suite to be Almasi, and we managed to hack the hotel's security cameras and we got confirmation. The other guy was Almasi's right-hand man, Bahar. The next day both men took a flight to London, where they hired a car and went to a hotel in the city for four hours, before heading back to Heathrow and taking a flight to DC.'

'So, they're here.' Muertos looked to Walker.

'They got into the US without any problems?' Walker said.

Overton nodded. 'Neither is on an official watchlist, and each entered with false papers and biometrics.'

Muertos said, 'Which we know Almasi's contact here can arrange.'

Overton nodded again.

'Do you have any thoughts as to why would he come to DC?' Muertos asked. 'This is the lion's den of security services and surveillance. Why not JFK and get lost in the masses, where we know he'd entered before?'

Overton shrugged and sipped her wine.

'Because he's not afraid,' Walker said. 'He knows someone up high has his back, so why not walk right in through the front door.'

'That's what we figured,' Overton said. 'And there's less onerous TSA screening here than in JFK.'

'And here could be closer to his US contact,' Walker said.

Overton nodded; she'd had plenty of time to think about it all and clearly had come to the same conclusions.

'So, what happened from here?' Walker asked.

'That's when we were shut down,' Overton said. 'Two hours after they'd landed in DC.'

Muertos said, 'But surely you can somehow get back into the tracking system and—'

'Rach, I'm sorry, but there's really no way to access it,' Overton said. 'Homeland wiped the track. There's no way to re-run the trace, because the nano-trace puts out a one-time code, designed so that we can track thousands – and one day potentially millions – of targets at once. Homeland ordered it wiped, and we had to comply. So it's gone. Irretrievable. Believe me, I tried to get it back up and running – it's gone.'

Walker saw hope fade from Muertos. She remained silent. The French fries arrived, and the waiter topped off the wine glasses and departed. Walker watched Overton closely. She was holding back on something. And it was beyond disappointing a friend. There was hurt there. Real pain. Something personal, and the stress of it was writ large in her mannerisms.

'Sally . . .' Walker said. 'What is it?'

Overton looked at him over the rim of her glass.

'Tell us,' Muertos said.

'We had an agent ghost him from the airport and the rest of the day,' Overton said. She took a gulp of her wine. 'Secret Service. A favour. That I cashed in – *I* asked her to do it. Off the books. It was her day off. I was going to take over the shift today. She was my subordinate – she felt she had to do it.'

'And?' Walker asked, but he could see the answer in Overton's demeanour: she'd lost an agent.

'She followed Almasi and his bodyguard from their pick-up to their hotel, then to a lunch meeting, and dinner.' Overton paused, looking down at her wine glass in her hands, and said, 'By the end of the night we'd lost contact. That was last night. She was due to call me every three hours at the most, and change over surveillance at five am. She hasn't checked in for about twenty-hours. She's gone.'

23

'These are the latest photos of Tareq Almasi, and his bodyguard, Abu Bahar.' Overton passed Walker her phone, and there was a slight shake to her hands. 'And this is Clair Hayes, my missing agent.'

Walker swiped through the three images on her phone, back and forth and back again. Memorised the faces. Almasi was all angles, sharp nose and squinty eyes and square jaw and chin, closer to fifty than forty – he looked aristocratic, not a street thug. His muscle guy was the opposite. The camera's watermark told Walker it was from the Homeland Security TSA automated entry point from Dulles airport in DC. It was taken front on, from the top of the shoulders up, looking directly at the camera as instructed. Bahar was an imposing brute. Flat face. Broad features. Neck thick with veins and muscle that came with steroids and heavy weightlifting. His trapezius, the muscles from his neck to his shoulder, were triangles the size of dinner plates. Buzz-cut head with a pale scar cut through the black stubble where a part might otherwise be. Dark shadow of a beard that looked like it could sand down hardwood. The final image was the official United States Secret Service photo of Agent Clair Hayes. She was young; mid-twenties. Blue eyes and blonde hair. A junior agent at the Secret Service, not long into the job and asked to do a favour on an off-books op by a senior agent to score some points. Now missing near on twenty-four hours. Walker felt a twist in his gut. He'd been in Overton's shoes, plenty of times. Being on the outside of it did not make it any easier. An agent was out there, either dead or detained by those two guys.

Walker said, 'Any way of tracking her?'

'Her phone is off the grid,' Overton said. He neck was flushed red.

'Destroyed?' Walker asked.

'Must be, there's no tracking it,' Overton said. 'It's as dead as it can be.'

'How about tracking her vehicle?'

'She was using her personal car, which Virginia State troopers found parked under an underpass in Stafford County this afternoon.'

'Where's that?' Walker asked.

'Forty-odd miles south, maybe fifteen miles beyond Quantico.'

'What's there?'

'Nothing much.'

'Any connection to your guys?'

'Nothing we're aware of,' Overton said. 'We've examined the car and the scene, but there was nothing. It didn't break down. It had plenty of gas. The tyres were fine. There was no sign of an accident or struggle.'

'Set perimeters,' Walker said. 'Door-knock. Talk to potential witnesses.'

'This is all on the way, *way* down-low,' Overton said. 'I've been forced to run an off-books missing-persons case with people I know can trust – people who are putting in their own time, and their own careers on the line if this comes out a bust. I started with three agents. Now it's two. And me.'

Muertos asked, 'Who are the other two?'

'Two Secret Service guys who are out there now, shaking trees, looking for their missing colleague.'

'Names?' Walker asked.

'Why?' Overton said, her tone harsh, defensive.

'In case we cross paths,' Walker said. 'A name and a photo of each would be good, so I know who's on whose side, if it comes to it.'

Overton unclipped a cell phone from her belt, a Blackberry, her official government-issue piece rather than the prepaid generic brand she'd passed over moment before. *On off-books op that went south, fast.* He pictured the possibility of Hayes tailing the Syrians, then being pulled over by a black SUV containing a couple of bent Homeland agents. They would ask her to get out the car, and she would, exasperated about losing her quarry and too preoccupied with thoughts of disappointing her boss to notice that the two Homeland agents had a complete disregard for her ID or explanations – until it was too late, when they would subdue her and take her someplace remote. Walker watched as Overton tapped and scrolled and came up with a Facebook post, which she held out so Walker and Muertos could see.

'This is Assistant Special Agent in Charge Blake Acton.' Overton then tapped and scrolled again and held her phone out. 'And this is Agent Jim Bennet.'

Walker nodded, satisfied. 'How about checking cameras leading out on the highway?'

'We found two separate sightings from traffic cameras, neither good because we're talking late at night, and they're just regular digital cameras designed for traffic management, not identifying occupants of vehicles,' Overton said, putting her official phone away. 'They showed Hayes following a black Lexus SUV, which she'd already called in; she called in the licence plates as soon as she started the tail, plates that were stolen yesterday from a white SUV from Connecticut. So, their Black SUV is probably stolen too.'

Muertos said, 'Any idea where they got the car?'

'We've got security footage that shows the car parked at a car park near an airport hotel, where they got the shuttle to.'

'So, they have help on the ground,' Walker said. 'Someone here knew they were coming and set it up for them. Probably some accommodation too.'

Overton nodded. 'The last image of Hayes we have was just ten miles out of town, to the south, on the second traffic camera. That's the last known sighting, at around one am. Thirty miles later they found her car on the I95, Stafford County, Virginia.'

Walker said, 'A lot can happen in thirty miles of darkness.'

Overton was silent. Muertos too. Whether they were thinking optimistic thoughts about what could happen in thirty miles of dark highway, Walker was unsure.

'Now's the time to put this out there,' Walker said. 'Missing person. Get the media to help spread the word.'

'I'm . . .' Overton looked at her near-empty wine glass and fell silent.

'You've long passed the point where you can protect your career,' Walker said. 'If there's any hope of finding your agent alive, you have to act fast, and be as loud and vocal about finding her as you can. You need to bring all your resources to bear. You have to own this, while there's still something of a trail.'

Overton nodded. She couldn't look at Walker.

'I've been in your shoes, plenty of times,' Walker said. 'Running agents in foreign countries. Some of them for years, and they became friends. I'd met their families, broke bread with them, had their kids jumping all over me. And too many of them fell off the grid, at some point. Sometimes it had a happy ending. They'd show up after being taken in and questioned – and being questioned in places like Afghanistan or Libya isn't fun for anyone – but they'd be back, and move on. Sometimes it didn't end so well.' Walker paused, seeing Overton take it in, and then he said, 'So, suck it up, Overton, and prepare for the worst – but right now, and all the way to the end, you need to do your best. Right? You have to stay on mission, all the way, and see it through to get the bad guys.'

Overton was silent.

'This was your call,' Walker said. 'You sent Agent Hayes out on this off-books surveillance, with your prepaid phones. You planned it and executed it. It's on you. Own it. That's the responsibility that comes with being in a position of command.'

Overton nodded. 'Okay.'

Walker said, 'I'm not saying it's easy.'

'I know.'

'But you have to stay functional, and do all you can to get your agent back.'

'I know. I know.' Overton looked down at her clasped hands and closed her eyes and said, 'Shit, I know.'

'So,' Walker sipped at his wine. 'That's it? All you've got on Almasi?'

Overton composed herself. 'Yes.'

'Okay. We'll see where it goes overnight. You've got a lot of work to do to get this out there.'

Overton nodded. 'You think we can find her safe?'

'She's worth something to them alive; insurance. And you're still inside the first day,' Walker said. 'And that big friend of Almasi's, Bahar? He's hard to miss. Once you run this through the media, get Hayes' picture out there, along with those of your two suspects? Think about it. A couple of Middle Eastern suspects listed as persons of interest in the disappearance of your all-American sweetheart Secret Service agent, that's going to make a lot of noise. I think they'll be forced to make a mistake, or they might reach out to make a deal. Hell, they've probably already made mistakes, like checking into a hotel. Night clerks usually have a TV running in the background. You might get a call straightaway from a hotel worker someplace in Virginia telling you that they checked in, that they're sleeping like babies.' Walker leaned forward and said, 'You get this out there tonight, and by morning you might just have your agent back, a couple of arrests, and we all get answers.'

24

'You really think that?' Muertos asked Walker as they climbed into the Beetle.

'Think what?' Walker asked. He kept his door open, pushing the car from the curb, then built up momentum along the street, about five miles per hour, and he jumped in, put the car in gear and dropped the clutch and the engine turned over.

'That they will quickly find Almasi and Sally's undercover agent?'

'It's possible.' Walker looked around the old neighbourhood as he drove. 'I doubt they're far away, and the eastern seaboard is full of surveillance and police and security networks – it's not a great place to hide.'

'Unless you're got friends at Homeland who are planting fake biometrics to match fake IDs when you're entering the country.'

'True.'

They drove on in silence for a few minutes, Walker working the gears and brakes as they wound out of the neighbourhood.

'Sally's career will be over,' Muertos said, her voice heavy, as though she was just comprehending the gravity of it. 'It's all she ever wanted to do.'

'Could be worse.'

'Yeah, you're right.' Muertos paused for a long beat. Thinking.

Weighing up. 'I think I'm less optimistic than you when it comes to finding someone who's missing.'

'These guys . . . If they're in a hotel, law enforcement will catch up with them overnight. But I'm a realist. They'll be off the grid, hunkered in a private house, or if they are in a motel or hotel it'll be under a whole new identity, and maybe they had the keys picked up from reception by a third party so they could avoid being seen.'

'You think they're that paranoid.'

'Maybe. Careful, not paranoid.'

'Why didn't you tell Sally that?'

'She'd know it already.' He entered the tunnel of the 395, headed south. Still well inside the Beltway. Forth gear and the engine topped out doing sixty-five. The carburettor in the little air-cooled engine was designed as a governor, favouring longevity over engine speed. 'But it'll go a long way to getting *to* them – forcing them to panic. Maybe the Homeland contact too. Someone will make a mistake. And until we have other leads, we need to watch how much noise the media and police and federal agencies will make to find Hayes – and then we look for the mistakes.'

'I imagine Fox News will have a field day with this.'

'Because the suspects are Middle Eastern?'

'Can't you picture it? They'll go nuts for it.'

'Well, that certainly won't hinder things. A Secret Service agent vanishes, abducted while working on a secret op inside the US. The airplay will be constant. No matter how high up the contact is at Homeland, it's gonna go stratospheric.'

'So, what do we do now?'

'We sleep.' He kept on the 395 heading south-west, towards Arlington.

'Where?'

'Hotels are generally a pretty good option when looking for a bed for the night.'

'What if they're looking for us – those cops from Annapolis, or the Homeland guys?'

'They probably are.'

'So, doesn't that exclude hotels? You said night clerks keep TVs on . . .'

'We be smart about it. Find a motel, not hotel. Something off the interstate. Somewhere busy but not booked out. A non-chain, where we can pay cash and not show ID. You stay in the car, I'll get the rooms. It'll be fine. There's wanted, and there's *wanted*. So far, we're the former. We won't be on any TV screens.'

'You sound like you've done this plenty of times before.'

'That I have, Muertos,' Walker said, checking his rear-view mirror. 'That I have.'

25

The motel was in Huntington, Virginia, south of DC and just outside the Capital Beltway, as though the I495 represented a big physical ring around DC and that while outside of that, Walker felt like they were less likely to be seen. In practical terms it meant that they had a little more room to manoeuvre; they could get on the Beltway inside a minute and be headed any which way, including further south, to check out the last known location of Agent Hayes. He pulled up the Beetle in the car park, shielded from view of reception by a van. Walker left Muertos in the car with the engine running and headed for the dimly lit reception.

The motel was made of an orange brick and dark tiled roof, single storey, twenty-eight rooms arranged in an L-shape with a car park in the negative space. Walker booked two rooms, paid a hundred and forty cash, which he figured was cheap for DC, but a decent tip for the night clerk who didn't record their details and didn't put the cash in the drawer. The clerk gave him two keys, rooms 13 and 14, and two photocopied discount vouchers for breakfast at a diner down the road. Walker parked the car in front of room 13, stalled the engine and passed Muertos a room key.

Muertos said, 'So . . .'

'Meet here at seven am,' Walker said.

'Okay. Then?'

'Then we grab breakfast and check in with Overton and see where we're at. Maybe grab some new clothes.'

'New . . . Oh, right. Shit, our bags . . .'

'Were back in the rental, in Annapolis.'

'Okay. Seven am.'

He waited for Muertos to enter and close her door, then he headed for room 14. The bright white energy-saving bulbs overhead threw stark shadows. Brick walls and built-in timber furniture from the seventies reminded Walker of many other such owner-operated motels across the United States. The double mattress was covered in a pastel quilt. Two flimsy timber chairs were arranged around a small table. Walker set the shower on and while he waited for it to steam he checked his phone and emails. Nothing. Before placing a call, he put the television on to block out any chance of his words travelling through to Muertos next door.

It was just after ten pm. He called Somerville's cell number, and the call was answered almost straightaway.

'Walker, I see you've entered another shit storm,' Somerville said by way of greeting.

'Who's saying what?'

'Homeland reached out to us two hours ago, asking questions about you,' Somerville said. 'They're looking for you. They've got you ID'd at a house in Annapolis, where apparently you spooked and shot at a CIA agent. That sound familiar?'

'He pulled the gun; them's the rules.'

'You know I really don't care about what they have to say,' Somerville said. 'Thing is, they want to question you – and I have to report any contact you make.'

'But you really don't care about what they have to say.'

'Not in the least,' Somerville said. 'But this is Homeland, right? This cell phone I'm on is encrypted, so they can't listen in, but they can get the metadata from it, like the numbers of the incoming and outgoing calls, and my location.'

'I'll trash this phone and call you on a new one tomorrow.'

'Right. So, where are things at?'

Walker gave her a rundown of the conversation with the Secret Service agent, and the APB that would be going out any moment on the missing agent. And then he shared his observations of Muertos.

Somerville said, 'Did you ask her about no longer working at the State Department?'

'Not yet.'

'It doesn't bother you? And skipping out of the hospital in Germany?'

'I'm waiting to see why she's withholding that from me.'

'Waiting for what – for fun?'

'I'll pick the time. I'm watching her.'

'Is there anything to suggest that this is related to a Zodiac attack?'

'No,' Walker said, seeing the cable news reporting boatloads of refugees arriving in Italy after being plucked from the ocean by the EU Coast Guard. 'Honestly, I think that my father was there to buy a family as some kind of cover, to travel with them. Or maybe to use them as some kind of face-to-face communications package to me or someone else here in the states. Can't think it'd be anything else.'

'But he told Muertos to find you. Why would he say that?'

'I assume because his plan fell apart. But just to say find me, and nothing else? That's what's bugging me. The old guy has always been cryptic and secretive, but this is something else. What's he telling me?'

Somerville was silent on the other end of the phone for a few seconds, then said, 'How long are you going to give this thing with Muertos?'

'Until tomorrow,' Walker said. 'We've got someone from the Secret Service looking into it, and it should turn up the two Syrians who got into the country yesterday.'

'The Secret Service?'

'Long story,' Walker said. 'Then, depending on what comes of that, I'll either quiz Muertos some more, or walk away. Can't be drifting around the country fixing everyone's problems now, can I?'

'Probably for the best,' Somerville said. 'I mean, who knows when the next Zodiac call might appear. You need to be up to it. How's the leg?'

'It's still there, right next to the other one.'

'Right. Talk tomorrow.'

Walker ended the call. He hung his clothes over a chair and opened the shower stall and stood under the hot water. The soap was tiny and near to useless. He kept replaying the conversation with Hassan, and with Overton. And Muertos. Distilling it, looking for a pattern. Human trafficking. His father wanting to buy a family. Did he really want to do that – or was he there for another reason? Could Muertos be the reason? *Find Jed Walker.* Was it relevant that she was the one who came to him, or was that just happenstance, that she was the only one from State to get out alive. Then his mind drifted to Agent Hayes, and the picture of her, and then the photos of Almasi and his thug, Bahar. He turned the water off. Dried with a thin towel. Wiped the fog off the small mirror over the basin and saw the reflection of a tired version of himself. His earliest memories of his father were of him being the age Jed was now, and the face in the mirror reminded him that the apple had not fallen far from the tree. He'd made so many of the same mistakes in his relationship that his father had made, because his work overrode his personal life. And here he was, in some cheap motel, trying to unravel something because his father had dragged him into it – and away from Eve.

Everyone's looking for somebody.

Her father helped my mother, a long time ago.

Find Jed Walker.

26

Walker woke at six am. Outside was dark, the sun barely a hint on an unseen horizon. He turned on the television, a small off-brand flat screen. He filled the small coffee pot with water and poured it into the drip reservoir, then put a paper-wrapped serve of coffee into the tray underneath. It started to steam and bubble and drip into the glass flask. As he dressed he flicked through all the news channels, changing and watching and listening for information on the missing Secret Service Agent Clair Hayes. He sat on the edge of his bed with a mug of coffee, flicking the news channels back and forth for another ten minutes. Still nothing. As he started on his second cup of coffee, he used his phone to check online news, and he even Google searched it. *Secret Service agent missing*. Nothing. *Secret Service agent abducted*. Nothing. *Secret Service Agent Clair Hayes*. Nothing.

Which meant that Sally Overton hadn't put word out.

Why?

He put on his jacket and walked out into the cool morning air and tapped on Muertos's door. It was six-thirty. His breath fogged in front of him. There was light behind her curtains. He heard the pad of feet on the thin carpet of the room, then her voice from the other side of the door: 'Yeah?'

'It's me,' Walker said. 'Can we talk?'

The door opened. She looked sleepy, like she'd not slept right through the night, and had only recently entered and then woken from decent REM sleep a few minutes before.

He held up a coffee for her. Black, steaming, as strong and hot as the machine in his room would make it.

'Didn't you say seven?' Muertos said. She was dressed in her clothes from yesterday, but her shoes and jacket lay at the end of her unmade bed. She took the coffee.

'Can I come in?'

'Sure.' Muertos stood back and Walker entered. Her television was on mute. MSNBC. The news ticker had nothing about the missing agent. 'What is it?'

'You been watching the news?'

'All night.'

'And have you seen any reference to Overton's missing agent?'

'No.'

'You should call her.'

'I don't have a phone, remember.'

Walker passed her his.

'Maybe she's busy,' Muertos said, looking at the object, then sipping her coffee. 'Organising the search, being debriefed.'

'Maybe, but I doubt it,' Walker said. 'I think there's two things that could have happened here.'

'And they are?' Muertos said, starting to punch in the numbers of Overton's cell.

'After out meet, Overton told her boss about what's happened,' Walker said. 'He or she is now working with the FBI on this, debriefing and briefing, like you said. And it's being all hushed up, perhaps for security reasons. Maybe they've already got a location and Hayes is captive and the captors are in their sights as we speak.'

'Almasi and his guy, Bahar.'

'Presumably it's them,' Walker said. 'So, that's one possibility.'

'And what's the other scenario?' Muertos watched him waiting to press call.

Walker looked absently at the television screen. 'Overton didn't make her report. No-one up the chain knows that Hayes is missing. No-one's looking for her.'

Muertos didn't respond to that, instead she pressed call and put the phone on speaker.

The call went straight to Overton's voicemail.

'She might be on her phone,' Muertos said, ending the call.

'Maybe,' Walker replied. 'You get ready, and try calling her again. Let's be out of here in ten, okay?'

Muertos nodded.

Walker left Muertos to get ready. In his room he sat on the end of the bed and flicked through the news and waited. He wanted to make a stop to get a new shirt and undergarments and maybe a sweater – the life of a nomad wearing the same clothes day in and day out wasn't for him. Next thing he'd be packing a folding toothbrush and letting his passport expire and living out of cheap motels across the country all his life, solving everybody's problems. He knew where he wanted to be – with Eve. Relaxing. Away from this kind of thing. The chaos of twenty years at the coalface to protect his country was more than enough. The last year of chasing the ghost of his father, who may or may not be driving the Zodiac terror groups but undeniably had a hand in creating them, was wearing him out. *Where would it end? How long would he give it – another twenty years?*

Not a chance.

He looked the room over, leaving the key on the worn timber table, and stood outside. He checked his phone: 6.42 am. The sun was a sliver on the horizon. The sky was clear and steel blue. The sound of traffic already filled the nearby interstate and the big cloverleaf that fed the Beltway. He opened the door to the Beetle, eased the park brake off and pushed it out to face the road, then push-started it across the car park and did his manoeuvre of folding himself inside and behind the wheel. The throaty garble of the tiny vintage engine cut through the morning air like a chainsaw. He flicked on the lights and the familiar yellow glow of the old lamps flared in the cool morning air.

Muertos emerged from her motel room and entered the car, the smell of soap and shampoo and coffee following her in. Her hair was wet and tied back in a ponytail. Walker put the heater on a low setting. The air took a while to blow warm.

'She's still not answering,' Muertos said, passing Walker his phone. 'So, she's either been on her phone all this time, or it's turned off – but I've never known her to turn her phone off.'

Walker could see that Muertos was concerned. That maybe a fate worse than the one Overton feared, the fate worse than losing her career, may have become a reality.

Walker said, 'Do you know where she lives?'

Muertos nodded.

'Okay,' Walker said, taking off onto the road. 'You navigate.'

27

Sally Overton lived in Lincoln Park, which was about as central a spot inside the Beltway as you could get, short of living in the White House. It took them an hour to get there. They crossed the Potomac, then the Anacostia, past the Navy yards, taking Independence Avenue SE to get into the neighbourhood. The Monday morning commute was on, the roads filling with kids on buses and in cars to get to school and mums and dads with steaming to-go cups and government workers getting their gridlock on. Walker eased the little Beetle to the curb, in a spot down half a block from Overton's four-storey 'row house' home, a typical design of many old Washington DC neighbourhoods, here attached to adjoining buildings of similar look, all set back behind wrought-iron fences and gardens.

'Overton have a family?' Walker asked as he shut the Beetle's door and made for the footpath.

'Her boyfriend is posted to Boston,' Muertos said, falling into step next to him.

'That'd be her car,' Walker said, pointing to a shiny black Chevy Caprice parked out the front of Overton's house, with government plates and discreet lights on the back and front dash. He felt the hood as he passed and it was dead cold, the windows slightly frosted.

Walker went to the front door and found the buzzer button marked Overton. It chimed a two-step chord, three notes at once, repeating twice. Four sounds, ding-dong, ding-dong. He listened for a minute, then repeated the procedure, this time with a knock of knuckles on the door. He looked around. A couple of people were walking dogs. A kid rode by on a bike. Cars passed by every thirty seconds.

'Which apartment is hers?' Walker asked.

'Second storey, that window over there is her lounge room,' Muertos said, pointing up and to the right, to one of the two picture-frame windows on the next level up.

'I'll go see what I can see,' Walker said, then he put his hands over his eyes to shield out the sun's glare from over his shoulder and looked at the window beside the entry door. The interior of the townhouse was dark. No movement. He passed Muertos his phone. 'You wait here. Try calling her phone again.'

'Maybe she's out.'

'Not without her car.'

'A colleague might have picked her up.'

'Maybe,' Walker said, 'but since we're here we have to check.'

'And what if there's no answer?' Muertos replied. 'Break in? Steal her car while we're at it?'

'If we have to,' Walker said.

'We could try buzzing all her neighbours, see if they'll let us in the building.'

'Maybe, but that won't help us get in through her apartment door,' Walker said. 'The window is our easiest bet.'

'She's probably at work.'

Walker exhaled, looked to Muertos, and said, 'It's okay. Let's just check things out while we're here, okay? Just in case she's inside and needs our help.'

Muertos took a moment, then said, 'Okay. Try the window.'

'Right. Wait here, I'll buzz you in.'

Walker went through into the garden next to the entry. Smooth white pebbles the size of chicken eggs crunched underfoot as he headed to the first-floor window. Birch trees lined the fence next to the footpath, already brimming with new pale green leaves. There was a basement level, and the house was raised, so the first floor was actually about mid-thigh level, half a floor above street level. Walker heard the hiss of a fan under there, either connected to a boiler or gas ducted system. Walker pulled himself up, then used the first-floor window architecture to climb up and reach the sill of the second-floor window. He did a chin-up and hauled himself up.

He looked inside Overton's front window. It was a lounge room beyond, hard to see into for the sun being behind him and reflecting against the glass. There was a lamp on inside. Maybe she was home – would she leave that on all day if she was headed out? Maybe she'd gone for a morning run to clear her mind. He sat sideways on the window sill, then put the tips of his fingers under the bottom of the casement window and lifted.

Nothing happened. The window was locked. Either that or it was painted shut. The window frame looked as though it had been painted over every election year.

Walker could see through the lounge to another room, and beyond that a window. A window that was slightly open. He dropped himself down to the gravel, gave a signal to Muertos to stay put, and ran around the block. This street faced onto the green space of Lincoln Park, and the houses were mostly detached and yet to be converted to apartments. He counted his paces to match those of Overton's apartment, and went through the front yard of a white timber-clad colonial mansion, taking the paved side throughway to the backyard. There he climbed over a gate, and then, beyond the manicured courtyard space and over an eight-foot brick fence, was the back of Overton's building. He could make out the window that was open about a hand span. The back of the house had a steel fire escape that serviced each apartment, some kind of mandated twentieth-century add-on. He hopped the fence and dropped down to a small yard, full of outdoor chairs, a couple of grills and a lonely potted citrus.

Walker scaled the fire escape and looked through the back door into the kitchen.

The lights were on. And the oven, too – he could see that the dial was turned to grill, and the dim light of the oven was the same yellow glow behind the glass of the Beetle's headlights.

There was something else, too. Smoke. Clinging to the ceiling. Dark grey. Like something had burned to charcoal some time ago and was hanging around and slowly seeping through the gaps around the light fixtures. A fire alarm flashed a red light, but no sound emanated, as though it had long ago run out of effort in alerting anyone.

Walker couldn't see Overton, but his gut told him this wasn't right, and he tried the door handle. Locked. He went for the window, opening it silently and climbing inside. The smell inside was one of burned greasy food. The smoke was coming from the oven, a very fine stream of dark vapour. He saw on the bench an empty packet for frozen fries. They would be little more than black dust by now. He figured they'd been in the oven a few hours. There was an open bottle of pinot grigio on the counter, half-empty. Walker pictured Overton getting home, thinking about the calls she had to make, and opening some wine to build up courage. Some kind of last supper before kissing her career goodbye, or searching for some solace in food and alcohol before making a midnight call to her boss to report the missing agent Clare Hayes.

Then what? Or was she waiting for someone? He couldn't see any glasses to accompany the wine bottle, but there had easily been two glasses poured out.

Maybe she did call it in. And someone came over to get all the details. And they drank while talking it all through . . .

Walker headed up the hall, through the silent apartment. To his right was an open doorway, and it was a bedroom, and the bed was made. He continued onwards, towards the lounge room and the big bay window that he'd tried to open. The hall opened up to the lounge. To his right was a desk and computer set up in a corner as a little home office. The front door was next to that. Its chain was on, which meant she hadn't left through the front door.

But then Walker discovered that she hadn't left at all.

In the lounge there was another smell, this one different to smoke, but to Walker, just as familiar.

Death.

28

'No . . .' Muertos saw the look on Walker's face and she started to cry. She put her whole body into it, and Walker went to put an arm around her but she shrugged it off and wiped her tears to a sleeve and pushed through the open front door and across the room, where she stood suddenly still, looking down at her friend's body.

Walker stood next to Muertos. She was still crying, but they were now silent tears, the saline streams running down her cheeks in a constant flow.

Walker looked down at Overton, splayed out on a rug. Gunshot wound to the head, her service automatic near her open hand, her body arranged like a chalk outline. It was a well-lit room, leaving nothing to the imagination. The contents of her head had turned from pink and red to a dull red-brown. It was at least four hours old. Somewhere between ten and four hours ago, because it was just over ten hours ago that they'd said goodbye to her.

'She would never have done this, if not for me,' Muertos said. 'No. No. I can't believe it. Not her. No. Not like this. No. Oh, Sally, why . . .'

'She didn't do it,' Walker said.

Muertos looked at him.

'This was a clean-up crew,' he said.

'She . . .' Muertos's mouth opened and closed a few times with no sound coming out.

'She didn't shoot herself,' Walker said. He surveyed the room – no obvious sign of a struggle – and then looked back to the body. The entry wound was under the chin, a blackened burn mark around the small ragged hole. An unlikely spot for a suicide. You'd put it in your mouth, blow out the back of your head. There was something final about biting down on the steel barrel, and that way you couldn't miss. Under the chin, you'd worry that the weapon wasn't aimed properly – a couple of degrees off and you'd shoot out your cheek or eye socket or a corner of your brain and be left forever incapacitated, forever reminded of your failure.

In this case, the shot under the chin was dead-on. The contents of Overton's skull were mainly on the cream-painted ceiling, although a lot of it had then fallen onto the beige couch and armchair. Globs of brain matter clung like stalactites, chips of skull pierced into the plaster ceiling, and the blood splatter was a four-foot diameter piece of absurdist art. Secret Service used the SIG Sauer P226, in many variations; in Overton's case, the compact P229R version, to better fit her hands. The result of the .357 bullet at close range was devastating. It must have been loaded with some sort of hollow-point rounds. All that explosive kinetic energy in a mushrooming piece of metal obliterating Overton's head. The firearm was on the floor near Overton's lifeless right hand, and it looked clearly enough like that was where it had fallen from her grasp as she'd collapsed to the floor a split second after pulling the trigger.

'But she shot herself.' Muertos looked back down. 'In the head.'

'No,' Walker said. He put a hand on Muertos's shoulder and waited until she looked at him before saying clearly, 'Sally didn't kill herself.'

'But—' Muertos glanced down, then back up, and closed her eyes tightly, as though if she tried hard enough she could un-see and undo the scene before her.

'She was killed,' Walker said. 'Shot close range. It was quick. They didn't hurt her badly.'

'They didn't hurt her – *badly*?'

Walker nodded.

'What does that even mean – how do you know?'

'There was a struggle.' He looked from her and walked the room, then squatted down near Overton. He used his phone to push up Overton's open shirt cuff of her gun hand. 'See here – the bruise marks on her wrists? That's where someone big and strong held her. Probably before questioning her, and then forcing her own hand to make the shot. And the way she was shot tells me it wasn't suicide. If it's any consolation, it was quick.'

'Quick?'

'She'd know how to fight, and she didn't get the chance.'

'But . . .' Muertos looked down at her friend. Her shoulders slumped, but there was something in her face, her eyes, that said it was more bearable, more palatable, if her friend's life had been taken, rather than the alternative. 'Why would someone make it look like this?'

Walker was silent.

'I should have been with her last night,' Muertos said. 'I should have been there for her.'

'There's nothing you could have done, so don't feel any shame about this.' Walker stood and looked around. 'Anger, sure, directed at those who did it. If you'd been here, they'd have killed you too.'

'You don't know what.'

'I know we'll catch up with them soon enough.'

Muertos did a quick pace of the room. 'There's no other signs of a struggle.'

'The front door was locked and the chain was on,' Walker said. 'And the rear door to the fire escape has a slide-across bolt.'

'So, if there was a killer they exited through the window?'

'Yes,' Walker said. He found a wine glass, near the computer. Just one. 'But how'd the killer get in? She either let them in, which means she trusted them, or he got in the same way he went out.'

'Her bruised wrists could be from anything,' Muertos said. 'Training maybe?'

'No,' Walker said, moving back to the body and again using his phone to push Overton's hand to the side. 'It's recent, still swollen. A hand gripped around her right wrist and forced it to the firing position under the chin. A large hand, almost as wide as her firearm is long. See, those are marks from the tips of someone's fingers? A big, strong grip. Very strong. Maybe even fractured the bones in the process. Holding her by the other wrist too, maybe at first to talk, then to comply with the shot.'

'So . . .' Muertos stood by the front door and looked at Walker, who stood and faced her. 'A CIA team or medical examiner will see through this just as quickly as you did,' she said. 'So, why bother setting it up to look like this?'

'To buy a little time,' Walker said. He went back to the computer and tried it. It was dead. And not just for lack of power – the casing was loose, and when he lifted it up he saw that the hard-drive and mother-board were missing. If she had a government-issue laptop, that was gone too. 'Forensics will get here, work the crime scene and send the body off to full autopsy. They have all kinds the procedures to follow, boxes to tick. And because it's one of their own, they're going to take their time here. First responders and crime scene will pick what I've seen, sure. They'll *suspect* it. Proof, and finding the perpetrator, is something else. So, they'll follow their procedures. Take photographs, dust for fingerprints, collect fibres, DNA, the works. It'll take a day or two for the full report from here and from the morgue. And sure, they'll know from the get-go that she was held at the wrists, but not beyond reasonable doubt in a court of law that it was part of the action that killed her until they run all their tests.'

'So, they'll *suspect* it, they'll *assume* it, but it'll look like an *apparent* murder until then?'

'Yep. They'll be preparing for a murder, sure. They'll get uniformed DC Metro cops door-knocking for witnesses straightaway, because Sally was one of their own and they'll want to do all that they can within the limitations – but they won't be able to go nuclear until the official report is in.'

'Nuclear?'

'Figure of speech,' Walker said, standing up. 'They won't put it to the media, they won't set up perimeters on the interstates and beef up security at airports to catch suspects, they won't subpoena all security video footage from local houses and businesses, they won't get drones in the air overhead, that kind of thing.'

'So, staging it this way buys them a day or two from all that.'

'Yep, and that's a day or two longer than they would have had if Overton had gone to her supervisors last night, and a day or two longer than if the killer had simply gunned her down in the street.' Walker stalked the room, his eyes darting around, searching.

'So, the killers need a day. Another day, to get away from the area, or to do whatever it is they're planning.'

'Or they're planning something long term,' Walker said, crouching down and looking under chairs. 'And this is about cleaning things up so that the trail ends as soon as it's begun.'

'Who's they?' Muertos looked at Walker. 'Almasi and his big goon?'

'Maybe.' He looked to Muertos. 'That's the million-dollar question. It's related to them, it has to be. But was this done by them? Or someone else they're working with.'

'Like those two Homeland guys?'

'Maybe.'

'You really think a couple of corrupt Homeland agents kill a fellow Fed?'

'Depends how bent they are, and what's at stake.'

'How'd they find Overton?'

'Perhaps they got Clair Hayes to talk, to give Overton up. Then they came here and did this. That's my bet, but we don't know for sure yet. That's why we need to move fast.'

'Fast? What do we do now?' Muertos said. 'Sally was our only hope.'

'Look for her cell phone. Not her official one. The burner. And her handbag. And if you see a laptop or tablet computer or notebooks, grab them. Phone bills, Post-Its. Anything she might have recorded info on.'

'That's all evidence at a crime scene – a murder scene.' Muertos was careful not to look at the body of her friend as she spoke.

'And the authorities don't need it,' Walker said. 'But we do. They'll have access to all the content on her phone and computer – it'll all be backed up to a cloud and in phone records and data servers. It's only useful to us – we need to find what we can, and then we'll try to reach out to the other two agents Overton said she was using on this off-books op.'

'Okay. Okay. I'll take the bedroom.'

Walker carefully patted Overton's pockets with the back of his hand. Nothing. He checked the couch and lounge chairs, under and behind loose cushions. He saw Muertos head out of the room, heard her in the kitchen, then the bedroom, moving with heavy feet. Overton was her friend. *She's like a sister to me. Her father helped my mother a long time ago.* He wondered how Muertos would cope with this over the coming hours. *Would she fall apart? Or become a liability in confronting someone they suspected?* Walker stared at the bookcase that lined a wall around a covered-up fireplace. *Should he cut Muertos loose? Now that the killing had started, she was well out of her depth – she'd been an analyst at the State Department, not a field officer. Maybe she should stay here, or near here, and call in the murder. She could then brief Overton's Secret Service colleagues . . .*

'No handbag,' Muertos said, re-entering the room. 'No cell phone, no laptop or tablet. Whoever did this must have taken it.'

'The killer made away with the hard drive and Overton's official phone,' Walker said. 'But maybe not the burner phone she'd used to contact her missing agent and two colleagues. Keep looking.'

Muertos started taking books off the bookshelf. Walker looked down at the body. The way it was splayed, her left arm pointed up above her head, her right arm down by her side. He crouched down again. Looked around at ground level.

'I think—' Muertos stopped herself. Looked down to Walker. 'You hear that?'

'Yes,' Walker said.

He moved around the room. Then stopped. Not nothing. He heard a sound. Not the ringing of a phone. A vibration. Constant. Brrrrr. Nearby. Low. He listened near the body. No. He moved to the right. The bookcase. The sound was getting louder. He kneeled down and looked underneath. The cell-phone screen was lit up, the little device shifting on the floorboards – and then it stopped. He scooped up the phone, probably a prepaid Walmart special, untraceable, off the grid, mission specific.

The missed call was from Jim Bennet.

Walker said, 'Our next lead.'

29

Seventy miles away a phone rang.

'Yes?' Almasi answered.

Harvey said, 'Have you cleaned it all up?'

'The operation is still in play,' Almasi replied.

'What do you mean, *still in play*?'

'My man is still in the field. Working.'

'Have him work faster. This mess ends with those agents. Then we can talk about finding you a new role.'

'I'm working as fast as I can.'

'Lewis wants to shut this down today.'

There was a pause. Almasi looked out the back window. A black mare was running with its foal across vivid green grass. 'And is that what you want?'

'I want this to go on until we're finished,' Harvey said, 'but it's not entirely up to me.'

'I will get this done today. Will that make a difference for your colleague? Might he rethink the pull-out of Syria? It is still a gold mine . . .'

'I think Lewis is too spooked. This might be the end of things in that region. This has got far too close, with what's now happening here at home.'

'Funny he should be squeamish about that,' Almasi said.

Harvey was silent.

Almasi said, 'Then it's the end?'

'It's lasted longer than we expected.'

'Because we've been lucky.'

'I like to think we make our own luck. It's been a lot of hard work.'

'For me too.'

'You've been well compensated.'

'But what now?'

'Look,' Harvey said, 'if this is cleaned up quick and fast, maybe we can get you back out there. I might be able to sell it to him.'

'Thank you.'

'You're sure you don't need my assistance?'

'Absolutely. My guy is very good at this sort of thing.'

'It might take more than one guy?'

'He knows where the targets are. It's like a, what would you call it – a staged hunt?'

'That's assuming you really know where they are.'

'We have our methods.'

'We do too – if you had given me their names, I could have given you the addresses of the targets inside a minute.'

'My method works just fine.'

There was silence for a while, then Harvey said, 'Your method involved getting the information from the agent you picked up?'

'Of course. She's proving most helpful.'

'You should have – wait,' Harvey said. 'She's still alive?'

'For now.'

'Jesus – I don't want to know.'

'Relax.'

'She probably lied to you and—'

'Relax. She knows not to lie to me.'

'Okay. Well, make sure she's gone as soon this is cleaned up. And don't leave any trace of her where you're staying.'

'I'll see to it personally.'

'Right. Well, all going well I'll see you tomorrow night.'

There was a pause. 'But what about tonight?'

'Tonight won't work,' Harvey said.

There was silence.

'Get done what you need to get done,' Harvey said. 'And wait for me. And until this is all cleared up, and you're sure you're clean, I mean really sure, there's no chance in hell you can meet Lewis.'

Almasi said, 'You said I could meet him tonight.'

'And you said you'd have those agents taken care of by daybreak. This is a delicate task. Until it's all cleaned up for sure. Tomorrow is just one day away. You'll meet him soon enough. Until then, it's too dangerous for you to show your face in DC.'

'It might be too dangerous for you too.'

Harvey laughed. 'No, not for me.'

'Okay.' Almasi watched the horse and its foal disappear into a tree-line. 'Tomorrow.'

•

Walker pulled over two blocks from Overton's house and kept the Beetle idling as he looked over Muertos's shoulder. 'What's in the phone?'

'Four numbers in the call log.' She scrolled through the phone, the only piece of intel they found in Overton's apartment. She handed it to Walker. 'There's your cell number, all the missed calls from your phone from earlier, and three others.'

'The three agents Overton used for her off-books op,' Walker said, scrolling through the call log. The times of the calls over the past forty-eight hours were at three-hour intervals, just as Muertos had said. Her three friends calling in. After around nine pm, there had been many calls to one number, spread over the next four hours, which narrowed the time of death even more. He passed the phone back. 'One missing agent, Clair Hayes. The other two numbers are Bennet and Acton. Four missed calls from Bennet in the past hour. We need to talk to him, warn him.'

'I'll try calling him, then Acton and Hayes.'

'Try Hayes first.' Walker watched as Muertos tapped each number. She put it on speaker and they both listened: calling – then straight to voicemail.

'This is Clair Hayes, leave a message or send one.'

'It's not an official message,' Muertos said, ending the call and dialling the next listed number. 'They're not giving their title, or employer, which means the three numbers belong to their operational burner phones, right?'

Walker nodded. 'Acton?'

The next number also rang through to voicemail.

'You've called Blake Acton. I'm busy right now, but leave a message and I'll get right back to you.'

The tone sounded, and Muertos looked to Walker, and he nodded.

'Blake, this is Rachel Muertos, a friend of Sally Overton. You need to call back me asap on this number.'

She ended the call and scrolled down to the third number. Pressed call. They watched the screen. *Calling.* Waited.

Then, a voice answered.

30

'Overton, I've been worried,' the voice on the phone said. Male. From Connecticut, to Walker's ear. 'Overton? Can you hear me?'

Muertos said, 'Agent Bennet?'

'Yeah,' he replied, wary. 'Who is this?'

'I'm afraid I need to—'

'Who are you? Where's Overton?'

'I'm a good friend of Sally Overton. My name's Rachel Muertos. I'm with the State Department – she might have mentioned me?'

'No.' The voice was still wary. 'Where's Sally Overton?'

'She's . . .' Muertos stopped talking.

'What's going on?'

'Buddy,' Walker said. 'I'm sorry, but we have some bad news. Sally Overton was killed. Sometime in the past few hours. You may be—'

'Who is this?'

'My name's Jed Walker. We were just—'

'*Where's Overton?*'

'At her house,' Walker said. 'On the floor of her living room. Single gunshot to the head with her own service sidearm.'

There was a long pause, then Bennet said, 'She would never do that.'

'We know,' Walker said. 'And she didn't.'

'How'd you get this phone?'

'We were just there, at her house.'

'Who are you?'

'I'm with Muertos,' Walker said. 'We were—'

'From the State Department?'

'Agent Bennet, listen up,' Walker said. 'We met with Overton last night. We know about the off-books op, because we're working on it from another angle. We know about Agent Hayes and her disappearance sometime before midnight two nights ago. And now Overton's dead. Someone shot her and made it look like she did it to herself. Whoever did that will be after you and Agent Acton. We just tried his cell number and it went straight to voicemail – you need to warn him, and get someplace safe yourself. You need to do that right now. Someplace safe, you understand? Do that and call us back in thirty minutes.'

There was silence on the other end of the phone for fifteen seconds. Walker watched the screen of the phone, the duration of the call ticking over.

'I just tried calling Acton on my government phone,' Bennet said. 'You're right about the voicemail. But his house is just a few blocks from my apartment. I'll pay him a visit. See what's what.'

'I wouldn't do that,' Walker said. 'Call your superiors and have them send a tactical team to Acton's place. And you need to get out and watch your back and contact us when you know you're clear.'

'Why would I do that?'

'Because,' Walker said, 'Muertos and I are working on the same case you are, just from a different angle. And right now, as far as we know, you're the only person who knows about this who's still alive. So, if you want to stay that way, you watch your back, and get someplace safe.'

Silence. Then the sounds of movement, like the agent was walking, shuffling his feet. Then, in a hushed tone, he said, 'I think someone's at my apartment door. But I didn't buzz anyone up.'

'Don't answer it,' Walker said, putting the Beetle into gear. 'Get out the window or balcony or however you can. What's your address?'

Silence.

'Hello?' Walker said.

Nothing. The phone call ended.

31

'What do we do?' Muertos said. 'Wait to get through to him again?'

'We call in favours,' Walker said. He dialled Fiona Somerville's cell number, got through and asked for the residential address of Secret Service Agent Jim Bennet. He set the phone on speaker while they waited and he drove out of the neighbourhood; it took three minutes for the information to come through.

'Okay,' Somerville said, and gave them an address in Cherrydale.

'Thanks,' Walker said, Muertos punching it into the map on the phone.

'And Walker, about that other matter—'

'I'll call you back soon,' Walker said, ending the call. He pulled a U-turn and drove towards the dot on the map, which was a predicted fourteen minutes away. He'd try to make it in eight.

'Who was that?' Muertos said.

'A friend.'

'A friend who can get the address of Secret Service personnel over the phone in a couple of minutes?'

'A well-placed friend,' Walker said.

They drove in silence as Walker kept the revs of the little old engine high and used the brakes as little as possible through the morning rush hour. When the congestion forced them to stop at an intersection, Muertos finally spoke.

'That was Fiona Somerville, of the FBI?'

Walker glanced at her, then back at the road. 'Yeah.'

Muertos paused, then continued. 'I saw her name, and title. In an email, on your phone.'

'I figured as much,' Walker said.

'I didn't mean to pry. I meant to look something up, and when the browser opened I saw it was logged onto your email, and my name was in the subject line, so I read it.'

'And?'

Muertos remained tight-lipped.

'You want to tell me anything about that email?' The road ahead cleared and he kept his eyes forward, his hands on the wheel and his foot on the gas.

'I guess I owe you an explanation.' Muertos looked out her side window as she spoke. 'I'm not in the State Department anymore. Haven't been for a few months.'

'I got that, from the email,' Walker said, hitting the brakes and making a hard right turn to make a red light. 'So, why lie to me when we met?'

'It was unintentional.'

'I'm calling BS on that. You mentioned the State Department because you wanted me to take you seriously. You'd read my employment file, the heavily redacted version. But the file you read gave you clearance that covered the year I spent with the State Department.'

'Yes, and yes,' Muertos said. She held onto the dash as he sped through the gears, up and down as they accelerated then slowed for another turn. 'Look, Walker, mine is a long and complicated story – but the short version is: State busted me out.'

'Busted you out?'

'Yeah. I had some – some issues, okay? And I wasn't coping, but I insisted on staying. Then my boss said something to me that made it impossible for me to work there anymore. He said: *You're either on leave, or you're fired.*'

Walker manoeuvred around an empty school bus.

'That was four, almost five months ago,' Muertos said. 'But the joint-taskforce team on the ground in Syria didn't know that I was out. I called in favours, forged my order papers, went over there, worked with them, the whole time not flagging anything back here.'

'I need to know why you did that,' Walker said, and he glanced across at her. 'What's driving you?'

'Because . . . it was always my baby, from the ground up – and I want to stop these people from doing what they're doing,' Muertos said. She spoke quickly, as though the information might not come out unless she pushed it out. 'I've spent my life working with State in people trafficking, liaising with Customs and ICE and Homeland and whatever they want to call our border-protection agency every few years.' She laughed without humour. 'It's like they think that in rebranding it they can say to those up the chain: look what we've done – we've arrested more and recovered more and saved more than anyone in the history of this outfit. It makes me so furious.' She was quiet a moment, reflecting. 'And beyond work, it's personal, always has been, okay? My mother was an illegal, from Mexico. She informed on the smuggling ring that brought us into the US, after she was caught up in an immigration case – she was being held as basically slave labour with dozens of others, and she did that deal for me, so that we could become legitimate citizens. That was thirty years ago, and now here I am, paying it all back, getting the scum that preys on profits from trafficking desperate people like my mother.'

'Overton's father worked that case,' Walker said, glancing sideways at her. 'That's what you meant last night, when you said he helped your mother.'

'Yes. He's a good man. He went above and beyond, made sure that my mother's deal was stuck to. We even lived with the Overtons for a few months in San Diego. I . . . I really should call him. About Sally.'

There was silence between them for near on a minute, Walker driving Muertos thinking about her loss. Then he said, 'What department was her father in?'

'He's well retired,' Muertos said. 'He was DOJ, and later helped form ICE.'

'Okay.' They were stopped at an intersection along Arlington Boulevard. 'And why'd you get busted out of State?'

'I think the official reason was insubordination, along with accessing compartmentalised data I had no clearance nor orders to access.'

'They kicked you out for that?'

'It was three-strike thing.'

'So, you had form.'

'Let's just say I used up all three strikes in one epic disaster of a day.'

'Unofficially?'

'What?'

'You said that was the official reason.'

'Yeah, I mean, that's what was on my letter of termination,' Muertos said. 'There was more to it. More than they knew. I'd spent the best part of two weeks doing the same kind of thing – it's just that day I got caught.'

'What drove you to do it?'

Muertos took a deep breath and said, 'I was desperate.'

'About?'

'About helping someone I care very deeply about.'

'Really?'

'Really.'

'Okay.' Walker hit the gas and took a left.

'Okay?'

'Okay. I can deal with that. And we can talk about it more later. Right now, try calling Bennet again.'

'I hope he answers,' Muertos said as she went to the call list.

'Me too.'

32

Muertos dialled the number and it went straight to voicemail:

'Jim Bennet. Leave a brief message after the tone.'

'What now? Just show up at his address?'

'Now dial Somerville back so we can give her Acton's name, in case Bennet's house call was something innocent and he's now going to check on Acton,' Walker said, but Muertos was already onto it, again putting the call on speaker. He overtook a line of cabs and blacked-out town cars, a few beeping his illegal manoeuvre.

'Fiona,' Walker said, 'time's ticking fast on this one – I need the address of Agent Blake Acton, colleague of Bennet and located just a few blocks from his apartment.'

'Walker, I just called in a big favour to get that last address for—'

'Life or death, real-time,' Walker said. 'Tell the Service that too, if you need to – just get me that address.'

'Okay, hold . . .'

Walker was heavy on the brakes at a jammed-up intersection, the skinny tyres of the Beetle leaving tracks of rubber on the road. He looked over his shoulder as they came to a stop, then reversed the little car as fast as it would go, pulling on the hand-brake and completing a J-turn, taking the first left between traffic. Muertos rattled around next to him, holding the dash and the phone and trying not to be thrown out of the vehicle.

'Walker,' Somerville's voice came loudly over the phone. 'I'll text you the other address asap.'

'Thanks.'

Muertos ended the call and punched in the new address as it came up.

'It's close, just north of North Pollard Street. About another mile north from here.'

'Got it,' Walker said, taking a left through an intersection, the tyres squealing in protest.

'What do we do when we get there?' Muertos asked.

'You wait in the car,' Walker said. 'I'll check on Bennet, and if he's gone, then we'll bug out to Acton's.'

'Okay.'

'And keep the engine running, we might need to bail out fast.'

'You think they got to him?'

Walker didn't answer.

33

Walker crossed the road, leaving Muertos behind the wheel of the idling Beetle. He stepped up onto the curb, looking around as he moved. Bennet's apartment building was anonymous in a forest of mates – an orange-and-white painted concrete mix of seven- to eight-storey towers sandwiched close together, either studio apartments or single-bedroom units, each with a tiny balcony poking out over the street. The kind of place populated by low-paid single government employees or couples trying to make a start of it before moving to something bigger. He found the building number and stopped at the glazed entry. The address he had for Jim Bennet was apartment 532: level five, apartment thirty-two. The security door was accessible via an electronic lock attached to the buzzer, or with a resident's electronic key fob. The glass in the aluminium frame was half-inch-thick tempered safety glass, conforming to whatever safety code DC demanded in such a setting – the type of glass they used in shop-fronts and commercial spaces that would not break or shatter short of a car hitting it, and still, when broken, it would shatter into safe little cubes and hold together for the plastic laminated between the two panes.

Walker wondered about the possibility of an unknown number of assailants getting up there, how Bennet had said someone was outside his door but he'd not buzzed them up. *Had the assailant buzzed at random, asking to be let in? Or he might have followed a resident in, or ducked in after someone exited for work.* Walker figured there was a fire escape or car-park entry around the back, which could conceivably be forced open or the lock picked to gain entry. Walker didn't have time to go and look, so he started to buzz. He'd buzzed four apartments on the fifth floor by the time one of them replied.

'Hey,' said Walker, 'this is Jim from thirty-two – I've locked myself out, any chance you can—'

The buzzer sounded, and the door's electronic lock made a loud click.

'Thanks.' Walker entered and pressed the lift button. One lift. It was coming down, currently at level seven, then six, then it stopped at five. He headed for the stairs, took them two at a time, got to the first landing and then stopped.

The lift. He had to see. To be sure.

He turned back and went down through the lobby and waited by the lift, out of sight, opposite the building's glass doors; there was nothing but a tall table with a bunch of plastic flowers in a fake Ming vase and a few square feet of empty space – the dead-end place a person wouldn't look if they got out the lift and headed straight towards the light of the day outside, to the only exit.

The lift was at level two.

As Walker waited he relaxed his heart-rate; kept his hands, arms and shoulders loose; shifted his weight to the front of his feet. He could hear the mechanics of the lift working, the counterweights and cables shifting. The bulk of the steel lift in the shaft. The slight grind as it came to a stop.

The lift doors pinged, and a single figure stepped out. Male, six-five, 250 pounds, shaved head. Familiar. He headed for the exit.

'Buddy?' Walker said, already moving forward.

The guy turned to look – through the waist, a glance over his left shoulder as he moved towards the door.

It was the guy from Overton's picture. Bahar. Almasi's muscle. Most likely Overton's killer. A clean-up guy. He was bigger in the flesh; shoulders wider than the doorway; arms hanging by his sides like an ape; a neck as thick as Walker's thigh. A brute of a man with a shiny scar snaking across the top of his head.

There were plenty of options to take the guy down, and Walker knew he would be armed – he wouldn't have gone to a Secret Service agent's home with the intent to kill with just his bare hands, no matter how big and strong those hands were. But bare hands were all that Walker had at his disposal, and he regretted it immediately. In one respect it was fine, because he didn't want to kill the guy.

Not yet.

But it was easy to kill someone with your bare hands. Walker knew that, because this was far from his first fight. It was too easy to kill someone, really. Accidents happened, especially in hand-to-hand combat, especially when the stakes could quickly escalate in the moment to become literally life or death. He knew if he hit Bahar too hard in the head, he might die. Get in to tussle and wrestle, his neck might snap. Well, maybe not that particular neck, but it principle it was a possibility. Crash into him and take him off his feet and Bahar's head or neck might come to an abrupt end against the thickly laminated glass door, and the mass and impact point of the two would be similar to a car crashing into it, and that force would easily snap a neck or crack a skull. And with their combined mass and his kinetic energy, it would be a big impact.

So, all things considered, Walker was cautious. And he acted fast, because he knew that whatever transpired would be over inside a few seconds.

Walker moved in. Took aim.

Not at the head. Not at the neck. Not to engage a wrestle. Not to crash-tackle Bahar into the doors.

His first move was to kick down at the back of Bahar's knees with brute force, a single blow of Walker's size fourteen left boot, the impact horizontal, obliterating both knees at once, hard and fast. Walker thought he heard the sound of an ACL or MCL snapping in Bahar's right knee, which bore the brunt of the force. All that mass, hitting the tiled ground at speed. Speed was again the damaging factor, multiplying that mass on impact. The guy hit the ground hard, on his knees, and Walker heard cartilage and bone shatter and crunch.

But Bahar was not done. He was far from being done, that much was clear as the surprise left his eyes and was replaced with calculated fury. Clearly not his first fight, either.

Despite now being on his knees, despite the pain that must be coursing through him, Bahar continued to turn at the waist, his face grimaced in what might have been pain or anger or a combination of the two. In the same motion he lifted his right arm to reach under the left side of his jacket, where, no doubt in Walker's mind, a sidearm was holstered. Probably a silenced 9-millimetre automatic, because silencers worked better on the 9-millimetre round than on heavier calibres. A silenced pistol meant a long pistol, and a long pistol meant a long, slow draw, giving Walker a couple of seconds. But that was a guess. Walker couldn't rule out that after doing his job upstairs the assassin unscrewed the silencer so the weapon wasn't as cumbersome to conceal – or use, in a hurry, if it came to it. That was probably the case. Walker would have done the same. If so, sans silencer, Bahar could draw the firearm quickly and shoot at Walker through his jacket. Not an ideal situation for Bahar or his tailor – and that suit had to be tailored because suits that big didn't come off the rack – but effective. Perhaps he'd even shoot while the weapon was still holstered, which he could if there was enough play in the holster, which would be an even quicker action. A second maybe.

Walker erred on the side of caution and determined that the gun was stowed without its silencer. And that, given Bahar's size, there would not be much play in the holster – he imagined it would be tightly strapped around his shoulder and back, played out to its maximum size because the manufacturer didn't make them any bigger, or it was custom made, like the suit.

However the weapon was stowed, Walker figured he had a second before it could be brought into play. And a second was a long time, in a do-or-die fight. And up until now Walker didn't want to kill him, but having the gun involved altered that mindset.

Walker side-stepped to the right as Bahar was still moving to his weapon and still twisting at the waist to look over his left shoulder. It negated the firing of the weapon while still holstered, and Bahar knew that and adapted, twisting around to relocate his moving target and bring out his right arm. Out, and up, a huge black pistol in his hand, still with silencer attached: a H&K SOCOM, a massive .45 calibre automatic originally designed for the US Special Operations teams, and it looked like a child's toy in Bahar's oversized fist.

So, not a 9-millimetre. This was something with more firepower. A specialised killing machine. And the custom silencer meant the weapon as quiet as anything else on the market. The perfect tool for an assassin.

Bahar didn't get to use it that morning – at least, not in the lobby of that apartment block.

Walker had inside a second before the weapon was trained on him, so he had few choices. Plan A – beating information out of Bahar –had gone completely out the window. He went for the swiftest, and potentially less lethal. Call it Plan B. He still didn't want to kill the guy if he could help it – not yet.

Walker jabbed hard and fast, his fist hitting the giant's Adam's apple, the impact making a sharp cracking sound.

The pistol dropped to the floor and Bahar put both his hands to his throat, his mouth opening and closing like a fish out of water.

But still, he wasn't done. Perhaps realising that worse was yet to come, perhaps knowing that he couldn't allow himself to be captured and questioned – maybe both those lines of thought being born out of specialist training in a paramilitary outfit back in the Mid East – Bahar lurched forward for his pistol.

Walker had little choice, in that split second. Plan B was on the scrap heap with A. So, Plan C it was. He hit Bahar hard in the back of the head with his elbow – using his fist against a head like this guy's would be akin to punching a granite boulder, and broken hands were not in Walker's list of desirable outcomes. Plan D would have seen him kicking him in the head, lining him up like a soccer player looking to kick the ball across the pitch – but he still didn't want to kill the guy, not if he could help it.

The impact of the elbow was awesome, and the force shuddered up Walker's arm and through his shoulders. The giant continued his path forward, the momentum of Walker's blow adding to the effects of gravity, and he hit the tiled floor of the foyer face-first. The shiny white porcelain tiles cracked on impact. He was out, destined not to come to for some time, and even when he did, he wouldn't be going anywhere on his feet and Walker couldn't imagine him dragging himself back to wherever he'd come from.

Walker looked around. There was a security camera in the corner, the ubiquitous little black plastic dome. He had no doubt that the scene had been captured and recorded, probably on a digital archive somewhere off site, and that feed would soon enough be in the hands of Homeland Security via their ubiquitous Trapwire program.

He had two choices. He could drag Bahar upstairs to Bennet's apartment and question him when he came to – which might take hours, even if he could speak through his crushed thorax. And that was time Walker didn't have, not to mention the possibility of witnesses coming through the lobby or on level ten at any moment.

So, Walker made do with the other choice, which was to search Bahar and take anything useful, then check on Bennet and get out of there. He checked the SOCOM pistol: two bullets missing. He sniffed the end of the silencer: it smelled faintly of gunpowder and gun oil. He patted down every pocket, finding a folded wad of cash, two spare clips for the SOCOM, two spent .45 cartridge casings, a combat knife sheathed to Bahar's ankle, a cheap-looking cell phone and a set of car-keys. He left the weapons and took the rest.

34

Walker found the door of apartment 532 ajar. The peep hole was blown out, as was the lock. Big ragged holes left behind by the .45 calibre rounds.

He entered, and saw Jim Bennet on the floor in front of him. His head was blown apart and there was blood splatter coating the small entry hall. Walker didn't need to check for a pulse. Instead, he pulled the door closed, and backtracked to the lifts.

In the lobby downstairs he stepped over the unmoved body of Bahar, and used the guy's right thumb-print to unlock the cell phone, then headed outside.

On the street Walker pressed the button on Bahar's Lexus key-fob. He couldn't see any flashing lights, nor any Lexus parked on the street out front, so he figured it was tucked away behind the apartment block, or in one of the side streets. He headed across the road for the Beetle, approaching it from the back. Exhaust coughed out of the tiny tail-pipe in small blue-tinted smoke rings, like it was burning minute amounts of oil with every cycle of the pistons. Muertos was in the driver's seat. He opened the passenger door and got in and said: 'Drive around the block.'

Muertos pulled from the curb and took the first left. She was good at driving a stick; fluid with the clutch and gear changes. The size of the pedals suited her better than Walker.

Muertos said, 'Agent Bennet?'

'We were too late,' Walker said. He dialled 911 and gave them the address and said an armed man was unconscious in the foyer, and to check apartment 532, then he ended the call and took out the phone's sim card and battery. He snapped the phone in half and started to toss pieces out the window as they headed around the block.

'Slow down,' he said, seeing a parked Lexus SUV, matt-black paint and blacked-out windows. When he pressed the key-fob the flashers blinked yellow. 'Pull up behind, we're changing cars.'

'Bennet is unconscious?' Muertos said as she stalled the engine. They got out of the Beetle and headed for the Lexus, the two crossing paths behind the car as they switched seats – Walker getting into the driver's seat, Muertos in the passenger.

'Bennet's dead,' Walker said, pressing the ignition button on the dash.

'You're sure?' Muertos asked.

'Pretty sure,' he replied, then looked at her and said, 'Yes, he's dead. Head shot. It was Bahar, Almasi's guy. He's the unconscious guy.'

Walker started up the sat-nav system in the centre console. 'It's a clean-up operation, and he was the final link. He went in and out and did his third kill of the night.'

'Third kill?' Muertos said. 'You think Acton is dead too?'

'We can't reach him, and he's made no attempt to contact to Overton on her burner, so it's a fair assumption. We know Bahar killed Overton at least four hours ago, and then he's here, so he's had a lot of time in between, and he wasn't sitting at Dunkin' Donuts killing time.'

'We don't know for sure.'

'I'll have Somerville call in to the Secret Service for us, tell them to check in on their agent Acton.'

'Shit.'

'There's nothing we can do about it,' Walker said, and he took off from the curb. The car was devoid of engine noise. A hybrid. 'But we can find Almasi. You up for that?'

'Find him how?'

Walker tapped the sat-nav system.

'Whose car is this?' Muertos asked.

'Bahar's.'

'You think this is a smart move?'

'He won't need it.'

'Because he's unconscious?'

'The cops will pick him up. He's out of the picture.'

'Did you question him?'

'Didn't really get a chance.'

'Then now what?' Muertos asked, her voice cracking with desperation. 'That was our last lead. Sat-nav won't do you any good if you don't know where . . .'

'Here,' Walker said, working the controls of the sat-nav screen. 'This will lead us to Almasi.'

It showed a destination labelled HOME, a rural spot in Virginia about seventy miles south, on B-roads off the I495 and Route 1, which ran parallel to the eastern seaboard. Right in the very direction and along the very highways on which Clair Hayes' abandoned car had been found. The sat-nav system also showed recent map searches: the three addresses of the three agents stored. Bahar's hit list, his journey through night and into the morning, from rural Virginia to Overton's and then on to the two agents. Incriminating. Useful.

'Now,' Walker said, as two Metro PD cars flashed by them in the direction of the apartment complex, their lights flashing but sirens off, 'we go *home*.'

35

'And when we get there?' Muertos looked at the sat-nav screen, to the blinking dot of HOME, seventy-four miles south, then across at him. 'How do we deal with Almasi?'

'We question him. And hopefully find Agent Hayes.'

He glanced at her, then back to the road. The Lexus felt anonymous, just another big blacked-out SUV ploughing through the streets, full of power and refinement and entitlement. The heated seats were plush and the engine nearly silent, the noise of the outside world blocked out. The complete opposite to the Beetle.

'You think Hayes is still alive?' Muertos asked.

'Yes.'

'Why?'

'Insurance.'

'In case she gave false names and addresses of her fellow agents?'

Walker nodded.

'Bahar might have called it in as soon as he'd completed the job,' Muertos said, 'telling Almasi to get rid of her.'

'I doubt it. He was about to make a call as he left the building,' Walker said. 'The phone was in his hand. I stopped him from making that call.'

'He may have called Almasi after killing Acton,' Muertos said. Then, a moment later in a quieter voice, 'And after killing Sally.'

'Maybe. But, I doubt it. A guy like that, a job like that, he'd go out, get it all done, call it in once it's complete. Radio silence in between, if all was going to plan, which it was, up until he met me. Check the call log.'

Muertos did so, saying as she scrolled down, 'Is that how you would have done things when you were in the CIA?'

'Well, contrary to what you see in the movies,' Walker said, overtaking a truck to make a green light, 'we don't just tool around assassinating people.' He stopped at the next lights, his indicator signalling he was going to turn left, where he'd soon merge to the I95 and head towards HOME. 'At any rate, these days the CIA has got an army of drones in the sky to do their targeting killing for them.' He glanced across. 'Anything in that call log?'

'Last call was to Acton.'

'Because that's not Bahar's phone.' Walker glanced down. 'Does that phone look familiar to you?'

'It's the same as Sally's.'

'Correct. Identical. And I bet the other two agents had the same too. Burners. Used for this op only. She probably bought all four handsets in bulk at RadioShack or Wal-Mart. Gave them out to her volunteer workforce a couple of days ago, so that they could report in on the movements of Almasi and Bahar and stay off the official cell network. See what other numbers are in there.'

'Three saved numbers, with the initials of our other three agents.' She looked across at Walker. 'So, Bahar killed Bennet and then took this phone. This is evidence, Walker. You should have left it back with that guy so the cops could log it.'

'Log it?' Walker said, easing on the accelerator as he made the turn and headed for the Beltway onramp, which he would take until he could split off to head south on Route 1. 'So it can sit in some cardboard box in an evidence locker for a case that'd likely never get to trial?'

'You left Bahar alive back there,' Muertos said.

'Are you suggesting I should have killed him?'

'If he killed Overton, I certainly wouldn't have minded if you'd said you killed him. Instead, he'll be arrested, and he'll be charged with the murder of Bennet, if the evidence supports it, and maybe Overton and Acton too. I just don't want to jeopardise whatever justice is coming his way.' Muertos went silent for a while, staring out the windscreen. 'That'll lead to trial. Then what? They might have him on camera at murder scenes of three federal agents. Maybe he left some DNA behind at the scene to make the cases watertight. You think he'll be put away and they'll throw away the key?'

'He might post bail. A big one, sure, maybe in the millions. But they've got money, this crowd, so he'll have a high-powered lawyer, right? Then he'll disappear.'

'Unlikely.'

'True. But you know what? I think the whole scenario of Bahar seeing a police interrogation, let alone a courtroom, is fanciful. More likely is that he'll be under guard in whatever hospital he's taken to, getting some bones and ligaments fixed, and while he's there his group will either bust him out, or – and this is where I'd put my money – they'll get rid of him.'

'You're talking like this is a gangster movie. Killing people in hospital – one of their own?'

'It's how this world works, Muertos. This group is connected, and they have reach. Or did you forget those two Homeland guys in San Francisco?' Walker took the freeway entrance, shooting the Lexus down the ramp, the electric motor now working in tandem with the petrol one – which Walker could hear and feel as it kicked in.

'I doubt they'd have killed us.' Muertos looked across to Walker, who remained silent. 'What? You think they would have killed us in the hospital?'

'No. They'd have us drugged and bagged and wheeled out and questioned.' Walker glanced to Muertos, then back to the road. 'Look, you know how it works, and you've seen far worse, even if it's been in reports and photographs of what happens to illegal immigrants desperate to make their way to new countries. And we know that Almasi and Bahar are intent to kill federal agents. Maybe their contacts at Homeland are too.' It was not outside the realm of possibility, but to Walker, as the bodies piled up, it seemed more and more likely that someone at Homeland was bent. Probably for money. If there was as much money in this as Muertos and Overton said, that would be more than enough incentive to the right person. 'I think we've stumbled onto something sensitive for Homeland, and they wanted to shut us up while they dealt with it.'

Walker glanced at the sat-nav screen as they settled onto Route 1, headed south. At highway speed they were forty minutes from the dot labelled HOME. It seemed to be in a rural area, which posed a problem. Surveying an urban target was easy, in terms of being able to blend in and remain inconspicuous amid the clutter and hubbub. A rural property, which may have no visible neighbours, and a mile-long driveway, and likely open farmland surrounding it – well, that posed all kinds of tactical problems, least of which was that he and Muertos were sitting in one of their target's cars. Which, Walker figured, he would have to make the most of. He started to think that he should have taken the SOCOM pistol, but shook it off, because it was probably the murder weapon of at least one agent – Bahar wouldn't have got close enough to all three agents to shoot them with their own sidearms, and at least two shots had been fired this morning. He pictured Bennet: talking to Walker when he heard someone outside in the hall; a light knock on the agent's apartment door; Bennet going to the peephole. Bahar waiting in the hallway, pistol ready, the silencer pressed against the peephole, waiting for the light on the other side to disappear – then *pop*, a silenced shot right through the head. The sound of Bennet's body hitting the floor, then Bahar shooting out the door to make sure his job was done.

'What do we do when we get there?' Muertos broke the silence and Walker's reverie.

'We get Almasi talking,' Walker said, 'and find out what's going on.'

'Find out how your father fits into this?'

'That's what I want to know.'

'I want to know a few things too.'

'You'll get your chance.'

•

Harvey called Lewis and said, 'It's done.'

'Done?'

'I spoke with our man from abroad. The situation has been cleared up.'

'And Jed Walker and Rachel Muertos?'

'I have Krycek on it.'

'Good. I've never trusted the Syrians. I want them gone today as well.'

Harvey was silent for a while, then said, 'You're sure? Once Muertos and Walker are gone, we can keep this going, right? We can keep Syria open, it's been a—'

'We've got enough,' Lewis said. 'Trust that. Think back to when we started out, what we hoped to achieve. We've got more than we need to bring this country to its knees.'

36

Walker took the west-bound exit off Route 1 as the sat-nav instructed. This highway was a two-laner, winding with gentle curves through semi-rural farmland. This was no Ohio or Indiana or Oklahoma or Texas, where Walker had driven through several times and seen farms that stretched for hundreds of miles, with harvesting equipment that worked on, quite literally, an agricultural scale. Here it seemed there were more estates, hobby farms, houses on modest-sized acreages that the owners agisted out to farmers who ran dairy cattle and horse stables.

The sat-nav announced five minutes to HOME.

'What do you want to ask Almasi?' Walker asked.

'That's what I've been thinking this whole time. What to ask him. I'll start with the meet in Syria. And then . . .'

'And then?'

'Who's his American contact.'

'Good. And I want to know what Almasi's contact with my father was. And what's happening here, killing Overton's agents – was it just because of the tail, or were they getting too close to unravelling their little people-smuggling party?'

Muertos nodded. 'I want to know who his US contacts are, and anyone he worked with back in Syria. I want to destroy the network, right back at the root. Then I want to salt the earth. Put them all out of business.'

'You've said that.' Walker glanced across at her. 'There's more to it, though, right?'

'Don't be so sure.'

Walker looked back at the road. 'Would you kill them, given the chance? If that's what it took to shut it down?'

'I doubt I could do it,' Muertos said. 'But I'd rather they were dead, if that means they're shut down forever. Do I want to do it? Maybe. Could I? I really doubt it. But the world would be a much better place for them being gone. For all this kind of thing to be shut down. To send a message to those who may prey on future refugees. That's the real problem here, right? Those fleeing persecution we lock away in camps, and those who profit from it remain free.'

'Have you ever killed anybody?'

'No.'

'Try to keep it that way.'

'Would you do it? If it came to it, like if Almasi or Krycek were in your sights?'

'In self-defence, sure. But I'd rather they got justice.'

'Justice? We've established how much money these guys must be worth. What about defending the defenceless? All the people they're making money off? The thousands of refugees they're trafficking around the world? That's not enough to make you happy to pull a trigger?'

'I've never been happy to pull a trigger . . .' Walker trailed off. It was true, at first thought. But if he spent time really going back over some events in his life, there were certainly people he was happy to see in the ground, and he didn't regret his part in it. In those circumstances, not regretting and being happy about the outcome weren't that far apart.

'I think your best bet will be to find out who that contact is, and pass the information to ICE or Customs or Homeland,' Walker said. 'Or some old colleagues in State. These scumbags will get what they deserve, and you'll probably be reinstated.'

'You think?'

'Sure, why not? You'd have proved your worth to them, that you can operate just fine in the field.'

'Because you said yourself, just before,' Muertos said, 'that people like this, with their money and influence, are able to make things disappear.'

'Maybe I've still got a little more faith in the system than you do,' Walker said, slowing the car and making a turn down a B-road, headed further inland. Farmland stretched as far as he could see, with bands of trees along streams and brooks and hedging around buildings. It seemed to be all farmland, the closest town Burnley, eight miles away. 'If they're as big a fish as you say, the Feds will make a big song and dance about busting them up – they'll make news all over the world, and there'll be no hiding or shirking from what's coming to them.'

'We'll see,' Muertos said.

Walker knew that there was more left unsaid, but he didn't press it now. HOME was down a driveway, a hard right two miles down the road. The terrain was not becoming to any kind of slow and sneaky approach. He started to run through his options of overpowering to Almasi in a remote farmhouse. None of them was good.

•

Almasi filled a pot of coffee with water. A heavy stainless-steel pot, which would percolate the water up through the fresh coffee grounds and into a reservoir at the top. He checked his watch, a Patek Philippe that had been his father's. Bahar was taking much longer than they'd planned. He poured the beans in an electric grinder and set it on. The machine burred away, and the smell of the fresh grinds filled the air. He turned it off, filled the coffee and tamped it, then assembled the coffee pot. He was headed to the stove when he stopped.

A noise from outside. A car, approaching, the sound of tyres on the gravel driveway.

He put the coffee pot on the bench and headed to the front door. Out the window to the side he saw flashes of the black Lexus through the rows of conifers that lined the drive.

Almasi smiled and went back to the kitchen, where he turned on a gas burner and set the coffee on the stove top, all the while whistling a tune from an Italian opera he'd seen in Damascus before his home country had imploded. Out the kitchen window the black mare had returned and was nuzzling its foal. He was happy with America, happy with how things had panned out. He could get used to life here.

37

Walker had seen a glimpse of the house from the B-road before he turned onto the tree-lined driveway. It was like a transplant from Connecticut, all white timber and slate-grey roof and shutters on its two storeys of windows. The gravel driveway was a mile long and lined with conifers that were tall and thick with dark green needles. Dairy cows grazed in the fields each side. There were no cars visible but there were lights on inside the house, giving the place a warm and inviting glow, and smoke rose from a chimney, the puffs darker grey than the sky. Walker noted a large barn to the west, which might have been used as a garage, or perhaps this was a working farm when not occupied by terrorists. No sentries were visible. No security of any kind. No vehicles. No army of bad guys. And it was, unmistakably, where the vehicle stated was HOME.

Heat flared up Walker's neck.

As he neared the house a thought occurred to him – this vehicle might be stolen, and HOME might well be Ma and Pa in retirement, the vehicle boosted by the killer last night when the two oldies were tucked up on their couch watching *Jeopardy*. They might still be there, oblivious to the fact that their car had been taken. Walker kept up speed along the driveway, thinking as fast as the wheels turned. There was no name on the letterbox, which was an old milk can painted white; just a number. The driveway had a gate, made from galvanised steel and set at each side onto concrete posts. A serious gate. The type of thing that people might have on a holiday house that they locked up for extended periods of time. Retirees hitting the road or going overseas, perhaps. But it had been left open. Inviting. Or careless.

Walker slowed the car a little.

'What's wrong?' Muertos said.

'Almasi might not be here,' Walker said.

'*What?*'

'I've assumed that he was here the whole time, waiting for Bahar to return.'

'And?'

'Assumptions can be wrong.'

Muertos said, 'So, what are you going to do?'

The crunch of gravel under the low-profile tyres was barely audible in the plush cabin. Outside, on either side of the driveway, was green rolling pasture, largely flat but for very gradual undulations and, to the east, a crevasse that sprouted saplings munched by the cows. Patches of white frost had formed in the gullies, brilliant crystal droplets of dew on the rises. Wire fences and bands of trees delineated different owners on the lots beyond. Visibility all around, especially from the vantage point of the house, was good.

Walker said, 'I'm going to knock on the front door.'

'Are you serious?'

'I think so.'

'You *think* so?'

'This place is hardly Osama Bin Laden's compound in Abbottabad. No guards, no cameras. Look at it. Sweet little country pile. Maybe this is home to this car, but maybe home is not where Almasi is.'

'But Almasi *could* be in there,' Muertos countered. 'With other guys. And they could be armed. And they might shoot you before you reach the door. Or shoot you when they open the door and see you, like Hassan almost did.'

'It's possible.'

'So, what? Turn around and watch the place a while?'

'It's too late. Whoever's in there has probably heard or seen our approach.'

'This is crazy.'

'What would you have me do?'

Muertos was silent.

'This is a bad place to recon, and it's too late now, we're committed,' Walker said. He drove slowly – but not too slowly. Five seconds to the front door. He'd stop close, so that the journey from the car to the door would be a few strides at most. 'In other circumstances, we could stake it out, but we don't have time for that.'

The house was three seconds' travel time away.

'We do if it keeps us alive,' Muertos said, her voice rushed. 'You can turn around and bug out.'

'No,' Walker said. He came up to the house in a burst of speed and then braked hard at the last moment, the tyres dragging grooves through the gravel, pulling up to a stop just in front of the door of the house. 'Sometimes surprise is all the protection you need.'

38

Walker was on foot and paused at the door. It was timber, painted the same slate-grey at the shutters and the roof. Solid. No peephole. Why would you need one, out here? You wouldn't. This was friendly territory, not a big city. Friends and family and neighbours and the occasional delivery person would be the only people to come knocking. Half those people probably just opened up the door – which might be left unlocked all the time that the residents were at home. He didn't knock.

He tried the handle. It turned, and he pushed the door open, keeping out of view to the side. The door moved and stayed fully open, silent on big, expensive brass hinges. No reaction from inside. No bullets flying his way. Nothing.

Still none the wiser if he'd find Ma and Pa in the house, or Almasi, so he took a moment to listen. No click-clack of Ma or Pa raking a shotgun to welcome him. No sounds of any inhabitant. A faint hissing inside the house, coming from the back, a kind of domestic white noise. The smell of coffee in the air.

Walker slipped his boots off and entered, his socked feet silent on the highly polished hardwood boards. He was in a grand entry, where a wide staircase took centre stage as though the owners might like to make big entrances as the help invited the visitors in. But there was no sign of Ma or Pa, or their help, or Almasi. Walker went by the stairs, moving silently, and down the hall, towards the back of the house, which he could see was a kitchen and informal dining area. He knew it was informal because to his left was a formal dining room with settings for twenty around an oval table. The noises of cooking cut through the house – the clang of a pan, something dropped. A curse word, short and sharp, from a man. *Was it Pa or was it Almasi?* Something was burning – toast, Walker thought. It reminded him of Overton's apartment, of the smell of carbonised food left in the oven for hours. But this was a fresher smell – and the clang of a pan and the curse signalled it was a current affair, an unfolding situation. He was almost at the doorway when he heard a voice call out:

'Making a late breakfast, American style.' It was a male voice, deep, accented, educated in America. 'How'd your mission go?'

Walker entered the kitchen to see the speaker: Almasi. He had his back to Walker. He was alone, cooking eggs in pan and juggling burning toast and a stainless pot of coffee bubbling on the gas burner. He was either speaking with someone who was out of sight, or he'd seen the car approach and thought Walker was Bahar returning from a night of killing. Either way, it gave Walker time to act.

Walker moved fast. But not fast enough.

39

Walker took in the kitchen scene as he made his advance. His peripherals and senses told him the room was clear but for Almasi. To his right was an empty room with an informal dining setting, the table hewn from a slab of timber from a giant California redwood. The kitchen, to Walker's left, was set out in a U-shape, with the oven and stove against the far wall to his left, running ninety degrees off that was a bench with a sink and a with a view out to the fields. The bench made another ninety-degree turn to form a breakfast bar, the counter-tops made from polished red granite. Steam rose from the stovetop. Almasi was six paces away, his back to Walker. Walker moved quickly and silently and then threw caution out the window as he knew he was being made.

Almasi's head rose from where he'd been looking down at the sizzling pan. His eyes level, Almasi saw Walker in the reflection of an overhead glass-fronted cabinet. They locked eyes for split second, and he turned as Walker was halfway across the room – and in that motion Almasi threw what he had on hand.

Walker was four paces away by the time Almasi turned to face him. The Syrian made a pirouette, spinning around on the ball of his right foot, fast. In his right hand the coffee pot – a couple of pounds of searing hot metal and boiling liquid – was thrown in a fluid motion, a slinging action that carried through Amasi's turn.

Walker raised his left forearm and the stainless-steel pot bounced off, hitting the floor, but on impact with his arm the lid popped open and the boiling coffee splashed his jacket. He felt the hot liquid soak through his sleeve and the front of his T-shirt, searing his skin and sticking his shirt to his chest. He didn't stop his advance, though. He took two more strides by the time Almasi's motion stopped and began in a different direction.

Almasi's empty left hand grabbed a knife from the chopping block and he swung back, the opposite direction his arm and body had just moved through. An agricultural slash, arm outstretched, seven inches of carving knife slicing at Walker.

Walker halted his forward momentum and moved his midsection back a split second before the knife sliced through the air where his stomach would have been. But Walker didn't stop. Not completely. His socked feet and the wet floor combined to keep his feet sliding forward, out of control, and the motion of bringing his mid-section out of the way of the blade unbalanced him. Walker's feet continued onwards, as his body, torso and head, moved backward.

Walker slipped over. On his back. On the floor. Prone.

Almasi smiled and tossed the knife between his hands like it was a toy. Like he was comfortable with a blade, any blade. Like he'd used a knife on a man before. He had that look in his eyes.

Damn.

Walker hadn't wanted to kill Bahar, and he'd succeeded in that. He certainly didn't want to kill Almasi – if anyone had answers about what went down in Syria, and about his father's involvement, it was the guy standing above him with a knife. But Almasi really wasn't giving him much choice.

It was the coffee pot that did it.

Almasi dropped forward towards Walker, the carving knife out in a double-handed stabbing action that would bury the blade to the hilt into Walker's chest.

But Walker was having none of it. He didn't want to die. Not today. Not for many thousands of days. So, he reacted, improvised. Saving his life in that moment was more important than preserving Almasi's. His right arm raised and slowed Almasi's fall by catching him in the chest. At the same time Walker reached out to his left and grabbed the handle of the overturned steel coffee pot and swung it up and across his body, using the swiping motion to deflect the blade away to his right, and it made a metal-on-metal noise as it was smashed from Almasi's hand and buried a half-inch into the timber floor next to Walker. The handle wobbled on the impact, and kept vibrating side to side for the full second it took Almasi to react.

Almasi reached quickly and drew the knife and sat up, his weight on Walker, Walker's free hand gripping the front of Almasi's shirt at his neck, the knife rising in the air for another plunging attack—

Walker swung the pot. It was a backhanded motion, reversing the arc over his body, this time swiping from left to right. The pot hit the side of Almasi's head and the bulbous bottom of the stainless-steel jug made a dull clang as it hit the man's skull.

Almasi's eyes rolled back and he fell to Walker's left, onto the floor.

Walker checked for a pulse, but he knew there would be none. The blow had caught Almasi in the temple, where the skull was thinnest. There was a big dint there, the concave shape matching the base of the stainless-steel coffee pot. A trickle of blood ran from Almasi's nose.

Walker got to his feet, swearing under his breath. He turned off the stove and turned around to saw Muertos enter the room. She looked spooked. Walker was about to explain the situation – then stopped. Muertos wasn't spooked by Almasi's death.

Behind her were two guys dressed in suits. Each had a pistol drawn.

40

Walker and Muertos were each ordered at gunpoint to sit at the huge timber table, and plastic flexicuffs were placed around their wrists. The two guys were official, which had Walker worried. Official in the sense that they were employees of the federal government. Homeland Security, Walker figured, but different to the pair he'd seen yesterday. Yesterday's crew were big and tough and hard-edged, the of choice for getting the hard work done. These two were different; the older one seemed like he'd spent the best part of the past couple of decades sitting behind a desk. Which of itself wasn't a bad thing, nor something to worry about. The issue was that they were either working for someone in addition to Homeland, with an agenda related to Almasi, or someone bent at Homeland. Walker knew this because of their reactions, and because one of them was on the phone, allowing Walker and Muertos to hear every word. Sure, they only caught one side of the conversation, but it was enough.

'So,' the agent said into his phone, 'this Walker guy did our work for us. No more Almasi. Yeah . . .' He poked Almasi with the toe of his scuffed black shoes, turning the dead man's head to inspect the dint. Then he looked at the puddle of spilled coffee, then the stainless steel pot that had rolled to a stop in the middle of the kitchen floor. 'He killed him with a coffee pot. Yep. Coffee pot. Yeah, in the head. What? No, one of those steel ones you put on a stove. Percolator, yeah, that's it. A percolator. I don't know – you want me to check? No. Right. Looks expensive. Shiny stainless steel. Yeah, not one of those angled aluminium ones, this one's round and shiny. Right. Yep. Ah, not now, no. Yeah, got them here, bound, seated, not going anywhere. Sorry, what?' He looked over to Walker and Muertos, seated around the huge timber slab of a dining table on the other side of the room, then back to the body of Almasi, then out the window out at the grounds. His voice went quieter when he said, 'Really? Yes, that's right. Yep. Right. Okay. Yes, I know. But that's not what we're – okay. Okay. Leave it with us.'

He ended the call, then motioned for his colleague to follow him out to the hallway. Walker couldn't make out what they were saying, but they were animated.

Walker was weighing up options of getting to a knife in the kitchen when the two agents came back in.

'Up,' the one who'd spoken on the phone said to Walker. His partner had his Glock drawn and pointed at Muertos's head – a sign for Walker, taller and bigger than either of these two, someone they knew was capable of killing a man with a coffee pot, not to make any kind of break for it.

Walker stood.

'Now you,' he said to Muertos.

Muertos stood.

'Back to back,' he said.

Walker turned and took a couple of steps backward to Muertos, then bent at the knees and felt Muertos's hands touch his.

'Keep still,' the guy said.

Walker kept still. Muertos was shaking. He felt the guy pull their arms tight together, looping a couple more cable-ties through their connected wrists.

'Now get down to the floor, on your butts,' he said.

Walker and Muertos went down, back-to-back, sitting on the floor, and the guy then flexicuffed each of their ankles.

'All right,' he said to his partner. 'Help me scoot them over.'

As the other guy holstered his Glock, Walker saw a Homeland Security ID clipped to his belt. The two agents pulled and slid a collective four hundred pounds across the polished floor until the captives where hard up against a leg of the table.

'Now what?' the other guy said.

'We put the table leg through their flexicuffs.'

The guy looked at the table. 'We're gonna lift *that* table?'

'Sure, why not?'

'Nu-ah. I've got a bad back. And that table's gotta be the best part of a tonne. Look at it. That's solid mahogany or something. I bet they built the house around it. Maybe it was made from an old stump that grew here, and it was too hard to entirely remove, so they just pushed it over and hewed it in half and polished it and called it the dining room table.'

'Hewed?'

'Yeah. Like hewn. Past tense.'

'Not sure hewed is the right word.'

'Well, anyway, my back's sore just thinking about all this.'

'You got any ideas?'

'Just shoot them.'

'With my service pistol?'

'Right.' The guy looked around. 'You could use a knife. Or choke 'em out.'

'*You* choke 'em out.'

The two men stared at each other in silence for a minute before the first one said, 'How many flexicuffs have you got?'

'Rest of the pack.'

'How many's that?'

'The pack minus the three we've just used.'

'Jesus, just get them out and count them.'

'All right. Jeez. Don't get your whatever in a whatever.'

'My shorts in a hewed?'

'Ha di ha.'

Walker watched as the second guy took a packet from his jacket pocket and emptied the contents onto the table. Clear plastic, like they'd been bought at a discount store. Walmart probably sold them for hogtying whatever Walmart customers hogtied. Walker watched as the guy counted out seven more sets of flexicuffs. Each was made out of half inch-thick ribbons of near unbreakable plastic. They seemed content to leave them shackled here. Probably then call in to the local cops. The two of them found at a murder scene, with a Syrian national sprawled out on the kitchen floor. That'd attract the interest of the FBI, or Homeland Security – perhaps even these very two fine agents. These two may even get a legitimate promotion out of it.

'That'll do it,' the other guy said, doing a quick count.

'For what?'

'Link a few around the table leg, then use the rest through those and theirs, make, like, a chain out of them.'

A few minutes later Walker and Muertos were attached, via virtually unbreakable plastic ties, to the table that weighted close to a tonne.

'You boys want to tell us what's going on?' Walker asked.

The both looked at him, as though they'd been unaware that he could speak – as though he and Muertos were little more than training dummies and this whole thing some kind of drill.

'Ignore him,' the senior guy said. 'Help me move the body.'

Now Walker was worried. Without Almasi, this was no longer a set-up for a local cop to come and find. So, what then? Leave them here to starve to death?

The senior guy went and picked up Almasi's feet. He waited, hunched over, for his comrade to come and help. When that didn't happen in a hurry he looked up.

'You get the legs?' the other guy said.

'Just grab him under the armpits and carry him out to the car.'

'But my back . . .'

The agent who'd been on the phone said something under his breath and moved positions, so that he was now crouched down and had his hands under Almasi's armpits. Together they lifted the dead weight and shuffled it out of the room and down the hall; they were out of sight to Walker, but he heard a thud and some swearing and some rearranging.

'What do you think they're going to do with us?' Muertos asked in a whisper.

'I'm not sure.'

'What should we do?'

'Nothing, yet,' Walker said. He heard a car boot slam shut, and then footsteps nearing, crunching on the gravel outside; no need for a quiet approach this time, their outside grit-covered shoes stomping up the hallway. 'Just wait and see what's what. We can't give them an easy excuse to kill us.'

The two agents came back in, and immediately one started to rifle through the kitchen drawers while the other turned on all the gas elements on the stove, then the oven, leaving the door open.

'Bingo,' the searching agent said, holding up a barbecue fire-lighter.

'Okay, start it in the front room,' the other guy said. 'We want the gas to fill the house right up before it goes boom.'

41

'Walker?' Muertos said as the front door of the house slammed shut.

'Yeah?' he replied, shifting his weight and testing the resistance on the ten flexicuffs that bound them together and to the table.

'What do we do?'

Walker heard the agents' car drive off, the tyres spinning on gravel. 'We get out of here before the place goes boom.'

'I can already smell the gas.'

'And I can smell the fire they started at the front of the house. Plastics and nylons – the curtains in the sitting room, probably. It'll spread to the carpet next, then the sofas and soft furnishings. And that's about it before things go kaboom.'

'How long have we got?'

'Minutes.' He looked at the stove and oven, the kind of industrial eight-burner cooking machine that just might have been dreamed up by Martha Stewart when she was sitting in a cell with nothing better to do.

'How many minutes?'

'Maybe ten.'

'*Maybe?*'

'Gas dissipates evenly – it's spewing out of this room and all through the house. It'll take a bit of time to build up to a point where it'll ignite.'

'Ten minutes is a bit of time?'

'Maybe five.'

'Five!'

Walker's shoulder was hard against the under-edge of the table, and he tried to get some leverage by drawing a leg in and then sliding it under his butt and pushing upwards – but it was no use. That table was going nowhere. Lifting his weight and that of Muertos on one bent leg was one thing; the huge slab of timber was another.

'Lie to your side – your left side, on the floor,' Walker said.

Muertos did so, and Walker lay to his right. He moved, trying to use his leg to press the table up. If he could get it just a half-inch off the floor, he could work the flexicuffs under it. He twisted, pushed.

Muertos screamed.

'Sorry,' Walker said. He eased off the pressure.

'You almost broke my wrists.'

Walker looked up at the table, sweat running into his eyes. 'Okay, listen,' he said. 'I see two options. I can try again to lift the table, then you pull down on the cuffs to get them off the leg.'

'I can barely feel my hands.'

'You won't feel anything soon enough if we don't try.'

'Okay.'

'Or we can try to shift the table, towards the glass door, use it like a battering ram – and if we get it to bust out the door, a table leg might even push off the step and tip over.'

'Yes!'

'Okay. Let's try that. Sit back up.'

They sat up in unison, back to back. He pressed his right arm and shoulder against the foot square table leg and pressed the soles of his feet against the floor.

'Pushing now,' Walker said.

The table barely moved. But his socked feet did. It was useless. Muertos gave a little grunt and he heard her shoes squeaking against the polished floor in the effort.

'Stop,' Walker said. 'Go back on your side. New plan.'

They lay back. Walker on his right. Muertos on her left.

He braced his leg up, bent at the knee, his foot wedged under the edge as he felt the tension against his binds on Muertos. He calculated the extra angle he needed: a few more degrees. The gas and smoke smells were getting stronger, and he started to feel light-headed.

'Muertos?'

'Yeah?'

'I'm really sorry about this.'

'What? Wait – *what*!?'

Walker didn't answer. He moved fast. Turned further onto his side, working hard against the binds, to get more of his back against the floor. Muertos screamed at the pressure on her wrists, and he felt a pop in the binds behind him that gave him more freedom of movement. He lifted his leg so he could push straight up.

The table lifted a quarter-inch. He strained and pulled at the binds behind him while pressing up with his legs. The table lifted a little more. Muertos was screaming. He felt a stabbing pain in his stomach, and the back of his right thigh was burning and started to knot, his muscles tearing under the strain.

'Push your hands to the floor!' Walker shouted as he pressed up with his leg and gave everything he had, pushing his hands as close to the floor was he could and his arms towards the kitchen. He felt more play in the flexicuffs as they began to slide under the table leg. One of them snapped and he had more movement, and lifted the table a little more, now two inches off the floor.

Walker's foot was slipping. The angle of the table above him, his cotton socks soaked with the sweat of exertion, all combining to foil his effort. Muertos was quiet now, murmuring.

'Muertos,' Walker said. He felt nauseous as the stitches in his thigh give out and the wound open in a slow motion tear. Felt blood pouring from the newly torn skin and flesh. 'Muertos, try pulling the cuffs towards the kitchen. You have to. My side's close – but you have to drag your side out.'

He felt her moving, slowly, against the pain of at least one broken wrist. She grunted and whimpered and her back knocked against him as she moved.

Walker felt the cuffs sliding under the gap between the bottom of the table leg and the floor.

Then his foot slipped.

'No . . .' Muertos said, her voice shaky.

Walker shifted and tugged at their binds and felt freedom – the flexicuffs had slid clear under the base of the table leg. The gas seeping through the house was nearing the point where it was saturated enough in the air to ignite against the fire raging in the front room.

'Quick, we're getting up,' Walker said.

He did most of the work, and Muertos cried out as they stood, the movement shifting the broken bones in her wrist.

'Back door,' he said, and they moved sideways like a crab, around the table, to the glass-panelled French doors, and Walker tried the handle but it was locked. 'I'm gonna lift you.'

'What?'

Walker didn't answer. He bent his knees lower, found purchase under Muertos's waist and lifted, then tilted forward and took her full weight onto his back, then kicked the door. His heel connected with the timber frame, just above the handles, and the doors flew open with pieces of timber frame splintering out. He took the two steps down to an area paved with red bricks and kept moving, as fast as he could through the pain in this leg, carrying Muertos on his back. Beyond the deck was lush green lawn, and he kept running in his forward-leaning crouch, fifty feet, then a hundred, then started to head to his left, around the side of the house, towards the only decent shelter around – the big barn. The grass was slick underfoot, and he welcomed the gravel of the driveway as they neared the barn. The stones and grit bit at his socked feet but he felt he had good purchase, and made better time, and he went around the front of the barn to the other side, away from the house.

He gently set Muertos down around the corner of the barn and kept crouched down so to not move the restraints against her broken wrist. The whole front of the house was ablaze, the curtains a mess of orange-red flames and black smoke seeping out the eaves. The fire had worked its way up into the gable windows and pitched roof, through the ceiling cavity and along the timber joists holding up the second storey – the house would explode at any moment.

The barn was timber-clad, rough-hewn inch-thick pine planks set vertically, covered over with as many paint layers as the house. At least thirty feet wide by sixty feet long, double storey, with a hay loft. Three windows and a door along each side, agricultural-sized double doors at each end big enough to drive a tractor right through. The roof was shingled and coated in tar.

Walker picked Muertos up and moved up the side of the barn, where he set her down again, gently, and she gave a whimper as the motion disturbed her wrist; there was no doubt that the bones in her left forearm just above the wrist were snapped clear through at their thinnest points.

Muertos said in a small voice, 'What now?'

'We need to get into the barn so we can cut ourselves free,' Walker said, trying the door handle. It was locked.

'You broke my arm.'

'I'm sorry.'

'You had to.'

Walker took that as a statement. 'Move away from the door a little and turn so I'm facing it.'

'Okay.'

They moved around until Walker faced the door. He moved to kick it, but then stopped—

The door was hung so that the jamb was on the inside. Maybe it was constructed like that for hurricanes or tornadoes. He didn't think they had any of the latter here in Virginia, but maybe the guys who built the barn back in the Depression era were from Oklahoma or Kentucky or someplace withe lots of tornadoes, and they built barn doors this way so the force wouldn't blast the door open but rather push it closed. The door was made from the same heavy pine as the barn, but smoother, the joins tighter. No-one could break that door down.

'Walker?'

'We need to find another way—'

Walker didn't finish, because at that moment a huge explosion rocked the scene.

42

The shockwave from the blast shifted the barn, the structure creaking and moaning in protest at the sudden assault of the immense pressure wave. The sound spread out through the countryside and made distant percussive claps as it hit and echoed off far-away buildings. The gas explosion sent debris high into the air, and it took ten full seconds for the pitter-patter of falling timber and construction material to cease.

'Let's move,' Walker said, and he and Muertos side-shuffled to the front of the barn.

The house was gone but for a far-corner wall supported by a stone fireplace and chimney. A cast-iron bathtub was imbedded deep into a flowerbed. All that remained of the house were flaming timber stumps. The huge oven was nowhere to be seen, but the hardwood table stood close to where it had been before. The Lexus was on its side, the duco sandblasted back to plain metal sheets.

Burning litter was scattered over the barn roof, and one of the main barn doors sagged off its hinges, forming a triangular space at one corner that was big enough to get through at a crouch.

Walker and Muertos shimmied through, back-to-back, ducking and scraping.

It was dark inside but for the dull light of the overcast day spilling through the small windows and broken section of door. There were no cars parked in there, no tractor, no livestock. Nothing but timber-slat livestock stalls each side, an empty loft and the fluttering of birds or bats in the gloom, spooked out of their perch or slumber by the brutal cacophony that continued to ring in the ears of all in the immediate vicinity, their movement filling the space with dust caught at the rays of daylight.

There was a long workbench on the southern wall, a heavy timber slab of wood that looked like it had been carved out of the same tree as the dining table. This one was dusty and well worn, with two big vices set into it, and above it was a shadow-board with an assortment of tools: bow saws and claw hammers, screwdrivers and wrenches, chisels and files. Walker used his foot to knock down a two-foot bow saw, and then they sat on the floor. He fumbled with the tool and eventually found suitable purchase to work away at their binds. It took all of three minutes and they were cut free, then he used some tin snips to get rid of the rest of the flexicuffs. Muertos cradled her wrist in the front of her shirt. He moved with a limp now that the adrenaline of survival had worn off and the pain from the injury announced itself.

'I'll splint your arm,' Walker said. He used duct tape, old and not as tacky as whenever it was made, but along with four broken sections of a fold-out timber rule it did the job of keeping Muertos's wrist immobile. He knotted two rags together and fashioned it around her neck to form a sling. 'That'll be as good as it gets until we get you to a doctor.'

'She might have been in there . . .' Muertos was looking out the cracked window to the wreckage of the house. 'Agent Hayes.'

Walker was silent, joining her at the shattered window. If Hayes was in there, she wasn't any more, and there was nothing they could have done to save her. His mind went to their next steps. First, he wondered if he could flip the Lexus back on its tyres, and if those tyres were still good, and the fuel lines intact. Wondered if he'd find his boots sitting there on the front step, smouldering but wearable.

He wasn't hopeful on either count. Which left him with the barn. He turned and looked around the dark interior.

'We need to find a way to get out of here,' Walker said, then stopped.

'What was that?' Rachel said, hearing the noise and backing towards the door.

Walker put his finger to his lips, then waited. He heard it again. A rustle of movement. Perhaps a critter of some sort, a big one, moving about somewhere out of sight in one of the stalls. Then something else, a muffled sound, definitely not a critter. Walker took a claw hammer from its nailed spot above the bench and made a *wait here* gesture to Muertos, then headed down the centre of the barn.

There were five stalls either side. Each was gated, about five feet high, made up of vertical lengths of timber, constructed from the same heavy pine planks as the rest of the barn. The first two stalls to his right contained rectangular hay bales stacked neatly and tightly. The first two to his left held a ride-on lawn mower, a forty-four-gallon drum of gas with a hand-pump attached, and tall tanks of natural gas. The rustling sound had stopped. The next stall to his left was empty but for a few rakes and shovels and pitchforks leaning to one side. The stall opposite that—

Held a woman.

43

Walker recognised Agent Clair Hayes from the photo on Sally Overton's phone. Her wrists were tied with the same plastic twine as used on hay bales, multiple loops of it, wrapped around tightly then hogtying her to a similar application of twine at her ankles. A grimy rag was tied around her head as a gag. She had a bruised eye and a swollen lip. There was straw in her blonde hair, dirt and grime on her skin and clothes, panic in her eyes. Walker made a gesture of putting down the hammer and showing her his open hands, and moved slowly towards her. Her blue eyes followed his. As he got closer he could see that her white shirt had been ripped open, that she had scratch and bruise marks around her neck.

'We're friends of Sally Overton,' Muertos called out from behind Walker's shoulder, and he saw in that announcement relief flood through Agent Hayes.

Walker used tin snips to cut her free, then he and Muertos helped her move, on unsteady feet, to the entrance of the barn. Walker took a bottle of water from a stack of others in a plastic shopping bag in a corner, and she drank greedily.

'Almasi?' Hayes asked. 'Bahar?'

'Almasi's dead,' Walker said. 'Dead, and in custody.'

'How did they get you here?' Muertos asked.

'They . . .' Hayes nodded, a spooked look in her eyes. 'I was tailing the Syrians. Then I was pulled over, on Route 1, by a couple guys posing as Homeland Security agents.'

'What'd they look like?'

Hayes gave a description which matched the pair that had come for Walker in the hospital in San Francisco.

'They tasered me,' Hayes said, 'and I woke up here, bound and gagged. That's when . . .'

Hayes fell silent.

'They were Homeland,' Walker said.

'You're sure?'

Walker nodded. 'They're out of the picture now. But there at least two others—'

'Three, with Krycek,' Muertos added.

Walker nodded. 'Right. At least three, two of whom turned up here not long ago and tried to blow us up in the house. They must have been in the area, surveying the Syrians. They came in to get rid of Almasi, but I'd done that for them already.'

'Who are you?'

'Just a guy. I'm Walker, this here is Muertos.'

'I was probably Sally Overton's longest friend.'

Hayes looked deflated, and it hit her in the gut. 'Was?'

Muertos nodded, and fought back tears.

'I . . .' Hayes looked from Muertos, to Walker, then at the dusty floor. She explained how Almasi and Bahar had extracted the information out of her; none of it was pretty, and Walker was glad Almasi was dead and hoped that Bahar would either rot in a supermax jail – where he'd be shived or shanked soon enough by patriotic prisoners who didn't take kindly to guys like him killing US federal agents – or maybe someone in his organisation would get to him and do the job, like those two bent Homeland agents who'd come for Almasi. 'What about the others? Bennet and Acton?'

'Bennet is dead,' Walker said. 'Bahar shot him. Overton too. And we presume Acton, sometime in between.'

Walker felt bad giving her that news; she'd now know that her actions had led to their deaths. It was the type of news that would haunt her to the grave, but there was no way of avoiding it – she'd find out soon enough, and he had no good reason to lie to her. The best he could do was sugar coat it.

'They're all . . .' Agent Hayes couldn't bring herself to say the word *dead*. 'Because of me.'

'You held out longer than almost anyone would,' Walker said. 'You did all you could. Your colleagues knew the risk.'

'I should have lied to them,' Hayes said, her head in her hands. 'I should have given them different addresses.'

'Then innocent people might have been killed.'

'Maybe.' Hayes wiped her face with the sleeve of her shirt. 'Or it might have bought time – time for my colleagues to find me.'

'Unlikely. They've got some Homeland guys helping them out, at least five agents that we know of,' Walker said. 'Who knows how many more, or how high this goes? They're doctoring the biometrics at customs so people like Almasi and Bahar can enter the country. Probably doing the same for the high-paying illegals they're facilitating stateside. Those Homeland guys could have given them the addresses of Overton and Bennet and Acton with a few keystrokes on a government computer, all in real-time, so don't for a moment feel guilty about it.'

'But not their names.' Hayes sleeved away more tears. 'They wouldn't have known their names.'

'They had your burner phone, with the numbers in it, and the agents stating their names on the voicemail. Homeland would have taken two seconds to get their details – they can find anyone, thanks to the Patriot Act. You know that.'

Muertos moved over and sat on a hay bale next to Hayes and put her good arm around her shoulders.

Hayes looked from her, found a small reassuring smile and reciprocated, then looked up to Walker and said, 'You found me. My friends would have found me too. I gave them away. How do I live with that?'

'With time, you'll find a way,' Walker said. He crouched back down to look her in the eye. 'And I only got to you because I used a car from a guy I almost killed. Bahar.' He saw Hayes flinch, memories playing behind her eyes. 'There were no laws holding me back when I took him down. I left him out cold, with a heavy concussion and shattered arm and knees. We took his car and headed straight here. And you know what, if it had played out differently, and Bahar was arrested and Almasi knew that? What do you think he'd have done then?' Hayes was silent. 'My bet is he'd have finished you and bugged out of here, fast.'

'You don't know that.' Hayes composed herself. 'That's all hypothetical.'

'But it's a reasonable assumption,' Walker said. 'Agent Hayes, look: I'm sure that your colleagues, your friends, if they'd somehow apprehended or evaded Bahar this morning, they would have got to you as fast as they could. But it would have been too late.'

'He's right,' Muertos said, still with her arm around the agent.

'I've been around long enough to know how these people operate,' Walker said, and he started looking around the bench and checking jars and cans full of nails and screws and nuts and bolts. 'No matter how much they tried to coerce Bahar, he'd have held out. It was writ large all over the guy. He was a hard nut. Sure, they would have eventually found his car, and checked the sat-nav, then driven out here like we did – but that whole process would have taken longer, far longer, because they would have had procedures to follow, and a guy to question, and by then you would have been dead.'

Hayes looked at the floor of the barn. 'You don't know that.'

'We do,' Muertos said. 'Believe me, Agent Hayes, I feel your pain. And we're not going to stop until we get justice served against everyone involved.'

Hayes nodded, closed her eyes, found some measure of resolve and said, 'Where's Bahar now?'

'I left him in Bennet's apartment lobby, with the murder weapon nearby,' Walker said. He found what he was looking for stored away in a tin can, then loosened his jeans and sat up on the bench. 'We called it in, so DC police would have picked him up within minutes of us leaving. They'll have found Bennet, too, because I mentioned him. Bahar won't be going anywhere.'

'You think these corrupt Homeland agents will get rid of Bahar to clean house?' Hayes asked.

'That's my thinking,' Walker said. He used some superglue to stick his leg wound closed.

'That's disgusting,' Muertos said, cradling her arm and watching him wrap his thigh tightly with a rag.

'That's what it was used for in the Vietnam war,' Walker replied, getting to his feet and fixing his jeans.

'Well, I say let them at him,' Hayes said, getting to her feet.

'We have to get to him before those Homeland guys,' Muertos said, standing next to Hayes. 'We need to question him. Work up the chain to get the US contact, because outside the Homeland guys, he's the sole lead we've got.'

Hayes seemed nonplussed.

'First we need to get out of here,' Walker said, 'before the fire department arrives, because once they see the wreckage of the house they'll call the cops, and all that's going to slow us down. We get the two of you treated, then we find Bahar.'

•

Harvey walked past his secretary at St Elizabeth's Homeland headquarters, holding up a hand to motion that he was in a hurry, and he shut his office door behind him and rushed to his desk. In the locked drawer was his burner phone, which had a missed call from the field. He pressed the number and it was immediately answered by his agent.

'Bahar was picked up, here in DC.' Harvey said, then spent two minutes explaining the situation, of the arrest, the transfer, finding Bennet's dead body, the weapon. 'He's under guard at a downtown hospital. He's unconscious, and as long as he stays that way it's okay. But you have to hustle. I'll send you the details. Get there, and clean it up. Understood?'

'Yes, sir.'

'Bahar must not be allowed to get out of his current state. I can't tell you how important that is. I've made sure that you'll have two hours from now before the Secret Service takes over his supervision.'

'Yes, sir, but, we, ah . . .'

'What?'

'We've already got a body in the trunk. Almasi. You don't want us to dispose of him first?'

'*This* is first,' Harvey said. 'Leave Bahar's body behind. People die in hospitals all the time. Then dispose of Almasi.'

44

The Lexus was beyond undriveable. The tyres had melted off the alloy wheels. Spot fires were all over the undercarriage. The gas tank would likely soon catch fire. His boots, which had been outside the front door, were nowhere to be seen – either obliterated by the blast, or sent into the sky with the smaller debris.

'Okay,' Walker said as he headed back to where Muertos and Hayes stayed by the barn. 'The car is not an option.'

'Waiting around is too risky,' Hayes said. 'What if those Homeland guys decide to come back to have a look-see?'

'My thoughts exactly,' Walker said. 'They didn't have the guile to kill us in cold blood, but they might just circle back to make sure their plan worked out.'

He looked back at the house. The echoes of the blast had long gone, and initial the force of the explosion had snuffed out the fire by removing all the fuel but for the few remnants that remained ablaze at the site, which was now no more ominous than a teenager's weekend bonfire or farmer's burn-off, and wouldn't be out of place in the cool grey spring sky in an area of farmland.

'Or,' Walker said, 'we can make our own way along the eight miles to the closest town.'

'I don't think I'd make that,' Muertos said, looking down to her arm. 'It hurts every time I move.'

'Not by foot,' Walker said. 'We take the ride-on mower.'

'How long will that take?' Hayes said.

'Quicker than walking,' Walker replied, moving down the stalls and stopping to look at the decade-old John Deere.

'I'm in,' Hayes said.

Muertos nodded.

Walker topped up the ride-on with gas, and sat in the driver's seat. The engine turned over on the third try of the key and a few pumps of the gas pedal. The exhaust spewed blue smoke, but the mechanics and drive gear seemed in good order – the tyres were all pumped, and the engine didn't miss. Muertos sat on the forward section of seat between Walker and the steering wheel, her broken wrist cradled tightly in front of her, and he could see clear over her head. Hayes sat on the steel cargo rack behind the seat, her back to Walker, her feet resting on the small tow-ball, her hands holding on to the metal tubing.

He eased the vehicle out the barn, then along the driveway and eventually merged onto the black-topped B-road, where he sped up and gave the engine about seventy-five per cent throttle. The engine was either automatic or had just one gear, and the pedal was two-stage – push down with his toes for forward, and push down with his heel for reverse. He took the left when they got to the two-lane highway, and kept to the shoulder, which had just enough tarred surface to fit them, and there he pressed the pedal fully forward. There was no speedometer, but he calculated that they were doing maybe fifteen miles per hour, by figuring the uniform distance in the fence posts counting the time it took to pass them. Twenty minutes to town, going flat-out like this.

Muertos leaned her back against his chest, while Hayes pressed her back against his. As much as he wanted to continue to help them, the fact was the more he got into this, the less likely it seemed to be connected to the Zodiac terror-cell network. People-smuggling just didn't fit the mould of a significant and immediate threat to national security. His father's involvement was most likely nothing more than covering his own butt in transit by posing with the refugee family.

But the fact remained: David Walker had *told* Muertos to find him.

And the 'why' that came with that kept itching at him. So, he had to know – he had to unravel this, to take it to its conclusion. At the very least, he figured, he'd chase this through until they found that US contact, to see if something Zodiac-related popped its ugly head in. Until then, there was some justice to dish out, on behalf of the fallen agents, and those refugees taken advantage of by this group. The sun had broken through the cloud-cover and the world had a golden hue. The engine hummed along as he motored flat-out towards town. There were worse ways to spend his time.

45

Thirty minutes after leaving the farmhouse, Walker dropped off Muertos at what passed as the emergency room of the local hospital, which was little more than a couple of doctors and a few nurses working out a double-storey brick building with a single ambulance parked in a bay. The staff were used to treating minor farm-related injuries, which judging by the wait in the emergency room seemed to be frequent, and being the first responders to road accidents, and mending the usual kind of things that happened around households and schools. Anything more serious or that needed specialist attention or surgery was sent north on Route 1 or I95 into the outer suburbs of DC. Muertos had been told that, all things going well, and save any more serious emergencies presenting, the wait would be two hours for her X-ray, set and plaster. Unless she needed a plate inserted, which they could do, but she'd be there until that doctor was out of surgery in the late afternoon. They gave her something for the pain and she sat in the waiting room, alone.

Walker delivered Hayes to a diner on a corner of the feeder road back to the interstate, where she ordered scrambled eggs on a short stack with potato hash on the side, and a bottomless cup of pale drip coffee. She waited anxiously for Walker to return to his requested order of coffee and burger with a side of mac-and-cheese – anxiously because she wanted to use a phone to call her office, and there was no payphone in the diner. Before he'd left, she'd discussed her next steps with Walker, who agreed it was the best course of action: call in to a trusted senior agent at the Secret Service, come clean about the side-operation run by Overton, and see where that would lead. Her goal was to ensure that as much information could be worked out of the detainee, Bahar, as possible. Walker suggested that she work with whichever police agency had the Syrian detained, by dishing out her knowledge tit-for-tat, and she agreed.

Walker wasn't in the waiting room of the hospital, nor sitting in the window booth of the diner, because he needed shoes. *Eat when you can, sleep when you can* only got you so far when you didn't have shoes. So, after dropping off Muertos, then Hayes, Walker steered the little green John Deere down the main street and looked for options. There were a few, even a Walmart, which he drove right on by without a second glance, and after doing a full lap he made a U-turn through bemused traffic and parked the ride-on in front of a family-run hardware store, where he figured he could get a sturdier pair of boots than at the local menswear store, and he was right. Sixty bucks later he laced up a pair of steel-capped work boots, suitable for building sites – and just as suitable for kicking the crap out of bent Homeland Security agents – and the store owner threw in a free pair of socks when he saw the state of Walker's. He broke his new footwear in on the walk back to the diner.

There were at least a dozen cars in the car park next to the diner, with one vehicle coming and one going every other minute. Walker figured it was busy for the traffic peeling off the interstate to grab gas and use bathrooms and get food and coffee before the grind of getting closer to DC. There was no sign of the two bent Homeland Security guys. No wailing siren of a fire engine. No threats at all.

It was a typical all-American diner so often found in small towns off interstates, and from afar it was clear it was either made to look like a time capsule from the 1950s or was immaculately kept. When he got closer he discovered it was the latter. Plenty of shiny chrome and red vinyl, and black-and-white linoleum floor tiles, a skinny laminate counter that spanned forty feet with a couple of guys behind it tending to the dozen or so customers seated on stools at the bench, and a couple of waitresses bussing the rounds on the floor where patrons were seated at tables and booths.

He saw Hayes seated in a window seat in one corner, her back to the wall, a fire exit close behind her, an unimpeded view of all and sundry, exactly the seat he'd have chosen. She looked more relaxed, inquisitive even, as though the big bright outside world was hers again, as though she'd come close to giving up hope of freedom until they'd found her an hour ago. Walker paused outside the diner, his phone to his ear.

His first call was to Somerville. He filled her in on what had played out at the farmhouse.

'I just checked online, as you've been talking,' she said. 'Bahar was picked up, unconscious, by DC Metro. He's currently in a downtown hospital, listed as John Doe. Under police guard. The note in the system has him as being found in possession of an illegal firearm.'

'Mention of the dead Secret Service agent at the scene, Jim Bennet?'

'No. Nothing. But it's the Secret Service we're talking about, so they're probably taking their time examining and cataloguing the crime scene. The murder charges against Bahar will come, but the illegal firearm is enough to keep him locked up until then. And when they eventually ID him, that'll ring more alarm bells, because you said he got into the country a couple of days ago using false ID?'

'Yep. And soon enough they'll start finding the other bodies,' Walker said. 'Overton, and Acton. And this whole situation will become so intense and tight that we'll have no way in. So, we have to move on Bahar, fast.'

'What are you thinking?'

'I've got to get to him, question him,' Walker said.

'This isn't your fight,' Somerville said. 'Unless something from Zodiac has popped up?'

'No, nothing yet.' Walker looked at Hayes, who was absently pushing her half-eaten meal around her plate. 'I know it might well be unrelated, but I've gotta do it.'

'Because of your father.'

'He was there. He told Muertos to find me.'

'Okay. But for the record, there's already dead Secret Service agents and a corrupt element from Homeland.'

'Your point?'

'It's dangerous.'

'Noted.'

'And Bahar might be unconscious for quite a while,' Somerville said. 'The first-responder report had him unresponsive due to a heavy blunt trauma. He might be out for hours, or days – maybe longer, if he's got swelling on the brain and they have to induce a coma. You know how these things can go.'

Walker said, 'I know.'

Somerville added, 'Not to mention that they've got him sedated and shackled and under guard.'

'I know,' Walker repeated, looking through the big plate-glass window at Hayes. She was cradling a cup of coffee in her hands, her gaze set forward, some kind of middle-distance stare that spoke of friends lost and her immediate future full of unknowns. 'I'll contact you when I'm at the hospital, looking at Bahar. Conscious or not, he's the lead we have remaining.'

'I'm gonna head to DC,' Somerville said. 'I've already had it cleared. You're going to need official support on this, and I can at least wait around the hospital with you. Call you when I land.'

Walker's next call was to Eve. She didn't answer. He didn't leave a message. He was about to – he listened to her voicemail greeting, and waited for the beep, and opened his mouth to say, *Hey it's me* . . . but he stopped himself and ended the call. He didn't know what to say that wouldn't further disappoint her. It's not like he could tell her when he would be home, or what it was that he was doing – because he didn't even know. *Hey, it's me. I'm pulling at a string of a threat or conspiracy or cover-up that's cost several lives in twenty-four hours and I'm gonna keep pulling and pulling at threads until I unravel the thing and, well, no, I don't know when it will end, let alone where it will lead or how things will pan out – but it has something to do with my father, so I have to do it.*

So, Walker headed into the diner and sat opposite Hayes, ready to tell her that he was going to go, alone, to Bahar. Muertos would be easy to leave behind. Hayes might put up a fight, so he had to be tactical about it. The smells of the diner were familiar and comforting. The waitress poured coffee and left a fresh pot on the table and he ordered a serve of scrambled eggs and pecan waffles to go with his burger, which he started in on. Then he drank his coffee and poured another, and the sum of it all was an arrival at a calorie-driven *America: hell yeah!* moment, the kind that makes you want to jump up onto counter and recite some lines from Walt Whitman, or *The Star Spangled Banner* – oh say can you see – and he looked around at the satisfied diners and thought, *You know what, I doubt I'd be the first.*

'What's next?' Hayes said.

Walker drained his second coffee, and told her why it was that she had to wait to contact anybody, and why she had to wait around for Muertos while he went to interrogate their remaining lead.

'Fine,' Hayes said. 'It'll postpone me getting fired for a few more hours.'

'We're gonna set this as right as we can,' Walker said, and the rest of the food arrived, and he ate fast. 'Whether it comes from Bahar, or whoever they send to silence Bahar, we're going to know a lot more about who's behind this before this day is out.'

46

The town didn't have a car-hire company and Walker didn't have the time to wait for the next bus, nor the inclination to hitch a ride. He didn't even have time to take a cab, because a cab would travel at or below the speed limit the entire way into DC. So, he started out on foot, following the traffic leaving the diner, which saw him walking four blocks east and two north, and came to a busy junction, where one road led to the interstate and another had a sign pointing to the local high school. Being Monday, and not a holiday, school was in. Drop-off was well over, and the car parks were full, and he stole his third car in twenty-four hours. It was an older model Ford sedan, from the 90s, mid-size, basic spec, a smaller chassis and engine than a Crown Vic or Taurus, and he figured it would be the easiest to hot-wire for the lack of an alarm or engine immobiliser.

Three minutes later Walker was on Route 1, doing eighty-five: fast enough to get a ticket, not so fast as to be arrested for a misdemeanour.

Muertos would get to the diner and Hayes would tell her that he had split – and what then? She'd be pissed, no doubt; first he breaks her arm, then he leaves her behind. But he figured that she'd found him once – if she tried hard enough she could find him again. And the truth was, he couldn't see any useful need to have her around.

But what happened today would depend on what he could get from Bahar or whoever went to kill him, and where that led. A name, a contact of the stateside operation. Beyond that, via Somerville's assistance, he planned to get access to headshots of Homeland agents and go through them, looking for the four guys he knew to be operating against their mandate, and run a search on a fifth, for which he had a name, the big guy Muertos mentioned, Agent Krycek.

•

The Homeland Security agent with the bad back answered the call from Harvey.

'How far from wrapping this up are you?' Harvey said on speaker.

'About thirty minutes from the hospital, depending on traffic.'

'You should have been there by now.'

'We're getting there, boss,' he said, and glanced across at his partner.

'What's that mean?'

'We had to stop, for gas, and coffee.'

'Whatever. Listen. The computer records at the hospital were just touched.'

The agent said, 'What's that mean for us?'

'You need to hustle. Someone just snooped all DC hospital records for in-patients in the past six hours, searching for male John Does brought in under police guard.'

'And what? You think it's the Secret Service?'

'No, it's not them,' Harvey replied. 'They'd ask us to do it.'

'Then who?'

'There were only two people looking into this from the outside,' Harvey said. 'Muertos, and Walker. So, I figure it was one of them.'

'Uh-uh,' he said, looking again to his colleague and grinning. 'Walker and that chick from State are toast.'

Harvey paused, then said, 'What's that mean?'

The senior agent replied: 'You told us to take care of them.'

'But this looking in the John Does for Bahar,' Harvey said. 'I need to know this wasn't them.'

'It's not them. No way it was them.'

Harvey said, 'Tell me how you dealt with them.'

'Okay,' the senior agent said. 'So, we rigged the house – with the gas, from the stove. Set a fire. The two of them in there – restrained. It took all of maybe, what, ten minutes? We pulled over before the highway to make sure. The house blew. Big. We were six miles out and felt the concussion. So, they're . . . toast.'

Harvey was silent.

The other agent said, 'You told us to take *care* of them, boss.'

Harvey said, 'So, you two didn't see the bodies?'

'Things were happening fast,' the senior agent replied. 'We had a murder scene to take care of, and two targets. And you said you wanted no trace of Almasi or Bahar left behind. This dealt with all those issues.'

'Did you look for Agent Hayes?' Harvey said.

The two agents shared a look, then the senior agent replied, 'We didn't see anyone else. But if she was in the house she's well and truly out of the picture now.'

Harvey again fell silent.

'Sir,' the agent driving said, 'it's actually a good result, if you think about it. There's no immediate evidence at the scene; nothing even that'll be dug up until they start combing through over the coming days – and they're not gonna do that unless they find a chunk of flesh or bone, and I doubt that, because it was a big kaboom. But even if they did, it's going to take some serious DNA testing to find out or who or what the flesh or bone belonged to. So, yeah, all considering, we did good.'

Harvey said, 'You know whose house that was?'

The agents looked at each other. 'No. Whose?'

'Doesn't matter. I'll deal with it. Get to the hospital. Deal with Bahar. Make your work there untraceable. Try not to burn the whole hospital down.'

47

Walker pulled up at the hospital bordering on the Chinatown district of Downtown DC. It was a six-storey yellow-brick building taking up half the block, built in the 1960s. Its windows from the second floor up were narrow slits with concrete frames, to prevent jumpers, giving away its original purpose as an institution for mental illness and one of hundreds closed down by the Reagan policies in the 1980s, which poured tens of thousands of mentally ill out onto the streets where they ended up either homeless or in jail. Repurposed as a general hospital, the exterior had barely changed but for the signage: white steel letters had been placed over the removed but still painted-on sign, which ghosted through the more recent paint job.

Walker parked the Ford across the street and watched the comings and goings. There was no obvious police presence. As he'd reasoned before, maybe they'd not made Bahar as a suspected killer of three Secret Service agents yet, or maybe the Secret Service was taking its time. Or there was a third possibility: that the Feds were here, ferreted away inside the building and crowded around their suspect, their vehicles parked out of view to the front. So, Walker waited. This wasn't the farmhouse in rural Virginia where he'd opted to use surprise to its fullest. This was reconnaissance first, action a cautious second.

His phone bleeped. A text message from Paul Conway, a computer genius who owed him.

Your guy's in room 304. Third floor, north-east corner.

Walker was parked to the western side of the hospital, so he couldn't see the windows of that room. He got out of the car, waited for the traffic and then crossed the street. He attempted a jog but the pain in his leg bit at him. The way he'd glued his wound closed had created a messy knot of skin that didn't want to be disturbed. So, he walked, and did a quick lap of the block, checking cars and people as he moved. Nothing doing. The eastern side of the hospital was a large service area, the wall blank and devoid of windows, brickwork all the way up and down and across but for the lines of concrete slab that denoted each floor. Two chimneys at the top, maybe one for a furnace of hazardous waste, the other a boiler for heating, the latter currently spewing out a cycloning plume of grey steam. He got to the south-west corner and looked side to side along the street. No official-looking cars. No CCTV that he could see, which meant this wasn't a secure medical centre where the cops or Feds sent high-value suspects – more likely, it was the closest hospital to the scene that responded that it could take an unconscious patient with head and other body trauma. Walker kept looking over the hospital, noting the emergency and staff entry and exit points – he needed a lay of the land, options for exfiltration in a hurry, if it came to that; routes back to the car; places he could get another car; somewhere with a view to hole up and wait; somewhere to disappear to, places to hide.

There was a multi-storey car park to his left, on the eastern side of the hospital, a laneway between the two structures. People came and went across a skybridge at the third storey, a concrete path that was glassed in on the top and sides to keep the weather out, like an airlock between the open car park and the hospital. Most the people were in hospital garb. Change of shift, maybe. Or lunch. But there weren't many people in plain clothes coming and going. Perhaps the skybridge was only for official use, and visitors had to access the building through the front doors, on the other side of the building.

He found yesterday's newspaper on a bus-stop seat with a view of the skybridge, which held the only real activity to observe. He held the *Washington Post* in front of him and watched the stream of people. Five minutes passed. Then ten. The flow of staff was lessening. Change of shift closing, or the scheduled lunch break over. He'd seen enough here. He was about to get up and go around the front to the main entrance. But he didn't. Because that's when he saw them.

48

Walker watched as the two Homeland Security agents from the farmhouse made their way across the skybridge. They were walking out, not in. Job done. Something about their gait. Hurried, but not overly so. An air of confidence in their demeanour. Free of task, after a job well done. Like a couple of guys who'd just tied up the last loose end and were on their way to a bar somewhere to celebrate. Walker zoomed his phone's camera as far as it would go and took photos of the two men, one on side profile, the other facing the camera as he'd turned to talk to his partner. They disappeared from view as they entered the car park.

Walker ran. At least, he did his best job of moving fast, his damaged right leg never quite matching the stride of his left. The exit for the car park was on the north side of the block. His car was parked to the western side of the hospital. A fair distance to make up, when invalid. As he moved in an uneven skip he emailed the pictures, twelve in all, to Paul, asking for an urgent ID of the corrupt agents, including the name of the person to whom they reported. He got to the small Ford, still parked where he'd left it, still unlocked, still with the bare wires under the steering column where he'd bashed it open and wrenched them from the ignition switch. He connected the wires and the engine kicked over and started, and he dropped the lever into drive and took off, driving up to the corner and slowing, looking right.

A black SUV was at the exit gate of the hospital car park. The two agents were inside. The way that the front tyres were turned towards the right, as they waited for the boom gate to rise, was all Walker needed to convince him to make a right turn, heading east, the direction they'd soon be taking, and as he drove he watched the gate lift and the SUV pull out and he was now behind them, half a block back, driving east. The faded silver Ford sedan was as near to being invisible as anything else on the road.

His phone rang.

'Those pictures are terrible,' said Paul.

'Can you ID them?'

'They're with Homeland?'

'Yep.' Walker made a left turn after the SUV. The guys drove as though they had nothing else to do that day, and he fell back, even slower, to try not to arouse suspicion. 'Two of their not-so-finest.'

'How badly do you need this?'

'Badly. Why?'

'My search will be mining data on Homeland severs, and it will leave breadcrumbs. Electronic fingerprints. It's okay, but it's a risk – on my part. Means I'll have to scrap a few favourite servers that I like to use.'

'I need this.'

'Okay. I'll go in and see what's there.'

'Time frame?'

'I'm typing as we speak. Minutes, not hours. I'm going into their facial-rec program, running it against their own personnel records. And after this?'

'Yeah?'

'Get yourself yet another a burner phone. I will too. These ones are cooked. Go to the site and let me know the new number.'

Walker paused and looked at the cell phone on speaker on the passenger seat. 'You sure this phone's done?'

'Because of what we've just said, we've triggered a whole bunch of flagged key-words, and I'm looking at your number popping up in their system right now,' Paul said. 'Homeland will put in a request to trace and transcribe all calls in and out of cell towers that your phone has connected to, including placing you in the vicinity of that house you were at before. I see NSA processing this command as we speak. You can thank the Patriot Act, and related surveillance bills. They'll have all the metadata off that device, and soon. Who you called, where you were you when you called them, where you are right now. Basically it's like you've got a tracking device in your hand, because that's exactly what it is, with GPS, accurate to within a metre anywhere on the globe – unless you plan to take your investigation underwater soon? Didn't think so. So, your phone is constantly singing out into the world, saying, *I'm here, I'm here* to the nearest mobile tower, and that tower makes a permanent record of that activity. They know everywhere you've been, they know everyone you've been in contact with: on the basis of this they'll know all of your associations – including my number. And even if you switch the phone off, they can still activate the microphone and camera. So, is it cooked? You betchya.'

'Okay, I'll ditch it when I hang up.'

'Ain't tech grand?' Paul said. 'They know who you talk to the most. They know when you talk to them. They know when you're awake. They know when you're sleeping. They know when you're working. They know how you get to work. They know where you shop. Your pattern of life. Oh, and your new burner? Avoid using it to make calls. Download apps for your phone. Use something like WhatsApp, which isn't perfect but it does encrypt your communications end-to-end, so it's much more difficult for the Feds to crack. Keep front of mind where you might be exposed, protect yourself where possible.'

'Right.' Walker slowed a little to match the speed of the Homeland vehicle, two cars ahead. 'Can they track you?'

'*Please.* I've lasted this long in this business by outsmarting those fools. But like I said, new phones at both ends, encrypted comms if it's keyword sensitive. Let's reconvene in an hour, I'll have your guys made by then.'

'Okay. And Paul? Thanks.'

'You owe me a lot of beer.'

The line went dead. Ahead, the traffic lights changed to red. The Homeland Security SUV stopped. The van between them stopped. Walker put the driver's-side sun visor down and pulled up close behind, hoping the van would keep him out of view. While he waited he pulled the cell phone apart and cracked the sim card in half, then he opened his door an inch and tossed it all onto the road under the car. There was little other traffic. None coming the other way through the intersection. Then, suddenly, the Homeland SUV took off through the red light. The van rolled forward and stopped.

Walker watched, knowing there was little he could do. If he ran the light after them, they'd see it in their rear-view mirrors. He couldn't afford to have them make him, but he couldn't lose them either. He watched them run the red light at the next intersection, in a similar move. They then hit their brakes, indicated a right turn. The traffic lights Walker was stopped at were still red as, two blocks ahead, the agents turned. Out of sight.

Walker hit the gas and turned the wheel. He went around the van and kept his foot planted as he ran the red, the little Ford's engine buzzing with the strain. Through the next intersection, where he braked hard and took the right. The SUV was nowhere to be seen. He kept to the speed limit as he checked right and left at every intersection. Nothing. Up ahead was a feeder road leading to Interstate 495, the Capital Beltway. Decision time. They'd either headed northeast towards the capital, or south-west – where they had come from earlier that day, the farmhouse in Virginia.

Walker made his decision. Instinct guided him into the city, not out of it. There were plenty of federal government installations on the other side of the Potomac, and these two had the air of those headed back to base. Within a mile, as he neared the Woodrow Wilson Memorial Bridge, slipping between cars to make up some distance, Walker reacquired his target. He slowed, let a few cars in and out of the gap ahead, always keeping the top of the Homeland SUV in sight. The Capital Beltway was thick with traffic but it was flowing and he kept the tail going around the turnpike and headed north on the 295. They drove past the sprawling campus of Joint Base Anacostia–Bolling, close on a thousand acres of military land along the Potomac, the result of base realignments during the belt-tightening years of the Iraq and Afghan wars. The Defence Intelligence Agency building was to his left, then to the right the newly completed headquarters that was the grass-roofed command of the Coast Guard. Beyond the trees was a taller, black-green glass structure – and Walker knew then where they were headed even before they took the exit.

Home. The black-green glass building was the newly developed Homeland Security Headquarters, known as St Elizabeths Campus. Formerly a massive psychiatric hospital operated by the federal government since the 1850s, which had over the years been reorganised and rationalised down to the point where the empty grounds could be repurposed by branches and departments and functionaries of federal government.

Commercial aircraft flew in low from the Atlantic on landing approach at the Ronald Reagan Washington National Airport. Walker kept an eye on the black SUV ahead while rounding the exit and taking in the expanse of the project to the west. The St Elizabeths site was by far the largest construction project in Washington since the Pentagon, and easily the largest excavation project the city had ever seen – hinting at what was unseen, being built underground, secrets and archives and Big Data all buried away from prying eyes and ears. The old brick buildings of the campus were kept intact, giving the new inhabitants a sense of history. Walker didn't miss the irony of the paranoia-driven Department of Homeland Security and its twenty agencies assimilating a psychiatric ward in an attempt to have some kind of cohesive corporate and sharing culture.

This place presented a big problem for Walker. He could follow these guys on the open road, but not into St Elizabeths. He tailed the Homeland agents' vehicle, with two cars between them. Heading here meant any number of things. Was this where they were stationed, and they were coming home to report in after a mission completed, now that, in their minds, the morning's little clean-up operation was all taken care of? Or were they headed here for a meeting or some other, unrelated assignment? Maybe it was part of an alibi, should it ever be brought to them by an investigative party. *Where were you when Bahar died in hospital? Who's Bahar? We were here all along . . .*

He wondered about how many Homeland Security Special Agents there were, and what kind of oversight they had, and how closely they were supervised. Surely they had all kinds of watch commanders and Special Agents in Charge, and Deputy Directors and so on, making their time accountable. Which made him wonder further. Were these two, and those in San Francisco, just moonlighting as contract muscle and killers on the side, unknown to anyone else in there? Or did the corruption go up the food chain, their butts covered by someone higher up the command structure who was tasked with keeping track of their performance and whereabouts? In the days of tight budgets and accountability, metadata was a two-way street: the government could track the bad guys, and their own. For performance enhancement purposes, on the face of it. And to keep tabs.

Walker pulled to a stop and waited. He was on the shoulder of the road just before Gate One, a walled-in entry point fortified with concrete bollards and blast screens. Not a great place to stop, and he knew as soon as he hit the brakes that he should keep driving on. There would be security cameras he couldn't see, tracked on him, watching him, and questions would be asked as to why there was a car parked out there by the gate, and maybe they'd think he'd broken down but it'd be a long shot because it was too much of coincidence for a lone man of military age to break down so close to one of the nation's most security-conscious places. He imagined the security force would come out with hands on their side-arms, or armed with sub-machineguns, if he hung around any longer than it'd take for him to get out and walk around the car and kick the tyres as though checking for a flat. Then he thought about them using the camera feed to check his registration, which on the face of it wasn't bad because who'd think of a high school teacher as a threat to national security, but then there was the chance the car was already reported as stolen.

Time to move.

Walker waited for a gap in the traffic so he could merge.

Then, two things happened at once.

The first thing was two security guards emerging from the guardhouse and standing clear of the blast wall, where they stood and eyeballed him. One had his hand on a radio that was clipped to his chest, with a cord to the main unit on his utility belt, and he was talking down into it, like he was reading out Walker's number-plate and relaying the information. The other had his hand on the butt of his holstered automatic and stood, waiting, watching. Not as a threat, but ready to draw down if the need arose.

The other thing was a car pulling out of the gate. It wasn't the car that was unusual, nor was it the way it was being driven. It's who was doing the driving.

Walker saw a dead man.

49

The man driving the car was Blake Acton. No doubt. He'd seen the picture of the Secret Service agent on Overton's phone, and now here he was. Which meant that Bahar hadn't killed him between Overton and Bennet, nor any other time, because he was alive and well, driving a car, and Walker had never been one to believe in reincarnation, nor in zombies.

Walker had to act fast, because Acton was driving his vehicle like it was a government car and it was his last day on the job before handing in the keys. Walker dropped the gear selector in drive and merged with the traffic, then pulled a U-turn as soon as he could, and was in pursuit. As he passed the guardhouse he saw the two security guards saunter back to their post, as though they'd called in the plate and been told that it belonged to a law-abiding teacher from Virginia, and that was that.

The little Ford's engine whined as he pushed it to catch up with Acton's Chevy Caprice. The other traffic was rolling slowly as Acton overtook two cars and ducked back into the lane and took the onramp onto the Beltway. Walker eased off the gas, not only because he knew where Acton would be – on the I 495, and there Walker would put his foot to the floor and wind out the car's little engine – but something else caught his attention.

A big black SUV, in his rear-view mirror. Growing bigger by the second. The two Homeland guys, the one with the bad back, and his friend, sitting inside it. Closing in fast, and Walker didn't know if they were after him or Acton.

•

'Where's Walker?' Muertos asked, sitting down opposite Hayes and resting her plastered arm on the table.

Hayes was nursing her fourth coffee, and had read the *USA Today* cover to cover. She folded the paper and said, 'He had to split.'

Muertos did a double-take, and looked around in a slight panic, then said, 'He left?'

Hayes nodded, said, 'He went back to DC. He said for us to catch the next bus in, once you got back.' Hayes looked at the old clock above the kitchen pass. 'It leaves in fifteen minutes.'

The waitress came and refilled Hayes' coffee, then poured a new cup for Muertos and left a menu. When she left, Hayes said, 'What's your connection to this?'

'This?' Muertos used her one good hand to pour sugar into her cup, then stirred it, put the spoon down and picked up the steaming cup. Her hand shook as she sipped. Nerves, adrenaline, and a degree of anger directed at Walker.

'So,' Hayes said, 'you're State Department. Walker's ex-CIA. Overton is – was – an old BFF of yours. How does it all fit together?'

'Does it seem like it fits neatly together?' Muertos tried to smile.

'Right.' Hayes crossed her arms, leaned forward a little. 'I mean, did you bring this to Overton in the first place? Or did she involve you?'

Muertos said, over the top of her steaming cup, 'How about we finish this coffee and I'll tell you on the bus ride.'

'Okay. The bus stop's right outside.' Hayes watched her. 'I didn't mean to sound like I'm looking to pass on the blame or anything like that. I'm just trying to understand the fuller picture.'

'Secret Service is going to put you under the griller, aren't they?'

Hayes nodded.

'Well, Walker and I will back you, every step of the way.' Muertos looked around. 'Did Walker say why he was leaving?'

'He wanted to try to get to Bahar in hospital, before those two Homeland guys who blew up the farmhouse got to him.'

Muertos nodded. Drained her coffee. Put her empty cup down. 'Let's go wait for that bus.'

'There's no hurry. We'll see it arrive.'

'I need some air,' Muertos said, standing. 'Did Walker say where to meet in DC?'

'He said you'd find him.'

'How am I supposed to do that?'

'He said you'd done it before.'

•

Walker was struggling to keep up the chase and remain inconspicuous. As were the two Homeland guys in their SUV, who were now in front of him – the guy with the bad back, and his pal, keeping a tail on Acton out in the lead, none the wiser that Walker was there. Their little speeding convoy took the Georgetown exit, Acton at a far-out lead.

Walker knew the Georgetown area well – it was where his father had kept an apartment, near where he'd worked for the better part of three decades. Walker had stalked the streets on long weekends and school holidays, taking the Amtrak or Greyhound from Philly. He'd imagined that he was a junior spy, and practised tailing 'suspects', and making dead-drops in conspicuous places; he'd write out passages from his favourite books and fold up the pieces of paper and put them in mailboxes before surreptitiously marking the side with chalk to symbolise that the drop had been made, and that it was to be collected by an imaginary contact or handler. When he told his father about it, it soon became a game, and David Walker would come home after work and hand in all the notes he'd found on the neighbourhood walk back from the bus stop. All that play, all that time, Walker had never known that his father, a career academic, was truly part of the nation's Intelligence apparatus, working for the CIA, a path that he would one day follow. Nor could he have imagined that he was playing around those very streets at the very time that Rick Ames, the CIA's worst traitor, was doing it for real, making dead-drops of US intelligence to the Russians. He later wondered if there were Russian agents out there with obscure passages from *Huckleberry Finn* and *Moby Dick* and *Catcher in the Rye* and *To Kill A Mockingbird*, scratching their heads trying to unpack cryptic messages from classic American literature.

Off the Beltway, the three-vehicle convoy was all halted up at traffic lights. The Homeland SUV was four vehicles ahead, Acton a couple of cars ahead of that, and Walker two cars behind them.

The lights changed, and the traffic flowed. Their convoy was constrained by the small streets and other cars, but Walker kept both vehicles in sight. A couple of miles later, Acton took a right. The SUV followed Acton. Walker followed the SUV. Three more intersections straight ahead, and the traffic gods seemed pissed because they got red lights at every intersection.

When they reached the next suburb over from Bennet's apartment, Walker remembered Bennet saying that Acton lived in a house here.

Acton was headed home.

50

Walker watched the Chevy Caprice take a side street lined with two-hundred-year-old oaks that were budding heavily with spring, the branches touching above the street to form a leafy tunnel. Walker slowed at the turn, and saw Acton's tail-lights flare as he brought his high-powered sedan to a stop outside a house. The black SUV drove by Acton and took the next turn, disappearing from sight. Walker knew the play – the Homeland guys would circle the block to get a good vantage spot to keep an eye on Acton's car. That's if this was just about surveillance. But the very real possibility was that this was something else – that they were casing the scene before going in and taking care of a final loose end, a loose end that Bahar had failed to tie up this morning; maybe Acton had been out, or Bahar had not got an opportunity to get here because Walker had got to him first, at Bennet's apartment. Whatever the case, Acton seemed oblivious to the danger he was now in.

Walker slowed along Acton's street in time to see him walk up the stairs of his house and be greeted at the front door by a woman and two children who'd been waiting, expectantly. They embraced and entered their home. That moment, and the fact that Acton had not made the Homeland tail, said to Walker that, wary as the agent may be, he'd likely not heard the worst of the news yet – that two of his colleagues were dead. Walker parked the Ford a few houses short and exited, moving fast, making the stairs just as the door clicked shut. He knocked. There was a pause. Down the street Walker saw the nose of the black SUV round the corner. The Homeland guys had U-turned on the side street and were coming back, for surveillance, or an assault. The front door half opened and Acton looked Walker up and down and went to speak—

Walker pushed open the door and stepped into the house.

Acton shuffled back and drew his sidearm and pointed it at Walker – who had his hands up to show that he was unarmed and not a threat. With his foot he closed the door behind him. Behind Acton was his wife, holding two children close, one crooked under each arm. The little boy was about four, the girl maybe six. Acton and his wife looked mid-forties, nearly a decade older than Overton, which Walker thought odd, given she had been the one calling the shots to her little rag-tag off-books team. Either she was a shooting star in the Service and outranked Acton, or he was a rung or two above her and helping her out. The latter seemed odd, but Walker would have to wait to find out.

'Agent Acton, listen to me: Clair Hayes is alive,' Walker said.

Acton, eyes wide and a two-handed grip on his pistol steadily pointed at Walker's centre mass, said, 'Who are you?'

'My name's Walker, and last night I met with Sally Overton,' Walker replied. 'I know about your off-the-books op, with Bennet too. I know about the burner phones, the three-hour check-ins, about Hayes going missing and her car being found on Route 1. I'm here to warn you, and help you.'

Acton didn't move. His sidearm still ready. His family still behind him.

'Check out the peephole.' Walker tilted his head towards the door. 'A Black SUV doing a drive-by. Two guys inside. They're the bad guys here. They followed you all the way from St Elizabeths. You need to get your family to safety.'

Acton paused. 'That's crap. That car? Those guys? I was just on the phone to them. They're Homeland, and were assigned as close personal protection to me and my family.' He got a little more comfortable in his double-handed grip, the business-end of the weapon directed at Walker's heart. 'So, the question remains: who *are* you?'

'Those two guys?' Walker said, his voice low and calm. 'They rolled into St Elizabeth moments before being assigned to protect you – literally no more than a couple of minutes. Let me guess – it was *them* who rang *you*?'

Acton was silent.

'Right. Well, before that?' Walker said. 'They were at a rural property in Virginia, near Burnley. Check the news – it looks like a bomb site now. Agent Hayes was there – but I got her out.'

Acton watched Walker closely, taking it all in, and he said, 'Where is Hayes?'

'She's fine, she's safe. Almasi and Bahar had her captive out there. Almasi is dead.'

Acton backed up a step, towards his family. 'Dead how?'

'Coffee pot.'

'What?'

'And I'm pretty damn sure Bahar is dead too,' Walker said. 'He was taken to a hospital in Downtown DC, just after I took him down at Bennet's apartment block this morning. You can check that out, to confirm my story. Where he was picked up, and where he was taken – and his current, real-time status. You'll find out I'm telling the truth, and you'll also find out that these two Homeland guys visited his room about forty minutes ago to make sure he never talked. I saw them leave and followed them – to St Elizabeths. Call the hospital. Check my story. But beware these two guys out there, okay?'

Acton kept his pistol trained on Walker. He didn't attempt to move to his cell phone, which Walker could see was clipped to the outside of his belt, next to his Secret Service badge and empty hip holster with spare mags for the Sig. Walker knew the Service preferred

.357 and larger-calibre rounds over the 9-millimetre, and that at this distance the agent wouldn't miss, and Walker wouldn't live because these agents were trained to shoot to kill, and at this range the .357 was a devastating round.

'You knew that already,' Walker said. He could see it, in Acton's face. Some kind of conformation, a light tell, in his eyes, which had gone from searching Walker to staring at him in a middle-distance kind of stare that said he was thinking, hard. 'That Bahar was dead.'

Acton nodded, met Walker's gaze. 'A friend at Metro PD told me on the drive over here. Can't say I'm sorry for him.'

'Well, you can check with the hospital staff,' Walker said, hands still raised. 'Ask them if those two Homeland guys were there. I saw them come out, walking to their car. Swaggering. All the time in the world, because they were almost done, cleaning this up, and they knew you were at St Elizabeths – why *were* you at St Elizabeths?'

Acton was silent. For a full five seconds, which was a lot of time, in that moment.

'Anyway,' Walker said, motioning over his shoulder to the door. '*You're* their last loose thread, because they think everyone else involved is gone. They went into that hospital and they pulled the plug on Bahar, or smothered him, or injected something into him. They set the house to blow, with Muertos and me in it. They took Almasi's body – he's either still in their car, or they dumped him on the road. But the latter's unlikely, so check their boot. They'll dispose of him later, along with you. Maybe in a furnace, or in a drum of hydrofluoric acid, or however guys like that make sure bodies don't get found.'

'Muertos?'

'A long-time friend of Overton. She started all this. She's with the State Department.'

'Where is she?'

'With Hayes.'

Acton didn't say anything, but he nodded.

'Look, Agent Acton?' Walker said. 'In their minds there's only one loose end remaining – *you*.' He motioned again to the door behind him. 'Those two Homeland guys are going to come in here and finish the job – in front of your family, if they have to.' Walker made a show of motioning to Acton's wife and kids but the agent just kept his gaze and gun trained on Walker. 'Or, if you're lucky? They'll ask you to go along for a ride – so that they can do what they have to do away from your family. Maybe they'll say that they have to take you to a safe house, or to some Homeland office to give a bullcrap statement. That's a maybe – I've met these guys, they've been squeamish before. But they might just do the job in here, the lot of you, make it look like a murder–suicide, because you couldn't live with what had happened to your colleagues – better yet, they'll make it look like you were the one cleaning house after an illegal operation, and they'll heap some half-baked conspiracy on you, that you were bent all the time and you killed your colleagues and Almasi and Bahar. Dump Almasi's body in here with you four.'

Acton glanced to his family. His wife was quiet and stoic for the kids, who were hustled in tight to her dress.

'Bahar killed Bennet and Overton, but I'm guessing you know that already?' Walker said.

No reaction from Acton, but Walker could see the tell again, the agent's eyes glancing to the side, almost non-existent, but it was there.

'Right,' Walker said. 'These two Homeland guys are working for someone off the books, just like you were for Overton – but for them, it's turned into a clean-up operation, and that means you're in danger. So, what's it going to be?'

Then, Acton's cell phone rang. He kept the pistol on Walker and used his left hand to unclip his phone. He glanced at the screen.

Walker said, 'Is it them?'

Acton ignored Walker and answered it. 'Yeah?'

Walker watched and listened.

Acton listened to the phone, then said, 'Right. Okay. Wait a minute, okay?'

He pressed a button on the phone, and looked from it to Walker, then back to his family.

Walker said, 'What do they want you to do?'

'Take a ride with them,' Acton said. The colour had drained from his face, and a glean of sweat beaded his forehead. 'To go talk with Bahar, who they say has now woken up.'

'Is there a basement under those stairs?' Walker asked.

'There's an old cellar,' Acton said, holstering his weapon and turning to hug his family.

'Your family needs to get down there, and find cover towards the back,' Walker said, turning and looking out the peephole. The two Homeland guys were standing by their parked SUV, across the road, one of them with a phone pressed against his ear. 'Tell them to come in and wait while you get ready.'

'Okay,' Acton said, moving fast. He first directed his family, closed the cellar door under the stairs after them, then spoke into the phone and relayed the instructions, then ended the call.

Walker watched out the peephole as the two Homeland guys conferred, then the older one shrugged and gestured towards the house and they both headed across the road.

'You don't have to be part of this,' Walker said. 'You can head downstairs too.'

'This is my house, my family,' Acton said, reaching down to his ankle and unholstering his secondary weapon, a small Glock hidden under his suit trousers. He passed the Glock to Walker. 'And I want to hear first-hand what these two have to say.'

51

Walker stood back as Acton stole a look out the door's peephole, then the Secret Service agent leaned back and whispered, 'Five seconds.'

Walker could see that the guy was nervous.

'Take a deep breath and settle yourself – don't alarm them,' Walker said. 'Open the door and let them in. Usher them through and tell them to wait for you in the lounge. I'll take the lead from there.'

Acton nodded.

Walker backed down the hall and into the lounge room and checked the small pistol Acton had passed him. It was a Glock 42 sub-compact automatic, chambered for the .38, and with its short barrel and single-stack six-round mag it fitted neatly in the palm of his hand. He stood out of view from the front door, his back to the wall. The floorplan was almost a mirror image of the layout of Hassan's house in Annapolis, although this place was wider and the hall was deeper. It would be a full five strides for the two Homeland guys to get from the doorway to the lounge room.

He heard a knock at the door, then the sound of the door opening. Nothing was said, but he guessed Action had given them a gesture to head for the doorway, up the hall, because Walker heard footsteps headed his way, and then the two Homeland guys sauntered into the room. Their backs were to Walker, and before they had the chance to turn around and react he shouted: 'Down! Down! Down!'

•

Lewis called Harvey, and Harvey cringed and said, 'You've seen the news.'

'The fucking *news*!' Lewis's voice boomed. 'They blew up the house! How the *hell* did this happen?'

'My guys were in a bind, and they reacted to a rapidly changing situation—'

'Bind? A *bind*! You know whose house that was?'

Harvey held the phone out away from his ear to avoid being deafened. He waited two seconds, put the phone back to the side of his face and said, 'Yes, I am aware. It's been reported as an accident. Faulty gas tanks. The local fire department put out what remained of the fire, and I already have a team there who have taken over the site and are cleaning it. It's all okay.'

'Okay? O*kay*!? If this gets linked back—'

'There's no link.'

'If it comes back in any way.'

'It won't come back.'

Lewis was silent for a while, then said, 'There was an off-books investigation, following Almasi and Bahar.'

'And it's been taken care of, trust me.'

'How many agents are you using on this?'

'I started with five of my own, down to three, because of San Francisco.'

'You should have just used Krycek, the man's a wrecking ball.'

'He has his uses, and this time they weren't needed,' Harvey said. 'Look, the people I used are loyal to a fault. Don't worry about that. And any thread that could possibly be drawn back to us is gone.'

There was a pause, then, 'Gone?'

'Gone. Finished. No more Almasi, no more Bahar. Their involvement in our operation has come to a dead end. Along with Walker and Muertos. Okay?'

'They're – you can't just . . . they were all out at the house?'

'It's been a fluid thing, and it's done now. Okay?' Harvey leaned back and looked out at the view from his office window, across the tops of trees to the Potomac. 'You knew lives would be lost in the course of this.'

'I couldn't give a shit about *lives*. It's having this unravel before my eyes when we're so close to finishing what was started so long ago.'

'It was an operational call. An imperative. I'm the man on the ground handling logistics and manpower, you're the one planning the operation. You've never questioned my methods or motives before. You need to relax about this.'

There was a pause, and then his voice was lower, as though that would stop eavesdropping of the encrypted call: 'You can't get rid of people, and houses, without it being looked into. Too much attention and this will blow up in our faces.'

'Please, listen,' Harvey said, trying to make his voice sound soothing. 'It's too late for any of that, right? And who do you think will look into it?' Harvey went silent, and Lewis was too. 'What I think is this: it's *time*. For us to use what we've got. To go operational, with what we've already imported.'

Lewis paused a moment, then said, 'We're not where we need to be.'

'It'll work,' Harvey said. 'Trust me. We've got enough from Almasi to do more than we ever dreamed of. What we've got will shape the news for years to come. You'll be driving policy, building a mandate, taking us to where we belong.'

'You really think that?' Lewis's voice was wavering, as though he wanted to believe it too, to be reassured.

'Yes.'

'I hope so. Maybe you're right. Maybe we have enough. Let me look at what we've got, and I'll decide.'

Harvey smiled. He liked saying *news* to the man. Being confident. Putting the situation and decisions back in Lewis's lap. The line went dead. Then Harvey hung up. He watched the news playing on one of the screens in his office. Waited for a final call from the field. Imagined where he would be a couple of years from now.

52

In Walker's experience in the military – which was ten years all up, from training at the Air Force Academy in the mountains of Colorado, to the dangerous built-up streets of cities and towns in Iraq, and in the frightening mountains and villages of Afghanistan – there were two kinds of reaction to quick, powerful force: fight, or flight. To react with force, or to comply without trouble.

Usually, when a person heard the repeated command 'Down!' shouted up close and personal, the reaction was to comply, to be wary, to raise hands and make it clear they weren't making any trouble, to make eye contact out of curiosity and probably fear, that basic human tenet that made it near on impossible *not* to turn and look.

The other reaction was to fight it. Walker had seen that happen a few times. The most spectacular had been when on leave in Kuwait, where a troop of drunk Marines were being arrested by MPs. The setting was a bar, which Walker had always considered a bad place to make an arrest because the arrestee was likely inebriated and thereby *non compos mentis* to the authority being brought to bear upon them, let alone being up to a fair fight. In that situation, the group of Marines decided to take the appearance of four MPs with batons ready and shouting compliance commands as a cue to start a full-scale bar fight. No lonely man was safe. A fight that Walker and a fellow Special Ops soldier had to put to rest after a few minutes of bemused viewing. Those Marines ended up in the hospital for the night, rather than a military cell, because of their choice of reaction.

The reactions of the two Homeland guys were somewhere above and beyond that, setting a new benchmark for Walker's future reference. At least with the Marines there was predictability – you could see where their minds were going well before their inebriated fists and elbows and knees and feet started to flay about. These two Homeland guys responded like they'd never been arrested before, like they'd never been threatened, like they'd never had to comply with an authority greater than their own. They were about to learn an important lesson.

The agent closer to Walker was the younger guy. His reaction, to fight, had been in sync with the older agent, but his movements were faster. They'd both reached to their hips at the same time, both made to turn around at the same time. The thing was, their expectations, and therefore their reactions, were way off. They'd expected Acton to be the one doing the shouting, because he was the obvious choice, and they knew from the walk from the front door that the Secret Service agent was a couple of paces directly behind them. Neither considered the possibility of there being another man there, out of sight, and in the context of this fight far closer to them. In effect, their reactions were rendered mute well before they could be of any use.

Walker's first movement was to drop his Glock pistol and take a step forward, grabbing the faster guy's rising arm in a tight grip around the elbow joint; he then put his other hand at the agent's back, between the spine and the shoulder blade, and pulled until the shoulder joint popped out and tendons tore and snapped.

That Homeland guy dropped his pistol and fell to the ground, hollering in pain.

The second agent was halfway through his turn, sidearm drawn, when he reacted the way most people would when their partner had just been put out of the fight – his motion slowed and he turned his head to see what was unfolding right next to him. Walker could see this reaction, because he was watching him as soon he'd made contact with the first agent, never taking his eyes off him, reading his every move. He saw the agent weighing decisions as events played out seemingly faster than real-time: another threat in the house, his comrade down. And then confusion gave way to recognition – he *knew* the perpetrator, a guy he'd assumed he'd killed in a gas explosion earlier that morning. He needed to alter his original plan of turning and shooting back through the doorway he'd just walked through. Walker saw it all register, calculate and compute – the guy was a dinosaur, an analogue man lost in the digital age. By the time the agent had changed his mind about how to act, it was far too late. By the time he'd shifted his feet and turned to square up to Walker, he was collected under the chin by a rising uppercut, then yanked forward by his tie.

Walker pulled him in and down, a sharp yank that ended when he felt the guy's nose and face connect with his rapidly rising knee. A broken nose, loosened teeth, shattered cheekbones, fractured orbital sockets, concussion – the sum of it all being: lights out. The second agent fell to the floorboards with a heavy thump.

Walker didn't stop there. He kicked the younger agent's pistol away, and hefted him up with one hand, using his other hand to grab the small Glock from the floor. He buried the snub of the barrel under the guy's chin, pinning him against the wall, lifting him up onto his tiptoes. The agent's face was twisted in pain and he put up no fight as he cradled his loosely hanging arm across his body.

'Talk,' Walker said to him. 'You need to talk.'

53

'You're . . . dead.' The Homeland agent with the bad back was trying to make sense of the apparition in front of him. A guy he'd left tied to a table of solid hardwood to be blown to bits in a gas explosion. His partner's bright idea.

Walker was silent. He let the Glock do the talking – he pushed it harder under the guy's chin, letting go with his other hand and patting him down, pulling out a wallet and throwing it to Acton.

'Agent Matt Kingsley,' Acton said. 'Department of Homeland Security.'

'Okay, Matt,' Walker said. 'Talk time. Who are you working for?'

Agent Matt Kingsley did not speak.

'Matt, come on . . .' Walker said, and brought his free hand to the guy's wrecked shoulder and squeezed. Kingsley let out a yelp. 'Talk to me. You're just an amateur here, so you don't need to die, or suffer. Jail, sure. You deserve that. Sweet little federal agent like you in jail, you're gonna be a popular boy, passed from cell to cell. Imagine your back then? So, use these last minutes of freedom wisely, so that Agent Acton here can put in a good word for you for cooperating. Who are you reporting to?'

Kingsley stayed silent.

Walker squeezed Agent Kingsley's shoulder and there was an instant reaction – he stepped aside as Kingsley puked.

'Oh man,' Acton said, looking at the result. 'Not on the rug.'

'Matt. Matt. Listen to me,' Walker said, slapping the Homeland agent's face to get his attention. 'You and your buddy here attempted to kill Muertos and me this morning. That was your first mistake. I know you're squeamish – you two couldn't bring yourselves to do it by hand, so you rigged the house to blow. That was your second mistake. You left the scene before making sure the job was done. Mistake three. Should I go on?'

'That house blew, big,' Kingsley said. 'How'd you—'

'Forget the past, this is happening *now*,' Walker said. 'Someone's giving you instructions. Who ordered us dead?'

Kingsley just stared at him.

'It's easy, Matt, talk to me,' Walker said. 'One word after another. First and last name. Just two words.'

Kingsley looked Walker steadily in the eye as he spoke. Two words. 'Fuck you.'

Walker smiled. 'Look, bud. Your friend there? As soon as he wakes up, *he's* gonna talk to us. You just *know* he will. He'll talk because he's been around longer than you and he knows the score on something like this – the first to talk gets preferential treatment. He gets in front of the legal storm that's coming down, he gets the leniency when it comes to indictments and sentencing. This moment right here, right now, is your one and only opportunity to be the smarter one here – all because you're the one who's conscious right now. So, what's it gonna be? Hmm?'

Kingsley looked from Walker to Acton. There was worry in his eyes.

'I didn't kill anybody,' Kingsley said, 'and I didn't know anyone would get killed, I swear. I mean, apart from the house thing, with you. Look, my partner, he took care of the Syrian in the hospital. But that's a good thing, right? That son of a bitch killed your friends, Overton and Bennet, right? I – I've had no choice in this – no choice – I'm just following orders, man. Please, you gotta believe that.'

'Just following orders . . .' Walker repeated, unconvinced.

'Yep,' Kingsley said. 'That's all. Doing as I'm told.'

'Okay. Matt? We need a name,' Walker said. 'Who's giving you these orders?'

Kingsley hesitated.

'Come on,' Acton said, standing close next to Walker. 'You talk, you'll be looked after. Tell us who's calling the shots. Who gave Bahar the addresses and kill order on my colleagues?'

Agent Kingsley was silent.

'Who told you to clean up at the farmhouse?' Walker asked. 'To get rid of Bahar and then Muertos and me? Tell me what we need to hear, and I can help you out. One-time offer, pal. Tick-tock.'

Kingsley looked pale.

'One-time offer . . .' Acton echoed Walker's words. 'I'd take it. Because your partner, old smokey here, when he wakes up? He'll be smart enough to jump on it, and he'll dive all the way in. Old timer like that, he *knows*. So, take the offer – talk to us. Give us a name.'

Kingsley looked from Walker to Acton, then nodded. Walker eased the pressure on the guy's shoulder.

'Okay. Daniel Harvey. Okay?' Agent Matt Kingsley of Homeland Security said, and he looked down at the mess he'd made on the Oriental rug. 'Homeland Security Deputy Director Daniel Harvey. I helped out, right? Please – you guys gotta keep me safe.'

•

Muertos and Hayes got off the bus at Arlington, Virginia. Inside the Capital Beltway, originally a part of the capital district, handed back to Virginia before the civil war. Now the second largest city area of Washington – a good place for them to stop and take stock. They found a convenience store and bought a pre-paid cell phone, which Hayes used to call her office; within seconds she'd ended the call and dialled another number.

The voice answered and said, 'This is Blake Acton.'

'Acton!'

'Hayes?'

'Yes. Oh my god, I can't believe it. You okay?'

'It's bad, Clair. They got Jim Bennet. Overton too.'

'I know. We have to get these guys,' Hayes said.

Acton said, 'I've got two of them detained in my front room.'

'I mean put them down,' Hayes responded. 'Into the ground.'

'Hayes . . . where are you?'

'I'm at Arlington, just got off a bus. With a friend of Sally's, Rachel Muertos. Is Walker with you?'

'Yep,' Acton said. 'Jump in a cab to my place. We'll be waiting.'

'On it.' Hayes ended the call, and then dialled for a cab.

'Walker's there with Acton?' Muertos asked when Hayes updated her.

'Yep,' Hayes replied. 'At Acton's house. It's not ten minutes by car.'

'What are they doing?'

'Didn't say,' Hayes said, looking at her companion. 'Why?'

'I just thought I'd be up against a dead end, in finding Walker again,' Muertos said, sadness in her voice. 'It was Sally who got me his location before.'

Hayes put an arm around Muertos. 'Rachel, we'll get every one of the sons of bitches behind this, I swear on everything that's holy. Mark my words: whoever was behind the killing of Overton and Bennet will not see the inside of a prison cell. We look out for our family.'

54

'Deputy Secretary Daniel Harvey of Homeland Security,' Acton said to Walker, quietly, after having watched his wife and children head upstairs with snacks, off to play games, oblivious to what had unfolded behind the closed door of the lounge room but for the few thuds they'd heard through the floorboards. 'He's a big fish in this town.'

'Know him?' Walker asked. They stood in the hallway, the door to the lounge room now open, keeping an eye on the two Homeland agents, the senior guy still unconscious, the guy with the bad back and wrecked shoulder still moaning. Acton had field stripped the Homeland weapons, laid the pieces on a side table, neat. Walker was going through their wallets and phones. They each had two phones.

'Reputation only,' Acton said. 'And those phones? The Blackberry is government issue.'

'And the other ones are burners,' Walker said. Then he called out to the Agent Kingsley: 'Password to your burner phones?'

'One-two-three-four,' Kingsley replied, his voice distant and dejected.

'They didn't even change the pre-set passwords,' Acton said.

'They never figured they'd get caught,' Walker replied. With the screens unlocked he saw that each phone had only two numbers stored: Kingsley's had *PJ* and *DS*. The other agent's had *Kingsley* and *DS*. And Walker knew that agent's name was Peter Jennings, because he'd just seen his ID. The call log in each burner phone had started yesterday, when this little clean-up operation was put into motion. AD was giving them orders. 'Is DS for Deputy Secretary Harvey?'

Walker looked at Kingsley and waited for a reply. When none seemed forthcoming, he repeated: 'Matt. Matt. Look at me. That's it. Who's DS?'

'Yeah, it's DS Harvey,' Agent Kingsley replied. 'He gave us the phones.'

'You sure?'

'I'm positive.'

'How many of you are there?'

'Huh?'

'How many phones did he give out?'

Matt hesitated, then said, 'Five. Us two, two guys on the west coast, and his go-to man.'

'Go-to man have a name?'

'Krycek. And believe me, you don't want to try getting a jump on him.'

'Yeah, well, he's the only piece Harvey's got left on the board,' Walker said, then looked to Acton. 'I took out the two west coasters yesterday.'

Acton nodded, his expression distant.

Walker watched Acton. 'What about DS Harvey's reputation do you know?'

'He's ex-Army,' Acton replied. 'A big shot from West Point, pedigree going way back. He worked in the Rangers until he made Major, then went over to Intel, made full Colonel and in charge of intel for CENTCOM out of Qatar.'

'Military Intelligence?' Walker asked. He'd been to Central Command bases in Qatar several times, and had never heard of a Colonel Harvey – but the personnel there was close to fifteen thousand permanent forces, with a similar amount often rotating through.

'Yep. The notion of intelligence in the military always seemed an oxymoron if you ask me. Why you ask?'

'The NSA has a big presence in Qatar. But if Harvey stayed in the Army, heading on-the-ground CENTCOM intelligence, then you're right – he's a big deal. The Army's Military Intelligence Corps is about the same size as the CIA.'

'Well, as far as I know,' Acton said, 'Harvey went civilian, some kind of specialist military liaison for the DEA, became a big deal in town, some huge busts of international drug syndicates that were funnelling funds to al Qaeda and the Taliban.'

'So, he was civilian, working for the feds in the DEA, but still using all his military channels in and out of Afghanistan and the Middle East.'

'Yep. That made him a poster-boy for what could be achieved when various government agencies worked in sync. He was poached by the then Vice President to be an integral part of the Homeland Security rollout in '02 and '03 as the chief military advisor, and to oversee the roll-out of Synergy Centres across the US – places were various agencies and the military and law enforcement all come together and share resources and information. He's been there right from the start, then as Assistant Secretary of Immigration Customs Enforcement, and he's now Deputy Secretary.'

'That sounds like a political appointment.'

'It is,' Acton said. 'What's that matter?'

'Just as he's transitioned from military to civilian in the form of going to HSA,' Walker said. 'Now he's the second in charge of Homeland. Next step is either heading Homeland, or jumping over that for a cabinet position, like Sec Def.'

'Look, Walker, I don't see the relevance of any of this,' Acton said. 'If Harvey's our guy, we gotta just pass this up the chain and have someone question him. This is so far beyond my pay grade, it's lunacy to think you or I could touch him. As far as we know, he's running a Homeland Security operation that we not only know nothing about – but we're getting in the way of.'

'I'm looking for his motivation,' Walker said. 'You really think Overton and Bennet were threats to national security?'

Acton was silent.

'I worry that if Harvey is pivoting for a political position,' Walker said, 'then why jeopardise that by taking the massive risks like this clean-up, and killing a couple of Secret Service agents? Could he be trying to bury a secret that would end his ambitions? People have killed for less, here, and all through time.'

'I don't know, Walker,' Acton said. 'He's a big fish. Doing this for ambition? I don't buy that.'

'I've seen, first-hand, governments rise and fall all over the world after a few well-placed assassinations. Look at what we did in Iran. In Libya. Iraq. Look what they do in China and Russia.'

Walker looked at the Homeland agents in the front room. He started to think through possible scenarios to get to Harvey. To question the guy. Alone.

Acton said to Walker, his tone hushed, 'This woman, Rachel Muertos?'

'Yeah?' Walker looked across to him.

'How well do you know her?'

'I've known her about twenty-four hours. Why?'

'What do you understand of her involvement in this?'

'She's tracking a people-smuggling outfit out of Syria, trying to find Almasi's contact back here,' Walker said. 'Something I also have an interest in.'

'Right. I know nothing about that,' Acton said. 'To me Almasi meant money-laundering, not people. Others at Homeland can worry about people-smuggling. What else do you know about Rachel Muertos?'

Walker paused a beat, trying to read the look on Acton's face for some kind of clue as to what he was getting at. 'What's that mean?'

'I mean, what do you know about her husband?'

'That he was State, and was killed while on duty.'

'Right. Well, you need to know more.'

55

'Steve Muertos,' Acton said to Walker. 'Did Rachel tell you he was Secret Service, once upon a time?'

'No,' Walker said. 'And Hayes didn't mention that this morning.'

'Hayes is a newbie; Steve Muertos was way before her time,' Acton said. 'When Overton brought this to me, the favour to get access to the nano-tech trace we've been developing, and then the off-books surveillance? I gave her the okay without a second thought. I let her bring in Hayes and Bennet. It was meant to be twenty-four to forty-eight hours, tops, of us putting in our off-time to share the watch duties. I said okay because I knew Steve Muertos, and I like to think he'd have done the same if the situation were reversed.'

'What's his story?'

'He was a quiet guy, but solid, and rose quickly in the Service, ended up running the Boston Field Office, then went through a change of life when he met Rachel.'

'Change how?'

'He barely survived a joint-taskforce raid on a group in Boston; it was a shoot-out, all the perps killed after their intel was compromised and they lost all tactical advantage. He got shot up some, and lost a couple of his agents, and post-recovery he bugged out – he moved sideways to State, working a desk in DC, which is where he met

Rachel. I'd gone through initial training with him – he was a close friend of mine, and Rachel was a close friend of Overton's, because Overton's dad used to be a Fed and he helped out Rachel's mum way back.'

'She told me that part.'

'But Steve?' Acton looked down at his hands 'After starting at State, it's like he was born again; a totally different guy. He loved it. He'd always butted heads in the Service because he was never a riser, never really wanted to stick his neck out and get noticed and fight people for promotions. He just wanted to do his thing, in his own time. But he found his *thing* at State.' Acton looked up at Walker. 'He once told me over drinks that being at State gave him the room to move the way he wanted, get ahead of crimes and be more preventative. I didn't ask him to explain it more, but he went on this different path and he enjoyed it. Then he was seconded to the Mid East when the Arab Spring became a thing, along with near-on everyone else at State who had a background similar to his—'

'Similar how?'

'He was Kurdish, from Iraq, came out after the first Gulf War, where he'd served alongside our forces,' Acton said. 'As far as I know he hadn't touched a firearm since leaving Boston, and didn't want to go into the fray, but State had him on their first flight over there – they sent everyone they had, until Benghazi happened, and they flew near-on everyone back until things cooled down. Wasn't until recently that he got a posting back there, doing some consulting work out of our new compounds.'

'Where was he working?'

'State sent him to Egypt, Libya, Syria, all the fun places, going back and forth and doing ground work for our diplomatic missions to reassert their influence.' Acton crossed his arms. 'Six months ago he disappeared. Officially listed as KIA, as a UN convoy he was in was taken out by a terror cell. I'm told they never officially ID'd his remains, but the four-vehicle convoy was near enough to vaporised.'

'And Rachel Muertos going over there was, what?' Walker asked, watching the young Homeland agent cradle his arm. 'A fact-finding mission, to see for sure her husband was dead?'

'I don't know,' Acton said. 'But I heard she was over there, with State, on assignment. That came from Overton, who I owed a couple of big favours, and so when she asked me to help keep eyeballs on these two Syrians, I didn't think twice about saying yes. And now look where we're at. Rachel's back here, with unknown motive. I've lost two colleagues. And then there's these two crooked Homeland agents in my living room.'

'And there's two dead Syrians,' Walker assed. 'All in the space of twenty-four hours.'

'What's it all mean?' Acton's eyes searched Walker's.

'I'm planning on finding out,' Walker said.

'But you trust her?'

'I've had no reason not to,' Walker said.

'But you've known her for what, twenty-four hours?' Acton said, looking into the front room. 'I don't think these guys know anything beyond what they're told to do. And I think if Harvey is calling the shots, then he's got a legitimate reason.' He looked back to Walker. 'I don't think the rot is there. I think there's something bigger that these guys, and we, aren't privy to. And I don't think butting heads with a guy like Harvey is the way to go forward.'

Walker nodded. He wasn't so sure about how best to deal with Harvey. But having Homeland agents try to kill him meant Harvey wasn't going on his Christmas card list anytime soon.

'I mean, Acton said, 'with a guy in Harvey's position, what do you think you can do?'

'I'll do what I can.' Walker scrolled through the agents' phones again. 'So, Steve Muertos goes to Syria and is killed by terrorists – and Rachel gets herself over there, attached to a legit op looking into people-smuggling, with what in mind? To see his body for herself? To search for a ghost? To find answers? Justice?'

'Could be any of those,' Acton said. 'I think you need to find that out, before you go after Harvey.'

Walker nodded. 'Any American in Syria had a big fat target around their neck.'

'I know that. Maybe Rachel can't deal with it all. It's understandable.'

Walker said, 'When did the convoy attack occur?'

'About six months back,' Acton replied. 'It looked like there were no survivors. But then there was a possible sighting, in Syria. He, and Overton, and Rachel, all went back a long time. I'd worked with him, so I was involved from the get-go – I was happy to help out. But this was meant to be a few hours' worth of surveillance apiece. Hell, Almasi's small fry compared to what's on our books right now.'

'You were Overton's senior agent in the Service?'

Acton nodded. 'I'm Special Agent in Charge of Counterfeit Investigations.'

'So, what do you think happened with Steve?'

'Dead. Kidnapping gone wrong, drone strike, IED, stray bullet from any one of dozens of different forces fighting there – take your pick; we'll never know. State assigned him along with a dozen others to make contact with the opposition groups that Washington thought they could bear to do business with post the current regime. He was there to dole out money to the so-called "good guys". One day he didn't report back. That's the game over there.'

Walker was silent. Taking it all in.

'I told Overton that,' Acton continued. 'And I was there when she told Rachel that her husband must be presumed dead. But I figure she wouldn't buy it from us, so she left, to go and see for herself. I got the feeling that until she had a body to ID, she'd never believe it.'

'I've met people like that,' Walker said. 'I get it.'

'So, what do we do with this?' Acton looked to Walker. 'If I even mention to someone up the chain that we need to look into Deputy Secretary Daniel Harvey, it's gotta be iron clad.' He gave a nod towards the two agents in his living room. 'Given this guy's injuries, he'll lawyer up and plead the fifth and whatever he's told us will be tossed out as information given under duress. It'll go nowhere.'

Walker said, 'How much time can you buy me?'

'Time?'

'How long can you keep these two guys locked up, and shut off from communication?'

Acton searched Walker's face for a clue as to what he was thinking but he found none beyond the obvious. 'You're going to go after Harvey yourself, despite everything I've just said?'

'The thought crossed my mind that he and I should have a conversation.'

'You're mad, Walker. Harvey's as good as untouchable. Leave it to someone else, high up, in the system.'

'Who would that be?' Walker said. 'The Secretary of Homeland Security? She'll look at me and you like we're something stuck on her shoe. Tell her that her star recruit is corrupt and – and what? – that he's part of a conspiracy that stretches back to Syria, but we don't know what it's about, or what the endgame or ramifications might be, let alone his motive?'

Acton said nothing.

Walker continued, 'But if Harvey is indeed the guy who ordered me dead at the farmhouse, and if he's behind this – and may have other answers that I'm after – then I want a chance to hear it from him.'

'You can't just barge into his office and demand answers,' Acton said. 'He'll have you arrested and on the first ghost flight out to some country where you can easily be disappeared without any form of oversight or recourse – he's got *that* kind of power when it comes to national security.'

'I'll find a way to get to him one-on-one,' Walker said. He looked at Acton hard, wanting the guy to come around. 'But I need a *window*. I need time, just a little, to manoeuvre.' He gestured to the two Homeland agents. 'How long can you keep a lid on this?'

Acton looked pained as he glanced at the two guys in his house, one conscious, one not, then down at his feet, then up at Walker, like he'd calculated it all and weighted it up. 'Best case: forty-eight hours.'

'I'll take it.'

'I said forty-eight hours was *best case*. Who knows when these idiots have a check-in? It could be in a couple of hours, right? I can only stall so long, if it really does go all the way up to Harvey.'

'Fine with me, just string things out as long as you can.'

'I need to figure out where to transfer them to. They need medical attention.'

'You'll find a place,' Walker said. 'Maybe take them back to where they whacked Bahar?'

'It's not that simple. This might get out of my control,' Acton said, again looking over at the two Homeland men. 'Someone might fret over these two a-holes – if not their agency, then Daniel Harvey himself. If they come looking here for them . . .'

'Put your family in a safe house, and keep a low profile,' Walker replied. 'Leave the rest to me. I *want* Harvey worried about these two, I *want* him wary, because that's when he'll make a mistake.'

Then, before Acton could agree or disagree, they both heard a knock on the front door.

56

Hayes and Muertos stepped into the hall, looked at Walker and Acton, then took in the scene in the front sitting room. Hayes and Acton embraced. Muertos looked from the two Homeland guys to Walker, then Acton, with whom she shared an awkward hug. Then she stood close to Walker, looking up at him, her expression tinged with guilt or apprehension, or something else entirely.

'How's the arm?' Walker asked.

'Fractured clean through both bones.'

'I'm sorry.'

'They set it without hassle, said it will heal fine. I think I'm still high on the pain meds.'

Walker put a hand on her shoulder. 'You know I had to, right?'

'You had to,' Muertos said, nodding. 'We've have been killed otherwise, I know that. Though you could have tried breaking your own wrist.'

'Pretty sure my bones are indestructible,' Walker replied. He was glad to see that she was in good spirits, all things considered.

She pointed at the Homeland guys. 'How'd this go down?'

'They got to Bahar at the hospital, and then were coming here to get to Acton.'

'Their final target to clean up.'

'Yep.'

'Have you figured out who they're working for?'

'A Deputy Secretary at Homeland,' Walker said. 'Daniel Harvey.'

'Never heard of him,' Muertos said.

'I have,' Hayes said. 'You're sure?'

'He's our next lead,' Walker said, then updated Muertos and Hayes, right up to his plan to find Daniel Harvey.

'I'm going with you,' Muertos said.

Walker nodded.

'How are you planning on doing this?' Acton asked. 'Make an appointment at St Elizabeths and roll on in to question their second in charge?'

'I'm gonna reach out to him,' Walker said. 'Get him someplace neutral. Get him to talk, pressure him to make mistakes.'

'Walker, I don't think you understand who it is we're talking about,' Hayes said. 'The superstar Deputy Secretary of Homeland? He's not going to *meet* with you. And if this *is* some grand conspiracy he's involved in, he'll send a tactical team to put a bullet or ten between your eyes. Or a drone and a missile. Or all of the above, just to be sure.'

'I don't think so,' Walker said.

'Why?' Acton said.

'Because of you two,' Muertos said, and Walker nodded. 'You're alive, and soon you'll be somewhere secure and off the grid, and that's going to piss him off, right? Plus, you've got these two. So, you're insurance, and as long as it stays that way Walker and I will be fine.'

'Well,' Hayes said, 'I'm just saying, I think you'll get as far as the front door before all kinds of legal threats come flying at you.'

'She's right,' Acton said. 'Even with this agent's testimony, if it holds, which I doubt because of the injuries he's sustained, it'll get nowhere. Harvey's untouchable.'

Walker smiled. 'Something I've learned, first-hand, many times over: no-one is truly untouchable. I understand what you're saying. A guy like Harvey is above the law, because he *is* the law. Which is fine by me, because I don't plan on using the law against him. That'll be something that you have to do, in the aftermath.'

Acton said, 'How are you going to do that?'

Walker looked to Muertos. 'I'm going burn his house down.' He let the silence hang in the room for a moment before he continued, saying aloud what they were all thinking. 'You guys all need to decide what happens next, and be at peace with it. If the buck stops with Harvey, then I say he deserves what's coming to him, because he's killed two of your friends, as well as being up to something seriously no good. So, if you have objections to this being done my way, the hard way, then speak up now.' He looked at Acton and Hayes, then to Muertos. 'Rachel and I want some answers. You two deserve some vengeance. And none of that will happen if we play this the nice way, because Harvey sure as shit won't be playing nice.'

'Do it,' Hayes said. 'Whatever it takes. For Sally and Jim.'

Walker looked to Acton, who seemed ambivalent. They all looked to Muertos. She was silent, and still.

Then, she said, 'How do we get to him?'

57

Walker and Muertos stood inside the open front door to Acton's house, the two Secret Service agents alongside them. He looked again at the burner phones of the two Homeland agents, which he was taking with him.

'You guys had pre-paid burners too,' Walker said to Acton and Hayes.

'Overton got them from Walmart,' Acton said. 'Four handsets, paid in cash. For this op only.'

'But no matter the phone's pedigree, it shows a lot, right?' Walker said. 'The government can subpoena the information and gain access to all the metadata, like which number called which, when and for how long, where the caller was at any given time.'

'Yep,' Hayes said. 'But there's no need to get a warrant; all the information is available to government agencies under the Patriot Act. It's all online, in the Intellipedia portal. You just have to fill out a form and state why you need the data – like, it's a suspect involved in an imminent attack, or a person of interest – and it's all available inside five minutes. But if you want access to Intellipedia you need someone on the inside to access the secure LAN at St Elizabeths, or one of their Fusion Centres.'

'I know a guy with access,' Walker said.

Hayes nodded, then looked to Acton.

'I'll take my family to a hotel we use for witness protection,' he said. He looked to Hayes. 'Can you accompany them, while I make some enquiries about Overton and Bennet, and deal with these two Homeland idiots?'

Hayes bit her lip. 'Of course.'

'I'll have another agent come help deal with them,' Acton said, then passed Walker a handwritten note. 'Here's my cell number.'

Walker took it and pointed at the Homeland guys. 'Where are you going to move them?'

'I'll figure it out when they're in a car. I've got a few options,' Acton replied. 'You better trash their cell phones. When Harvey can't reach them, you can bet your life that he'll have some tech heads at Homeland run a location trace on them.'

Walker nodded and passed Acton the Homeland agents' wallets, minus the cash, Kingsley's ID and a credit card, all of which he put in his jacket pockets along with the Homeland burner phones.

'I'll contact you tonight,' Walker said. 'See where things are at by then.'

Acton nodded. 'Good luck.'

Walker headed out the door, and Muertos followed right after. He went to the little Ford sedan, and tossed her the keys to the Homeland agents' SUV. 'Follow me. Take this phone, call me if we get separated.'

'Borrowed another car, have we?' Muertos said.

Walker smiled, climbed into the Ford and started the engine. He waited until he saw Muertos cross the road and get into the SUV before he headed up the street. He kept Muertos visible in his rear-view mirror and enjoyed the silence as he drove to the feeder road towards DC. Shortly after, they both pulled into a car park beside a gas station and in the front of group of shops. He used some of the Homeland agents' cash to buy a pre-paid cell phone from an off-brand Radioshack-type of store, along with a small set of binoculars. When he returned to the cars Muertos was waiting with two cardboard cups of coffee.

As he removed the packaging from the phone and put it together with the sim card, Walker said over the roof of the Ford, 'Why didn't you tell me about your husband being killed in Syria?'

Muertos looked away, first towards the gas station or something beyond, then down at her coffee, then up to Walker. 'It didn't seem necessary to tell you,' Muertos said, now looking around the car park, her breath, warmed from the hot black coffee, fogging in front of her. 'That's my driving force, sure. I want to know what happened to him. It was a set-up, did Acton tell you that?'

'No. Set-up how?'

'I'm trying to find out, and just like you and your father, I want answers from all involved, which now means Harvey.'

'Do you think Harvey could be the US contact for Almasi?'

'When I heard of his involvement the thought crossed my mind. You?'

'It's looking that way.' Walker sipped his coffee and looked around the lot. 'But we need motive. It's important, to understand, to be sure.'

'Well, nothing's changed between you and me, has it?' Muertos said. 'I'm sorry I didn't tell you my motive before, from the get-go. Now you know. We both want answers. For both of us, it's personal.'

'You should have told me.' Walker headed away and tossed the empty phone pack in the nearest trash can, then joined Muertos at her side of the Homeland car and took his cardboard cup of coffee from the roof of the Ford. He powered up the cell phone; the screen lit up and told him it had fifty per cent charge. He went to the browser and typed in the webpage he used to contact Paul.

'So, I'm telling you now.' Muertos looked up at him. 'This has been very hard for me.'

Walker was silent, waiting for the page to load.

'It's just superfluous information, isn't it?' Muertos said. 'We each have driving forces. Your father. My husband.'

'Motive is important.' Walker sipped the coffee, black and strong. The site loaded, a gamer discussion group on the dark web, something Paul used for communications, a site never found on any surface Internet searches, and something very innocuous to anyone looking on. He went to the open discussion link and typed in his usual greeting, along with a basic code that was the alpha-numeric numbers to his new phone. Paul would get an automatic ping on one of his computers in near enough to real-time, then call him on his own new burner phone.

'If it's that important to you,' Muertos said, 'then you should have asked why I was doing this.'

'Pretty sure I did, when it was clear you weren't working on this with State.'

Muertos shrugged.

'Okay,' Walker said. He put the new phone's ringer volume right up, pocketed it, and looked at Muertos. 'Clearing-the-air time. What do you think happened to your husband?'

'It's complicated,' Muertos said.

Walker paused, then said, 'We've nothing else to do just yet, so try me.'

Muertos nodded. 'Okay. Look, one of his jobs in Syria was assessing which groups the US would arm and supply. He was paying and organising for the Department of Defence to supply arms and munitions to friendly rebel groups who were anti-regime and non ISIS or ISIL. He gained knowledge on those getting the Syrian population out of the conflict zone – through official refugee channels, and through back-channels for those who had the money to pay their way into the West.'

'Almasi's group?'

'He brought them to light.'

'You think Almasi ordered the hit on your husband.'

'I now think Harvey of Homeland Security ordered the hit on him, yes.'

'Why would he do that?'

'That's what I want to know.'

Walker weighed it up. It was looking that way. Some kind of corruption on the ground, leading to the contacts moving back here, and a clean-up operation. 'What do you know about the attack on your husband's convoy?'

'They knew exactly where they'd be, and when – and all that information was compartmentalised, and being run by the DoD, so I've known since the get-go that it had an inside connection.'

'Harvey could have accessed the info.'

'Accessed *and* actioned.' Muertos sat on the bonnet of the Ford. 'But the thing is, the joint taskforce I got myself into ran a lot of Syrian agents, to keep eyes and ears open for anything like that happening again. And there was a trusted source who swore that they saw my husband two weeks after the attack, alive and well, in Aleppo.'

'Could anyone verify that?'

'No.'

'Maybe he told you what you wanted to hear, thinking it might get him a bigger payday or some other favours.'

'No.'

'How can you be sure?'

'Because no-one knew of my connection to him, because we had different operational names in the field, and no-one there knew me.' Muertos paused, then said, 'Walker, before I was there, what drew me there – there was this Syrian agent who came in and named my husband, an American that he'd dealt with before, and said he was headed north – *after* his death. I read that report and I headed over there, and I didn't give a shit if they found me out and put me in prison for it. I had to *know*. I went there, and I checked it out as much as I could – but that was it, the only reference, until the day I met your father.'

'Do you think your husband is alive?'

'It's possible. I thought it. Now it's a distant possibility. I got into Aleppo with an NGO convoy, and I spent six days talking to every source that he could give me, but it all came up cold. So, I tried the human-trafficking front, talking to all those who were to go on to the border or coasts via the coalition forces fighting the regime. The only ones who had seen an American man attached were linked back to the group that Almasi was running. So, I went back to Damascus, and got myself attached a State joint taskforce battling human trafficking, and two weeks later I went to the meet with Almasi in attendance.'

'Being thought of as dead could give your husband a lot more room to move as an undercover.'

Muertos nodded. 'And until recently, I thought he might have gone dark to find out who was behind the hit. Seriously, I'd thought he may have done just that. Four other Americans were killed in the attack on the convoy, as well as a bunch of internationals from Médecins Sans Frontiéres.'

'And now you think it could be because he made Almasi's contact here. Which could well lead back to, or be, Harvey.'

'Yep. Think about it. If Steve found out about Harvey, he could have gone out there, off reservation so to speak, gathering intel to get him – and then the attack on his convoy. It's the sort of thing he'd want to do. He loved undercover work, blending in, disappearing and then emerging with a big win. But whether he was killed on that convoy, or if he survived and went dark . . .'

'You think he'd do that to you, pretending to be dead for this long?'

'Didn't your father do that to you?'

Walker nodded. 'Yeah, he did that. To me, and my mother. Because of something he had a hand in creating, which then got set loose among terror outfits, something called Zodiac.'

'Well, I think Steve just might do it too, to protect me, especially if he suspects Harvey,' Muertos said. 'Part of me thinks: what if he knew who was doing all this, and didn't get the chance to tell anyone? I mean, after all, the Secret Service is run by Homeland.'

Walker was silent.

Muertos sipped her coffee then tossed the cup and said, 'What? *What*, Walker? Is this suddenly too much, because I didn't tell you everything from the get-go?'

'No,' Walker said. He headed around the car to face her.

'What then?'

'I know that this has gone from shit to worse,' Walker said. 'I know that. Look at what's happened in the past twenty-four hours: all the *dead*, and those *surviving*. It's a *wreck*. Harvey, known operationally to his guys as *AD*, is clearing house. He's near the end of his objective, and we still don't know what that is, although it has something to do with human trafficking. So, where we currently find ourselves in this story is right at the grim end, and I've gotta tell you, Rachel, these kind of stories – where you're holding out hope against despair – they're doomed. I've been here so many times, had agents I've been running disappear in the field because something they were all touching on suddenly came to a close. I've seen it, lived it. It never ends well, and you seldom get closure. I'm saying this because there might be no satisfying end for you, so steel yourself for that. You might never find out the truth about your husband. Or you might find out what happened – but that knowledge might well be something you'd rather forget.'

It was the first time he'd called her Rachel, and it was the familiarity and care as much as the content of what he'd said that made her eyes water. It got to her, it was personal, as if the gravity and weight of all that she'd lost, all that perhaps she might yet have to lose, arrived in that one moment.

'Are you telling me to walk away?' she said. 'To let you fix this?'

'I'm saying that you can. It's an option. I'll get to Harvey. I'll get what answers I can, exact what justice I can. You don't have to be there.'

'I need to *know*,' Muertos said. 'I need answers. Not justice, though if – if Steve's really dead, and it comes back to Harvey? And if that in turn is connected with Sally's death? Then, sure, I want *justice*, Walker. I want it *bad*.'

'Okay,' Walker replied. He looked around the car park. 'Okay. Just stay behind me, the whole way. We'll both get answers.'

Then a phone rang in Walker's pocket.

58

'Breaking protocol,' Walker said into the phone.

'And we're gonna need new phones after this convo, because I have news,' Paul said. 'I've got the info on the owner of that farmhouse that blew. You sitting down?'

Walker said, 'Do I need to?'

'My search led to a company, registered to a tax office in the Caymans,' Paul said. 'Took some digging. But in the end, there's a paper trail that leads to one Senator *Charles Lewis,* of Connecticut. He's a big shot, Armed Services Committee, Ways and Means, and Intelligence Oversight. Got his fingers in powerful pies all around town. Might be a good time to leave this thing alone, my friend?'

'Let's never mention *powerful pies* ever again.'

'Noted. I'm sending you a dark-web link to a site I created to house all his relevant info.'

'Okay, thanks,' Walker said. 'And I've got a new name for you to look into.'

'Why am I not surprised . . .' Paul said. 'Okay, shoot.'

'Deputy Secretary of Homeland Security, Daniel Harvey.'

'Okay, great,' Paul said. 'Let's make some more enemies in high places, shall we?'

'Can you do it?'

'What do you want, his social-security number?' Paul was getting exasperated. 'Or how many times he goes to the toilet each day? I can get info, sure, but you know what? *Behaviour* is still harder to find out about, yes, even online, unless the target's house and office are wired up the wazoo.'

'Paul, I want you to see if he has connections to any of our Syrian friends.'

'Okay. I'll email you the link to site where I dump the Senator's info, and I'll do the same for this Harvey guy.'

'Anything jump out at you in the Senator's background?'

'I'm not an analyst, but he looks like any other federal politician, I'd imagine,' Paul replied. 'By that I mean he's led a boring enough life. Old-school money from New England. Family has deep ties in industry and politics all the way back to the *Mayflower*. Had family serve in the Revolutionary War, the Civil War, then pretty much every other war after that. That said, he's got *big* money backers, as anyone would have to have to get to that level of politics. That's one place you could look? Big money does funny things to people, and to get the kind of money they need to run for office and keep it, they've often done some not-so-funny things, right?'

'Did you get access to the Senator's security-clearance files?'

'Yep.'

'That's where I'll start,' Walker said. 'They've already done the leg work for me – if there's areas of concern, they'll be in there. See if you can get the same for Harvey, as well as any worries that may have come up inside his military records.'

'Hacking the Pentagon, sure, why not, I'll put that on my list,' Paul said. 'When do you need all this?'

'Now.'

'Okay. So, I've been up all night doing this. You know, there's these weird people I've heard of who need this thing called sleep.'

Walker ended the call. He pocketed the phone, then checked the two Homeland agents' phones. Neither had received a call, but he figured that would change pretty soon once those guys didn't check back in with Harvey.

'What do we do now?' Muertos said.

'Let's leave the borrowed Ford here and take the Homeland vehicle,' Walker said. He took the acquired Homeland cash out of his shirt pocket, about five hundred and change, and tucked it under the sun visor, then put the keys in the side pocket of the car and locked it. He felt bad for the high school teacher in Virginia, but figured the car would be noticed and towed soon enough, and would find its way back, and eventually that teacher would find the nice little bonus. Walker liked teachers. He'd married one, once. His distant thoughts of Eve soon turned to Muertos and her husband Steve, and while he had the new phone in hand he sent a message to Paul to look up Steve Muertos of the State Department, formerly of the Secret Service, for a deep background check.

Sure, Paul replied. *Add it to the list.*

Walker drank his coffee. It was just checking over noon, and he shook off what had happened inside twenty-four hours and knew he needed to find a way in to Harvey – but then figured the guy had six or more hours of office work ahead of him, and as bent as Harvey might be, he would have all kinds of official demands on his time. Walker tossed his empty coffee cup in the trash, and then went to the Homeland SUV and held the passenger door open for Muertos.

'Where we headed?' she asked.

'Watergate Hotel.'

In his lap he held the two cell phones. One of them rang silently, vibrating, the screen lit up with one word: DS. It stopped after about thirty seconds. Then, as long as it might take someone to call the other phone, the other one rang. Same thing, same caller – DS – then it stopped.

•

Deputy Secretary Daniel Harvey ended the call for a second time. He looked out the window at the sprawling campus of St Elizabeths. They'd missed their check-in, but they were likely still operational, too close to the target. He'd figured he'd give them another two hours before sending Krycek to their location.

59

'Really?' Muertos said, looking up at the infamous landmark. 'The Watergate Hotel?'

'I'm a sucker for history,' Walker replied. 'Who doesn't like a good 'gate suffix. Nipple-gate. Monica-gate. Panama-gate. In fact, since Rio in '16, I think we've come full circle.'

'How about we're going to get killed-gate.'

'Not today, Muertos, not today.' He instructed the bell boys that he wanted to access his car once it was parked, then walked through the doors opened by staff in smarted-up versions of old-world-opulence-type uniforms. 'This place works, logistically, for what I want to do, because it curves back and looks onto itself. That, and we're nice and central – there are plenty of places we can bug out to, if it gets to that.'

He remembered something Bloom had drilled into him: *Always know the layout of a place you're going to use when making a critical contact become a tactical advantage.* He'd been here twice, as a teen, and remembered the basic layout of the building. Despite the recent renovations, the building's footprint remained the same, and the exits and entry points seemed familiar.

'And we're doing what here?' Muertos asked as she followed Walker, and he checked in using Agent Kingsley's licence and credit card. He booked a corner suite on level six, and was handed two key cards – stencilled with the tongue-in-cheek note: Watergate – *No need to break in.* She followed Walker across the lobby to the business centre. 'Is that wise? Won't Homeland track it?'

'Soon enough,' Walker said. He sat at a computer and typed in the URL that Paul had sent to his phone, and opened the security-clearance file for Senator Lewis. He hit print, and as pages started to stack up in the printer tray he turned to Muertos. 'I need you to go and get another room, on level seven or eight, that looks back at the suite, and we'll work there. That way we can see them coming.'

'You *want* Harvey to come to you?'

'Yes.' Walker collected the paper as it was spat out of the laser printer, then hit print on what Paul had found so far on Harvey – his military records, and security-clearance forms with dozens of pages of background checks.

'What'll having more people come after us achieve?'

'I want to know how they respond to losing their guys,' Walker said. 'And it might spook Harvey, and it will diminish whatever resources he has left. They might see the booking I made in Kingsley's name and think he and Jennings are still tracking Acton.'

'But they're not answering phones,' Muertos said. 'Which will eventually ring alarm bells.'

Walker nodded. He logged out of the webpage and cleared the browser history, then stayed by the printer, taking the pages from the output tray each time it neared capacity. He watched as Muertos went to the reception and booked the other room, then returned with two more key cards.

'If Harvey is running these agents on the side like this,' Muertos said, 'having them kill people? Well, what's stopping him from just sending a SWAT team to the location to get us?'

'He doesn't know we're alive, remember?' Walker replied, looking out the glass-boxed office in the foyer, taking in the exits and vantage points. 'When his agents don't reply, he'll send someone here to investigate. But Harvey won't risk a big visible take-down because whatever he's up to he's now winding down, not escalating. He sent those two guys to deal with Almasi and Bahar and us, then on to Acton, because I took down his better guys yesterday at the hospital.'

Muertos looked uneasy. 'He still has Krycek.'

Walker nodded. 'And he'll be here on the east coast by now.'

'But you think he'll send him here, to check in on his other two guys?' Muertos looked around the foyer, full of nervous energy.

'Yes.' Walker tapped the couple of hundred printed pages in his hands and headed for the door, Muertos in tow. He strode across the foyer and hit the lift call button. 'And in the meantime, we've got some reading to do.'

•

Harvey tapped at his desk, the burner phone on it, waiting for the call from agents Kingsley and Jennings, a call that was now two hours overdue. He typed an email including the phone numbers of his two missing agents, and demanded an immediate request for location of those phones, and sent it to the tech department. The reply came back within two minutes: both phones were at the Watergate Hotel, where they'd been for over an hour, unmoving.

Now, why are you at the Watergate . . . He called his best operative, Krycek. He had failed in San Francisco, and today was his chance at redemption.

'Get to the Watergate Hotel,' Harvey said. 'Kingsley and Jennings are there. They were meant to be taking care of Acton. See what they're up to.'

•

It took an hour of reading and arranging and Walker stepped back to admire the scene he'd arranged on the floor of the hotel room. Muertos passed him a cup of coffee made in the room's machine. The room was actually three rooms: a king-sized bedroom, an ensuite with an oversized spa bath and a walk-in shower, and a room that served as open-plan living area with a galley kitchen, and a balcony with an outdoor seating for six. Walker had moved the furniture around in the living room to create a twelve-foot space in which he could arrange his thoughts on paper, reorder the information to look for a pattern not immediately obvious.

'What's it all mean?' Muertos asked. 'What are you looing for in this mess of papers?'

Walker pointed to an area of printouts that were connected. 'My father, in Syria. And Bloom. You. Almasi. All there at the same time.' He pointed to the Senator and Harvey. 'These two have a few connections. The earliest connection I can see is that they're both part of the Society of Cincinnati.'

'What's that?'

'A hereditary club,' Walker said, picking up a piece of paper. 'A rich-old-white-guy thing, going back to revolutionary days. They meet up right here in DC.'

'You think the club's connected to this?'

'I can't see how. But it shows that they've known each other for at least twenty years, when they became members following the deaths of their fathers around the same time.'

'Their fathers probably knew each other too,' Muertos said. 'If the club is as exclusive as you say. So, the Senator and the Deputy Secretary may have been friends since they were young.' Muertos picked up a stack of bio notes on Senator Lewis. 'Think we can reach out to him, ask him about Harvey?'

'We can,' Walker said, 'but what if they're they working together on this?'

'Or was Harvey using the Senator's country house without his knowledge?'

'That's the question I'd like an answer for,' Walker said, 'before we approach Senator Lewis.'

There was a knock at the door.

60

'My agents are in place,' Fiona Somerville said as she walked into the room. 'Any sign of the guys from Homeland?'

Walker shook his head.

'This is Rachel Muertos,' he said.

'I'm Fiona Somerville, FBI,' Somerville said, and the two shook hands. 'Where's the target room?'

Walker passed Somerville the small binoculars and pointed at the room across the way, where the hotel curved and looked back on itself. Somerville looked to where Walker pointed, saw the cell phones on the bench in the suite on level six.

'How's it going to go down?' Walker asked.

'I've got six agents in the building, and another four in vehicles outside.' Somerville handed the binoculars back to Walker. 'When your guys show, we'll take them down, and we'll keep them out of the picture for eight hours. Max. But then that's it – they'll be out on the street, unless you can find evidence to warrant charges, because Harvey will know we've taken his guys, and he'll move on me.'

'Eight hours will do,' Walker said. 'And there's an Agent Clair Hayes who will ID them as her abductors, so if it comes to it maybe her Director, or the Attorney General, will step in to keep Harvey off your back until we can get to him.'

'That's all well and good, but as long as Harvey retains his power and influence, there's not a huge amount we can do – he can have all this classified as some bullshit training op, have it filed it away under national security, sweep everything under a rug.'

'He's ordered the assassination of two Secret Service agents,' Muertos said.

'Don't worry about Harvey,' Walker said, looking from Somerville to Muertos. 'He'll get his.'

'You better be right about this,' Somerville said. 'If you don't take down Harvey, you can bet he'll do all he can to take my job after I arrest his guys here today.'

'Don't worry about your job,' Walker said.

Somerville smiled. 'So says the guy with no job to speak of.'

'Take if from a pro, unemployment is vastly underrated,' Walker said, checking the scene again with the binoculars. 'Besides, I'm so busy, I couldn't possibly fit in a job.'

Somerville laughed, then looked at the scene on the floor, hundreds of pages all laid out like someone threw a thick file at a ceiling fan.

'This looks like a typical Walker mess,' Somerville said.

'Organised chaos,' Walker said. He took ten minutes to brief Somerville on everything they had, and all they'd experienced, over the past twenty-four hours. As he spoke he again checked the scene across the way with the binoculars. There was no activity. The two Homeland agents' cell phones remained on the kitchen bench of the corner suite. Muertos poured more coffee. Somerville perched on the arm of a sofa, listening.

'You really think Harvey is funnelling back-door illegals into the country?' Somerville said. Walker nodded. 'For what?'

'Money,' Muertos said. 'And perhaps the power that comes with that.'

'I don't buy it.' Somerville squatted down and scooped up some pages, part of the security clearance of Senator Lewis. 'And the Senator?'

'We'll soon find out,' Walker said. 'He and Harvey go way back though.'

'We need proof of his involvement,' Somerville said.

'Almasi and Bahar were using the Senator's house,' Muertos said. 'Isn't that damning enough?'

'But we can't yet assume that he's part of this,' Somerville said. 'That he knew Harvey was using the house for the Syrians. Unlike Walker, I need iron-clad proof at every step of the way. Something that will hold up in a court of law. And we're talking about taking down two men who help *make* the law.'

Muertos said, 'So, they're innocent until proven guilty? Even Harvey?'

'Afraid so,' Somerville said. 'Have either of you seen on the news any comment or reaction from Lewis that his house is no more?'

'No,' Muertos said.

Walker shook his head.

'Maybe he's buying the line on the news that it was a gas accident,' Somerville said. 'Maybe he has no involvement.'

Walker pointed to a picture of Harvey. 'But we know definitively that Harvey sent those two Homeland agents there to kill Almasi and Bahar at the country house, and that while there they detained us, called Harvey, and got instructions to kill us.'

'And how'd you get that information from the Homeland agents?' Somerville asked Walker.

Walker gave a guilty shrug.

'See?' Somerville said. 'I think until I catch one of these Homeland guys in an illegal act, my hands are tied.'

'The guys from San Francisco looked like they had a very different skill set to the two that tried to kill us this morning,' Muertos said.

'What's that mean?' Somerville asked.

'Muertos is pointing out that they were the A Team,' said Walker, 'sent to silence her, and by extension, me, because she'd mentioned my name to the big Homeland guy, Krycek, back in Germany. I took one out of the fight, we got away, and then Harvey was forced to clean house on the west coast, using his two B Team guys.'

'What about Agent Hayes?' Somerville asked. 'Who can she identify?'

'Almasi and Bahar, both dead,' Walker said. 'And the two Homeland guys from San Francisco.'

'They were the ones to pull her over?' Somerville said.

Walker nodded. 'The timeline is: they picked her up, dropped her to the Syrians, then they came after us. The Syrians were then tasked with taking out Overton, Bennet and Acton, while those guys headed west to take care of us.'

'But you messed things up for them,' Somerville said.

'Least I could do.'

Somerville took the binoculars and checked the view. All clear.

'Right,' Somerville said. 'I can use testimony from Hayes and Acton. And the unconscious so-called B Teamer, if I can get him to talk. The one who spoke to you will be inadmissible.'

'You'll get a chance to interrogate the two A Team guys soon enough,' Walker said.

Somerville motioned across to the empty suite. 'You really think they'll turn up there?'

'I think they're close,' Walker said. 'And you need to make sure they're completely out of the fight this time, until I get to question Harvey.'

Somerville nodded, but she didn't look sold, like letting Walker get to Harvey first would be a bad idea.

'Walker,' she said. 'You know that even though your father was there in Syria, this might have nothing at all to do with his Zodiac terror program, right?'

'I know.'

Somerville nodded. 'You can question Harvey. But don't jeopardise my case, okay? If the buck stops with him – or even Senator Lewis – I want to throw the book at them, okay?'

'Deal,' Walker said.

'That big one scares the hell out of me,' Muertos said. 'Krycek.'

'He's just a big bully, and uses his looks to intimidate. He'll learn his lesson soon enough.' Walker pointed to the piece of paper he'd marked HAYES. 'But what's bugging me is that the connection is missing. I don't believe that Hayes was made by chance, tailing Almasi and Bahar. How'd they make her, if Overton's little four-person operation was so close-knit? They got a jump on her, with the two A Team guys. We need to figure out how.'

'Maybe while she was tailing Almasi out of DC,' Somerville said. 'The two Homeland were also tailing him, as an escort of sorts, to make sure he got to the Senator's house safe and sound?'

'I'm not so sure,' Walker said. 'I think there's a missing person here, someone who connects them. Someone who told Harvey about Overton's off-books surveillance op.'

'This is Homeland Security and Washington DC we're talking about here,' Somerville said. 'They can pretty much watch anyone they want, even Secret Service agents on a side project.'

'I think that person is going to turn up in the suite next door when they track those Homeland phones.'

'Maybe.' Walker took the small binoculars and surveilled the suite. The door was still closed, the room empty of people. He stayed behind the curtains, watching.

'So, what's your next step?' Somerville asked.

'Short of getting whoever turns up to talk, we need to dig deeper on Senator Lewis,' Walker said. 'There are too many unknowns in his background. He's been a Senator for fourteen years and was in banking before that – his life before politics is largely vacant but for some social events. Harvey's the opposite: he's all there in his service records and security-clearance forms. Four years in Kabul. Made a name for himself for getting things done. And you know what area he excelled in?' Walker pointed to a page. 'Handling the flood of people-smugglers, and the drug trade out of Afghanistan, the two shadow economies often overlapping. He stamped out a bunch of human traffickers. Rooted them out and smashed their networks. Ruthless – he had a good team of private contractors kicking down doors and executing the top guys throughout Afghanistan, Iraq, Libya and Syria. So successful they sent him back during the Arab Spring to report on the refugee streams out of the Mid East and northern Africa, keeping eyes on all known and suspected traffickers. He spent a couple of years in the region, and his recommendations led to networks in each country being shut down by a specialist taskforce that preceded the one Muertos here was on. So, when Acton said Harvey was in Homeland from the get-go, he was wrong, technically. He was still Army until six years ago, but he'd been their military liaison with Homeland Security since 2002, as well as working across DEA taskforces. And we've got all his postings, all his secrets, laid bare from the moment he joined the Army at West Point, to twenty-four years later when we arrive at today.'

Walker fell silent. He re-arranged the piles of paper, some of them twenty pages thick. There was no reference to an Agent Krycek, so he figured he might be an off-books private contractor personally reporting to Harvey. The two Homeland guys from San Francisco were both ex-Army. Both had served in Afghanistan, with the 110th, which wasn't Harvey's unit, but there were tens of thousands of Army guys rotating in and out of Afghanistan and Ira and JSOC over the first decade of the wars there, so they may have made contact prior to Homeland. Walker had been in Kabul overlapping the times of all three of them. He'd cross-checked records, and there was nothing indicating that they had been attached to Harvey's anti-people-smuggling outfit. But they'd been attached to a lot of door-kicker units looking for HVTs, and no doubt a lot of the human-trafficking king pins were rated as High Value Targets.

'Senator Lewis was on Intelligence Oversight, and came out smelling real good when Harvey did his work,' Walker said. He held up a picture of the Senator shaking Harvey's hand in Kabul, dated just before the Senator's first re-election. The then Vice President was in the photo too, along with his entourage. 'It was a big political win, because he'd fought to give more funding to the project. It enabled Senator Lewis to get on all sorts of powerful committees, where he's remained entrenched as a real powerbroker.'

'So,' Somerville said, 'he definitely benefitted from Harvey's work.'

'Acton mentioned something about Harvey having political ambitions,' Muertos said.

'Yep,' Walker said. 'And looking at all this, and knowing the ambitions of each man, I'd put a C-note on a joint ticket of Lewis and Harvey. One's got the power and influence of the political class, the other military and Intelligence experience and who has recently segued into the political appointment of Deputy Secretary of Homeland.'

He put the papers down on the floor and studied them from afar, and then went back to Harvey's posting dates.

Somerville's cell phone rang, and she answered it, listened, then kept the line open.

'Two Homeland agents are in the lobby, they're getting the manager to provide a master key,' Somerville said. 'One of my agents on the desk says they sound like your pair: one really big, scar on his head, and one regular sized, both hard-cases.'

'That's them,' Walker said. He held the glasses to his eyes and watched the scene across the way. Waited. It didn't take long. Inside a minute, the door to the apartment opened. But it was too soon for the Homeland agents.

A single figure entered the room, pistol drawn.

Secret Service Agent Blake Acton.

61

'What the hell?' Muertos said. 'Why is he there?'

'I'm gonna find out,' Walker said. He used the hotel landline to call one of the burner phones and watched Acton through the small glasses. He could have called Acton's cell, but he preferred it this way.

Walker watched Acton stare at the phone on the table when it started to ring, just as he'd entered, as if he was thinking, *That's a coincidence.* Then another moment, another ring, and he looked at the number and saw it had a local area code. Then on the third ring Acton looked around, checking for the set-up, a camera or something, but saw nothing. Then came the fourth ring, incessant, and Walker watched Acton calculate that he had no other lead to go on, so he picked up the phone and answered it.

But he didn't speak. He answered the call with his left hand, his right still holding a large Glock pistol, not his Service-issued Sig, and not his back-up compact, so it was a burner gun, for a dirty job. Acton put the phone to his ear and listened.

'How did Bahar miss you on his kill op this morning?' Walker said. He pressed the speaker button and then put the receiver on the table.

Acton remained silent. But he looked around the hotel suite. Saw nothing. Did a double-take at the windows – then ducked out of view, behind a small wall by the entry. They could hear him breathing. Big guy, big breaths. Adrenaline pumping. Decisions forming.

'He didn't miss you, did he?' Walker said. 'You were never on the hit list. You weren't on it, because *you* sold out your own people. Overton and Bennet. And Hayes. But they kept her alive. And that added a complication for you.'

Still, Acton was silent.

'My question is: why'd you let me leave your house?' Walker said. 'If you're in this with Harvey, why'd you let Muertos and me out of your sight?'

Again, silence.

'I can guess it was two things,' Walker said. 'You wanted to keep up appearances to get your family out, and to look good in front of Hayes. Because the other option was to kill us all, and you couldn't do that, you're really not that capable.'

Finally, Acton spoke. 'Why don't you come in, Walker,' he said, his tone sharp, direct. 'Meet me. Let's talk about all this. Work something out. You'll be well taken care of. They'll even find a good job for you. You've got talents.'

'Who's they?' Walker asked.

Acton was silent.

'Lewis and Harvey?' Walker said. 'They'd never invite me on the payroll.'

'Why's that?' Acton said.

'Because I'm the kind of guy they hate.'

'A patriot? They'll love it.'

'Incorruptible,' Walker said.

Acton was quiet a beat, then said, 'Look, Walker, you've got this backward,' Acton said. His breathing and voice changed, from one of calculated reasoning to one of urgency, clutching at straws, trying to change tact. 'I'm here at the hotel because I had the phones tracked to this location. I'm here to help you out.'

'Then why have the gun drawn?' Walker said.

Silence from Acton.

'Whose Glock is it, anyway?' Walker asked.

Silence.

'If you want to help,' Walker said, 'there are two of Harvey's guys headed to you right now. How's that going to play out? You going to arrest them? Or work with them?'

Silence.

'Or you can leave,' Walker said. 'If you want to help, you can talk to the FBI, tell them everything you know, everything you've done. Help us arrest Harvey.'

'Now, why would I do that?' Acton was walking around, looking for a hidden camera. 'Why would I help the FBI arrest a guy like Harvey?'

'To avoid two counts of being accessory to the murder of two federal agents, for a start. Aiding and abetting human trafficking. Should I go on?'

'Is that what you think this is about?'

Walker looked to Somerville, who motioned him to go on with the questioning, and he replied, 'What else it is about?'

'*You* assaulted those Homeland guys at my house,' Acton said. 'One of them saying Harvey's name under duress means nothing in court, you know that. You're in trouble here, Walker. Me talk to the FBI? Please. How about you give yourself up to me and I can help you out. You're a smart guy, this is your chance to get on the right side of all this.'

'Nice try. Those two idiots back at your house were the B Team, and they tried to murder Muertos and me, two innocent citizens. And they had the body of Almasi in their car. Notice I said *had*. It was in their trunk. Now we have it.'

Acton paused for a beat, then he said, 'Homeland can trace their own vehicle. They'll clean up.'

'It's no longer in their car.'

Acton paused a beat, then said, 'Where'd you dump a body in broad-daylight DC?'

Now it was Walker's turn to fall silent. He wanted to give Acton room to speak. To reveal.

'Where are you?' Acton said.

'A step behind you,' Walker replied. He could sense another shift in Acton; he was spooked.

'I can find you,' Acton said. 'DC is a small place. Washington is the most surveyed city in America. How long do you think it'll be before we catch up with you?'

'Agent Acton, if you're part of this, and I think you are, now's your chance to come clean. One chance. I'm not the law. But you can come clean and get out of this. But if you're in my way, and you're a part of this, you're going to leave a wife and kids behind.'

Silence. Just Acton's heavy breaths. Then, 'I'm coming for you, Walker. You hear me. You have no idea what you're into. And you know what? You're nothing. And this is *my* town. I'm going to destroy you.'

Walker let Acton hang a moment, then said, 'Good luck, buddy. And my advice, for the sake of your family? Up your life insurance.'

'You want answers, I get that,' Acton said. He was breathing fast now, pacing across the room. 'This thing with Muertos's husband, with your dad, with the dead guy – what was his name? Bloom? He was like a father to you, right? You really want to find Almasi's American contact who's running it all, for what – vengeance? What's that gonna do? What's that ever done?'

'Seems you know a lot about all this all of a sudden.'

'I checked you out, Walker. And you've got a choice here. You're already on the outer. Come chat with me. Let's work something out.'

'It's about justice,' Walker said. 'And it's coming your way.'

Then there was a noise, and Acton moved towards the centre of the suite's living room, facing the door.

The two Homeland guys had gained entry, and they stood facing Acton. One was Krycek, the other was from the hospital back in San Francisco and he had a silenced pistol pointed at Acton. They were having a little pow-wow, but Acton had ended the call, so Walker and the others could no longer listen.

Somerville spoke into her phone and ordered her agents in for an arrest.

Walker watched through the glasses. The two Homeland guys facing Acton, the three of them talking. He kept expecting half a dozen FBI agents to storm the room. He watched, waited.

The wait was long. Two seconds. Three. Four. Then it happened.

The smaller Homeland agent kept his silenced pistol at Acton - then his hand jerked, and Acton's head become a cloud of pink mist as his body fell to the ground like a puppet whose strings had been suddenly cut. Two seconds later six FBI agents rushed the room, weapons raised, commands yelled, and the two Homeland agents put their hands on their heads and dropped to their knees. Walker watched them being cuffed, disarmed and then led out of the suite.

'Acton's down,' Walker said, passing the glasses to Somerville.

'He deserved it,' Muertos said.

Somerville looked to her, but she was listening to her agents via an earpiece connected to her cell phone. 'Clean arrest of those two. Confirmed, Acton's dead.'

Walker said, 'Tell them to check the master suite's wardrobe.'

Somerville relayed the message.

Walker watched through the glasses as a pair of FBI agents moved to the bedroom, where they opened the slide-across mirrored wardrobe – and jumped back as the body of Almasi fell out.

'Okay,' Walker said. 'We'll move on Harvey and Lewis.'

'Eight hours,' Somerville said. 'Harvey will be all over this. He'll have footage from the hotel of his guys being taken in by FBI agents, and we'll all be ID'd, and then he'll call my Director and demand answers – and his two men will walk. My bet would be that they'll have a way to put all this on Acton, claim that he went rogue and killed his colleagues, and Harvey will come out of this a hero.' She looked at Walker for emphasis. 'Eight hours, Walker. You better do this right.'

62

Somerville left the hotel room, and it was quiet for near on a minute. Across the way, one FBI agent remained at the scene.

'That was neat, right?' Muertos said. 'Acton was the link that sold out Overton, and our Homeland threat is out of the picture. Two birds with one stone.'

'Nice when things go your way.' Walker checked the time on his watch – just after two pm – and went back to his mess of papers. 'I learned early on that you gotta use the law to your benefit.'

'The FBI knows who Almasi is,' Muertos said. 'He's on a watchlist, and when they make out that he entered the country via a false ID, passport, biometrics, the works, it's got to point to someone inside Homeland, right? Maybe even directly to Harvey.'

'We can hope, but all that might take time we don't have,' Walker said, leafing through his notes on Senator Lewis. 'Sure, Almasi's prints and face will match immigration's electronic records from when he landed in DC the other day. They'll run his name and it'll bounce up that it's bogus. They might even trace some digital trail that leads back to Harvey, though I doubt it.'

'But when they run Almasi's prints and mug shot through global police databases and discover he's really Tareq Almasi,' Muertos said, 'a globally wanted human trafficker, and that he was until recently was a person of interest to a joint taskforce in Syria. Then all kinds of questions are going to be asked, like how'd we let this guy into the country when he was on a watchlist? And that's got to lead to corruption at Homeland, because they run the borders.'

Walker nodded, kept reading.

'And then they'll look at Syria again,' Muertos said, 'and find out what *really* happened to my team, that the plane crash was bullshit.'

Walker nodded. 'A false passport is easy enough to get, but Harvey changing the biometrics in the system, something he's doing for his well-heeled illegal immigrants too? There's got to be a digital trail someone can trace, now that they've got Almasi as an example, highlighting the manipulations to the immigration database at the point where they're finger-printed and retina-scanned on entry.' Walker paused. He was seeing something in the mess of papers, but he wasn't. *Find the pattern*, he heard Bloom say, years ago, more relevant now than ever. The careers and lives of Lewis and Harvey spread out in paper form at his feet, carpeting the suite. 'The question remains: is Lewis in the know?'

'I think so.'

'Me too. But we need proof.'

Walker looked to Muertos, who in turn was looking at the image of Harvey in his service record.

'Harvey spent a lot of time in the Mid East,' Walker said. 'He was working there for DoD, then for Homeland.'

'He could be the US contact for Almasi,' Muertos said. 'But like Somerville asked: why? More than money?'

'He comes from old money,' Walker said. 'Senator Lewis too. Harvey from old money in Boston. Lewis from Connecticut. Asset tests and listings are part of their security clearance. Harvey's family trust runs into the tens of millions. Lewis is worth even more; he's got two sisters, they've got a bunch of kicks, extended family share in it, they're collectively valued at around three-hundred million. Both Lewis and Harvey have a lot of the same kind of stocks and companies. KBR and Halliburton types.'

Find the pattern . . .

'They're both pedigree,' Walker said, seeing the family trees he'd mapped out on the paper. 'Their connection goes way back. Harvey's family were military all the way back to before the union. At least ten years' service for every male. Then industry. They were in steel, and construction. Made fortunes in the two World Wars. All the wars, actually, since the Revolutionary. Seems the family business is geared towards all that. Same for Lewis, although his family have Navy ties. But they're both part of families we'd think of as captains of industry. Both members of the Society of the Cincinnati.' Walker looked up at Muertos. 'Did your husband ever serve?'

'Yes,' Muertos said. She seemed a bit taken aback, as though her primary driving force – of finding out what happened to her husband – was relegated to running under the surface. 'Steve was Army. Six years, before joining the Secret Service.'

'Think he ever came into contact with Harvey?'

'I'm not sure. I'd never heard his name. The Army's a big place, right? There's what, about half a million in active and reserve Army? Tens of thousands rolling in and out each year—'

'Your husband was Army . . .' Walker was starting to see the connection.

'Yes.'

'What unit?'

'Rangers.'

'Shit.'

'What?'

'Harvey had been Rangers, once, even Acton said that,' Walker said, taking the printed service jacket off Muertos and going back to the start. He started with Harvey's enlistment date at West Point, a brief service in Military Intelligence, transferred to Airborne, went to Ranger school, was involved in a helicopter accident and went back to Intelligence. 'When was your husband in the Army?'

'He left about a year before we met, and after his next tour he transferred to stateside work with the Secret Service,' Muertos said. 'That'd be . . . fifteen years this August.'

'So, sixteen years ago . . . Here. Harvey had just made Major, in Military Intel. Was posted to Afghanistan the better part of the year, then he left to go to Homeland, but was still based in Afghanistan and the Mid East for the best part of the next decade.'

'You think that my husband *knew* about Harvey's involvement with Almasi?'

'He may have. Maybe he suspected something, and that was enough to put him in their crosshairs.' Walker looked again at Muertos. 'When we confront Lewis and Harvey, we need to know more, to be prepared.'

'Okay. How are you going to get to them?'

'Just like his Homeland guys, Tweedledumb and Tweedledumber over there,' Walker said, motioning to the suite. 'I'm going to make them come to *us*.'

63

For Lewis and Harvey to come to them, Walker had to find the pattern, and it emerged twenty minutes later. It had been front and centre the whole time and he'd read over it without really giving it much thought. It all came down to communications. Covert communications. The type of thing that Intelligence officers would do in the field to contact agents. Like the Georgetown dead-drops he'd played around with as a kid. It was the ways and means of Lewis and Harvey's communication.

Walker was flipping through pages and Muertos poured more coffee when it clicked. It was all about *contact*. Making contact, out of plain sight. Walker thought about how a guy like Harvey might reach out to a guy like Lewis. Not just for a casual hello, but to collude, to be in regular contact, because there was nothing on paper, nothing in their security clearance forms, to suggest that they were friends or connected. They wouldn't use phones or email or any electronic communication, because that was the easiest way to get caught. *Washington is the most surveilled city in America.*

'Lewis and Harvey,' Walker said. 'If they're part of something together, they needed to communicate on a regular basis – and they couldn't do it in public.'

'So?'

'So, what about doing it *not* in public?' Walker said. 'Behind closed doors. Somewhere off the grid where no-one can see or hear.'

'You sound like you're onto something,' Muertos said, passing Walker a coffee.

Walker nodded. He wasn't yet ready to articulate it. The ideas were still forming. Senator Lewis and Deputy Secretary Harvey were both old money, old family, always positioning themselves to be the beating heart of the US economy. He could track that all the way back to when there were thirteen colonies, and each family, the Lewises in Connecticut, and the Harveys then in Rhode Island, were major stakeholders in what were then chartered colonies, which meant that even when they arrived over to the New World from England they'd brought with them wealth and power. Those chartered colonies, systems of government separate to that of the thirteen, were granted rights by the British King to self-govern. It was ingrained in these two families from dozens of generations back that they could and should rule over all that they surveyed, that there was none equal to them and what and where they came from. The very originators of corporate America, where money and profit rules.

First the gold, then the railroads, and steel, and construction; and war: the revolutionary war, the civil war and then, in a big, big way, the wars of the twentieth century – they had stayed in the business of war for over a century. Their economic advantage was built of the back of planes and tanks and munitions and ships and bases and bombs and rations, from the World Wars to Korea and Vietnam and then the Gulf War and then the big one: the War on Terror. Never had so much money been spent on a war, and they made hay. They had fingers in every pie, supplying and producing the constituent parts of the machinery of the US war machine for over a hundred years, and they kept their family in and around government to ensure that the family businesses always thrived.

They wanted war. War eternal. And they still self-governed. Stoked the fires. Rubbed their hands together as the world burned.

And they had to talk. In secret. In person, in places where the NSA couldn't snoop. And in all the biographical notes he'd read, there were no obvious or unusual instances where the two titans of their families connected. The Senator's father, a Senator himself, had recommended Harvey for admission into West Point, although it was on the surface a mere formability, as the Harvey family were an institution there, and were among the campuses' biggest benefactors since its inception. The family home on the Palisades along the Hudson had served as an unofficial officers' mess for Christmas parties and the birthdays of successive Commandants for as long as anyone could remember.

In isolation, each man was a part of something elite and almost unfathomable – instigators of America as we know it. Together, they formed a pattern. Collusion. Conspiracy.

But there was one place that correlated between the two men. Each was part of a club. An exclusive club. Right here in Washington. The centre of power. A club of wealthy and powerful plutocrats within the club of wealthy and powerful that was the Capital.

The Society of the Cincinnati.

The Lewises and the Harveys were more than founders of the United States, they were owners of the United States. Always there, in the background and foreground, impervious, omnipresent, eternal. An immovable object.

The Walkers also had a long tradition, and as much as Jed was unsure of his father, he was sure of one thing: for hundreds of years, for many generations, the Walkers of the United States were good at setting things right. In the background and the foreground, they unravelled and destroyed armies and networks and conspiracies and injustice. An unstoppable force.

And sometimes an unstoppable force met an immovable object.

64

They left the Homeland agents' SUV and took a cab. Walker had a note from the concierge and gave the directions to the driver. Two addresses, two stops. Muertos had a folder from the hotel stuffed with all the papers, and Walker paused at the cab's back door and looked sideways at her.

'I'm not staying behind,' she said.

'You can't get into this club,' Walker said. 'It's a gentleman's club. Guys only. Not my rules.'

'Fine. I'll watch from outside.'

'We need to blend in,' Walker said.

'I know,' Muertos said. 'I'll figure it out. I've done field work.'

'Right.'

'And if you find it's where Harvey and Lewis meet, then what? You wait for them to show? Eavesdrop on their conversation? Beat them up? Where's that get us?'

'Let's get moving,' Walker said, and Muertos slid across on the back seat and Walker sat in close next to her. 'We need to know conclusively that these two are connected to what happened in Syria, right?'

'Almasi was using the Senator's home. And don't tell me you think he didn't know about it,' she finished, raising her eyebrow at Walker.

'I'm not saying he doesn't,' Walker replied. 'It's too big a deal for it to be something on the side on Harvey's part, without the Senator's knowledge.'

'And we know he and Harvey go way back.'

'But we need to hear it from them,' Walker said. 'You heard Somerville. Because there is the slim chance that Harvey's in on something and the Senator's in the dark, we need Harvey or Lewis to confirm it.'

'And your father?'

'I'll get answers. And you'll get answers about your husband.'

Muertos was silent for a moment while she nodded and looked out her window, then she said, 'How are you going to do this?'

'It won't be with Harvey,' Walker said. The cab driver was slowing down and checking street numbers outside on the strip mall. 'He'll stonewall. But a Senator is a politician, and by definition always vulnerable to scandal – so, I'll exploit that.'

'This is your first stop,' the cab driver called over his shoulder.

'Five minutes,' Walker said, and went into the menswear store, the cab double-parked out the front with the meter running and Muertos waiting. Walker took a black suit off a rack and found a shirt in his size and was headed for the tie section when his phone rang. Paul.

•

Harvey called Lewis with an update from the field.

'All these years and no phone calls, always meeting in person,' Lewis said into his pre-paid phone. 'Now these calls are becoming a distraction. What happened to the operational security you so steadfastly put in place all those years ago?'

'We should meet.'

'Tonight, as planned.'

'Okay. And you're right,' Harvey said. 'This has come to an end.'

There was a pause, and Lewis said, 'What now?'

'My last guys were picked up at the Watergate, by the FBI.'

'Even Krycek?'

'Yes.'

'Will that be a problem?'

'They won't talk, if that's what you mean,' Harvey said. 'And I'll have them back out on the street soon enough, but there are procedures to follow. But Walker is still out there. Rachel Muertos too.'

Lewis swore under his breath, then said, 'What can they do?'

'Walker will come for us.'

'Do you have another asset you trust to do what the others failed to?'

'I'll do it myself.'

'Okay. How will you find him?'

'He'll make contact.'

'This is really the end of the line, isn't it?'

'Yes.'

'Well, I say we move forward then. We've waited long enough. Zodiac ran better than I ever thought it would. It's time to take the next step.'

65

Walker had his cell phone to his ear.

'Your Senator?' Paul said. 'Lewis? There's some weird shit going on with him.'

'Define weird,' Walker said, moving the phone to rest between his ear and shoulder as he put his new clothes on in the change room.

'His original security clearance was redacted. I think that's the word. No, actually, it's not redacted, as that'd be an official omission of sensitive information. But the guy tasked with doing the background check found some stuff that, if I'm right, got him killed, though it was officially listed as suicide by firearm. That security clearance was then cleaned of whatever he found, and that's what was entered in the database, minus a hole lot of data.'

'How'd the clearance get through?'

'Beats me, but someone up high doctored it.'

'How do you know this happened?'

'Okay,' Paul said. 'The dead guy's wife? She brought it up a bunch of times, how her husband died in an apparent suicide, gunshot to the side of the head, through and through, with his own service sidearm.'

Walker's mind filled with an image of Overton in her apartment.

'This woman, the wife, she was pregnant at the time. She couldn't believe he'd do it, and she said so for years to anyone who would listen, like the FBI, but there's nothing more they could say to her.

I've seen the reports from the scene, and it seems a legit investigation was carried out by the OPM, his employer, along with the local county crime scene. This was three years after nine-eleven, when your then Junior Senator Lewis had to go through a more thorough security check to get onto the Armed Services Committee and soon thereafter Intelligence Oversight, which meant OPM checks and then DoD's Adjudications Facility grants the final clearance.'

'Who'd the wife go to?'

'The Office of Personnel Management, where he worked, and when she got nowhere she went to the FBI, and the Department of Justice. Got nowhere there as well. She then tried lawyers, reaching out to some ambulance-chaser firms, got nothing from that either. Tried the traditional media, from national newspapers to her local TV news outlet. Nada. Got nowhere with any of them. Then she started reaching out online. Must have got the interest of someone who knows their way around the digital world, and she ended up doing a couple hours of verbal interviews with a guy who runs an anti-government conspiracy-type site on the deep web.'

'Nut job?'

'With a lot of stuff, but seeing as these are raw interviews with the widow, I listened to them all. She was dead sure that her husband was killed for what he found, and she convinced me. And you know what else? The guy that runs this site? He had a heart attack and died in a car wreck not long after the interview went online. The site's been kept alive since by online friends of his, some kind of insurance policy against the government sending a wet-work operative that obviously didn't work out.'

'You think he was killed too?'

'Three deaths make a conspiracy.'

'Three?

'The wife, the widow of the guy doing the clearance report, died the same day as the deep-web guy.'

'Damn.'

'Right? Listed that she OD'd, but was not listed as a user, nor suicidal. So, that's where I ended up, doing a search on the dark web – and the Senator's name came up. Among pieces that the guy had done on how the government tracks us via flu shots.'

'Guys writing blogs on the dark web probably talk smack about every senator since LBJ.'

'True, but the timing is interesting. His deep-web site was wiped. But he was so paranoid he had it backed up every day, and it's been pinging around the dark web ever since, like a time capsule of fifteen years of his paranoia, never being able to be wiped by governments anywhere. It's a good set-up. But scary. It means if the Senator did have his background checks changed, the investigator killed, and then had the resources to reach out and hit a guy who has a dark-web conspiracy page? That's some reach.'

'Reach an Deputy Secretary at Homeland Security would have.'

'That, and some. Sceptical of government agencies and eavesdropping as I am, I don't believe they have a fleet of black helicopters flying around whacking people who threaten their positions.'

'You really believe this story?' Walker bundled his old clothes and walked out of the change room dressed in a new suit.

'On the surface it seems like just another nut-job conspiracy theory – but given that you're looking into him, it jumped out at me. Then I checked her background, which this guy with his conspiracy page didn't do. And her background was legit. So, what she was saying might be legit too.'

'What was she saying?' Walker asked. He handed over Matt Kingsley's credit card, the clerk ran it and Walker scribbled a signature. He left behind the old clothes, then headed out to the waiting cab.

'I know you think this might be a crackpot talking nonsense on the web,' Paul said. 'I mean, that's what I thought at first, before I saw that all three people involved in it are dead.'

'Okay. I admit, it's building the case that Lewis is deep into this with Harvey.' Walker paused at the open door to the cab. 'But could we use that as proof?'

'You want to take this to court?'

'Me personally? Probably not. What was she saying about the Senator?'

'She says that her husband found out that Senator Lewis was a terrorist.'

Walker did a double-take. 'What?'

'I know, right? She said that he was running something that her husband had dug up, and that it was going to rock the world. He said he was going to reach out to someone high up, well beyond his own superiors, because this guy was a Senator.'

'What was she saying he found on him?'

'She said that Senator Lewis was running something called Zodiac.'

66

Walker ended the call and sat in the back of the cab as it motored along Massachusetts Avenue towards Dupont. Sweat beaded his forehead. Anticipation. The unexpected. *Zodiac.*

Zodiac. A program of terror cells that his father had developed in a DC think tank of about eighty serving and former Intelligence officials, when he was part of an exercise to dream up worst-case scenarios that could damage, degrade and destroy the United States – a program that had in the past two years gathered a life of its own, perpetrators unknown, each terrorist attack initiating the next unlinked terror cell. So far Walker had succeeded in averting wide-scale damage during the first three attacks, but according to his father's plans, nine more would follow . . .

'Pass me that folder,' Walker said, and he took the thick ream from Muertos and started to flick through the pages.

'What are you looking for?'

'Dates.' His father was the key. Walker knew that Zodiac was developed during a war-game scenario in 2003, when Intel agencies and policymakers and the military were scrambling for larger pieces of the seemingly endless gravy train that was government overspending writ large. Brainstorming future terror events that would make 9/11 seem tame. These two guys, Lewis and Harvey. He found Harvey's record. Despite being onboard with Homeland, he was still Army, and he'd been deployed in 2003 to Afghanistan. He spent a total of three months back in the US, split over four periods. Lewis was in the Senate. These two were as close to running the US war on terror as anyone. Senator Lewis, a terrorist. Running Zodiac. Taking it from spit-balled ideas to actuality. Orchestrating cut-out terror attacks against the homeland? To generate more work for themselves? How did smuggling illegal immigrants fit into a terror attack? How did that create chaos – to bring war, eternal, upon the homeland, which is where their business interests were tied up.

'What is it?' Muertos said.

'This is bigger than I thought,' Walker said, looking up at her. 'Harvey and Lewis? They're connected, in the system, going way back. Personally and professionally. Looking out for one another. Creating paths forward for one another. Having each other's back. It's how they've been able to survive and thrive all this time. It's like you said before – this *is* like a gangster or mob thing, because it's *organised crime*. And this is at a federal level – the airlines and the Homeland Security databases, to human trafficking and planning terror attacks.'

'What does that mean?'

'It means you really should stay back,' Walker said. But he could see the resolve in her. That if there was now proof these two had a connection to her husband's death, he'd never be able to keep her away. 'I'll get out at our next stop. You should continue on. Make contact with Somerville, meet her, wait for me to call you both in.'

'I want my answers, Walker,' Muertos said. 'I deserve them. I've been doing everything I can for six months to find out what happened to my husband – I can't just walk away from it now.'

Walker was about to speak but his cell phone rang. He looked at the screen.

Somerville.

'Yeah?'

'Walker!' Somerville said. It sounded like she was running. 'The big guy. Krycek. He's on the run!'

'What?'

There was a pause, and he heard Somerville stop running, then she was panting to catch her breath.

'He used his cuffs to choke the driver. The vehicle crashed on the Beltway. The driver and my other agent in there are KIA, as well as the smaller Homeland guy – he'd taken on the agent in the passenger seat, and they were both shot dead in the tussle. But the big guy is loose – and he's armed. I've called DC Metro PD, we're locking down the area, but a guy like that, with his skills and connections, he's going to disappear.'

'Do what you can,' Walker said. 'And I'm sorry for your loss.'

'Walker, don't go up against these guys alone,' Somerville said. 'Where are you now?'

He could hear the sound of the highway traffic in the background of Somerville's location. Of tooting horns and the grind of air brakes of eight-wheelers. He could imagine the scene of the highway: the crashed FBI vehicle, maybe with blood splatter on the windows, maybe with a dead agent hanging out an open door, the traffic slowing to rubberneck at the scene.

'When I know more I'll contact you,' Walker said, and he ended the call.

Muertos looked across at Walker.

'That big scary guy, Krycek? He got loose.'

Muertos looked at him wide-eyed, said, 'Oh no . . .'

'You really should hang back. I've got this.'

Had his father known about a connection between Lewis and Zodiac?

Muertos was silent. The driver drove on.

Find Jed Walker.

67

The cab dropped off Walker and Muertos at 2118 Massachusetts Avenue, in the Dupont Circle neighbourhood of Washington DC.

'Now I see why you needed the suit,' Muertos said, looking up at Anderson House, home of Society of the Cincinnati. It was a stone mansion on Embassy Row, designed in the Beaux-Arts style, grand on every scale. Through one of the two iron gates was a courtyard, where they walked beyond tall colonnades and came to a sign listing the dress code. Suit jacket and tie at all times. Inside the reception area was a uniformed armed guard, as well as a suited man sitting at an elevated reception desk.

'Take my phone,' Walker said, passing his cell to Muertos, then pointed down the road. 'There's the hotel we just passed on Mass Avenue, The Fairfax. Go wait in there.'

'But—'

'Wait at the hotel bar. Call Somerville and let her know where I am. Tell her to bring some agents. Tell her I'm gonna bring Lewis and Harvey here. You'll get your answers, I promise.'

'Walker—'

'Tell Somerville that Zodiac ends here,' Walker said. 'That's very important, okay? Tell her that. She'll understand. And I swear to you, Rachel, that you'll get your answers. Okay?'

Her gaze searched his, and she eventually nodded. She took the folder of paper and the cell phone and turned and left, looking over her shoulder, hesitating, but she continued on, turning right at Massachusetts Avenue and heading for the hotel.

Walker moved inside. The receptionist asked if he was here for a tour of the museum section. Instead, Walker asked him for a pen, and transcribed the number listed as *DS* in the cell phones of the two bent Homeland agents.

'I need you to call that number for me, please,' Walker said.

'I'm sorry, sir,' the receptionist said. 'This is a private members' club. We have tours twice a day, but if you need to make a call, perhaps try the hotel—'

'That is the number of one of your members, who I am meeting here, and he's going to be pissed when I tell him I couldn't get in touch via his own club's receptionist.'

'Right, sir. One moment.'

'When he answers,' Walker said as the guy picked up his phone, 'tell him where you are calling from, then pass me the phone.'

The receptionist nodded. Walker didn't blame the guy for being short, or rude. Dealing with rich and privileged idiots all day, one was bound to develop a defence to it. He dialled the number. He spoke, then passed Walker the phone.

'Harvey,' Walker said, turning his back to the receptionist. 'Or should I say, Deputy Secretary Harvey, driver of Zodiac.'

There was a pause of three seconds, then: 'Who is this?'

'Jed Walker. Surely you knew this call would come.'

There was silence on Harvey's end.

'You know where I am, and I'll be waiting for you,' Walker said. 'Bring your chum Lewis. It's time we three talked, don't you think? Half an hour, or I take Zodiac to the press. And I have all the information on you, and Zodiac, off site, so show up in person. Both of you.'

He passed the phone back to the receptionist, who ended the call.

'Deputy Secretary Harvey and Senator Lewis will be meeting me here in half an hour or so,' Walker said. 'Is there a good place in the building for a private meeting?'

'Yes, of course,' the receptionist gave a slight bow, as though making up for his earlier dismissive gesture. 'If you will follow me, sir, after you sign in here, please.'

Walker scrawled a signature on the guest book and followed the receptionist out of the foyer. In the grand ballroom, classical music was playing quietly over the sound system. Vivaldi. Some tourists were milling about talking, their voices echoing, taking pictures. Vast tapestries on the walls. Crystal chandeliers overhead that twinkled in the light and must have weighed as much as a car. Walker followed the receptionist through a sitting room with ornate furniture and the walls adorned in portraiture and fireplaces at each end topped with baroque gilt mirrors. They took a doorway in the corner and headed up two flights of stairs, where they entered another small landing with a window looking over Massachusetts Avenue.

The receptionist opened a door that was eight feet tall and at least three inches thick, some kind of dark wood like mahogany, like it could have been made from the same tree as the table back at the Senator's farmhouse. Beyond was a sitting room of old. The air was stale, as though the windows had not been opened in years, and the drapes and carpets impregnated with all the cigars and pipe tobacco that had been consumed in here for over a century. There were two small timber tables with carved legs, four leather-bound chairs around each, and by the fireplace were well-worn plush armchairs for six. On the marble mantle was a heavy copper urn, and behind that the obligatory gilt mirror. The fire crackled with split logs of hard wood as they made their slow transformation to hot orange embers. The far wall was lined with leather-bound books, with a couple of chesterfield lounges arranged for reclined reading. A time capsule for the hereditary elite.

The receptionist stoked the fire and then left, and Walker busied himself with the room. The wrought-iron fire-poker was the best improvised weapon. He scanned the books; lots of tomes on the early history of the colonies. He made his way to a side table that was set with crystal tumblers and decanters, one topped off with whisky, one with water, and Walker went to pour himself a whisky but then stopped – he opted for the water. He needed all his faculties. He imagined a line of Socratic questioning of these two, now that he'd gone through so much of their history and backstory in the form of biographical information and security checks. Of weaving the truth out of them, if they stonewalled him. Of getting an admission.

He didn't have to wait long. Twenty minutes or thereabouts. He was standing at one of the two sash windows, looking out the bubbly old hand-made glass across Massachusetts Avenue, and had just finished his second water when the door opened. He turned around.

A lone figure stood in the doorway. Though it was an oversized doorway, the figure took up most of the space. It was not Harvey, and it was not Lewis.

It was the big guy. Krycek. Tweedledumber.

68

'I hear you're looking for a couple of guys,' Krycek said to Walker after closing the door. 'Friends of mine.'

'You have more than one friend?' Walker said. He stayed by the window, crystal tumbler in his hand. A better weapon than nothing. The fall behind him wouldn't be good, but if this guy drew a pistol he'd have a better outcome jumping out to the ground and breaking both legs. 'Where is your little buddy? The mini-me I injected yesterday in San Francisco, the one who just shot Acton? He's still with us, I hope? Oh no, he's not . . .'

The giant was silent. He took a couple of steps into the room and looked around, his big blunt head turning like it was on the end of a stick, his body not moving at all. It would take a lot of energy to move a body like that. Walker hoped he'd be slow, but he knew Krycek would be driven to succeed, on a personal and professional level, because he had a score to settle – not just because Walker had thus far evaded him across the country, but that his pal Tweedledumb was now dead.

'I could shoot you,' the big guy said, taking a couple of paces into the room. He pulled a Glock, which had recently belonged to an FBI agent, from the back of his belt and placed it on the mantle above the fireplace. 'But that would be too . . . merciful.'

Walker knew it would be useless to question Krycek. Sure, he'd be privy to some useful information, like the fact that Harvey was ordering him around the country to kill fellow Americans, but this guy was all that was left of the A Team, and he'd be all clammed up in terms of snitching on his boss. Especially since he was presently pissed and driven to inflict some measure of retribution. So, that left Walker with two choices: fight, or flight. There was only one door in and out of the room, and the giant was between Walker and it. The windows behind him weren't a good option, for the thirty-foot drop. And add to that Walker wasn't typically a flighter.

But he was a fighter, albeit one with a wounded leg. He kept his weight on the front of his feet, so he could spring forward or to either side, should the giant rush him, and he tried to rationalise that he only had to beat one man, and he'd surely fought bigger men before and won, but the truth was, this was the biggest guy Walker had seen in the flesh. Certainly the biggest he'd squared up against. But he had to fight, and win, because he needed to talk to Lewis and Harvey. He was sure that they would saunter in shortly after Tweedledumber crushed and bludgeoned the life out of him, if for nothing else than to see their grimy little clean-up job come to a close.

'Did Harvey tell you to leave me alive?' Walker said.

No answer. Walker moved to his right, so that his back was to the bookshelves, and the giant mirrored his move and stepped to the left; they were now opposite each other with half the room each, the windows to one side, the fireplace to the other, their respective targets dead ahead.

'There's some information off site that Harvey will need,' Walker said. He was talking to get closer to the fireplace, a few paces to his right. The Glock was at the Krycek's end of the marble mantle, which would be a few paces into the giant's territory for Walker. But the fire-poker was at his end, and it was by far the best improvised weapon in the room.

'You don't want me to kill you, is that it?' Tweedledumber said.

'Dude, that was, like, *ten* words in a row!' Walker said. 'Good for you! Who's a *big boy* . . .'

Krycek rushed forward. Walker threw his heavy crystal tumbler, but it pinged off the giant's forehead as he kept charging. Walker feigned left, then moved right. He felt like he was back playing football at the Academy, some big dumb linebacker headed straight for him to put his lights out. But this was no game, and there were no rules, and when life and death were on the line, snap decisions had to be made.

It turned out that Tweedledumber was no dummy. Krycek saw the feint for what it was, and he hit Walker with a lowered shoulder, hard.

The hardest that Walker had ever been hit was not some blindside on the football field. It was an IED, in Iraq, that had hammered their up-armoured Humvee and sent it flipping through the air and into the third storey of a building. A rewired five-hundred-pound bomb, some tech guy would later say as he surveyed their wrecked vehicle and the crater left in the street. The Airman next to Walker had been impaled by a shattered axle. Up-armoured Humvees weigh upwards of six thousand pounds. The axles are huge. That blast was huge. Walker had sustained shattered ribs and a concussion.

This impact felt similar to that. The giant's shoulder was the same size as Walker's rib cage, and the only saving grace was that very size, which spread the load – if that much force and mass had hit Walker with a smaller point of contact, he'd have had broken ribs and perhaps shattered vertebrate and collapsed lungs as the impact compressed his body. Still, the impact took all the wind from him and he was picked up clear off his feet as they went crashing into a Chesterfield sofa.

Walker, fighting for oxygen, didn't pause. You give in straightaway, you die. And there were no tap-outs in these kinds of fights, just like there were no asterisks in life: Walker fought well * *until he didn't*. No. Not today. There was no coming second in this fight. By the way they fell Walker's left arm was around the giant's neck, with the guy's head against the back of the sofa, and Walker squeezed. His arm barely fit around the Krycek's neck, but he gave it everything he had, as he managed to take his first inwards breath and expand his diaphragm against the crushing force.

Tweedledumber was having none of it. He stood up, taking the full weight of Walker hanging on around his neck – and dumped backward. As they were falling through the air, Walker let go, and pushed off the giant's back. He fell awkwardly, on his side, more air crashing out of him. The giant landed on his back, and it seemed like the whole building shook. The mirror certainly rattled. Hot embers spilled from the fireplace.

Walker took a heaving breath and rolled some more and got to his feet and picked up the fire-poker.

Krycek got to his feet and picked up a table.

Walker felt unsteady on his feet and felt at his left ear – his fingers came away with blood. He remembered back twenty years to a fellow cadet's snowboarding accident in Colorado where he'd fallen over on the snow and had blood coming from his ear and had to be airlifted to Boulder to have his spleen removed. The guy had been fine, and Walker knew you could live without your spleen, but you couldn't live if a giant buried a table in your head, so he moved, fast.

The fire-poker bored straight down in a double-handed grip that split the wooden table in half. Krycek threw the two halves at Walker: a hundred pounds of broken timber hit him, hard, and he went over. The giant moved in, kicked at Walker's head, a kick that would have made a field goal from two hundred yards. Walker rolled to his side as the kick swooshed through the air. He brought up the fire-poker and buried the sharp end into the underside of the giant's thigh. It went into the meat until it hit bone, where it stopped.

Then, two things happened at once.

The giant let out a shrill cry, high pitched, like a little kid squealing as loudly as they could just for fun.

But this was no game between little kids, and Krycek was *feeling* it. And then the second thing happened, as he was still squealing: he fell backward, his hands going to the poker, his leg raised, one leg on the floor and he dropped. His head hit the marble mantle, and the two-inch thick slab of stone cracked, as did his head, and he collapsed with a heavy thump that shook the floor joists. He was out cold, and his big shaved head was starting to steam from the heat of the fire just inches from it.

Walker got to his feet, then grabbed the ankles of the giant and pulled him away from the fire to the middle of the room. Not because he felt bad about the guy being burned alive – if he remained unconscious he'd not feel any pain – but he had no desire to smell flesh cooking in the room. Walker sat in one of the armchairs and caught his breath. His chest ached.

Then the door opened, and two people entered.

69

Walker recognised Lewis and Harvey from the files Paul had prepared. Whether they'd been waiting outside the room the whole time, listening to the tussle that had lasted just a couple of minutes, Walker did not know. What he *did* know was that he was staring down the business end of a Colt 1911, the much-venerated .45 automatic that had served the US military with distinction since its introduction in the 1920s, only superseded in the mid-1980s by the smaller-calibre 9-millimetre M9 Beretta. A fine piece of machinery, in the hand of an ex-Army Ranger. The weapon was in Harvey's hand, and he could be in any corner of this room, and Walker in any other corner, and he'd not miss. And the Colt .45 had awesome stopping power, so Walker would be close to dead before the second shot got him. Walker stayed seated.

The two newcomers looked from Walker to their guy sprawled on the floor and back to Walker.

'Sorry about your giant,' Walker said. 'If I knew he'd squeal like a pig I'd have done things differently.'

Harvey moved around Walker and sat on the Chesterfield that had been crashed into earlier, and kept the .45 on him. Lewis went to the fireplace and used the tip of his highly polished Oxford dress shoes to kick the hot coals from the oriental carpet and back onto the stone hearth.

'Good idea,' Walker said. 'Don't want another of your houses to burn to the ground.'

'You think you're clever,' Lewis said, turning to face Walker. 'So, why don't you tell us what you think you know.'

'I know you're both cooked,' Walker said. He was still struggling to get his full breath back. It felt like the right side of his ribcage was on fire. It hurt to breathe, so he was taking small, shallow breaths that made him feel like he was never getting enough oxygen. He was beginning to feel light-headed, so he sat forward, his elbows resting on his knees, trying to take some weight off his torso. It helped, a little. 'This is the end of the line, fellas.'

Harvey chuckled.

'I know in 2003 that you two participated in a secret think tank of worst-case terror attacks, and you've since implemented a cut-out terror network called Zodiac.'

Walker watched for reactions. There was one. Harvey laughed. Lewis was silent.

'My father was there too,' Walker said.

'Your father's a dinosaur,' Harvey said. 'And he should have stayed dead. Like Bloom will, because he was a good man.'

'What do you know about that?' Walker said, staring at him.

'I know those two old sons of bitches were at a deal that went wrong in Syria,' Harvey said, the pistol unwavering. 'That Bloom's body was recovered among the dead. That your father's wasn't. Pity.'

A faint glimmer of hope flickered inside Walker. *These two guys are no fans of David Walker.* Which didn't put his father in the clear in terms of founding Zodiac, but it was starting to point that way. 'What happened to Bloom's body?'

'Burned, probably,' Harvey said. 'Did he mean that much to you? If you ask me, he was lucky he survived as long as he did.'

Walker thought about Bloom, and what he'd taught him. All those sayings. All those discussions over drinks. All the laughs, and all the wisdom. *Clear liquor is for rich women on diets. Friends – one to three is sufficient. A blowjob is not worth blowing your cover over – learn from my mistakes. Work the angles. Get in and get out. Play dirty, fight dirty. If you fight, fight to win. There are no asterisks in life. Eat and sleep when you can; you might not get another chance for a long time – and even if you do, what's the harm?* Bloom was a big man. A true gourmand. Six-five and three hundred pounds, who'd first made a name for himself as a young CIA agent helping Mossad hunt down surviving Nazis in the seventies. Quick of wit and handy with a blade. A handsome brute. And as much a father to him as David had ever been.

'You two have been running Zodiac,' Walker said. 'I can prove it.'

'Tell me,' Lewis said in a patronising tone. 'What is this Zodiac?'

'Nice try,' Walker said. 'You know all about it, Senator. And you know what? I know all about *you*, and your cooked-up security clearance.'

That got to him. Lewis looked to Harvey. Spooked.

'Got your pal Harvey here to take care of the poor bastard from OPM, the guy doing the background checks, because he touched on things in your life you wanted to keep secret,' Walker said. He saw the truth on Harvey's face – he wasn't nearly the liar that Lewis was. But he'd found their weak spot. 'I've got full transcripts from the widow, on file, off site. So, come clean on Zodiac, and we can make a deal.'

'A deal?' Harvey said. He looked down to his Colt .45, then back up to Walker. 'What on earth would we *deal*?'

'And you're in no position to deal, Walker,' Lewis said, regaining some composure.

'Oh really, Harvey, not even when your own Homeland agents are currently detained by the FBI?' Walker said. He saw a tick in Harvey's face. 'We know about your burner phones with your crooked agents, for your little clean-up mission. How'd that work out? I'm still here; Rachel Muertos is still here; Clair Hayes is still here. And we've got your bent Homeland agents, in custody. Kingsley and Jennings. And Jennings is already singing like a bird.'

'He knows too much!' Lewis said to Harvey. The Senator ran his hands through his hair. 'Shut him up!'

Harvey grimaced. Walker smiled.

'Why were you working with Almasi?' Walker said. 'Tell me that. Why were you trafficking people out of Syria and the Mid East?'

'I think we've heard enough from you,' Harvey said, and he stood up from the couch, the pistol still levelled at Walker's centre mass. 'Maybe, if you're lucky, you'll get to hang out with Bloom in some place where dead spies end up.'

'You don't care about all the information I've got off site?'

'Kingsley and Jennings?' Harvey said. 'You think they'll talk? They'll get theirs. They're nothing to worry about. You know who we are? Who I am? I make people *disappear*, Walker. Gone. Bloom. That Muertos bitch's husband, Steve. The OPM idiot who dug too deep during my friend's background check. Countless others. Not even names worth remembering. Gone. *Poof!* Into the ether, never seen or heard of again. Because they got in my way. *My* way!'

Walker paused before speaking, watching the tick in Harvey's eye, a vein pumping away in his temple. 'What'd you do with Steve Muertos?'

'Steve got too close,' Harvey said. 'He was a rogue element. Looked where he wasn't supposed to. He should have stayed the line. He was lucky with the way he went out; it could have been much worse.'

'You've killed a whole lot of patriotic Americans in your quest for money and power.'

'Small price to pay.'

'He might be taping this,' Lewis said to Harvey, his voice quiet.

Harvey smiled, looked at Walker. 'You taping this, boy?'

Walker stood, slowly, straining with the pain. He held his arms up. His right arm could barely move for the pain in his shattered ribs.

'Why would I tape you two idiots,' Walker said. 'It's not like you're ever going to see inside a courtroom. Look at you. I know who you are. You're untouchable. You can be embarrassed if some information gets released, but so what? You can spin your way out of it as quick as the news cycle refreshes on people's phones. But tell me. About Zodiac. You know it means everything to me. Explain it.'

'What about it?' Harvey said. 'What do you *think* you know, junior?'

'I know it's twelve cut-out cells, with no interlinking ideology other than chaos,' Walker said. 'That it was putting twelve separate worst-case scenarios together, each triggered by another in the chain, so it could never be traced back to one – or two – people. That it was being helped along, financed, by someone – or, evidently, two people. My question is *motive*. Look at you two.' He gestured around. 'Look at this place. You're meant to be as patriotic as any American can aspire to be. Your ancestors *created* this country as we know it. Or is all this just a cover to wreck things from within?'

'Harvey,' Lewis said, his voice now urgent, 'would you make him shut up.'

'Let's humour the kid. His father started Zodiac, right? We just have it a little nudge along, made it a reality.' He looked from Lewis to Walker. 'Right, Walker? You want to talk about *ancestors*? This was *your* father's brainchild. We just helped things along. Made it all it could be. And it's going to be glorious . . .'

'So, you admit it,' Walker said. His heart was beating fast. The way Harvey was telling it, this was all about them, not his father. David Walker's idea, his out-of-the-box worst-case scenarios, let's look out for it, let's be prepared. And it was all their *doing*.

'Attacks on the homeland are always going to happen,' Harvey said. 'Better it be from the devil you know.'

'There's more to it than that,' Walker said. 'You started in New York, you tried to take over the CIA from the inside.'

'Private spies,' Harvey said. He looked to Lewis. 'That was a good idea, you mark my words. Ahead of its time, perhaps. What else you got, boy?'

'You orchestrated the events in St Louis.'

'*Triggered*, boy,' Harvey said. 'Gave a nudge, to certain parties. Some funding. Some breadcrumbs. All they needed was the means.

They brought the motivation. That's always been the beauty of your father's plan, see?'

'Bringing down the Net,' Walker said. He felt heat rush up his neck as he wanted to take these two over-privileged sons of bitches down. 'The so-called abduction of an NSA agent, forcing the President's hand to enact the Kill Switch.'

'And you've been a pain in our butt every step of the way,' Harvey said. 'I give you props for that. Who knew Air Force could be so resourceful.'

Walker tried to smile, and he took a couple of steps towards the fireplace, away from Harvey, and to the left of Lewis, so that he was on the door side, and they were on the bookcase side. There was the Glock on the mantle, the weapon Tweedledumber had set there, out of view to the others for the large brass urn. Walker stepped over the sleeping giant. Let out a noise at the pain that shot through his ribs as he made the motion.

'Where do you think you're going, Walker?' Harvey said. He brought the pistol up, single handed, pointed again at Walker's centre mass. He'd shoot and drop Walker a clear second before Walker could grab the Glock and get a shot off. But it was the only good option he had. 'We missed out on putting a Walker in the ground once before. The same won't happen again, certainly not today.'

•

'We want everyone alive,' Somerville announced to the agents around her. They were assembled two buildings down on Massachusetts Avenue, and she strapped on a bulletproof vest. 'But if it comes to it, Lewis and Harvey are our bad guys. Your team got that?'

'Yes ma'am,' the leader of the FBI's Hostage Rescue said.

'Where the hell is Muertos?' Somerville said, looking around the hotel's driveway. 'I told her to stay put. Someone find her!'

70

Walker looked up when the door of the room opened. Two people entered.

Rachel Muertos.

And his father.

'David Walker, as I live and breathe,' Harvey said, keeping the gun on Jed. 'Come on in. Shut the door after you, and keep your hands in the air.'

David Walker shut the door and turned back to the room, his arms raised. Walker searched his face for a sign and found none. Muertos looked guilty, and after a quick glance she avoided Walker's eye.

'Now, take your jackets off, both of you,' Harvey said.

David Walker did so, Muertos too; Jed staring at the barrel of the Colt .45 the whole time.

Harvey moved towards them. 'Keep your hands in the air.'

David Walker did so. Staring at his son the whole time. Sadness in his eyes. That it had come to this.

'You too,' he said to Muertos. She did so. 'Turn around, both of you, slowly.'

He motioned to Lewis with his free hand.

'What?' Lewis said.

'Check them.'

'Check them?' Lewis said.

Harvey said, 'For a gun, or a wire.'

Lewis shook his head. 'I don't know how to do that.'

'Just have a look and feel to see if there's a gun or recorder on them.'

Lewis went to David Walker and Muertos. He patted them down, back and front, and nodded to confirm they were clean.

'What are you doing here?' Walker asked his father.

'Rachel called me,' David replied.

'When?'

'Half an hour ago.'

Walker looked to Muertos. He'd given her his cell phone, and she'd rung his father from the hotel next door. She'd known he was in town the whole time. They were in this together, somehow, for some reason. He hadn't just said *Find Jed Walker* and let her be. He'd been in contact, or at least contactable, this whole time. Using her to drive Jed. Using Jed to uncover who was controlling Zodiac.

'Did you even call Somerville?' Walker asked her.

Muertos looked at Harvey's gun and didn't answer.

Lewis headed back to Harvey's side of the room but stopped at the mantle over the fireplace when he spotted the Glock pistol. He picked it up.

Harvey looked to Walker, smiled. 'Nice try.'

'Let these two go,' David Walker said. 'They don't belong here. This is between us.'

'David, David, David . . .' Harvey said. 'There's no letting *go*. This is it. Your son said it before. Our clean-up over the past couple of days fell to pieces, several times – because of your boy. But now here they are, and we've got you too. Sure, Hayes is out there, and my two guys are in custody, but that's all an easy fix.' He looked to Lewis and smiled. 'Gimme that.'

Lewis passed over the Glock. Harvey put the Colt .45 in the concealed holster under his jacket, took the Glock, checked it, then with his free hand he picked up a book from the shelves. About an inch thick, leather binding.

Walker looked to his father.

'Jed, I didn't know it was these two,' David Walker said, meeting his son's gaze. 'I knew it had to be one of the eighty people on that secret think tank. I looked them all over, front and back, again and again. But I didn't know. I went to Syria to investigate. To get make contact with the people smugglers, see where the trail went. Then that all went to hell.'

'Well, now you and you son know the truth,' Harvey said. 'Ain't life just grand?'

'What are we going to do?' Lewis said. The guy was way out of his depth. Walker could see the Senator sweating, lines of it running down his forehead and face.

Harvey glanced across to him.

'What's the deal with you two?' Walker asked Muertos.

Muertos said, 'He—'

'I got her out of a jam in Syria,' David Walker cut in. 'I saw the opportunity and I took it. I gave Rachel a way to contact me, and helped her with a false ID and transport to get back into the US, and money to use to find you, and fund this mission.'

'This *mission*?' Walker said.

'Uncovering these two,' David Walker said. 'Stopping Zodiac.'

Walker pictured it in his mind. Muertos handing over the thick wad of cash to those guys in the SUVs for transporting them in San Francisco. The private jet across the country must have cost twenty or so grand. Her escape from that military hospital in Germany, and finding Walker's location by using a DoD computer before she'd bugged out. She hadn't had access to a false ID from the State Department – his father had supplied it for her. He'd been trailing her all along. He'd have known they were at the Watergate, might have even followed them here.

'Cut the bullshit, David,' Harvey said, bravado in his voice. 'Come clean for your boy. You've been working with us all along.'

'He's lying, Jed,' David said to his son, and looked him in the eye. 'I checked these two, separately, at the very start. There was nothing indicating it was them. But you found what I couldn't, because they've got sloppy, and you forced them to make mistakes. And now we know they're in it, driving Zodiac, together.'

'What's with the people-smuggling?' Walker asked his father. 'These two working with Almasi to get illegals into the country. I've seen their background – they don't need to do it for the money.'

'You think it's about *money*?' Harvey said.

'It's about people,' David said. 'They wanted *people*.'

'Shut him up,' Lewis said to Harvey. 'Make them stop.'

Walker looked to Lewis and Harvey.

'They facilitated the influx of people into the United States,' David said, 'through official channels, gave them new identities—'

'Harvey, would you please—'

'What, Senator, you suddenly going weak at the knees?' David said. 'You've known what you were doing since the beginning. Attacking your own country. Killing your own people. Own it.'

'He's right,' Harvey said, looking from David to Lewis. He passed him back the Glock. 'Own it.'

•

'We've got snipers across the road,' the leader of the FBI's Hostage Rescue Team said to Somerville. 'We've got visuals but no clear shot unless one of them gets right up against the window. And now with two more potential friendlies in there, it's a more difficult proposition.'

'So,' Somerville said, 'we have to rush the room?'

'There's one way in and out, the big wooden door,' he said, tapping a schematic laid out on the hood of their armoured vehicle. 'And we have four hostages between us and two armed targets. I'd have two of my team do simultaneous breaches at the windows, here and here. We'll attempt to take both targets down with less-lethal rounds, but there's every possibility they'll get their own shots off.'

Somerville was uncertain. 'There's too much risk.'

'We'd go in fast and heavy,' he replied. 'Survival rate of your three is pretty good, compared to doing nothing.'

'You really think that?'

'From all you've told me, yes ma'am, that's what I think.' There was finality to it. Confidence. The FBI's HRT were among the best in the world for this type of thing.

'If we wait?' Somerville said. 'Get a negotiator?'

'Due respect, that'll force their hand. We can wait and see if they'll take your people out as hostages, and we can take them down on the street with less-lethal weapons. But I'd rather we did this while we have them trapped. Out in the open, with them being armed and pressured by my team to comply, who knows how they'll react.'

'Block Massachusetts Avenue,' Somerville said. 'Let's prepare for them getting out. And be ready to enter the room as well.'

'Roger that,' he said, and relayed the instructions into his tactical radio.

Somerville said, under her breath, 'Come on, Walker . . .'

71

'The people they're bringing in?' David said. 'They're not refugees.'

'Can you shut him up?' Lewis said to Harvey. He looked to the gun in his hand, unwilling to use it.

'They're terrorists, Jed,' David said. 'That's what this Zodiac cell was. It's got nothing to do with people-smuggling en-masse, setting innocent parties up here for money. It's about getting terrorists *into* the country. Almasi was the facilitator, and presumably the leader of this cut-out Zodiac cell. They've been bringing in the worst of the worst that the Mid East has created since nine-eleven, and they're setting them up here in the US as sleepers, to be activated at any time, given a certain command.'

'Shut up, David,' Lewis said. 'I'm warning you.'

'You hid them in plain sight,' David Walker said, staring at the Senator, as though daring him to act. 'In suburban America. Working regular American jobs, with social-security numbers and medical insurance, given middle-class houses and cars, all of it approved by you two grand patriots. Setting these sleepers up with fake identities, having them wait for the time to emerge and play their role in attacking the United States from within. How are you activating them, Senator? Hmm? How many did you get into the country?'

Harvey and Lewis were silent.

'Why would you do that?' Muertos asked them. 'Why . . .'

Lewis looked ill. Not at what was said, but because it was being said out loud, that it was out there. Harvey was grinning.

'They're doing it because they're in the business of war,' Walker said. 'They want the frontline brought back here. They want to use it to elevate themselves to the highest office, to make their mark, to shape the future of the nation.' Walker took a step towards Harvey and said, 'You want all that will come with having a war play out right here on the homeland.'

'We're making America great again,' Harvey said with a big grin. 'Ain't it grand.'

'Too bad you won't be around to see it,' Walker said.

Harvey put the book to the barrel of the pistol – the book acting like an improvised silencer – and pointed it at Walker.

'Harv,' Lewis said. He moved closer to Harvey. 'Have some of your agents take these three someplace and make them disappear, yeah?'

Harvey kept his weapon trained on Walker, and side-stepped to Lewis. They spoke in hushed tones that Walker could not make out.

'Why not tell me about these two?' Walker said to his father.

'I was nowhere near sure, Jed. Since the start I've gone over everyone connected – I couldn't see what you found.' He looked to the floor, his voice quiet. 'I'm sorry it's led to this.'

'You set me up for this. You knew I'd follow Zodiac to the end. What that would mean.'

'I knew you wouldn't let it go. You can't. Because I can't.'

'I can't because you started it!'

David nodded. 'And all this time I hoped someone else would catch who was behind it.'

'And here we are.'

David looked up at his son. 'Here we are.'

Walker was silent. His father looked old. Like he'd aged twenty years over the past two years.

'I know what you'll do,' he said. 'And what that will mean. Son, you've got your life ahead of you.' He paused, watching his son. 'Don't ruin it, not for them.'

'What else can I do?'

'Don't. Let someone else handle it.'

'What can *they* do?'

'What can *you* do?'

'I can end it. Right here, right, now.' He gestured to Lewis and Harvey. 'These guys are where Zodiac starts and ends.'

'Oh, Jed . . .'

Then, inside two seconds, three things happened.

72

David Walker was the first to move. Forward, and to the right, towards Walker. He was just lifting his leg to make the move when Walker saw it, and he started to move, towards Harvey. Walker wasn't as worried about Lewis; the Senator wasn't as familiar with a pistol, and while he currently had the Glock in his hand, his arms were hanging by his sides, not ready for action. But he knew that Harvey would react, fast.

That was the first thing.

The second thing was Harvey's reaction. It took half a second. He was talking with Lewis but watching the three people across the room. His pistol was still trained on Walker, still snug up against the book. Harvey saw the first movement – David Walker – and he moved the pistol to a new target. Instinct. Muscle memory. Training. His reaction was to adapt to the unfolding situation, designate the new target and take action. Inside a second.

The Colt 1911 was set up for four pounds of pressure on the trigger to fire. The .45 round would travel over eight hundred feet per second. The distance from Harvey's pistol to David Walker was no more than twelve feet.

Harvey's finger applied pressure and the gun fired. The sound was a muffled boom. The book seemed to disintegrate – bits of paper debris filled the air. To Walker's left, his father fell. He'd managed to clear the body of the fallen giant, Krycek, still unconscious and spread across the floor like a speed-bump in the room between the two parties. David Walker had leaped the giant with his second stride, and the Colt had gone off, and he was pushed backward by the force of the first round, then he started his fall to the floor. The first shot got him in the chest. He was still flying backward as the second shot hit him, in the arm.

All the while, Walker was moving forward, towards the target, Harvey. Harvey started to turn his pistol back to the younger Walker.

Then the third thing occurred.

The windows behind and to Walker's right exploded inwards, and a figure burst through each. Clad head-to-toe in the dark green tactical operations gear of the FBI Hostage Rescue Team, each carried a suppressed Heckler & Koch sub-machinegun with laser sight, and each acquired their target as the first, most imminent threat emerged: Lewis, armed with the Glock, in the process of aiming it their way. Whether the Senator was planning to shoot anyone with the firearm would never be known, because his body was shredded with dozens of 9-millimetre rounds, and he was pressed against the far wall from the barrage of bullets, leaving a red mist in his wake.

That was how the first two seconds played out.

The next moments were scrappier and more drawn out. As Walker got to his target, the door to the room was blasted off its hinges and fell inwards, plaster and wood flying as HRT members rushed the room.

Walker hit Harvey low, hit him with everything he had. His left shoulder slammed into Harvey's chest and his body ducked under Harvey's arms, so the .45 aimed high when another round went off as they crashed to the floor between the Chesterfield sofas and the wall.

Harvey's reaction was to pull his arms down and squeeze at Walker, who was now on top of him. Walker heard shouts from the HRT members as they spilled into the room to subdue any further threats. He blocked their shouts out. Not intentionally; he started to black out from the pain exploding in his chest, his shattered ribs cutting into the internal organs they were designed to protect, sending all kinds of hideous feelings through the nerve clusters in his sternum and spine back up into his brain, his body telling him to stop, his mind telling him to stop, fighting some primeval instinct and desire telling him to beat his attacker.

He hit Harvey hard with the only weapon he could bring to bear – his head. His forehead connected with Harvey's nose and the quick snap smacked the back of Harvey's head against the thick maple floorboards. He saw Harvey's eyes roll back like he was a boxer who'd taken a heavy blow, but he only was dazed, not out of the fight. Harvey's constricting grip around Walker's body slackened, and Walker lifted his left arm across his body, clamping his hand around Harvey's elbow and pressed his thumb and fingers into the joint. He felt muscle and fat and bones and tendons, and he kept squeezing until he felt things move in the arm, muscle and fat and bone and tendons shifting in ways that they weren't supposed to, and the .45 went off again, and then Harvey dropped it to the maple floorboards, and his grip around Walker went limp and he shifted away from the fire of pain erupting in his arm.

Walker slumped off Harvey, and sat up. He looked at Harvey lying there, uncertainly in his eyes. Fear. He didn't know what to do. Maybe for the first time he could remember, he was on his own, and spooked, and unsure of his future. Once all the power and influence was stripped away, he was a man, as fragile as any other. His gaze went from Walker to Lewis, who was sat up against the wall behind Walker, lifeless, a smear of blood down the beige paintwork behind his body. Harvey closed his eyes as the FBI agents got to him, turning him roughly onto his face and placing flexicuffs on his wrists.

Walker turned to see the life fading from his father.

74

'I hope you didn't kill him,' David Walker said to his son.

'I didn't.' Walker sat next to his fallen father. He held his head up, and put pressure on the chest wound.

'You need to find out . . . who, and where, all the sleepers are . . .'

Walker knew then, for sure, that when it came to Zodiac, his father stood on the right side of history.

'He's alive,' Walker said. He shifted so that his father's head was resting in his lap. Walker had shrugged off the offered help of the FBI team and crawled across the room, over the giant, to his father's side. David's chest wound was catastrophic, and he was close to bleeding out. Walker kept pressure on the gauze. The HRT medic had started an IV, but shook his head when Walker had searched for news. 'You did it, Dad. I'd always questioned where you stood, but in the end, you did it.'

'I never doubted you.'

Walker smiled through some tears. 'I hated you for a while there.'

'I know.'

'For what you did to Ma, and me, and then this . . .'

'I know.' David started to cough. At least one of his lungs was shredded and collapsed and filling with blood. 'I'm sorry.'

His father didn't say anything else, but he stayed alive for another minute. They held each other's hands in one big grip. His father's hands, which had always seemed so impossibly large, looked smaller now. Walker knew that this was the end of so much of what had been his life, and as the life left his father's eyes, Jed thought of Eve, and what he and his job had done to her, and he knew he needed to start a new chapter. It was life, not death, that was triumphant this day.

EPILOGUE

The Walker family ranch was south of Amarillo, Texas. Right in the panhandle. The sun was rising not setting. Walker was crouched down at the grave plot, where three generations on his father's side were in the ground. And now both his parents. He'd put the urn of his father's ashes in a deep hole in the ground and topped it off with shovels of tightly packed desert dirt. The morning was crisp, his breath fogged. Fingers of light were reaching over the red cliffs of Palo Duro Canyon.

The long squat adobe house, empty for years, was brought to life today. The lights were on inside, the yellow glow of progress. Eve was at the kitchen window, making coffee. Her movements and expression reminded him of memories of her spanning over half his lifetime. That was his future, right there. The vermilion sun glanced off roof tiles. Birdsong woke the day. Somewhere distant a lonely bobcat called in a kill.

Walker kneeled down and finished scraping the barren desert earth over his father's plot. There was no headstone. He saw the movement of a rattlesnake as it sought the first rays of sun, slivering out atop a small hoodoo and curling up in a bright nook. *You know about Mojave rattlesnakes?* his father had once said to him, as a boy, when his dog had been bitten and died graveyard dead moments later. *Mojave rattlesnakes have a neurotoxic poison*, David had said.

You need to respect them. Walker had wanted his father to find and kill the snake. *We protect them,* his father had said. *We have come here into their world, they're letting us share in it. We must respect that.* He'd sat there, with his father, his dead dog in his lap, the two of them looking out over the vacant spaces of the desert canyons that looked the same today as they did that morning, thirty years before.

The crunching of the gravel on the path roused him from his memories.

'You think they'll know they're together down there?' Eve said.

'When you die,' Walker said, standing up, 'I figure it's the same as if everyone else has died too.'

Eve stood next to Walker and handed him a steaming cup of coffee, black. He wrapped an arm around her and drew her in. They watched the rattler loosen its coil to capture more sun.

'You really think it's over?'

'Zodiac is done.' Walker brushed the dirt off his hands. 'Somerville called late last night. They found data on a private email server at the Senator's house. Some obscure lines that meant nothing to anyone, but there was a pattern to it. It was my father's work, from the Zodiac think tank, meant to be destroyed, but the Senator had kept a copy. It's the smoking gun, and the blueprint to how Lewis and Harvey then planned Zodiac to unfold. So, yeah, it's over. The FBI are conducting raids all over the country as we speak. Our friends around the world too.'

They stood in silence for a while, Walker with an arm around Eve and holding her close. The proximity and the rising sun and the hot coffee pushed away the morning desert cold.

'What will you do now?' Eve asked.

'You mean what will *we* do?'

'You know what I mean.'

'Are you asking if I'm gonna get a job?'

'Can you really walk away from the life you've known?' Eve looked up to him. 'For good?'

Walker looked out at the shadows that lingered in the nooks and rocks, the remainders of night losing out to the slowly rising sun that snuffed them out with daggers of daylight.

'Yes,' he said. 'I like to think so.'

'Do you think you'll *know* so?'

Walker looked down at her. Eve's eyes were bright.

'You've left that life behind before,' Eve said. 'You've gone back. Again and again. You really think you can change? After all this?' Her eyes searched his for an answer, for reassurance, for certainty. 'I miss the person I met. Before the Air Force, before the CIA, before all this mess that's been twenty years of you, out there, fighting. I want you to fight for me, no-one else. For us.'

'I'll try.' He kissed her forehead. 'I promise.'

'Jed. You've tried before.' She squeezed against him, tight, her head against his chest. 'If *we're* trying *this* – being and staying together? – then you have to *do*. Okay? It's decision time.'

'Then consider it decided.'

'Jed . . .'

'I swear, on everything I hold holy. I'm here. For you. For us. Nothing else.'

'Okay.'

'Okay?'

'Okay.' She looked up at him and smiled, and put her hands to her stomach. 'So, I have news . . .'

If you enjoyed *Dark Heart*, read on for the beginning of the next book in the Jed Walker series . . .

THE AGENCY

PROLOGUE

'You make a mistake, you will die.'

Walker didn't take it personally.

'You miss your target, you will die.'

The instructor was just doing her job.

'You get a jam, you will die.'

Three weeks together and he could tell she was good at her job.

'You get distracted, you will die.'

And she was quite attractive.

'You listening, Walker?'

'Yes, ma'am,' he replied.

'Good,' she said, then looked up and down the line of seven recruits. 'Because you've been trying to finish first and only first, for three weeks – you think I didn't notice? You're the only Air Force out here, with these Army and Navy and Marine vets, the best they had to offer. Me included. And you know what they say about Air Force?'

'No, ma'am,' Walker replied.

'Me either. No-one gives a damn about the Air Force, so why talk about them?'

The six other recruits sniggered.

'Run the op again,' she said, looking to the staffers to confirm the training scenario had been reset. 'This time I want that building cleared and the objectives completed in under two minutes. *Two minutes*. You hear me, recruits?'

'Ma'am, yes, ma'am!' the seven replied as one.

She gave a signal to the kill-house training officer, and he blew a whistle. They had a minute to prep.

Welcome to The Point, Walker thought. It was the CIA's hands-on training facility, formally known as Harvey Point Defense Testing Activity Facility, a sprawling North Carolina campus owned by the Department of Defense. It was where the country's top front-line operators from all branches of the military and intelligence agencies were sent to hone their field skills. The place was meant to test and train the best of the best: Top Gun for door-kickers.

He rushed the house. They had already assaulted it twice, and had failed miserably both times. Seven going into a double-storey building up against an unknown number of hostiles to subdue, an unknown number of friendlies to protect and get out, and three marked objects to retrieve – last time it had been a briefcase, a laptop and a thumb-drive, the latter hidden in a stitched-in seam inside a bad guy's jacket, which they had failed to find. Six men and one woman going in and, like Walker, all were military. All practised at this kind of thing. All well trained. But this was different. This was designed to break recruits, to be near-on impossible, so that things in the field paled in comparison. Classic special-operations training.

However, this was even beyond special operations, at least as the DoD knew it; these new recruits had already been through the best the nation had out in the field: two Navy SEALS, two from Delta, a Force Recon Marine, an Army Ranger – and in Walker's case, an officer from the 24th Tactical Squadron, the Air Force's boots on the ground to Joint Special Operations Command.

Walker shadowed an ex-Army Delta Force guy named Clive Gowan, moving quickly to the rear of the complex. The other five were breaching the front doors and windows. They had their choice of silenced 9-millimetre weapons, and most, including Walker, were using an MP5 sub-machine gun. Good and accurate in close quarters. His secondary was a hip-holstered H&K USP 9-millimetre. The weapons fired blanks, and all wore laser tags. The flash-bang grenades and door-breaching charges were real, albeit dialled down. The people in the building were real too. Playing roles. Like the seven assaulters, they wore protective eye and ear coverings. Like the assaulting force, they didn't want to lose.

The whistle blew, twice. Go time. Two minutes on the clock.

Clive tried the handle of the rear door – nothing made an operator feel more stupid than kicking in a door that wasn't even locked.

Click.

It was unlocked. He opened it a thin crack, then used the back of his combat knife to slide from the ground up in that slim opening. Gently. He paused, about a foot from the ground, and shook his head. Walker closed the door. There was a trip wire, which in a real-life scenario might be connected to an explosive charge. In this case a smoke grenade, to signify an explosive charge.

Walker pointed to the window. Clive nodded, tried it, and it slid open. Safety glass, in case it smashed. Gym mats were positioned below each window, on the off chance someone fell through. The course was designed to break recruits, not maim them. Walker covered the Delta guy as he shimmied through, then saw the all-clear signal, and it was his turn. Clive was typical Delta: small and wiry, 180 pounds wet. Walker was taller and heavier, and didn't land with the same kind of grace as his fellow recruit.

A figure emerged in front of them, coming around the doorway to what was set up as a small kitchen. Clive shot him with his silenced MP5. And got shot in the process. Exact timing, couldn't do it again. Both were out of the game, and sat on the floor. Clive looked pissed. The instructor looked pleased, which told Walker that he'd done his job, and that meant that there were at least six hostiles still in here, each of whom had been tasked to take out a recruit.

He stepped around the instructor, then paused. He bent down, saw the lit-up area on the guy's shoulder where Clive had zapped him twice.

Walker whispered, 'That kill you straightaway?'

'Huh?' the instructor said.

'I guess not,' Walker replied, and he ditched his MP5, pulled his sidearm and then hefted the instructor to his feet. He pressed the end of his pistol's suppressor under the guy's chin, pinning him against the wall. 'Ever had a blank fired close-up against your skin?'

'You're mad.' The guy was an old Army sergeant. Green Beret. Walker liked him, and wouldn't shoot, but he wanted the intel, and he kept the pressure on the pistol.

'We fail this run, we're out,' Walker said. 'How bad do you think I want this?'

The instructor was silent.

'Imagine I'm now doing something especially nasty to you, to get the intel,' Walker said. 'Play along. Use your imagination.'

The instructor's eyes searched Walker's. He sensed something harder, and said, 'Upstairs, south-east room. Two captives. Three pieces of intel, all on the person in charge.'

'Number of hostiles?'

'You're on the clock,' the instructor said. 'Tick-tock.'

Walker lowered his silenced pistol, took a pace out the door.

'Asshole,' the instructor said.

Walker shot him in the torso, twice. The guy was lit up all over. Clive's laugh was drowned out by the loud boom as the front door was breached.

Twenty-one seconds down.

Walker was already moving up the stairs, and motioned for the two SEALs to follow him, and for two other recruits to clear the downstairs rooms while the remaining operator took up a cover position. As he ascended he led with his pistol in a two-handed grip.

He sighted and double-tapped the first two targets that emerged at the top of the stairs. Imprudent move on their part – they should have waited for someone to rush up. But they probably figured the boom from downstairs was the first entry into the house and they would be in position faster than the attackers. Fine by Walker.

Three targets down. At least three remaining. Thirty-six seconds in.

Walker paused at the hallway and provided cover, motioning to his colleagues to head onwards. He felt a pat on his shoulder, and watched as the two SEALs went past. They were competent operators, Walker thought, as they moved warily but quickly towards the northern end of the house, where four rooms branched off the hallway.

At the top of the stairs, Walker turned right, heading to the southern end. He didn't bother to check the south-west door. Instead he kicked in the door to the south-east room and rolled through the open doorway. Immediately he saw two captives seated on a bed, and a guy with a gun covering them. Walker sprang up and forward, rushed him, and as the trainer brought the gun to bear, Walker crash-tackled him, hard.

His college football coach would have been proud of the impact. He hit with his right shoulder, just under his opponent's ribs, and kept his force going onwards and up. He hefted the instructor off his feet, and kept going until they smashed out the window, the safety glass shattering into a million little pieces. The drop was twelve feet. Walker didn't want to get busted out for maiming a trainer, so he twisted as they fell, breaking the guy's fall with his own body as they landed on the gym mat. The downside was, 200 pounds of man crashed onto him, and Walker was winded and sore – but not regretful.

'Prick,' the trainer said, getting to his feet.

Walker stayed on his back and shot him, three times.

Forty-six seconds in.

Ten seconds later, the whistle blew.

Under a minute. A new record.

Walker stayed on his back. The other six recruits shuffled over. The SEALs had extracted the two captives.

'He's got the intel on him,' Walker called out, pointing to the instructor he'd taken out the window. His cohort patted the guy down and quickly found it all – documents, a thumb-drive, photos.

The chief instructor stood over Walker, smiled, then held out her hand and helped him to his feet.

'Welcome,' she said, 'to the CIA.'